PRAISE FOR
Wild Abandon

'Emily Bitto writes superbly textured prose, granular with detail. Here is her sumptuous, freewheeling riff on innocence and experience. *Wild Abandon* is thrilling and heartbreaking by turns—a glorious novel.'

Michelle de Kretser, dual Miles Franklin Award-winning author of *Questions of Travel* and *The Life to Come*

'Emily Bitto's *Wild Abandon* made me fall in love with fiction again. Reading this book is a rush and a thrill. I loved how the narrative kept shifting and changing, how it constantly kept me on my toes as a reader. The mastery of language and storytelling is exquisite, electrifying really. The compassion and generosity, and Bitto's humane curiosity, are profound gifts. Only a superlative can do it justice: this is a *great* novel.'

Christos Tsiolkas, author of *Damascus* and *The Slap*

'How thrilling it is to strap in for a ride into the unknown. It is rare to read a novel so full of risk and adventure, so exuberant in its language, so free of cant. You never know where *Wild Abandon* is going next, but in Emily Bitto's expert hands you know it will be worth the trip. What a fearless talent she has, and what an exhilarating novel this is.'

Malcolm Knox, author of *Bluebird*

PRAISE FOR
The Strays

Winner of the Stella Prize 2015

Winner of the Tina Kane Emergent Writer Award

University of Canberra 'Book of the Year' 2016

Longlisted for the International DUBLIN Literary Award

Shortlisted for the Victorian Premier's Literary Award for an Unpublished Manuscript

Shortlisted for the Dobbie Literary Award

Shortlisted for the Indie Book Award for Debut Fiction

Shortlisted for the UTS Glenda Adams Award for New Writing in the NSW Premier's Literary Awards

Shortlisted for the Historical Writers' Association Debut Fiction Award

Shortlisted for an Amazon Rising Star Award

Shortlisted for Walter Scott Prize for Historical Fiction 'Academy Recommends' Read

'Reminiscent of Ian McEwan's *Atonement*, Sybille Bedford's *Jigsaw*, or A.S. Byatt's *The Children's Book* . . . *The Strays* is like a gemstone: polished and multifaceted, reflecting illuminations back to the reader and holding rich colour in its depths.'

Stella Prize Judges' Report

'You could lift out any sentence in *The Strays* and admire the sheer artistry of its melody and composition . . . an immensely pleasurable read.'

Bookseller + Publisher (4.5 stars)

'*The Strays* is a marvellously accomplished and assured debut, announcing a major new talent. Rich in atmosphere and beautifully observed.'

Booktopia

'Told with impressive intensity . . . the strong bonds, bleak outcomes and moral struggles of its central female characters give *The Strays* its substance.'

The Guardian

'Treating this novel as historical fiction risks missing some of its breadth of insight. *The Strays* is an eloquent portrayal of the damage caused by self-absorption as well as a moving study of isolation.'

The Age

'Bitto writes beautifully, her prose supple and satisfying, her insights and extended metaphors worth lingering over.'

Adelaide Advertiser

'Bitto has a deep interest in the transformative power of memory, in how life's chaos is shaped into story, its each retelling laying down a fresh stratum of personal and cultural meaning. *The Strays* has the earthy feel of what David Malouf calls the most exotic place—the one we grew up in.'

Australian Book Review

'A perfectly crafted novel . . . an immediately engaging and tender story taking hold of the reader from the first pages. Emily Bitto is without doubt a writer to remember and follow in the future.'

Tony Birch, author of *The White Girl*

'Emily Bitto's hugely impressive first novel . . . magical. Bitto creates a world so densely imagined that it seems not just real but part of the reader's own past—and she does it in lovely prose.'

Michelle de Kretser, *Sydney Morning Herald*

'A terrific novel . . . I was certainly captured by it from the very beginning.'

Chris Womersley, author of *Bereft*

'Remarkable . . . Bitto's scenes of the Trentham commune are vividly written, almost painterly.'

New York Times Book Review

'Lyrical.'

Publishers Weekly

'Full of lush, mesmerizing detail and keen insight into the easy intimacy between young girls which disappears with adulthood.'

The New Yorker

'Explores with quiet passion both the cost of creative life on family and the definition of family itself.'

Kirkus Reviews

'Showcases a dazzling, gabby and ultimately doomed collection of stray human beings . . . *The Strays* invites readers into a world that is by turns disturbing and magical . . . Word pictures which elevate the ordinary to exquisite appear throughout Bitto's novel . . . With precise and graceful turns of phrase, Bitto reveals the bond of passion between the two girls, which seems unbreakable but inevitably snaps under all that can't be said. And she delivers all of this with a grace and eloquence.'

NPR Books

'[A] sparkling debut.'

National Book Review, '5 Hot Books'

'A haunting evocation of life-changing friendship . . . *The Strays* is a marvel of setting and characterization, re-creating a time of artistic revolution and personal revelation. Memorable and moving, this is a novel not to be missed.'

Booklist (starred review)

'Told in both the breathless voice of an easily infatuated child and the more measured tones of a wiser adult, *The Strays* is a powerful tale of the consequences of creativity.'

BookPage

'Its themes and characters provide universal resonance . . . *The Strays* is a thoughtful exploration of what happens when artistic genius and family life collide, and how a relatively short period in one's youth can shape personal and professional choices for a lifetime.'

Bookreporter

'Emily Bitto has written a very stylish and enjoyable debut novel.'

Sunday Mail

'Emily Bitto writes so well about art, childhood, infatuation, loneliness—you name it. *The Strays* is a knowing novel, and beautifully done.'

Meg Wolitzer, *New York Times* bestselling author of *The Interestings*

'Riveting, captivating, with a sense of foreboding threaded throughout. *The Strays* is such a daring look at art and love and family that you'll want to clear your calendar: you'll be reading it in a day.'

Whitney Otto, *New York Times* bestselling author of *How to Make an American Quilt*

'Emily Bitto's *The Strays* is a powerful and precisely imagined journey into the lives of two girls growing up in the avant-garde artistic milieu of post-war Australia. Like Elena Ferrante in her Neapolitan novels, Bitto entices and enthrals, probing the pathos of the heart and the unpredictable volatility of friendships and family. But above all, it is the writing itself that delights the reader: vivid, tactile, perfectly wrought, this is prose that weaves a lasting spell.'

Paul Kane, author of *Welcome Light*

Emily Bitto is a Melbourne-based writer of fiction, poetry and non-fiction. She has a Masters in Literary Studies and a PhD in Creative Writing from the University of Melbourne. Her debut novel, *The Strays*, was the winner of the 2015 Stella Prize. Her work has appeared in various publications, including *Meanjin*, *The Age*, *The Monthly*, the *Saturday Paper*, the *Big Issue* and the *Sydney Morning Herald*. In 2018, she was awarded a six-month Australia Council International Residency in Rome to work on her second novel and debut poetry collection. She has been teaching creative writing for over a decade, and is currently a tutor at the Faber Writing Academy. She is also the co-owner of Carlton wine bar Heartattack and Vine.

EMILY
BITTO

WILD
ABANDON

This is a work of fiction. Characters, places and incidents are sometimes inspired by historical events, but are used fictitiously.

First published in 2021

This project has been assisted by the Australian Government through the Australia Council, its arts funding and advisory board.

This project is supported by the Victorian Government through Creative Victoria.

Allen & Unwin
83 Alexander Street
Crows Nest NSW 2065
Australia
Phone: (61 2) 8425 0100
Email: info@allenandunwin.com
Web: www.allenandunwin.com

A catalogue record for this book is available from the National Library of Australia

ISBN 978 1 76087 913 6

Set in 12/18.2 pt Janson Text LT Pro by Bookhouse, Sydney
Printed in Australia by McPherson's Printing Group

10 9 8 7 6 5 4 3 2 1

The paper in this book is FSC® certified. FSC® promotes environmentally responsible, socially beneficial and economically viable management of the world's forests.

Personally I experienced steep variations myself, bad news, wasted expenditures, wicked dreams, wizard happenings like the appearance of animals in the heat of evenings to desert Fathers, still I am thankful to say that as I view it I was not harmed.

Saul Bellow, *The Adventures of Augie March*

Then I took off on the first stage of the second journey, the great seeking leap into the depths of America, wilderness dream of all poets and scoutmasters, westward to our manifest destiny, to sovereign red timber and painted sands, to the gold-transfigured hills, westward to match the shadows of my image and my self.

Don DeLillo, *Americana*

1
America

ON HIS FIRST NIGHT IN New York City, he sought out a man to give him something—as travellers and people in end times have long done before him—some rich hyper-distilled substance to help him feel at one with the seething glorious doomed mass around him or else to heighten his separateness into an exquisite reverie.

The foreign culture in which he found himself was not much unlike his own, was in fact imbued through association and servile reverence into the very fabric of his own, which sought to replicate all things touched by that talismanic word, *America*, as his father had revered and made his own young quest to *Europe*, and so they walked within the same parade of youths setting out into the world to find their fortunes and become men, the objects of their reverence notwithstanding, which were different from each other as one generation from the next. And yet he possessed the traveller's heightened sense-perception and saw and felt about him all that was foreign: the steam shooting up from the subway grates like some Dickensian miasma; the rumbling below his feet as trains shot their sleek heavy rattling bodies along tunnels stacked one above the other like sleepers tossing and turning on stacked and slatted bunks; the common sight of dark-coloured skin; the profusion of obese flesh of all colours and the responsible profusion of sweet and salt and fatty foods whose names were new and despite himself tempting: Applebee's, Shake Shack, Red Lobster, Olive Garden, Chipotle, Del Frisco's, sweetgreen, Melt Shop.

In the end, he thought, the difference was in this profusion itself, this bounteous bewilder of people and sights and smells and things to eat and buy which made him feel at once that Australia was marked indelibly by a probably-British restraint and proud conflicted frugality even in its lust for this American plenitude.

He had arrived greasy and nauseous from the flight and stood swaying at the baggage carousel, somnambulant and still emerging pupa-like from that necessary snug hermetic of long-haul privacy, until a woman wearing a *Save the Whales* t-shirt said to him, 'If you stay back, then the people behind you can see too,' and he stepped away chastened and indignant, and himself now unable to see. He watched an elderly man attempt to haul a hard-shell Samsonite monstrosity over the rim of the conveyer belt and then let it go, whether because it was too heavy or because the man realised it was not his own, he could not tell, but because of the Whale woman he did not feel disposed to help his fellow man and he crossed his arms as the case wobbled off on another tedious round. He realised at last that his own backpack had passed him twice already—it looked so small that he hadn't recognised it—and he felt at once so small himself and unprepared for the reckless dashed headlong on which he had embarked unthinking, impelled by twin engines of heartbreak and humiliation.

All around him people wheeled their property with such heft, the armoured cases reaching to their thighs and resembling nothing so much as small refrigerators or dishwashers propelled about the world, protection from weightlessness.

He took the airport train and then the subway to Astor Place and then walked with his pack to the East Village, reviving only in the balm of dusk air from his body's brief unnatural modern hibernation. At the corner of East 9th and Avenue C he collected the keys Paul had left at the coffee shop across the street and dragged his vagrant body up the seven flights to Paul's apartment, where he planned to stay a few nights and then keep moving, to where he did not know, movement itself being the only aim and target of his heartbreak breakneck thrust.

The apartment was a one-bedroom but Paul had said he could crash on the couch for as long as he liked. He dropped his pack and had a look around: the dark short hallway from which Paul's bedroom opened to the right; the square foot of terrace that faced out on community gardens; the black-and-white-tiled bathroom with a small window set at head height in the shower recess; the thriving fern that hung there in the frame; the box of matches on the toilet cistern; the kitchen tucked into an alcove off the hallway—copper pots and pans hanging from hooks and a watercolour painting of a woman squatting with her knickers around her ankles, her cunt a gaudy pink—and the final abbreviated L of the living room, where there was a round table, a green corduroy couch he wasn't sure would accommodate his length, and a huge potted palm. That was the extent of it and it was stylish within its limited reach, curated in a kind of masculine near-opulence that did not accord with the Paul he had known in childhood: his older brother's best friend and the source of much cruel torment.

Paul had left him a note on the kitchen bench:

Hey mate,
Welcome! Make yourself at home, take a shower etc. There's beer in the fridge—sit on the balcony, or there's a rooftop upstairs. Wifi is Celebritychef, password: oink69. See you at Dante or msg me if too knackered.
—P

Paul had told him to come west, to meet at midnight in a bar called Dante near Paul's work. But that was hours away and jetlag was beginning to stroke him into a warm, unwise seduction. He found a towel in the hall closet and took a shower, standing in the rising steam and gazing out at the new Old World (or was it the old New World? he wasn't sure) through the square window as the day struck its final match.

—

The contact in his phone was listed simply as 'the dude', which was how it had come through from Violet. She had been connected with this dubious personage by her friend Holly, an Australian living in New York whose name he had been instructed to drop when he messaged the dude like an old-fashioned calling card, though he had never met Holly, knew her only from the high-filtered images in Violet's Facebook album titled *Violet eats the Big Apple*. He had bought a cheap prepaid SIM on the way to Paul's so that he could use maps on his phone and not appear too much of a tourist, could call Paul or call home in an emergency. And for this purpose too.

He had no idea how to address a New York dealer, but surmised that to err on the side of cryptic was wise and so, with much backspacing, he composed and eventually sent the following message, omitting certain punctuation marks, to seem less like the careful young man he was:

> Hi my names Will. I'm visiting from Australia and my friend Violet gave me ur number. Hope thats ok. Shes a friend of Holly . . . Wondering if we can meet up. Cheers

The message came back almost immediately:

> Hey, those aussie girls are crazy. No problem we can meet up round 8 ok?
> Where u at?

He replied:

> East Village but can meet u wherever . . .

The pause was slightly longer this time, but the message came back, as sure as commerce:

> East Village is fine. Will msg when nearby

That particular ambivalent task accomplished with the requisite haste, he was abruptly uncoupled from all purpose and found himself let loose into time and space, feeling the suppressed panic of the astronaut who pushes off into the deep black reaches of the gravity-less universe with just a small engine strapped to his body to propel him, when the time comes, out of that chill infinity.

Now, the sole vain task was not to think of her, and while he waited for the dude, and nightfall, he found an ATM and then the nearest bar, a strange and (if he admitted it, which he did not) disappointing replica of a Western saloon in the midst of Manhattan, with a rough wood counter and rows of bottles lit by candle lanterns and cut-glass tumblers and a soundtrack that was either Ryan Adams or Justin Townes Earl or some other indistinguishable phenotypic variant of the alt-country genre (he had an idea for a piece he might write about how that ubiquity of sound and repudiation of originality might represent a key convention of the genre, and what its function might be).

The cocktail list was long and contained many drinks *washed* or *scented* with unknown American ingredients—Douglas fir and buffalo grass and chokecherry and hickory—and he spent some time looking through it to make himself busy, but when the waitress came he ordered a beer. He downloaded the New York Subway app that Violet had recommended and tried to familiarise himself with the many coloured lines that snaked their way down the long form of Manhattan like an outdated computer game.

He still had hours before he was due in Greenwich Village and would have to find some interim occupation, and he canvassed several ideas to see how they felt. He knew that he would try out the drugs alone because he was not an especially seasoned drug-taker and wanted to test his response away from all risk of humiliation, which took for him both the general form of human witness and the more particular form of Paul, whose association with his childhood and his status as a younger brother heightened the potential for such humiliation, for that old buried feeling of being under an unremitting keen malign scrutiny. Perhaps, since he was at this moment so truly anonymous, he might put aside his scant sophistication and deep-set fear of gaucherie to plunge once and briefly into the quintessence of sightseeing and emerge unmarked before midnight, and he looked up Times Square on his phone and mapped his thrilling incognito course there.

He was on his second beer and the bar was filling up when his phone buzzed again.

In East Village now. Where u at?

He stood abruptly and the passing waitress looked at him and asked, 'Can I get you something, babe?'

'Um, just the bill, please,' he said.

'You want the check?'

'Yes please, the check, thank you,' he replied, re-seating himself and turning back to his phone.

On Avenue C. Not sure of number but near cnr of East 9th st.

Ok be there in 5

He did not know how much to tip, but the bill came complete with his total and three options in percentage and dollar amounts and he chose the middle option and signed the credit card receipt and went outside to where the black car was waiting.

With some pride and trepidation, he opened the passenger door.

'Will?' said the guy at the wheel.

'Yeah, hi.' He slid into the dark leather interior.

'Welcome to New York. What can I get you?'

'Um, some coke, please.'

'Sure. How much?'

'Um, I don't know, I've got like a hundred and fifty bucks. Is that enough?'

He pulled out his wallet and handed over the notes, and the dude reached into the front of his pants, just as Violet had said he would, and pulled out two small baggies and passed them low over the gearstick into Will's hand.

'Thanks. Thanks heaps,' Will said. He reached for the doorhandle.

'Sure thing. You've got my number. Have a good night.'

'Thanks,' said Will again. 'You too.'

He jammed the baggies into the front pocket of his jeans and got out of the car.

He had done it. The fear was past and the night was instant-lit with adventure. He got out his phone once more and orientated himself and began to head back along East 9th towards Union Square. The dark was sleek and warm and populous and he strolled through Tompkins Square Park where people were walking their dogs and jogging. He passed a group of young black guys with a portable speaker playing Kendrick Lamar and he drifted through chained pools of scent—dog pee and sullage and sweet weed smoke—fingering constantly the ziplock edges of the baggies in his pocket.

At the corner of his overhyped ebullience, he knew, hovered the threat of despair, like the shadow of a finger at the periphery of a photo, the pink obliterating blur that draws the eye away from the smiling foreground. But he was confident that tonight at least, with its novelty indomitable and heady and hammering at his senses, he could keep despair at bay.

He checked his watch but he had not adjusted it, and it was still on Melbourne time: 10.23 am, and at once he saw her—the agent of his flight—going about her morning life, watering her many potted plants and making her second stovetop coffee for the day and pouring in the Bonsoy and drinking it with that beaming pleasure that never flagged, as if each cup was the first and an exquisite new discovery, and then, as though flinging a blanket over a kitchen fire, he smothered this vision in a whoosh of urgent haste.

Instead, he pictured his mother, at the cheap computer table in the lounge where she sat to do her household budgeting, the beige carpet deeply marked by the wheels of her chair, switching on the old desktop with that boing-and-static modem sound, and he heard her call out to his father in the garage, 'No news from Will yet.' She had told him to email when he arrived, but he would not, and he felt a flush of cruel and childish pleasure and knew that he would wait some stubborn days before he made contact, to punish his parents for what they had unwitting and by their very natures brought to pass. He counted back the hours—8.23 pm—and he began to walk faster and with comforting purpose towards the subway.

*

The interval of descent into rank warm determined non-intimacy endured and over with, he emerged at Times Square. But oh, the dear disappointment he experienced in that place of light, that civic monument to the evolutionary death of anything as subtle as the subliminal, to advertising elevated to sightseeing, to the undeniable victory of capital. He stood and absorbed it: the mega-watt spectacle that overpowered even irony; the mass of pocket-sized screens focused on their end-point archetypes.

Not that he had expected to be awed; despite his low origins, he belonged to that association whose documents of membership are cynicism and a taste for unconvention: those possessed of 'cultural capital', hard-won in his own case and amassed with the diligence and utter seriousness that a nineteenth-century dandy might have brought to his education in opera and the delicate wielding of cutlery. His training had equipped him with a strong and avidly displayed aversion to mass culture in any context that did not involve enough irony to cushion him from derision (it was acceptable, for example, to watch reruns of *Friends* and admit to it as long as one was stoned or coming down). Yet he had not expected quite this depth of disenchantment, and he did not stay long, and made his way now aimless-east in search of touristic charm of a more refined or humble nature, capable of beguiling a twenty-two-year-old man in a state of emotional strife that exacerbated his already entrenched imposter syndrome and his developing pretension.

Who is he, then, this fresh and vulnerable protagonist of his own life, this end-times tourist of the falling West, fitting his own desperate headlong to the desperate headlong world and yet, and yet, so filled despite himself with the pheromonal drug of sweet young hope? Late-born son and younger brother; a small-town boy until his recent migration to Melbourne—to the fastball game of fakery and the slow spirit-whittling rot that was its consequence—in which metropolis he awoke to culture like a nightmare of public nakedness; awoke to all he had to learn and acquire and pretend he had always possessed. And to love, the swift shock removal of which has spurred this striking out from his antipodean home. He arrives heartsore and humiliated, the latter emotion for which he feels a particular sharp familiar aversion. Better, then, to cry on the plane, his cold grey eye mask applied like an ineffectual compress; better to flee the friends who know him and, worse, know Laura.

Laura Laura Laura Laura Laura.

It is all he can do to keep the door closed on that pain we feel but once and never allow again, that profound quotidian pain of first love repulsed.

In the region of Radio City Music Hall he returned to his body and to the blunt reality of hunger, and he swerved impulsive into a diner and ordered a burger and another beer. The place was desolate, unable to compete with the nearby smorgasbord of plasma and neon, though its own screens were plentiful enough, Will thought, and showed baseball and gridiron and basketball and hockey across the four corners of the room. Still, the diner displayed the necessary uncalculating semiotics, called up some prelapsarian New York out of Don DeLillo's early novels, and he imagined businessmen in polyester suits coming here for lunch, being served by the kind of large-breasted waitresses who don't seem to exist anymore, probably engaged in some protracted class action against that fallen god, the 'Boob Man'.

He sat down at one end of the bar, a polite three seats away from two men eating steaks, eyes raised in parallel to the baseball screen.

'Disaster,' said one man, chewing viciously with his mouth open.

'Annihilation,' said the other.

He could not help watching, himself, and found the screens a relief from the need to appear occupied when dining or drinking alone. In the ad break, a beautiful woman spoke silently at the camera, which zoomed in on her perfectly symmetrical face, her white singlet, her skin, which Will supposed epitomised the adjective 'mocha', though he wondered if it was racist to use or even think such a term. The image cut to an island paradise, to a coconut falling in slow motion, spilling its juice in an awkward symbolic gesture of ejaculation, and then the mocha-skinned woman was back, pouring a tetra pak of coconut water down her extended supple throat.

The small-breasted waitress set down his burger, along with a plastic basket that contained cutlery, napkins and an array of foil sachets of condiments: ketchup; American mustard; hot sauce; mayonnaise. The burger was terrible—the meat watery and grey—and the chips were thick and still tacky-raw in the middle, but he ate everything on his plate, opening three sachets each of ketchup and mayonnaise and drowning his fries in the red and white sludge. He had not taken a shit since before he got on the plane and now that he was sated and in a state of post-consumption tristesse he regretted putting more bowel-clogging carbs down his gullet and knew that there was pain to come. Was something added to the in-flight food that suppressed digestion? It seemed desirable, he supposed, not to have a thousand people shitting into the dry vacuum toilets over the course of sixteen hours. Once they were off the plane the internal blockage of those thousand people was of no concern to the airline. He shook his head at his own inanity and wiped the salt from his hands. It was time.

He paid and then went into the bathrooms and tapped out a line, choosing a crumpled American ten to snort it through, not his last Australian plastic twenty. He looked at himself in the mirror to see if his pupils were altering, but it had not come on yet, and so he wandered into the street, feeling more alone than he had ever felt before because it had been cold implacable defiant hurt that had made him leave his home and now, while he walked the hot dark congested aisles of the unknown world, she went about her day drinking the same strong soy latte and carrying the same brown leather backpack and drinking the same rosé at the same bar with Maddie and Ronnie, by turns laughing and talking intent and fierce from their sure embattled femaleness and all he had succeeded in doing was to make literal the distance that was now the truth of their unconnection.

On a whim, he bought a ticket and rode up and up inside the elevator to the top of a tall iconic building as his heart began to beat faster and a feeling of goodwill began to wash over him at last. He stepped out with a crowd of people onto the windy platform and saw the lights of the city spread out around him and was overwhelmed despite himself. He was a country boy still after all. He took a photo for an Asian couple who smiled with such sincerity that he could only be happy for them, and he looked over at the lights of the Chrysler building that was both exciting and boring at the same time, so familiar was its image, and down at the slow-moving phosphorescence spilling out in every direction below him, red one way and white the other, like lines of illuminated ketchup and mayonnaise. He thought that this was how it was to be alone in the world and yet content. It must be because I am here, at the centre of everything, he thought, and then he laughed at himself and thought, No, of course it is because of the drugs, and tomorrow I will wake again with that throat-ache grief of missing her. Still, he could not perforate the aura of luck around him in this moment, and he continued to gaze at the lights of this vast significant city, and he thought that it was unlikely anything could ever again surpass his fantasy, not a city and not a girl, and this made him feel a little older and wiser, but in a detached, filmic way, as if he was viewing himself from an external vantage point, the lights all out of focus around his face. He thought, in the smooth profundity of his coke high, about the concept of the simulacrum, which he had been introduced to in last semester's cultural studies class, and supposed that even New York was a simulacrum of some non-existent prime *metropolis* and to be awed by it was to fall victim to something, but nonetheless he could not summon up any trace of disappointment or disdain.

He stared at the lights for a long time, transfixed by the idea that every light in every window and every point in the ant-march of traffic represented a person, and that so many others were in darkness or crowded three or four into a single glowing vehicle or room. How do they go about their lives within the knowledge of such teeming populousness? How do they move so silver passive and so fast in their seats below the city, side by side in their thousands with their unacknowledged fellows like grains of sand tumbled endlessly along the ocean's seething bed?

He imagined the sea of light suddenly extinguished. The ravenous blackness that would open up below him like a maw. Even the awesome terrible stars blinking into view above could not fill the void, were no match for this plenitude of light. Even light, he thought, is excessive here.

He felt that old unvanquished religion rearing up in him, and he looked around him at the people pressed against the railings, all gazing at the same luminous dehumanising spectacle of humankind, and saw that it was impossible to do other than resist the knowledge of oneself as speck. As the bleakness and exhaustion began to tingle at his edges, he went inside to the bathroom, where he waited in a rising stench for the single cubicle to be evacuated, and then he chopped and lined up and inhaled the powder, to feel again the benevolence that he knew he had been born lacking and had found only briefly in Laura and now could only synthesise by half-hour intervals in the otherwise eternally mean sardonic synapses of his interior chemistry.

He did not return to the viewing platform, but descended once again in the tight-packed elevator, leaning in his inviolable trance against the mirror-panelled wall and exiting last.

It was almost 11 pm. If he walked from here, he might arrive to meet Paul at about the right time and have regained some sense of equilibrium for the meeting, of which he was somewhat apprehensive, Paul having spent most of their shared childhoods heaping shit on Will, pretending to punch him in the face and then laughing when he flinched, deriding his clothes and music and his inability to excel in sport of any variety and turning his own brother against him, too. But that was long ago, and they were both men now; Paul had been gone six years, was successful here, and had been nothing but welcoming over the phone.

He set off with fleet foot and firm purpose and a clenching jaw, the movement propelling the drug through his body and making the high more diffuse, but also less at risk of becoming unpleasant in its intensity. He was happy for now to close the gateways between his body and the world and exist as just a set of legs and sinuses, a sensation of chemical pleasure, and he walked 5th Avenue from West 49th Street to Washington Square Park, a mere organism in the cooling night, the air going in and out, being permeated by the world only in the usual unobtrusive ways. By the time he got to the park he had pounded himself sober again and his brain was sparking in brittle flashes deep within like lightning in a dense thunderhead. He consulted his phone and skirted the park and on a street of bars found the one Paul had told him to come to. It was one minute past midnight and the timing revived his sense of good fortune and he prayed to no god that his time in this city would blast away the phantom of Laura.

—

The first time he met Laura, he had been wearing what he'd come to think of privately as his hipster uniform or, more accurately, disguise. He sometimes wondered how things might have been different if he'd come dressed as his authentic or former self, in cheap straight blue jeans and a country town surf shop shirt with pearlescent press-stud buttons, perhaps with Rosie at his side, though dogs were not allowed in rental accommodation. Perhaps they would have turned him down and that would have been the end of it: he would have gone back to college and moved out later with Dobbers and Matt. But Jack, who he'd met that semester in a philosophy elective, had told him his best friend Tristan was looking for a housemate, and he was desperate to move out of college, away from the other country kids, and to meet some actual Melburnians.

And so he'd dressed the part, in his new skinny black jeans, short in the leg so that a band of pale ankle was exposed above the formal brown shoes he had paid an exorbitant sum for in a vintage store, for the service of having them accredited as acceptable in all their details of colour (chestnut, not chocolate brown) and shape (long and tapered at the toe, but definitely not squared off at the tip like those the college boys wore out to the clubs, announcing their cluelessness) and shine (high) and lace type (thin, round). He wore a white shirt and over his shoulder was slung a brown leather satchel of a shade equivalent to his shoes, but with a battered matt finish.

He pulled the D lock from his back pocket and fumbled his bike up against the pole of a street sign, clipping his helmet onto the crossbar. He ran a hand through his flattened hair.

It was hot and he knew his cheeks were flushed more than their usual pink from the ride. The street was wide and typical in its *inner north* way, lined with single-storey Victorian terraces and plane trees whose shed filaments were banked in the gutter like dirty snow. He felt the hay fever scratch at the back of his throat. Three milk crates sat on the front porch, and between them a wooden wine box stood on its end with a full ashtray and an empty bottle of Coopers Green on top.

As Will stepped up to the porch, the door opened and a girl came out. She was dressed in a hipster uniform too: very high-waisted jeans with a tucked-in stripy t-shirt, her hair up in a bun and a gigantic woven basket over one shoulder as a handbag. She was waving and smiling vigorously at the guy holding the door open.

'Thanks, Georgie,' said the guy. 'We'll give you a call as soon as we've made a decision.'

'Okay, no worries,' she said. 'I'm super keen, so just let me know.'

'We will. Take care.'

She didn't look at Will, but pushed past him, her basket rasping against his arm.

'You must be Will?' said the guy.

'Yep. Hi,' said Will, holding out his hand.

'I'm Tristan. Come in.'

They walked down a narrow dark hallway that smelled of mildew, past two closed doors and two bikes leaning against the wall. The salmon-coloured carpet was flat and threadbare down the centre and edged with dust bunnies against the skirting. They passed another door, this one open to an empty room with mirrored built-in robes.

'That's the room,' said Tristan. 'I'll give you a tour once we've had a chat.'

They came out into a sunny lounge that led onto a small kitchen and a paved back courtyard. There was a 'sofa' against one wall, made out of two mattresses partly covered with a woven rug. On it sat two women. One, incongruously, was knitting. Both scrambled up.

'This is Maddie and Laura,' said Tristan.

The girls held out their hands. Laura was the knitter. She wasn't as good-looking as Maddie, but there was something open and likeable about her. She had a lot of curly hair of a nondescript pale shade, a pale heart-shaped face with slightly pudgy cheeks, and a genuinely welcoming smile. She had several piercings up one of her ears and a gold hoop in her nose. 'It's Maddie and I who live here,' Tristan continued. 'Laura's just here pretty much constantly, so we thought she should be involved in the selection.' They all laughed. Will felt instantly despondent at the word 'selection', aware of the disadvantage his upbringing put him at with these easy city kids and sure already that he would not be chosen. Georgie had probably just engaged in an effortless exchange of the cultural codes that seemed to Will a language he would never be fluent in.

'Okay, let's do this,' said Tristan. 'Have a seat, man.' He gestured at a dining chair placed opposite the mattress sofa and sat down on another.

'Cool,' said Will. He felt like he was in a job interview. Why did they insist on making the process so formal?

'Sorry about the couch,' Tristan continued. 'We did have one, but it belonged to our old housemate and he took it with him.' He picked up a spiral-bound notebook and pulled a pen from behind his ear. 'Fuck, this never gets any less awkward, does it?' he said, smiling at Will.

'Nope,' said Maddie, smiling too. 'Don't worry, though, we liked the sound of you already from your email. And you're Jack's friend, yeah?'

'Yup.'

'So,' said Tristan. He turned a page of the notepad. 'You're doing arts at Melbourne?'

'Yeah. About to start second year. Not sure what I'll major in yet.'

'But you're almost twenty?'

'Yeah. I moved down from Newshepton at the start of the year. I had a year working after high school.'

'Where's that?' asked Laura.

'North-east. About halfway to Albury.'

She nodded as if she didn't know where Albury was, either.

'I'm at VCA,' said Maddie. 'Graphic design.'

'What about you, Tristan?' Will asked.

'Just working in hospo at the moment. And I'm in a band'—he made a sheepish face—'so I'm away on tour a bit.'

Laura picked up her knitting again. Will thought it was strange to see a young woman knitting; he had no idea that it was what everyone was doing, that he would soon see scores of hot girls pulling out their wool and needles at gigs and in pubs and parks and lecture theatres.

'So,' said Tristan again. 'What kind of housemate would you say you are? Are you a chores list kind of guy? Or more of a take-it-as-it-comes kind of guy?'

'Umm . . .' said Will. 'Well, I'm not a milk labeller, but I always clean up after myself. I guess I'd say I'm a shared stir-fry kind of guy, although I'm not a great cook or anything. I'll offer you a cup of tea when I'm making myself one.' Oh god, what was he saying? Tea! He wished he could come up with some witty epithet to describe his share house personality, but the truth was he didn't really know what kind he was. 'I've got good manners,' he continued, seemingly without conscious control. 'I can fix a leaking tap.'

'Ooh,' said Maddie. 'That's good! Our landlord is a complete tight-arse.'

Tristan nodded, making notes.

'And . . . you said you have a couch?' he asked, looking up.

Back out on the pavement again, Will had a sneezing fit under the plane trees and then unlocked his bike. No one else had arrived so far, but he was sure there must be millions of applicants. It was such a good location, and not too expensive either.

He wanted a reason to dislike Tristan and Maddie, but they seemed like nice people, which made it worse. He imagined what it would be like to live there, Laura and Jack coming over all the time to visit. There had been a record player in the lounge room and he imagined himself buying vinyl, going to Tristan's gigs, saying to people, 'My housemate's in a band. They're really great. I'll see if I can get you on the door for the next show.' He imagined them having parties, sitting on the porch together in the evenings after uni, drinking beers in the long sunshine. He thought about Laura knitting, and how it was kind of endearing, exhibiting a self-acceptance and comfort that allowed for actual *personality*, even a certain dagginess that somehow remained cool in its very confidence. It made him hope that he could be like that one day.

—

Paul was already seated at the bar when Will arrived, a cocktail in his hand, the red drink lit to a glow by the candescent backbar, where bottles of coloured liquid the full warm spectrum of amber to crimson pulsed among grass-green glass. The room was full and the only empty stool was beside Paul. Saved, presumably, for him.

He paused in the entrance to reassemble his parts, watching Paul, who put down his drink and laughed at something the white-shirted barman was saying, ice scoop raised. A waitress approached him and he gestured at Paul.

'You're Paul's friend?' She replaced her customer-service smile with a real one, a quick shuffle of cards.

'Yeah, I'm Will.'

'Ilona,' she replied, holding out a hand. 'Paul,' she called out over the noise of the room. He pushed his way over and Paul grinned and stood and they embraced, Will thumping Paul's back and then feeling foolish.

'Welcome!' said Paul. 'Hey, Stav.' He turned to the barman. 'This is Will. Closest thing I've got to a younger brother. He's my best mate Tom's little bro.' Stav held out his hand and Will shook it and settled himself on the stool.

'You made it!' said Paul. 'I kinda thought you might crash out on the couch. Are you shattered?'

'Pretty shattered.' As he said it, the tiredness loomed up from wherever he had locked it away, and his eyes began to water.

'Let's get you a drink, hey?' said Paul. 'I'm having a coffee Negroni. House speciality. Perk you right up.'

'Sounds amazing.'

'Al-*right*! Stav, two more please.'

Will didn't know whether he should mention the coke to Paul. He always misjudged these things. It would either be an affront or seem showy, an announcement of his desire to look cool in the eyes of this old ambivalent hero and tormentor.

Paul turned back to him, looking at him seriously with the uncanny pale blue eyes he remembered. 'It's been a while. What's been happening?'

'I know, right. Um . . . Where to start . . . I moved to Melbourne. Been there, like, three years now.'

'Great. Liking it?'

'Yeah, love it.'

Will realised this might not be true anymore. His life in Melbourne, his friends, the house he shared with Tristan and Maddie, the scene he existed within—a world of students and bands, of activists and home fermenting and backyard vegie gardens and doing paste-ups, of house parties and drinking beers in Edinburgh Gardens; his odd functional particular little ecosystem—it was all Laura's too, had been hers long before he stumbled into it out of pure dumb luck, and he had shared it with her and the others as a friend before they got together and now he would probably be banished, like some defeated adolescent gorilla chased out of the tribe to find his way alone in the predatory unloyal world.

'That's great,' said Paul. 'What else? Studying?'

'Yeah, just an arts degree. Not sure what I wanna do still, really.'

'Ah, you've got time.'

'I've been trying to get into a bit of music writing. I've done some gig reviews for the uni paper and I'm trying to get in with the street press. Tough competition, though.'

God, what a try-hard he sounded. Why had he mentioned it so early in the conversation?

'That's awesome!' said Paul, sounding genuinely interested. 'We'll have to see what gigs are on while you're here.'

'What about you? You've been here, what, six years or something now, haven't you?'

'Seven, now.'

'Seven! No plans to come home?'

'Nah, no way. I mean, never say never. I might turn around and decide I want a family and a fucking Hills hoist one day, but for now I'm happy here. Great job, great apartment, great friends. I've got a girlfriend. Who may or may not be the one. But I'm pretty crazy about her. She's super cool. An artist. You'll meet her.'

'Sounds great.'

'It is. And New York is fucking incredible. You're gonna have such an awesome time. How long are you planning on staying?'

'Not sure yet. I mainly wanna do a road trip. That's the plan. Maybe something like Route 66, but really just drive and get lost. But I'll definitely stay a few days, at least. If that's okay.'

Did it sound lame? Get lost? Route 66? He had left Australia with only the flimsiest structure of a plan, *On the Road* at the toe of his backpack, pulsing out some wishful compatriot energy of motion and heartless conquest. He'd fled only ten days after the breakup, long enough to secure a ticket and drop out of his classes and sublet his room to a friend of Tristan's and in a ferment of emotion detonate his life, as if it would somehow punish her; only now was he starting to wonder how he was ever going to return. It was a pantomime of heartbreak that made a mockery of his aspiring to the state of inviolable selfhood he secretly worshipped in Kerouac, the way women fell from him like ash shaken from the burning tip of adventure, cooling already as they paled and loosed and released while that pure core and engine of selfhood burned on.

'Of course!' said Paul. 'Like I said, stay as long as you want. You're practically family. Better than family! You'll have a great time. Justine—my girlfriend—has a show opening this week, so that'll be fun. Group show; big party. I'll have to be away for a night next weekend, unfortunately—booked a private gig. But that's still a week away. We'll have some time before then.'

'What do you mean a private gig?'

'Like, private chefing. I've been doing it a bit lately. Through my old head chef, who owns a bunch of places. Super zhooshy. Basically I get flown in by helicopter to cook for a bunch of rich cunts. The couple I'm doing this gig for next weekend, I've cooked for them four or five times now, and I haven't even met them. Never laid eyes on them. It'll be for their wedding anniversary or some visiting VIP or something, and they'll fly me up to Martha's Vineyard and I'll do a five-course dinner for eight people. That kind of thing.'

'Wow, that's crazy. You'd never get that in Australia.'

'Yeah, well, exactly. And I mean, they're rich wankers, but the pay is very good. Compared to regular hospo here, which is balls. And you get to work with some amazing produce, drink their wine, stay somewhere fancy, and usually have a day to yourself in whatever fuck-off beautiful location they've flown you out to. It's the only time I get to swim in the ocean, which I miss. Probably the only thing I miss about home.'

'Man, it sounds like a whole different world.'

'Oh, totally. You get that here, though. There's so much fucking *money* in this city, it's crazy. I'm seeing it in the art world now as well, via Justine. It's pretty fun to dabble on the edges of that kind of life, but I wouldn't want to reside there full-time. But it's all good. I used to pretty much always get laid with one of the gorgeous waitresses, too, before I got a girlfriend.'

'Man, I need to get laid.'

'Yeah, I heard.' Paul chuckled. 'Heard you're running from some kind of heinous breakup situation.'

'Oh, what?! Did Tom tell you?'

'He may have mentioned it.'

'Prick.'

'It's all good,' Paul said again. 'He's just looking out for you. Said I might need to show you a good time. So that's exactly what I'm gonna do.'

'Thanks.' Will took a big gulp of his Negroni.

'Speaking of good times,' said Paul. 'I'm going to powder my nose, if you catch my drift . . . You might wish to do the same?'

And so he did not need to confess, only to glide easily and with poise into the new narrative of tonight, and he nodded and Paul grinned and thumped his shoulder and said, 'Al-*right*!' and when he returned from the bathroom he passed Will an Altoids tin and said, 'Your breath's a bit funny, mate. Here, take a mint,' and although he knew it was a joke, he breathed and sniffed into his hand in the cubicle before he shook out the powder onto the screen of his phone.

He sat on the toilet seat for a few minutes and 'checked in' at Dante on Facebook. It wasn't something he would usually do, but he thought he remembered Tristan's boyfriend, who was a cocktail barman back home, mentioning this as a place he thought was cool, and Will hoped it would get back to his housemates, and to Laura, and help recast his trip as holiday rather than tantrum.

When he got back to his seat, Paul passed the tin on to Stav, who winked and said, 'Why, thank you, sir. Most kind.'

Will breathed in deeply. He felt the rush rear up behind him like a grizzly bear and enfold him in its arms. He looked at Paul and smiled, thinking how boyish Paul still looked for someone who had presumably been living hard for close to a decade. Paul looked like a Hollywood cliché of an Australian man, like the actor in *Gallipoli* who wasn't Mel Gibson: floppy sandy hair and pale stubble; broad shoulders and lean arms, which Will noticed were covered in purplish burn marks. He would have been a classic hunk except that his facial features were a bit too narrow and pointy. And then there were those eyes: Tom always joked that they were the eyes of a psychopath, so pale and cold-blue, but in truth they were more vulpine.

'Look at you, all grown up,' said Paul, and he ruffled Will's hair. Will winced, but Paul didn't seem to notice. 'Free Willy's all grow'd up,' he said in a stupid accent.

Oh god, here we go, thought Will. *Free Willy* had been one link in a chain of humiliating nicknames Paul had bestowed upon him in childhood, including—because his name was William Free—*Freeballer Willy*. He remembered his mother asking at the dinner table what freeballer meant, and Paul sniggering and saying, 'Yeah, Willy, explain it to your mum.'

'I wasn't sure whether to offer you the party parmesan or not, but you're obviously all over it,' Paul continued. 'Become a little bit of a hipster, too, haven't you? Look at those skinny jeans. You probably ride a fixie, don't you?'

Will tried to rally. 'No . . . maybe. I need to call my lawyer.'

'Guilty!' Paul crowed, picking up his Negroni and gulping from it like it was water.

Will nodded vaguely and looked around him. 'It's good to be here,' he said.

'Great to have you here! How's Tom? And your folks. They good?'

'Tom's good, I think. My folks are fucking killing me, though, to be honest. They came for a visit not that long ago and it was *so* painful.'

That was an understatement. But he wasn't going to get into the full story.

Paul laughed. 'Why? What happened?'

'Oh, just . . . I don't know. They're just getting so much more annoying as they get older. I mean, they were annoying already, but they're out of control now! Mum is *so* churchy. Even more than she used to be. Like, introducing her to my housemates, it was only a matter of time before she'd steer the conversation round to Jesus. It was *fucked*! And then Dad! He's so set in his ways. He doesn't want to actually *do* anything. Every time I took them somewhere he'd just want to go back to the hotel room and watch TV. And he won't *eat* anything! I don't know if you remember, but he doesn't eat fruit and vegies. Just, *doesn't* eat them. And Laura's a freaking vegetarian! So you can imagine how that was.'

Fuck, he was talking too much. He shouldn't have had such a big line.

'Laura? Is that her name?'

'Yeah.'

Paul laughed again and patted Will on the back. 'I'm sure it wasn't that bad. All parents are embarrassing.'

'You don't understand! It was *bad*! Dad actually said—'

'Remember your dad's "man cave" in the garage?' Paul interrupted. 'How we used to go in there and use his weights and watch Bruce Lee movies with him, and he'd always make us watch the fight scenes in slow-mo?'

'Oh god, how could I forget?'

'He'd rewound the tapes so much they were all stretched and fuzzy.' Paul let out a nostalgic sigh. 'Ah, I love your dad. What a kooky guy!'

'Yeah, well, you didn't have to grow up with him.'

'He's okay, as dads go. And I pretty much did grow up with him.'

Paul had come to live with them, when Will was twelve and Paul and Tom were in their final year of high school, because there was too much conflict at home. Between Paul and his father; between his father and his mother. His father had a mean streak, and Paul had inherited it, had been tough and vulnerable and cruel until a year in the benign kitsch chaos of Will's family softened him slightly, sitting down each night at the full mosaic dining table that had taken his mother six months to complete—six months during which they had eaten at flimsy card tables folded out and placed beside the big table with its growing plaster foundation and its wonky landscape of shattered tiles and button-shaped glass baubles and seashells that would soon spike the family elbows and make the surface unstable under glasses of tap water (or Appletiser at Christmas and birthdays) in domestic perpetuity, and were presumably still doing so in the reduced solitary mealtimes of his mother and father—while the Beatles or Grateful Dead played in the background at Will's father's insistence and Will's mother served up and said grace and then sat in a martyred silence that competed with the stereo, and his father kept a red plastic four-litre bottle of tomato sauce beside his placemat and brought every conversation around eventually to his last-days-of-freedom trip to London in the summer of 1972. By 8 pm his mother was at her sewing machine in the corner of the lounge room, the intermittent soft motor a familiar lull, and his father was back in his garage den practising his aikido moves or watching his videos and it was either homework or lights out by ten, take your pick.

All of that was between the two men as they sat in a bar in New York City, and Will felt suddenly that Paul was the perfect confidant: a stranger of seven years who also knew the asphyxiating shameful no-culture of his origins, who might understand his need to renounce those origins, heartless and entire, for at least the period of time it took to assimilate with the urban world. Paul surely knew the feeling and had in fact fled further and more effectively to the very throbbing *heart* of culture and had immersed and apparently surfeited himself in its plenty and emerged this cool self-knowing creature, clear-eyed and untainted by the wealth from which he daily drew his drip-feed sustenance.

'Another drink?' Paul asked.

'Sure. Why not?'

Paul held up two fingers to Stav, who returned a suave nod and began to squeeze and twist some long curling slices of orange peel, which he took from a mason jar that sat beside other identical jars containing pre-cut wedges of lemon and lime and sprigs of rosemary and lavender and dehydrated slices of apple, and beside them a small bowl of white and purple flowers that might—Will really had no clue—be orchids.

'So do you work this late most nights?' Will asked.

'Not always. I do brunch service most Sundays, and then if I'm lucky I get Monday, Tuesday off. Then I might do one lunch service and the rest are mainly nights. It's a bit rough on my love life, but it's probably good. Stops me getting too serious.'

Will couldn't imagine Paul getting too serious.

'Tell me about your girlfriend. What kind of artist is she?'

'Sculptor, mainly. She works with very messy, semi-liquid materials. Clay and silicone gel and shit like that. Even egg white. It's not the kind of thing you take home and put in your living room, but apparently actually *selling* art is unbelievably passé these days.'

'What?!' Will laughed. 'What do you mean?'

'Fuck, who knows. I'm just a spectator. A handbag, really. Or a doormat. A handbag that doubles as a doormat.' Paul paused and drank. His hand moved against the bar, a kind of spasm that betrayed strong emotion. 'Nah, I don't mean that. She's actually incredibly talented. I think her stuff is brilliant. She's super smart. The whole package. Except we can't seem to just *be*, you know. I'm not sure it's gonna work out, to be honest, even though the idea of not being with her makes me go out of my brain . . .'

'Why? What's the issue?'

'I wish there was *the issue*,' Paul said, making inverted commas with his fingers. 'There are a few, let's just say. We're both pretty damaged from a decade of shitty relationships, I think. Even though we know what we've got could be amazing we just can't seem to commit, you know.' Paul tilted his head back and inhaled. He was clearly quite high, as was Will. But this was going better than Will had hoped, and he tried his best to focus on what Paul was saying and nodded his head to show he was listening. 'We've both got one foot out the door all the time,' Paul continued. 'We've got our bags packed, is how she puts it. And we're constantly making sure the other one knows it. Like, that we'd be completely fine without each other. We've broken up a couple of times already. We've both semi-cheated on each other.'

'What do you mean *semi*-cheated?'

'Oh, just, you know . . . She still hangs out with her ex-girlfriend a lot, which she knows really pisses me off.' He paused and drank again. 'And then a few months ago she kissed her. I mean, I was there at the time. We were all really high, and it wasn't like she was doing it behind my back or anything, but I freaked the fuck out and told her it was over. Which lasted about a week, but in that time I fucked someone else and then *she* freaked out about that when she found out. Blah, blah, blah. It's all pretty tedious really, and I should probably just break it off, because we fight all the time. But I kinda just *can't*.'

'Man. That sounds complicated.'

'Yeah. Sorry. I talk a lot when I'm high. A lot of bullshit, basically.'

Paul drank and sniffed and cracked the joints in his knuckles and neck, turning his head with his hands as if it had no ability to move on its own. It was 1.30 am and the bar was packed. There was a big noisy group at a table directly behind them. The waitress, Ilona, had taken them round after round of Negronis, which Stav turned out with fast but unhurried precision.

The two men, almost strangers, almost family, slipped into silence, more comfortable now, in part because they had breached the shy unknowing that seven years had stacked between them, calling on the shared past like some benign (or at any rate, neutered) revenant invoked through these liquids and powders that constitute the magic of the modern age; in part because they had found at last that delicate elusive comfort point that consists in the precise balance of two competing substances and that resembles sobriety—strange aim though that would seem—yet differs in essential ways understood only by the proficient sybarite.

Paul looked over at Will with what he hoped was kindness. Christ, it was a relief to see that he'd turned out okay, despite the current heartbreak and the painful desperate trying to be cool, which he'd come through soon enough. Fuck, the guy was a flashback in human form, though; it was almost too much. Oof! Like some home-movie nightmare, and it took Paul back with all the inevitable bewilderment and friction of time travel. Shame and the name of the father; shame and his mother's purple violet yellow . . . and still she wouldn't . . . sent him off to Tom's like he was the one who . . . Oh, Tommy, Tommy, only true family of his heart and only friend. Where Paul would be without him he couldn't even . . . Shame and the constant diarrhoea. Shame and the thing with Grace that he'd never never told about: the older sister home for Christmas with her fucking *husband* and *Tom must not find out.* But oh, the seventeen summerness of it, the hotness and the terrifying love and then the smash like a fucking ceramic piggybank hit with a hammer and all those thousand thousand bits of him. That was where Will was now. God, he'd rather cark it right here on this bar stool than go back there. Women!

Will would be okay, though. Look at him, sniffing away and trying to act cool. It made Paul see it in his old self, too: that desperate bloody dragging yourself up and the gruelling effort of it just to convince yourself you're not marked forever by the very dirt of that church-fete-punch-up-drunk-dad-white-death town.

Paul felt his hand spasm, as it sometimes did involuntarily—so embarrassing—and he clenched it and cracked the knuckles. He knew he'd hassled this kid to a pulp, and yes he'd thought about that sometimes in his 3 am moments, but he was here now and smiling and maybe Paul could make it up to him, beyond getting him high! Oh dear . . .

*

'Bed, or keep going?' Paul asked, after more Negronis and more trips to the bathroom, after the big group had left and Ilona had called last drinks.

'Maybe bed,' said Will. 'I think I might have hit a wall.'

'You've done pretty well. This will help your jetlag, too. Sleep in a bit tomorrow and then stay up late-ish again tomorrow night and you'll be back on track.'

'I hope so.'

Paul drained his glass and turned to the bar. Will still had a good inch of watery red left, but he couldn't face it.

He reached for his wallet but Paul put out a hand.

'This one's on me. No protest.'

'But, Paul. You're putting me up at your place and . . .'

'Dude. Be cool. You just arrived, and I would like to buy you a couple of drinks. Would that be alright with you?'

'Alright. Thank you. I won't make a scene.'

'No, that's right, don't make a scene.'

They stepped out into the street where it was still as busy as a weekday lunchtime in Melbourne's CBD. It seemed to have rained while they were inside and the sidewalks were dark with wet and the road glistened, but the air was still warm, smelling of stirred-up dust and the juices released from leaves. Will knew that he was tired, but it was as if a row of spotlights sat between his rampant overstimulated consciousness and the dark truth of exhaustion.

'It's pretty much straight across town,' said Paul. 'So there's no real point taking the subway. I usually walk, but if you're too knackered, we can jump in a cab.'

Will hesitated. The idea of folding his frayed nerves into the dark motel-scented interior of a taxi seemed as luxurious as sleep right now, but he knew he had to be frugal, had seen the total of the cocktail bill and had virtually no savings. He knew, too, that this trip must last the full ninety days of his tourist visa or his self-respect was worthless, a commodity traded at more than its value.

'I'm okay to walk, I think,' he said.

'Okay, sweet. It'll straighten us out, too.'

Paul set off at a pace, and Will followed through green-perfumed air that was not what he expected of this mega-metropolis. There were so many small parks, slim interstices of wind-waved variegated leaf life between brick walls, giving the sense that each might link and merge in a labyrinth of garden, many-branching hive mind or wild emerald anima of buildings, the trees almost invisible in the dark but still perceptible by scent and by the swarm-movement of leaves and the way the breath of a million multiplied leaf lungs charged the oxygen as it moved through his own lungs' coralline labyrinth. Will longed to enter one of these portals and find his way to the city's heart, where perhaps some friendly minotaur or green-skinned goddess would waken him into a state of wisdom and he would emerge initiate and provisioned with those sure inner resources that were the expected outcome of this post-mythic hurtled quest to transform himself into the hero of his own story, though what form that might take—tragedy or melodrama or picaresque—he did not know.

And then there was the skyline, the thrilling familiar shapes created out of light that hung above their path, loomed almost, seeming too close because the closeness itself is the thing that cannot be reproduced (those futile stubborn repeat attempts to photograph the full moon, hanging like a paper lantern so pressing close that it is all we can do to refrain from reaching out to it, but which shrinks unaccountably in the image to just another chintzy pit-sized spangle among the ordinary spangles of the night). In real life, the New York skyline was somehow fake-seeming in its closeness, a cheesy pull-down backdrop in a tourist photo booth.

After this interval of skygazing and theorising in the over-awed manner of the drunk, Will once more submitted to the rhythm of walking and felt again the pure biological pleasure of effortless and continuous exchange through respiration that requires no thought or volition, and the two silent figures moved fast through the night towards their own small denning place.

WILL WRENCHED AWAKE WITH A cramp in the muscle of his left calf. He heard a shout in the still unconscious moment before he woke to the pain, felt the shape of the shout in the cavern of his mouth, and only thus knew that it had come from him. He ratcheted up, grasping the stone his muscle had become and flexing his foot until the catch released and the meat went slack again.

Paul appeared around the corner of the kitchen. 'Are you okay?'

'Yeah, just a cramp.'

'Probably dehydrated. I'll get you some water.'

'Thanks.'

Will threw his legs over the side of the sofa, the quilt gathered in his lap. His calf was tender, on the point of cramping again.

'Here.'

Paul handed him a glass and he drank, the clean water making his mouth feel rank and contaminated. Paul was dressed, and the smell of coffee came with him into Will's awareness.

'You look way too fucking chirpy,' he said.

'I'm off to work in a sec, unfortunately. You be right? There's coffee in the pot.'

'Thanks.'

'Any plans for today?'

'Nope. Any suggestions?'

'Um . . .' Paul held out his hand for the glass, a paternal gesture that made Will smile. 'Well, you could just go for a wander. Maybe even head up to Central Park. It's a nice day. And then, depending on the time, you could come in to my work for a late brunch. Let me know, though, and I'll bags you a spot at the bar. We get pretty hectic for Sunday brunch service.'

'Is it Sunday?'

Paul laughed. 'Uh-huh.'

'Okay. Sounds like a plan. Hey, what time is it?'

'Quarter to eight.'

'Jesus.' Will flopped back down and pulled the quilt up.

'Yeah, keep sleeping,' said Paul. 'I'm only on till five or six today, so I thought we could go out tonight. I'll be working most nights this week. You can meet Justine.'

'Okay, sounds good,' said Will, not lifting his head.

He lay with his eyelids closed and pink-lit against the day, feeling the way his brain ached and knowing, as his father had once told him, that his outer meninges had shrunk with lack of fluid and was squeezing the soft matter it was wrapped around, like cling film that has gone through the microwave.

He had to lie on his side with his legs tucked up to fit on the couch, and his body was sore from remaining in one position for so long. Still, there was comfort in listening to Paul's quiet noises of morning preparation: the juddering of the pipes in the wall, the squeak and gush and squeak of the faucet, the sounds of cupboards opening and closing and the thunk of a mug set down.

Paul came back into the room and said that he was going to open the window, just a bit. 'It's kinda funky in here. Some fresh air will help.'

And then the door banged and Paul was gone, and Will lay and urged his tender and shrunken mind to go back down to sleep, to lick its wounds and heal, but it only pulsed out painful admonitions and would not go down.

Sunday morning was just as quiet and breezy sweet in the East Village as anywhere and he even heard church bells, and the soft rhythmic vaguely sexual cooing of a pigeon close outside the window.

Eventually he admitted that he had woken into the awful spike in electric brain activity that follows the short blessed declivity offered by booze. He heard a door open and emit a dirty blast of house music from the apartment across the hall, where Saturday night carried on, oblivious, and he groaned and sat up.

Anyway, he wanted, though half-ill with the infusion of jetlag and comedown and heartache, to burst out into the light and air of Sunday, the single day in seven when he could seem regularly to rely upon his own cheer, either because of or despite the day's having been uncoupled from its association with worship by his startling glorious new-discovered agency at the age of thirteen, when he had taken perhaps the most definitive step of his life and told his mother that he would no longer go to church, and which felt always from that moment on like a lusty pagan holiday.

And after an interval he did burst out, damp as befits the act of outbursting, into the atmosphere of Sunday, with its sounds of birdsong (more voluble here, he noticed, in this mega-metropolis than in his own diminutive Melbourne) and its swishy leaves and its bicycles and strollers and its many dogs pissing in blithe freedom and sensual joy against the narrow trunks of gingko trees that sprouted from the pavement every three steps, each leaf the shape of a child-drawn tree and all of them moving moving moving as of course they would on a Sunday out of a glad collective quickening.

His first act in the sabbath worship of his free volition was to buy a coffee across the street and sit at an outdoor table from which he could see the community garden. He watched an old black man separating seedlings into narrow tubular pots and a bent ancient white woman with a mere spindrift wisp of white hair pruning a fruit tree with secateurs and a middle-aged Asian couple sitting on a bench with a thermos between them, and he recalled his high and green-lit garden fantasy of the night before, which seemed to him now as far-off and fantastical as a day-blasted dream.

A beautiful girl wearing denim shorts locked her bike and sat nearby. She crossed her long tanned legs, and her foot in its neat white tennis shoe hung in the air all showy languid grace as she took the elastic from her hair and shook out her short dark curls. And then she ordered a strong soy latte, and there was Laura, sprung up again inside him as fresh and close as pain.

How long would it be until the women stepped back into their myriad distinctness and stopped being Woman, until Woman loosed its tight connection with that one distinct woman, Laura?

The hurt was strong. It hit with more force than last night's drugs, and he thought he might actually spew. He stood and went inside, where seven customers typed on seven silver laptops, and he paid and drank a glass of water from the water station and left as fast as he could.

He would not let the Sunday feeling be contaminated by the ruthless predatory shade of memory, and he began to walk fast, away from the beautiful girl, feeling like a douche, but oh my god the tears began to prickle along the rims of his eyes and he looked up blinking at the branches and tried to remember that way of breathing—five-seven-eight? seven-five-eight?—that was meant to be calming.

He stopped on a street corner and like a drowner waved out of mute desperation and a cab pulled over to the rescue and opened its arms to him and he was enveloped, leaving the echo of his footsteps to carry on without him into Tompkins Square Park.

'Where to?' asked the driver, and he named Paul's workplace in the West Village and slumped back, texting Paul that he was coming in for brunch.

At the restaurant, he was treated like a VIP. A place had been reserved for him at the bar, and he was ushered straight in while the hostess at the door took phone numbers and told people that they would receive an SMS when their table was ready but unfortunately it would be at least forty minutes' wait, sorry, guys. Clusters of well-dressed people lingered on the pavement, some placated with coffees, and inside the room was all a-tinkle with cutlery and glassware and there were flutes of orange mimosas everywhere, Sunday-coloured against white tablecloths, and the air was crisp and flaky with the smell of butter croissants. Waiters hovered with big silver coffee pots, topping up cups.

'Hi, Will, I'm Daisy,' said the gorgeous waitress behind the bar. 'Paul told me to take extra special care of you.'

'Really?' said Will, keeping his tone free of the innuendo he wished was implied in Paul's request.

She looked perhaps Indian, with light brown skin, full lips painted hot pink, and a dark buzz cut. She wore big outlandish earrings, and was genuinely model-grade stunning. Stay back, phantom! Perhaps that would not be a problem, for the moment at least.

She put down a menu, a brunch cocktail list on top of it.

'Your first cocktail's on the house,' she said. 'Well, on Paul.' She smiled the widest smile, like Sunday itself.

'My *first* cocktail? Jesus! I could potentially still be drunk from all the cocktails Paul bought me last night.'

'Well, you know what they say . . .'

'Hair of the dog?'

'Uh-huh.'

He breathed out a big mock sigh, like a weary old lush, and raised the list.

'My pick's the marmalade Collins. Or the caraway bloody mary. Or if you don't like caraway, the dill pickle version.'

'Okay,' said Will. 'Whichever you think is best.'

'Do you like caraway?'

'Um, I'm not sure if I know what it is.'

She laughed. 'It's a spice. It tastes like rye bread.'

Will shrugged, helpless.

'Okay, we'll go for the dill pickle bloody mary,' said Daisy, sweeping away the cocktail list with a face that charmingly said she might find him trying if he weren't so adorable. She was very good at her job.

Will looked down at the brunch menu. He was hungry, but also felt gross and bloated and clogged. He still hadn't taken a shit since the morning of his flight. The menu was organised into sections: Broth, Grains, Protein, Vegetables. There were things like bone marrow with radishes and rye crackers; sixty-degree hen's egg with freekeh and taleggio; salmon rillettes with Belgian endive salad and bagel crisps; a wilted chard and chicory polenta mash. He longed for something plain, and wished that there was at least one item on the menu that he could confidently say he understood, and he was ashamed on both these counts.

A bloody mary was set down in front of him and he looked up and saw Paul, wearing chef whites and looking fresher and more awake than Will thought he himself might ever look again.

'Morning, sunshine.'

'Hi,' said Will. 'Thanks for the drink. I think.'

'Oh, come on. You're on holiday! And you're post breakup. By rights you should be unceasingly drunk for at least a month.'

Daisy joined Paul on the other side of the bar, which was raised, making the two of them loom over him like conspiratorial agents of vice, disguised by their general glow of wholesome vibrancy and sophistication and multicultural beauty.

'Daisy,' said Paul, putting his arm around her shoulders, 'my friend here is in a state of heartbreak and self-pity. We need to save him from himself.'

'Ooh,' said Daisy. 'I love a project.'

'Daisy is a mate of Justine's,' said Paul. 'She's how I got the job here.'

'Do you know what you'd like to eat, Will?' she asked, slipping out from under Paul's arm and turning her attention thrillingly—for our heartbroken hero is not far gone enough to be immune to attention—onto Will.

'Um . . . not yet, sorry,' he said.

'Jus and I are taking him out tonight,' Paul carried on. 'You should come.'

'Yeah, maybe. I haven't seen Jus for ages.'

Paul turned back to Will. 'You should get the variety burger. It's my recipe.'

'What the hell is a variety burger?'

'It's got beef brisket, chuck steak, heart and liver.'

'Oh god. I don't think I can do that, sorry. My guts aren't in the best shape after the flight.'

Paul made a cat's bum shape with his mouth. 'Ew . . . Okay, gotcha. Why don't you just let me feed you. I'll do you some greens. And you can have our prune shrub sour. That'll fix you right up. It's very popular with the over-sixty crowd.' He winked.

Will rolled his eyes. 'Okay, you can feed me. But not too much.'

Daisy looked from one to the other. 'We sorted then?'

'Yup, sorted,' said Paul. 'Get this boy a prune drink.'

'I haven't even started my freaking bloody mary.'

'Look, listen to your big brother. I know how to fix what ails you.'

'Are you talking about the heartbreak or the constipation?' Daisy asked.

'Both,' said Paul.

*

Three hours later Will was annihilated corporeally—perhaps even spiritually—by food and booze. He had drunk bone broth as well as four sundry breakfast cocktails and beheld, admired and consumed the over-rich succession of dishes that appeared in front of him, mysterious curated artefacts and symbols of the legitimised and lucrative debauchery of food culture, apex of privilege and apotheosis, as his mother would have it, of the sin of gluttony. And not even the peak of such debauchery; not the degustation menu, which Paul showed him when Will said he was feeding him too much, and which cost more and promised more and demanded more than Will ever expected to possess. Nonetheless, he was struck low when the check arrived and even with the twenty-five per cent discount applied and the first cocktail on the house the total was more than a hundred US dollars and that was before tax or tip and was officially and by far the most expensive meal he had ever eaten.

He thanked Paul and Daisy and told Paul he would come back to meet him by six o'clock and staggered out into the Sunday world that now seemed the very vision of uncorruption through which he hauled his bloated animal body, the reminder of his degradation.

If only he was less naive and more inured to decadence—if only he did not think in such retrogressive terms, was not the unconsenting vessel of his mother's Christian austerity and restraint and fearful rejection of all she did not know and would never try—he could have enjoyed this experience: being drunk and well fed, over-nourished by a friend on a warm Sunday at leisure, no duty or obligation but to refuse to languish in his heartache and self-pity.

More shameful then than excess was the fact that his very shame revealed him as he was: a bumpkin and an unsophisticate. A pleb and country boy whose ignorant associations with culture and metropolis were those of depravity and sin. He must and would learn from this time in New York: to enjoy, or at least season himself to, such excess. It would be for him a journey from innocence to experience, and he thought how fine it would be to return home acquainted and easy with decadence and he made a vow to open himself to whatever came his way, to free himself from judgement and become for this interval at least a newborn hedonist and yea-sayer, embracing all as part of the world in its glorious variegation and flinging off his mother's—his country's—stunted binarism like an outgrown garment to reveal himself free and breezy in a dashing new habit of wild and indiscriminate 'yes!'

He walked to Washington Square Park and lay down on the grass and a moment later he woke in shade and rose stiffly and checked the time and hurried back again.

Paul had knocked off already and was drinking a beer at the bar, his apron rolled up, the Altoids tin on the counter, and a powerful smell of miscellaneous food emanating from his person. He patted the empty stool beside him. 'Beer?' he asked. He looked tired, his hair flat, the skin around his nose and chin dry and flaky.

'Um, I dunno if I can move on to beer now after all that mixing of spirits at lunch.'

'Negroni?'

'Sure.'

Paul walked behind the counter and began to mix Will's drink. The restaurant was quiet now, and most of the tables were empty, re-set for dinner service. It was just after 5.30 pm.

'What have you been up to?' Paul asked.

'Fell asleep in the park.'

'Derro!' said Paul with affection. 'I thought you looked a bit rumpled. Did you enjoy brunch?'

'It was amazing! Thank you.'

'You're welcome.'

Paul smiled, and Will saw that he had pleased him with his sincere appreciation.

Paul set the Negroni down and cracked the joints in his hands and then his neck. The sound always made Will feel a little queasy.

Will inclined his head towards the Altoids tin. 'Are you?'

'Might have had a sneaky couple. Only way I could get through service today. Man, we got reamed.'

'Seemed like it. Is it always that busy?'

'Sunday brunch, yeah, pretty much. Hey, do you know it's the tenth anniversary of September eleven today?'

'Oh fuck, it is! I totally forgot. There was probably some kind of event or something.'

'Probably.'

'That's the only reason I could afford to come here, actually. I got really cheap flights because apparently no one wants to fly around this date.'

'People are idiots.' Paul finished his beer and went to get another.

'So, what's the plan for tonight?' Will asked.

'Well, Justine's having drinks with some girlfriends in Chelsea. So we could go and meet them. Or we could go somewhere to eat and then meet her after . . .'

'I don't think I'll need to eat again for about a week.'

Paul laughed, and Will thought how cheery and open he was compared to the hurt and hurtful boy he had been when they were young together. How had Paul reached such easy equanimity? How could he escape his own life's dumb defiance against the long-gone, never-gone past?

'Okay, cool,' said Paul. 'In that case I'll grab a bite here quickly and then we can head up and meet Jus. Sound okay?'

Paul ate a burger and fries and drank another beer and then a Negroni while Will sat on his one Negroni, and then they were off, walking to Chelsea with all its fertile associations of grunge and glamour, Will's fug lifting as he walked and his eyes wide open.

They came to a small and dingy bar and Paul led the way through, nodding to the barman, who smiled and motioned to the back. As they neared the door, they could hear female laughter, loud and captivating, the sound of desire and exclusion.

In the small bricked courtyard, hung with fairy lights and with grapevines growing over a wooden pergola, three women sat in various positions of hilarity, three martinis on the table between them. One was saying, 'So I'm lying there wiping my pussy with this fucking baby wipe!' and another snorted with laughter while the third brushed tears from the rims of her eyes, mouth pulled down as if she was putting on mascara.

The two men stopped, feeling shy and left out respectively, until the woman facing them noticed they were there.

'Your boyfriend's here,' she said, and the snorter came over and kissed Paul on tiptoe while the laughter of the other two subsided into sighs.

'This is Justine,' said Paul. 'This is Will.'

Justine stuck out her hand. 'Hi, Will. Good to meet you. I've heard lots about you.'

She was short, with muscled yoga arms and thick brown hair up in a messy bun. Her skin was a healthful international olive that could equally indicate Spanish or Israeli or Colombian heritage, or just a lot of time in the sun. She looked ordinary enough to Will, though Laura probably did to other men too, for that which inspires our obsession is not always evident to others.

'What are you ladies talking about?' said Paul.

'Oh god,' said Justine. 'Darla had a date with this guy the other night who she met online, and after they fucked he handed her a packet of baby wipes and started cleansing his cock. Like, actual baby wipes, with a picture of a teddy bear on the pack.'

'Wow,' said Paul. 'Clean freak.'

'More like misogynist,' said Justine.

'Why misogynist?'

'Well, clearly he's afraid of contamination. Of being contaminated by *woman*.'

'Mmm, interesting theory,' said Paul. 'I need a drink.'

'I'll get them,' said Will.

'Okay, thanks. Another Negroni, I guess.'

Will ducked back inside and ordered two Negronis from the barman, who was dressed in the Prohibition-era uniform of white shirt and braces, sleeves rolled up to reveal tattoos of bluebirds and anchors, and who sported the requisite carefully unkempt beard.

'I'll bring them out, buddy,' he said. 'You want to start a tab?'

'Sure.'

'Lemme grab your card then, bud, and I'll give you one of these.' He handed Will an oversized playing card. 'Queen of Spades. She'll bring you luck.'

'Will she?'

'Sure. That's my lucky card.'

'Cool. Thanks.'

He wandered back towards the courtyard, feeling intensely awkward. He wasn't in the mood to hang out with a bunch of strangers who all knew each other really well. Maybe a line was in order. That would certainly make him more talkative. Although he didn't want to be the only one high. Well, the only one besides Paul, who seemed to be the same either way. He paused at the back door and looked through the glass panel. Paul was sitting beside Justine, who was talking, moving her hands, looking around as if for backup. He pushed open the door.

'Why can't you just accept that he *could* be a misogynist?' Justine was saying.

Paul turned as Will walked out. 'Hey, this is my friend Will. He's visiting from Australia. Will, this is Darla and Kim.'

Darla was a scrawny redhead with long, very straight hair and bangs. Her face was sharp, almost slightly masculine, with strong cheekbones and jaw, freckles and a lot of bronzer across her cheeks.

She wore a black leather jacket, and Will found her immediately intimidating. Kim was African American, immaculately made up, with teeth that looked like they'd had a lot of money spent on them, but she seemed friendlier than Darla and smiled dazzlingly at Will. She had big gold hoops in her ears, and wore an emerald green silk shirt. Her hair was pulled back in a tight ponytail, and she could have come straight from an office.

The three women were almost comically different looking, and yet connected by their obvious confidence and radiant youth and coolness. They greeted Will, and he sat in the only empty seat, which was between Justine and Kim. Justine finished her martini and passed the glass to Darla, who ate her olives, and it was clear that this was what they did.

'How do you all know each other?' he asked, when he got up the courage to speak.

'Art school,' said Darla.

Justine turned to him. 'Paul told me how your family took him in when he was a *troubled teen*. He says you're like a little brother to him.'

He saw Paul looking at him.

'Yeah, he was definitely like a big brother back then . . . i.e. an arsehole.'

'*Arse*hole,' said Kim. 'Oh my god, you're so *Australian*!'

'He can still be one of those,' said Justine. She winked at Paul.

'Sure can,' said Darla.

'Hey,' said Paul. 'Easy.'

'So, what kind of work do you do?' Will asked Justine. 'Like, artwork, I mean.'

'I make sculpture, of a kind. It's ephemeral. Like, non-permanent.' Will nodded to show that he knew what ephemeral meant. 'I use materials that shift and change over time. And that eventually just slump into a pool on the floor.'

'And what's it about? If that's not too dumb a question.'

'What's it about?' She gave a patient smile. 'Um . . . well, it's sort of about sculpture itself, in a way. About what we want from it. Which, traditionally, has been permanence, solidity, grandeur, you know? Big blocks of marble that the artist forms painstakingly over years and years into the image of human perfection. So instead my work just sort of *melts* over several days or weeks to reveal an armature or a block of wood or stone.'

'Wow, that sounds fascinating. So how do you work out how long different materials are going to take to melt away? Or is that part of it, that you don't really know?'

'Oh no, I know. I've done a lot of research on that stuff. Viscosity and rates of flow.'

'Sounds like you'd need a science degree.'

'Ya-huh.' She looked pleased that someone had acknowledged the difficulty of her work.

At the rear of the courtyard the door opened and the barman appeared, two Negronis on a tray balanced on the tips of his fingers.

'Could I please have another martini?' Darla said as he set them down.

'Me too,' said Kim and Justine in chorus.

'Of course. Would you ladies like to start a tab?'

'Here, take my credit card,' said Kim. She opened the fat purse that was sitting on the table and pulled out a gold card that made her look, Will thought, hugely successful.

'I've got a tab going,' he said. 'Just put them on mine.'

'No, no,' said Kim, flapping the card.

'Seriously, it's fine. Put them on mine,' he said to the barman.

'Yes, sir. Same again? Gin, dry, olives?'

'And dirty for me,' said Darla.

'Thank you,' said Kim.

'Yeah, thanks,' and, 'Thanks so much,' said the other two.

Will suddenly realised that they thought he was offering to *pay* for them all, rather than just divide the bill at the end, and he felt mildly ill.

Paul lifted his Negroni and they all cheersed, though Justine and Darla's glasses were empty, Darla's with six olive pits at the bottom.

'Hey, when do you head off, Darla?' Paul asked.

'Next Monday. As in, not tomorrow.'

From the way she spoke to him, Will got the feeling that Darla didn't like Paul very much. There was a strong and circumambient energy to her, not precisely hostile but as if she anticipated hostility from others and so built up around her an aura of protection, a body language of crossed arms and a tone of scepticism, all of which fell away, quick as a smile, in the very instant of turning towards the two women whom she evidently loved and trusted utterly.

'You excited?' asked Paul.

'Of course. Can't wait.'

Will looked up, hoping to be filled in.

'So what will you actually be *doing* while you're there?' Paul asked, his tone, too, its own armour.

'I'll just be a regular volunteer. I mean, they know I'm an artist, and I'll be documenting. Whatever I can get permission for, anyway. But I'll just settle in first. I'll have to earn everyone's trust before I can start filming or doing interviews or anything.'

'Where's she going?' Will whispered to Kim.

'Oh, sorry,' said Darla. 'I'm going to spend some time in a rescue sanctuary for wolves, in California. They've got this program there where they use wolves to rehabilitate combat veterans with PTSD.'

'Oh, wow. That sounds amazing. And are you making a film about it or something?'

'Um . . .' Darla made a face that suggested it was too complicated to explain.

'Darla's art practice is all about the relationship between humans and animals,' said Kim. 'So her previous show was about bees, and the place they have in the ecosystem and the way humans have farmed bees for centuries. And about the symbolism we've constructed around them . . .' She paused and looked at Darla, who gave her an amused smile and said, 'Please . . . continue.'

'Well, it ended up as a kind of multimedia installation piece, with lots of different elements, including scent and sound. And she's just been asked to exhibit that piece in Europe, which is completely brilliant.'

'Congratulations!' said Will.

'So,' Kim continued, 'basically the point is I don't think she knows what will come out of this trip yet, but she's got an

NEA grant, and she's interested in this idea of wolves and the complicated relationship we've had with them culturally. Or historically?' She sat back and laughed. 'How did I do?'

Darla was bending over, lighting a cigarette, her hair shielding the flame. 'Great,' she said, exhaling smoke. 'Will you write the catalogue essay?'

'So, Darla—' Paul began.

'Where the fuck are our drinks?' Darla interrupted him.

Right on cue, the barman reappeared through the swinging door with the martinis. As he placed them down, Paul pointed to his glass and held up two fingers and the barman nodded.

Will stood. 'Bathroom,' he mouthed at Paul, not wanting to interrupt the conversation that had resumed about Darla's trip.

'Just inside,' Paul whispered. He pulled the Altoids tin from his jacket pocket and waggled it at Will, his eyebrows raised in question, and Will laughed and took the tin with a 'thanks', because it was too late now to tell Paul he had his own stash without looking like a weirdo.

As he headed towards the door he heard Justine say, 'Oh, so you guys are getting on it already? Why you holding out on us?'

Will drifted back to the table, to his waiting seventh cocktail of the day, glowing crimson in the sinking light, its big diamond-clear ice cubes sparkling with a beautiful false purity. He sat quietly, waiting for his high to kick in and enjoying the conversation of the women. It was something he had come to know when he was with Laura: sitting at a table somewhere with her and two or three of her friends, just listening to them talk, so different from the light disjointed chats he had with guys, which skipped across the surface of things like stones tossed over water, careful to keep moving and ignore the depth beneath, each brief touching down swiftlifted by a joke or a friendly jab at one or other of the group. These women, like Laura and her friends . . . they had *conversations*, diving deep and staying under.

'It's the cultural symbolism underpinning the whole thing that I'm interested in, mainly,' Darla was saying. 'There's this implied equivalence between the rescued wolves and traumatised soldiers. I mean, that in itself is fascinating. Soldier as wolf; wolf as soldier. Because, historically, culturally, wolves have always been seen as the enemy. One of the last predators. They're almost the archetype of the predator. In fairy tales, for example. And really the wolves are in there because we've destroyed their habitat, and have actually deliberately tried to destroy *them*, as a species. But in *this* case, there's a connection being drawn between the misunderstood, maligned wolf, who's now represented as actually this noble creature, just trying to survive, and these returned servicemen, who I guess they're saying are perhaps also misunderstood in some way.'

'Yeah, well,' said Kim. 'They're not treated like heroes anymore. Not in this bullshit war.'

'Yeah, for sure,' said Darla. 'I can see how it would be useful for those soldiers. That archetype. The innocent killer, or something. But on a broader cultural level . . . it's just interesting.'

'Yeah, fascinating,' said Will. He longed to contribute something impressive to the conversation, but all he could focus on was the numbness of his mouth and the sensation of his heart beating.

'And then there's the whole other part of it, which is this idea of the wild—in this case represented by the wolves—as a panacea for the human soul. It's seen to be inherently *healing* to commune with the wild. And then the gender stuff around that, too. Making these men feel masculine again. Like their trauma and PTSD is seen as feminising, and they need to be restored to full masculinity again through contact with this archetype of "wild nature", or something. Anyway, all of that's swirling around in my head, but I'm open to just observing them and seeing what they actually do there. There's a lot of ethics stuff that I need to be mindful of.'

'Full moon's gonna be a bitch out there,' said Paul, and he laughed and then howled stupidly at the darkening sky above them. Darla rolled her eyes.

Everyone had had a turn of the Altoids tin now, and Will had taken it twice in short succession and felt the sliding withdrawal of self-consciousness, the lifting of his mind into a sphere of frosted glass from which he could finally speak, the words slipping through like light and instantly diffused into no memory. His mind stretched out, ambient and open. As long as there was this within access, shyness was not a thing. He felt more comfortable and at ease than he had for he didn't know how long. Perhaps ever.

He wondered if he'd always seemed like a bit of a dickhead when he'd hung out with Laura and her girlfriends, as Paul did here. He remembered a conversation between Laura and her friends, who were all studying literature, and were talking about irony and how it represented the dominant theme of the 2000s, and he'd burst into that Alanis Morissette line about *ra-i-ain* on your wedding day, and they'd all just looked at him with this expression of total disdain. He'd replayed that conversation so many times in his head, and it never got any less painful to recall.

When he tuned back in, the talk had turned to the state of arts funding under Obama, and then they were discussing some guy called Marcus, who apparently lived in a millionth-floor apartment on Central Park.

'Do *not* tell me I'm gonna turn out like Marcus, please!' said Kim. 'That man is legit crazy!'

Justine turned to Will and said, 'Marcus owns the gallery I'm represented by,' and he knew she was throwing him a line into this buoyant circle of friends, that she was a kind person, whatever the complications between her and Paul. 'You'll meet him if you come to the opening,' she continued.

'Oh my god, I'm *totally* coming to the opening,' he said, like an idiot, and then, 'This Marcus guy sounds interesting.'

'He is interesting.'

'You fucking *worship* him,' said Paul.

'Oh shut up,' said Justine. 'Just because he's another man in my life who happens to be a lot more powerful than you . . .'

'Just don't take the pills he offers you,' said Paul to Will. 'You might wake up in some gold-plated bathtub covered in lube.'

'You are so *wrong* sometimes!' said Justine.

'Okay, kids!' said Kim. 'We should get moving. Are we all going to Tamar's party?'

Apparently they all were. Will wondered if he minded having his night determined for him in this way, and decided that he did not. He hadn't thought of Laura for at least an hour, and he liked this group of people and the world they inhabited, which seemed to be a good several rungs above anything he had even brushed up against in Melbourne. In fact, it was the very world most of his friends dreamed of being part of, back home, and perhaps if he could return bearing the spangled traces of this encounter with culture he might make up for the humiliation of his dashed departure.

Back home, he found himself pleasantly coke-philosophising, the circles of power and cool were like Venn diagrams that never overlapped; back home, the powerful people were white male baby boomers with distended bellies who played golf and lived southside, and their kids had gone to private boys schools with grammar in the title, and had been to Europe on family holidays, but were painfully out of their depth at share house parties in backstreet Collingwood, where everyone was working six days a week in hospo and making stencils in their spare time and could get much better drugs if the rich kids would pay, which they would, and the rich kids tried to take over the PA and put on Cut Copy and were laughed down and had to pretend they'd heard of Shabazz Palaces. Back home you could be rich or cool, but not both. But here it seemed that these young women were, if not genuinely powerful yet, at least next in line, and those they stood to inherit from certainly didn't sound like the golf-playing types. He was beginning already to fall in love with the image of itself that New York was spinning around him tonight, himself but a flimsy stick held, he hoped, long enough for the glorious gossamer sugar of experience to accumulate and envelop him in its pink cloud.

*

In the grey star-fade dawn, Will went to bed to the ghastly sound of birds calling on the day, with the experiences of the night still churning in his mind: the conversations overheard or mildly contributed to; the articulateness and cool of Justine and her friends; the almost impossible glamour of Tamar's party, in a warehouse loft, full of young men and women who all seemed to be living at a peak intensity he was not sure he could sustain even with the yea-saying spirit of the traveller and constant access to the Altoids tin; the way the dancefloor was like a video clip, everyone moving so smooth and sensual in their impeccable street fashion; the way that Paul seemed to flow from one such heightened moment to the next, lithe unresting symbol not of iniquity (that was his mother's voice) but of indomitable energy and keen amoral yet still discriminating hunger, without ever growing satiated or overwrought; the hotness of the girl he danced beside and wanted to kiss but didn't and who he later saw kissing Darla on the fire escape. And yet he knew that he had not really participated but only spectated from a distance created by his own provincial reticence and inability to let himself go, a product not of provincial Melbourne but his bog-provincial home town, where the Protestant and convict commingled and persisted with enough determination to produce in the twentieth century a figure such as his mother and many more like her, abnegant and fiercely plain, repudiative of pleasure and suspicious of ambition, and he realised with a sick feeling that his own climbing had merely raised his head to chin level above that pervasive element, his upbringing.

—

Over the next three days he tried to raise himself at least to chest height, and he waited impatiently for Thursday and the launch of Justine's exhibition, which Paul said was going to be *wild*.

Paul had Monday off and they spent the day together, what little was left of it once they woke from the sleep that began with birdsong and ended in clammy midday sun. Paul took him to Brooklyn, to a bar where there was an oyster happy hour, and he ordered each of them a dozen oysters, marking in the numbers of several East and West Coast varieties on the skinny order sheet they were given, like some ironic food hall self-ordering system, as well as French champagne at twenty-five dollars a glass. Will had eaten oysters only once before, when he had taken Laura out for a fancy dinner for her birthday. 'Ooh, shall we have some oysters to start?' she had said, and he pretended he'd tried them before and swallowed them down like soft enormous pills of fresh-killed grey and briny flesh. But he was determined to like them now and found that, with interspersed mouthfuls of heavily buttered bread, he did.

On Tuesday Paul was on a double, and Will walked the streets, observing the city with the heightened attention of the newly-in-love. He loved the serial repetition of corner delis with their displays of flowers and potted plants, and wondered at the profusion of psychics and how they could afford to rent their small shopfronts, decked out with red velvet curtains and crystal balls over which the non-existent customers would crane into their futures, on display to the passing foot traffic and performative as those gyms with rows of treadmills facing the street (walking in the evening he saw a psychic and her young son sitting at the small round table in the shop window sharing a pizza from a takeaway box, and he found the image unbearably poignant).

He went to Central Park and there he fell asleep again in sunshine on grass, exhausted by all this peak with no trough except that which lay over the inevitable but thankfully still-distant horizon, a crash he pictured as a growing shadow creature, but which could still be chased away a good many times before it loomed and turned and began to chase him back.

He went to Tom's Restaurant, where he ate a mattress-thick pastrami sandwich and a pickle as big as a dildo, and he took a photo and considered sending it to his father, *Seinfeld* being one of their few shared interests, but lacked at present the magnanimity required for such an act. He still had not emailed his mother.

Avoiding rumination, he made another call to 'the dude', and he bought his own tin of Altoids and concealed beneath the powdery paper his dubious powder bounty. He took it everywhere and remained drunk and high with a determination he had never previously mastered, and he made his way through this foreign city buoyed and alone in a state of awed unceasing openness.

He was besotted with the contrary nature of the East Village, where impeccable small cocktail bars persisted beside tenements with busted-out windows—or was it the other way around?—and where all those small green portals led him back to his midnight garden labyrinth dream. He walked, in love with grey squirrels that bounded and leaped and watched him from tall trunks with such intellect, and with the oily rainbow starlings and the chess players and rows of old ladies who sat with their vinyl shopping carts gripped like cellos between their knees in

Tompkins Square Park, where the sign on the playground gate read *No adults unless accompanied by a child*, and where the dogs likewise had their own exuberant domain, and in love with the fenced miniature plots of flowers around the bases of the telephone poles, and even with the mounds of black garbage bags stacked up on pavements like the evidence of some industrial holocaust of waste and overpopulation that would consent to neither forgetting nor disguise. He went to a record store the size of a regional Australian airport, where he flipped and flipped in a compulsive daze until he grew dizzy, but he knew this journey asked of him a lightness that he truly longed to obtain, and he walked out empty-handed into the bounteous city.

All this took him to Thursday night, when he was to meet Paul after work and go with him to Justine's exhibition opening. As he crossed Washington Square Park, very high, the sky going the chemical colour of Cottee's orange cordial, he was kindled with a peaking manic vision and felt he was being blessed by the spirit of the solitary quest, sensed the presence of an ancient guide beside him, bright and insubstantial as burning paper. He felt himself glow hotly and deep among the cold sleep-blind masses who passed him on the path, holding up their amulets of no-change—the paper coffee cup and the mobile phone—and he saw himself in a ritual of sex and violence, blood-smeared and naked, and knew that he was climbing still to the apex of his initiation.

He walked in thrall to this appropriated dream of primitivism, and he began to think about Paul, the expatriate. At first he had seemed a new man entire: sophisticate and fine, fitted precisely to this city as a piece of clay fits into a hole. But seeing him with Justine, Will had glimpsed that boy still there, incompletely buried: that boy who had made his own youth harder but who was hard and hurt himself and desperate to be shown welcome, who pushed away out of presumption that whatsoever solace was offered him in this world would last only until he grew to need it and then be twitched from him, as easy and smarting as a hair in a tweezer. Here, Paul had been kind. Perhaps he remembered. Still, there was a wariness in Will, even a faint urge to humiliate Paul somehow, though only in far outdated retaliation. Paul seemed, for the most part, to have changed, and this offered such relief to Will, still living every day engrossed in his desperate wish for metamorphosis, his dream that the past could be hatched out of and left behind, clean-broken and clingless as a carapace.

And there was the man himself, sitting at the bar rubbing his eyes, a Negroni in front of him. Daisy was pouring him water from a tall amethyst glass jug. He saw her lips move and they both convulsed into laughter, mouths open and bodies curving. Will was looking in from the pavement like a revenant, but he was electric with anticipation of the night. He pushed open the door and went to the bar and put his hand on Paul's shoulder.

'*Heey!*' said Paul. They hugged, and Daisy came around the bar and kissed Will's cheek. She smelled of some woody, almost masculine scent that made Will want to nuzzle into the soft convex between her shoulder and neck. He wondered how old she was. Older than him; maybe twenty-five? Twenty-six? Fuck, he needed to get laid, for wasn't that the surest way to obliterate the sweet intolerable memories that dogged him even now?

'How was your day?' Daisy asked.

'Yeah, great,' he said with some effort. 'Yours?'

'Mine? *Amazing*.' She rolled her eyes. 'I've only got a couple of hours to go, though, and then I'll come meet you guys. See Jus's show.'

'Oh, brilliant.'

'You want a drink before you head off?'

Will looked at Paul, who raised his full Negroni.

'Sure. Maybe just a beer, though.'

'Pussy,' said Paul.

'Hey, man, just pacing myself. I already had two beers with lunch and then a park nap, which seems to be my MO here.'

'Okay,' Paul said. 'Get the man a beer.'

'I've got a gorgeous IPA made in Williamsburg,' said Daisy.

'Nah, fuck that,' said Paul. 'This man is an Australian. No IPAs for him. Get him a real beer.' Paul's voice sounded as if this may not be his first Negroni of the day.

'I'm quite partial to an IPA, actually,' said Will. 'You really haven't been back home for a while, have you?'

'IPA shmy-PA,' said Paul.

Daisy was lingering, looking at Will.

'I'm really not fussed. A real beer is fine.' He winked at Daisy, who shook her head.

Paul pulled out the Altoids tin and set it heavily on the bar.

'One step ahead of you,' Will said, revealing his matching tin.

Paul laughed loudly. 'Re-*heally*?' he said. 'How'd you wrangle that? You should've asked me to hook you up!'

'Actually, I had a contact from a friend of a friend. I've pretty much been high for the last forty-eight hours. I could never afford to do this back home, so I figure I may as well take advantage.'

'Oh, man, I know. Only problem is when you live here it's so fucking cheap there's really no disincentive at all. I've been taking advantage for years now.'

Daisy set a bottle and a cold glass on the bar. She uncapped the beer and poured it. Her hands were slim and proficient and perfect. There was a large emerald ring on the middle finger of her left hand.

'Thanks, Daisy,' he said.

'You're welcome.' She flashed him a smile that made him feel as if he himself was a just-uncapped beer and moved off down the bar to serve some other lucky bastard.

'Fuck, she's stunning.'

'Daisy? I know, right.'

Will sighed.

'Don't worry, there's gonna be plenty of beautiful women at the opening,' said Paul. 'And the afterparty, which I imagine will get pretty loose. The last one did.'

'Justine's last opening?'

'Yeah. Actually that was the night she pashed her ex, so hopefully not quite as loose as that.'

Will felt a slight sting of insult at the fact that Paul had directed him away from Daisy, as if she wasn't even a possibility. Then again, who was he kidding? She was way out of his league. And maybe Paul knew she had a boyfriend or something.

'So . . .' said Paul in a tone that indicated an uncomfortable topic was at hand. 'I've deliberately left it alone so far, but do you wanna tell me about this breakup you're running from?'

'Don't we have to get going?'

'Not yet. Anyway, it's perfect timing. Spill your guts. Have a line. Go get laid. And see some art somewhere in the middle there.'

'I think I might swap the first two around,' said Will, picking up the Altoids tin. 'Gimme a sec.'

Paul grinned.

'So . . .' he said again when Will sat back down some short minutes later.

'Well . . .' said Will. He wasn't really high yet, hadn't even begun to feel the comforting trickle down the back of his throat. 'I mean, there's not a whole fucking lot to tell really.'

Laura. In all her plain golden ineffable wonder.

'Come on, you can do better than that. I had a total *Dr Phil* moment the other night, talking about Jus, so don't leave me hanging now.'

Will laughed and took a long slug of the beer. 'I guess I was just really in love with her. Probably the first time I've really been in love, you know?'

'What's her name again?'

'Laura.'

Laura, Laura,

Laura, Laura, Laura, Laura, Laura, Laura, Laura, Laura, Laura,
Laura, Laura, Laura, Laura, Laura, Laura, Laura, Laura, Laura,
Laura, Laura, Laura, Laura, Laura, Laura, Laura, Laura, Laura,
Laura, Laura, Laura, Laura, Laura, Laura, Laura, Laura, Laura,
Laura, Laura, Laura, Laura, Laura, Laura, Laura, Laura, Laura,
Laura, Laura, Laura, Laura, Laura, Laura, Laura, Laura, Laura,
Laura, Laura, Laura, Laura, Laura, Laura, Laura, Laura, Laura,
Laura, Laura, Laura, Laura, Laura, Laura, Laura, Laura, Laura,
Laura, Laura, Laura, Laura, Laura, Laura, Laura, Laura, Laura,
Laura, Laura, Laura, Laura, Laura, Laura, Laura, Laura, Laura,
Laura, Laura, Laura, Laura, Laura, Laura, Laura, Laura, Laura,
Laura, Laura, Laura, Laura, Laura, Laura, Laura, Laura, Laura,
Laura, Laura, Laura, Laura, Laura, Laura, Laura, Laura, Laura,
Laura, Laura, Laura, Laura, Laura, Laura, Laura, Laura, Laura,
Laura, Laura, Laura, Laura, Laura, Laura, Laura, Laura, Laura,
Laura, Laura, Laura, Laura, Laura, Laura, Laura, Laura, Laura,
Laura, Laura, Laura, Laura, Laura, Laura, Laura, Laura, Laura,
Laura, Laura, Laura, Laura, Laura, Laura, Laura, Laura, Laura,
Laura, Laura, Laura, Laura, Laura, Laura, Laura, Laura, Laura,
Laura, Laura, Laura, Laura, Laura, Laura, Laura, Laura, Laura,
Laura, Laura, Laura, Laura, Laura, Laura, Laura, Laura, Laura,
Laura, Laura, Laura, Laura, Laura, Laura, Laura, Laura, Laura,
Laura, Laura, Laura, Laura, Laura, Laura, Laura, Laura, Laura,
Laura, Laura, Laura, Laura, Laura, Laura, Laura, Laura, Laura,
Laura, Laura, Laura, Laura, Laura, Laura, Laura, Laura, Laura,
Laura, Laura, Laura, Laura, Laura, Laura, Laura, Laura, Laura,
Laura, Laura, Laura, Laura, Laura, Laura, Laura, Laura, Laura,
Laura, Laura, Laura, Laura, Laura, Laura, Laura, Laura, Laura,
Laura, Laura, Laura, Laura, Laura, Laura, Laura, Laura, Laura.

'She's the best friend of my housemate Maddie, so she was always over at our place. We used to hang out all the time: me, Maddie, Laura, Tristan—my other housemate—and Jack, who's a mutual friend of Tristan's and mine. He's how I ended up living there. Anyway, then Laura and I kind of hooked up at a party, and we decided not to tell the others. Well, like, Maddie mainly, because those two told each other everything. Just 'cause we didn't want to make things weird in the group. But then it kept happening, and it became this big secret thing for a while, which was actually kind of really fun, you know?'

Paul looked wistful, as if recalling some grand extinct clandestine passion of his own.

'It was sort of ridiculous,' Will continued. 'Like, she'd pick me up in her car from uni, or from Officeworks—I was working in the print shop there—and I'd hunch down in the seat until we got out of the area where we all lived and worked. We'd go on dates to the southside. It was so stupid.'

'Sounds hot, though.'

'Yeah. It was pretty great.' Will paused and closed his eyes for a moment. He'd had a massive line and the rush was intense, and yet it felt wrong, a false euphoria laid down over a foundation of grief. He could feel the pressure of tears collecting somewhere, in some sealed reservoir where they would pool and then be reabsorbed, leaving behind a salt residue. He could feel Paul looking at him. 'Sorry,' he said.

'Oh, man, don't be!' said Paul.

Will took another gulp of beer and tried to collect himself. 'Yeah, it all came out eventually, and then we were properly together for almost a year.'

'So what happened?'

'I don't know . . . I mean, I do, kind of. Well, there's her explanation and then there's my theory.'

'Your *theory*?'

'Well . . . Actually, you'll probably get this—see what you reckon. *She* said she didn't think I was ready for a proper relationship. But I *so* obviously was! And the thing is, she broke up with me *right* after she met my family, which is pretty sus I think . . .'

He looked at Paul, but he merely tilted his head.

'You know how I said my folks came to visit me in Melbourne a couple of months ago? I was freaking out about introducing Laura to Mum and Dad, 'cause her family are all total lefties and all super cool and relaxed. She's grown up in this inner-north bubble. And mine are *so* not that. I mean, you know Mum. And she's gotten a heap more churchy since you left.'

'Yeah, you said.'

'She's pretty full-on. And Dad! He was *so* bad!'

Will felt the core of himself floating up as he spoke. He felt the words pouring out loose and soft and apparently of their own volition, traitorous and with a feeling of physical release, the verbal equivalent of a cocaine shit. But he felt a long way from his body, as if he had climbed some crow's nest out the top of his skull and sat there, watching himself let go.

'I told you how he wouldn't *do* anything?'

'Yeah.'

'Laura was trying to plan all these activities and gallery visits and stuff, and he was just like, "Nope. Nope." And he was *so* fussy about where we ate! Laura booked us dinner at this really nice place. And he *literally* wouldn't eat anything on the menu. It was so embarrassing. And *then*'—Will paused, finding it difficult to face directly the humiliation of the next piece of evidence—'he got really drunk and started talking about his trip to London, of course . . .'

Paul spluttered with laughter, almost spitting his Negroni. 'Oh my god, I forgot about that. Is he *still* going on about London in the seventies and his one-and-only acid trip and whatever else?'

'Oh yeah.'

'That's the only time he's ever been overseas, isn't it?'

Paul was shaking his head in disbelief. Did he think Will was a complete loser? Probably. Fuck, he needed to stop talking.

'Oh, man, that sounds shit,' said Paul. 'The thing is, I get it. Totally. I mean, the idea of Justine meeting my parents. Well, my dad mostly. Well, no, both of them. It's just, like, *no way*! No fucking way.'

Will laughed despite himself.

'I mean, I'm way worse than you,' Paul continued. 'I haven't been back since I left. That's seven years. So I get it. But I've gotta say . . . that's kind of fucked if she did dump you over that. I mean, I know I'm biased, but your folks *are* actually really lovely people.'

Will shrugged and sighed. 'I think she just saw who I really was, you know. And didn't like it. She so obviously changed after that. I guess I was acting pretty weird and awkward when they were there, too . . . I'm still so fucking pissed off at Dad. I haven't spoken to him since.'

Will picked up his empty beer and tried to drain one more drop from the bottle.

Paul jumped up. 'Sorry, man, I'll grab you another one.'

'It's fine, seriously.'

Paul shook his head and went behind the bar.

'Sorry,' he said again, coming back with a fresh bottle. 'You were saying?'

'Oh. No, that's it really. Just that I probably did act like a real dick. I got all caught up in my head with this imposter syndrome thing I've got going on. Being from the country, you know? Not being cool enough.'

Will peeled away the label on the bottle, which he had been picking at as he spoke. It tore cleanly for about an inch and then the top layer separated, leaving an ugly white jagged shape behind. He started picking at the opposite corner. He thought he had finished talking, but then found himself continuing. 'She said she thought I wasn't *comfortable* with myself, and that she really liked me but that I *wasn't ready* for a real relationship.' Will held up his fingers in angry inverted commas and then necked his beer. 'But I just can't help feeling like, if she hadn't met them . . .'

Paul put a hand on his shoulder. 'Mate,' was all he said.

His high was going already, washed away by this ocean of words and pathetic emotion. Still, he was touched by Paul's response; by his kindness and seeming understanding of how it was to be ashamed of one's origins and family, to have tried to escape and to be reminded that you cannot; to thrash with dumb anger and humiliation and kick away everyone in the vicinity only to realise, in his own case, that if he had just been okay with who he was it would have been far better for him. He missed his dog, suddenly, and with a simple pang. Rosie! He should never have left her with his parents. He should have taken her to Melbourne when he moved there. Maybe then he could have shaped himself an entirely different identity, one of firm regional authenticity that could not be shredded so easily. With Rosie by his side at every barbecue and beach trip and Sunday drinking session in the park, perhaps he could have been himself—whoever the fuck that was—and Laura would have liked him. But he had felt himself too cool, or too uncool, even for his dog—those eyes she gave him, the way she lay with her nose between her paws, long kelpie body stretched out beside the door, while he packed his things for the move to Melbourne and away from everything he had been.

He sighed and shook out his hands in a spasm of involuntary purging.

'Look,' said Paul, 'I know you're hurting now, but maybe—just maybe—she did you a favour. I mean, you wouldn't be here otherwise, right? Maybe you would have just settled down and become like your old man.'

Will began to protest, smarting with the slap of Paul's comment, but just then Daisy came up behind them with the water jug.

'Shouldn't you guys get going?'

They both looked at their watches.

'Fuck! Yeah, we've gotta go, like, *now*,' said Paul. He sculled the dregs of his Negroni and stood up, cracked his neck and knuckles.

'See you there?' Will said to Daisy.

'See you there.' She kissed him on the cheek again.

Yes! thought Will. *Screw you, Paul!*

THE GALLERY WAS FULL AND even from the street Will could see that this was what he had come for; this was the centre to his eager yearning periphery. Inside, Paul was greeted by someone and became mired in small talk and Will took a breath and pushed out courageous into the tide of culture, which lapped at him with a sound that was in fact oceanic; a literal surf of voices.

He had already abandoned the vague thoughts of embracing an authentic regional identity and moved to more bitter hopeful plans of simple revenge: surpass his father; surpass Laura; surpass Paul; surpass Australia. There would be no fear of unmasking when he had become . . . become *this*.

The foyer was white-floored and white-ceilinged, white-lit and packed. Four doorways opened off it, and the bar set up along the rear wall was rammed with beautiful consumers of the liquids necessary to endure, let alone enjoy, such hectic and socially significant human proximity. There was not an ugly person in sight, though there was plenty that was strange and outlandish in a way that made him think of *Zoolander*: a woman in platform heels as high as soup-can stilts; a thick-muscled man in a suit that appeared to be made of scrunched brown waxed paper; a vast array of carefully damaged clothing that must have been torn and frayed by the hands of uncomprehending children in a factory somewhere; a man wearing a pinstriped suit and calf-high red cowboy boots.

He floundered towards the bar, where he ordered and suckled on a beer, drawing sweet malt comfort and feeling the sensation of his overused, aching feet. Then, the shock of hearing his name in this furthest promontory of isolation.

Kim and Darla stood beside him, holding flutes of champagne between thumb and forefinger, and if their faces were not exactly alight with warm welcome, they were at least composed in mild unhostility and that was good enough.

'Hi! Have you two just got here?'

'We've been here a little while,' said Kim.

'We came with Jus, so she wouldn't have to arrive by herself,' said Darla.

'Nice.' Will wondered if this was a dig at Paul and, if so, whether he was caught up as collateral. 'How's the show?'

The two women looked at one another.

'I think it's good, don't you?' said Darla. 'Of course, Jus's work is far superior.'

'Naturally,' said Kim.

'But I thought the standard was generally pretty good.'

'I liked Julia's work. It's in that room,' said Kim, pointing to the doorway to the left of the bar.

'Yes!' said Darla. 'Do you know her?'

'Not really. Just from around.'

The conversation was steering towards a place of no current, and Will decided to bail now and avoid the awful slow exit out of silence.

'I might go check it out,' he said. 'I haven't even seen Justine's yet. Just got here.'

'First things first, right?' said Darla, tipping her glass.

'Yep.' Will laughed, again uncertain of her implication. 'Which room is she in?'

'Front left,' said Kim, pointing across the dense-packed bodies.

'Okay, cool. Maybe I'll pop into the one you said was good first, before I try to shove my way back through all those people. This is a pretty great turnout, yeah?'

Kim made an unimpressed face. 'I guess. Most of these people would turn up for the opening of an envelope. They're just here to kiss Marcus's ass and then fuck off back to their boardrooms.'

'Wow,' said Darla. 'Sounds like someone is getting jaded already.'

'God, I just heard myself.'

Will shifted his feet and placed his empty beer bottle on the corner of the bar. 'Well . . . see you in a bit.'

Kim and Darla smiled and nodded and returned to that familiar multi-voiced unceasing chorus of impassioned female conversation that he would hear the world over and for the rest of his days and always be shut out of.

He edged sideways through the crowd towards the gallery that contained the work the women had praised. The space was smaller than he had expected and seemed to contain very little. In the centre was an enormous plexiglass box, and inside it what appeared to be a mountain of dust. The row of backs across the room suggested that there was also something on the rear wall. He looked around for a clue. To the right of the door sat a wooden plinth with a stack of exhibition guides on it, and he opened one as he walked towards the box of dust.

> Julia Lee is an artist of Korean, Hispanic and Irish descent, who graduated from CalArts in 2006 and whose work has been shown at . . . Themes of . . . Late-stage capitalism . . . race, class and gender as they relate to . . .
>
> For this project, *Dirt/Cheap*, Lee took a job as a domestic cleaner for six months, posing as an undocumented migrant. She was engaged by a couple to clean their apartment twice a week for $12 per hour, cash. Over a six-month period, Lee collected the detritus that she vacuumed from the floors of the apartment. She then returned the collected refuse to the apartment and photographed it in situ . . . Photographs and material traces . . . the viewer to reflect on the ways in which race, class, gender and nationality impact perceptions of the relative value of time and physical labor.

Will looked up from the glossy image of the dust heap to the real thing: a mound about navel height, a metre or so wide, piled into a rough peak, with an intricate terrain formed by clumps and snarls, mainly of hair, and with the occasional larger object: a balled tissue; a rubber band; a paper clip. For the most part, though, it was making visible through simple accumulation what was normally invisible, a billion tiny particles of . . . *what?* The stuff of which we are all just such accretions imbued with breath? It was this that caught Will's attention—the philosophical significance and to him real pathos of this act of bringing to light, almost if not quite to *existence*, through addition alone—though he was ashamed by this, and aware that if he was a woman or an immigrant he would no doubt feel a greater identification with the politics of the work. He thought about how he would explain the work to some undefined interlocutor—Tristan, perhaps—using terms like *ontological*. He really needed to get more into art!

He dust-gazed for a long while, noticing the threads of different colours, the occasional form of a moth or fly that only distinguished itself out of the composite grey after prolonged attention. Around him people milled and eddied, glancing, commenting, moving on; failing uniformly, he felt, to register the profundity of the dust.

He looked at the photographs on the back wall: the artist in her cleaner's uniform; the artist standing beside the dust pile in the middle of a lavishly decorated room; the pile replaced by a small stack of money—the amount, presumably, she had been paid for her labour over the six-month period.

What a strange, specific world this is, he thought. The art world; the food world—Paul's equally strange and specific niche. What a strange time to be alive. Or was it only this unfamiliarity, this seeing through the tourist's bright and credible gaze, that made things crystallise in this way?

Someone put a hand on his shoulder, and he turned and saw Paul holding two beers.

'Drink?'

'Sure, thanks.' Will accepted the beer and took a gulp. It was cold and highly carbonated and he felt the bubbles going into his nose in a crescendo of prickling effervescence that made his eyes water. 'I really like this.' He inclined his head towards the dust.

'Yeah, it's great. I got to see the whole show a few days ago. Popped by while Jus was bumping in.'

'I haven't seen hers yet. I didn't know which room it was in.'

Will realised he was telling one of those easy and inexplicable unnecessary lies that he was constantly telling because in the moment they somehow seemed to ease some subtle social pressure or anxiety. He needed to stop doing it, after the trouble it had caused him.

'Come and see it now,' said Paul. 'It's in the front.'

They passed back through the atrium. Will followed Paul's deft figure as he wove through the masses, slimming sideways as if to waltz a moment with the back-turned bodies. There was a nimbleness about him that Will remembered from boyhood, exhibited on the backyard basketball court, the site of many of Will's chief mortifications.

Ahead, Will saw Justine; she was talking to an elderly woman dressed in red, with long straight hair the colour of pewter. She caught sight of Paul and Will and held up her fingers in an odd childish wave that Will felt conveyed a desire not to be interrupted, a message Paul could not or would not read. He stepped up and laid his arm around her waist, an obvious claim-staking that Will found irritating on Justine's behalf.

The woman stopped speaking and looked at Paul without welcome. Someone nearby farted and Will stood there in inert pretence, trying not to breathe until the toxic cloud dissipated.

A man approached on Justine's other side and touched her elbow, and Justine turned and smiled at him. He was about to interrupt Justine's conversation with the grey-haired woman until he glanced at her; then he clutched his hand to his chest and laughed.

'Ellen!' he said. 'I was just about to drag Justine away to meet someone important, but I failed to notice that she was already talking to the most important person in the room.' The voice was soft and higher in tone than might be expected from the stature of this man; there was the trace of an accent: a slight international lilt.

'Oh, don't be ridiculous, Marcus,' the woman replied.

So this was Marcus: the apex of power and influence towards which the next generation doggedly, hopefully, with upturned faces climbed.

'How are you, Ellen?' Marcus asked, but the woman was already manoeuvring her way out.

'I've been monopolising you for too long,' she said to Justine. She put out an arthritic hand and grasped Justine's forearm.

'Oh, no,' said Justine. 'It's been wonderful talking to you.'

'I should really see the rest of the work,' said the woman, laughing, taking a step backwards. She turned to Marcus. 'Congratulations on finding this one,' she said, as if Justine was a seam of precious metal that Marcus had prospected out of the fulsome female earth. Will thought of the childhood joke that had felt back then so daring in its sweet blasphemy: *I found Jesus . . . He was behind the couch the whole time!*

The woman offered Paul a minimal nod and moved off.

'Hello, Paul,' said Marcus.

'Hey,' said Paul. 'Who was that?'

'Ellen Roche. Sometime art critic for the *New York Times*.'

'Whoa!'

'Yes. Quite the correct response. And she seems to approve of your girlfriend's work, which is excellent news for all of us.'

'Hey, this is Will,' said Paul. 'He's a friend from back home. From Australia.'

Will stepped forward and Marcus held out his hand.

'Pleasure,' was all he said, and the word befitted him entirely.

The smile he directed at Will was warm and proprietorial; *bestowed*. It conveyed that he alone was the host here, that Will was being welcomed into his domain, and Will found himself understanding utterly the power of this man, felt himself authorising it somewhere in himself as inevitable. He was in fact nothing like what Will had expected from the talk of Justine and Paul. He'd expected the gallery owner to be sleazy and petite, all his power located in his wealth. The man shaking his hand was better denoted by the word *potent*. He was thick and full in every feature: the hand that gripped Will's; his head and chest; his lips and hair and neck. His power animal was clearly the bull, his face taurine in its bearing: broad and placid and self-assured. He looked a lot like Javier Bardem, had the same coarse-grained European sophistication, the same veined hands and forehead through which the thick blood pumped almost visibly; the same sleepy eyes and square chin with its shading of stubble that could probably never be removed.

For his part, what Marcus saw when he looked at this boy, this friend (or brother?) of Justine's idiot boyfriend, was something that had become in his American ascendancy almost impossible to find—rare, as his mother would have said, as hen's teeth—and that he experienced as a relief, a glass of plain cold water after too much fine wine, and it was this: a true *naïf.* His face, this boy's, was wide open, beautiful in the rarest possible way, with no awareness of its own beauty. He could not recall the last time he had met someone beautiful who did not know it. His skin was smooth, as if he had not started to grow a beard, although he must be at least twenty-one, and there was a flush on his cheeks that evoked an erotics of innocent exertion. His hair was guileless, radiant: freshly washed and free of product. He was like a concubine raised in a tower, brought up by a very clever woman who understands precisely, so that she—the concubine—emerges at puberty intelligent, curious, trusting; educated in certain essential ways and yet utterly untouched by sophistication, that ubiquitous repugnant quality that defined his tiresome long-desired and now apparently inescapable life. Artless, yes, but the more perfect for it. He was Australian: that had been his tower. Though it must be more than that. Marcus had met Australians before, dealers and artists from Melbourne and Sydney. They were usually unsophisticated, true, but certainly not guileless. He had found their dominant character to be a careful self-deprecation, which he experienced as comical, so unserving was it to their purpose in the American art world.

Who was the clever woman who had raised this boy? he wondered. She must have been more cunning even than his own mother, who dreamed for him, shaped him for, the singular unimaginative refinement he had so easily acquired and of which he was now so very tired.

*

Will felt Marcus's eye fall on him, and he felt himself assessed, felt the movement of the older man's gaze and how it made him want to shrink. Was it sex, or just power, that made his gaze so palpable? Was this how it felt to be a woman?

'Justine, I must introduce you to someone,' said Marcus.

'Of course,' said Justine.

'Please excuse us. You'll come back to the apartment later?'

'Yeah, for sure,' Paul responded on Will's behalf.

Marcus smiled at Will once more and drew Justine away.

The title of Justine's show was *Flux Materia*, or perhaps *Materia Flux*, Will couldn't tell because of the way the words were arranged on the front of the booklet, the word *Flux* running from left to right towards the bottom of the page and *Materia* running from top to bottom along the right-hand edge. The work was lit like surgery and it was savage as a catheter to Will's abraded brain cells.

Ten poles of varying height and girth sat around the space. They seemed to be made of wood, either single blocks or smaller chunks stacked on top of each other, crude cut probably by chainsaw, totem poles to honour or invoke whatever gods Justine worshipped: gods of DIY; of fluidity; of the fraught exchange of ephemera for the hope of future money; of the right kind of uncompromised success.

Each pole was coated in a different material, listed in the guide, which also informed Will that each would shift and change over the course of the exhibition, some drying and cracking away, some flowing at various rates from their wooden armatures so that they ended in a slump on the gallery floor. These soft volatile substances included clear silicone gel (what must be several bucketloads), river clay, pitch and pigmented petroleum. The colours were either black or white or semi-transparent or neutral brown or umber, the textures predominantly wet-looking and somewhat sexual in this sense. They were slathered thickly, like raw industrial fondants on rough cakes of saw-cut wood.

Will tried to read the exhibition guide while Paul stood beside him, arms crossed, rocking back against the gallery wall and then pitching upright again like a fractious child, complaining about how he hated these events where Justine was ushered about from rich person to rich person like a dessert trolley while he had to just stand there and *behave*.

'Let's have a line, I'm getting antsy,' he said.

Will was getting nowhere with the booklet, which was full of quotes from Heidegger, who he'd read a bit at uni but couldn't be expected to decipher now in this riot of studio lighting and glistening lubricants, with the sound of neurons shrieking out for their next fix like so many baby birds, the sound actually audible in the channels of his ears even above the clamour of people who were here to . . . surely not *buy* one of these sticky things? He couldn't see one making its home in the apartment in Julia Lee's photos, for example, and how the hell would you dust it? He imagined himself picking up one of the goopy sculptures and hurling it into the dust pile in the other room.

'Okay,' he said, placing the guide back onto the stack.

They jostled their way to the unisex bathroom tucked into a corridor behind the bar, where there was also a small office, a glass box containing a young woman dressed in a canary yellow suit tapping away on a keyboard as if none of this was going on around her.

'So, answer me this,' said Will as Paul racked up two gigantic lines on the rim of the square pink marble basin. 'I haven't seen the work in the other rooms, but it seems like Justine's work, and the dust pile, aren't actually, like, *for sale* . . . So what I'm wondering is, how do they make actual *money*? How does Marcus make money from this?'

'Fucked if I know,' said Paul. He handed a rolled-up bill to Will and stepped back, examining his nostrils in the mirror, blocking each in turn and inhaling for clarity of passage to the soft membranes that would soon take another blissful beating. 'Nah, I mean, it's complicated. I don't fully understand it, but I think he does more commercial shows too.'

Will bent close to the bench. He could see the clumpy texture of the cocaine, the spaces between the tiny chunks. He felt a minor interval of hesitation, a shadow-sense of the deep patient utterly inevitable crash that lay in wait for him: a widening sink-hole; a debt accumulating; a counter ticking over, the numbers mounting, mounting. Here goes, he thought, as the tiny particles shot into his nasal cavity, ticklish and smelling of horseradish and petrol, each one acquiescing as it rose to the *yes* of his grit determined spree.

—

Later, it was as if he came to, slopped back into his cage of bones from some cloudland of incorporeal hovering above his own experience—drinking more; seeing with a hard buzzed distraction the work of the other two artists and registering nothing; the arrival of Daisy and the not talking to her; the dispersal of the crowd like the slow-motion herding of a flock through a single paddock gate—and when he registered again his own person he was in the front seat of a car driven by Marcus, his thick hand assured and paternal on the gearstick. The roof was open, letting in the bright dizzy flick and flick of the lit-up night, and there was house music blaring on the stereo and a powerful scent of leather upholstery. Paul and Justine and Julia Lee were laughing in the crush of the back seat, the women's legs bare and bent and colt-like, and Will closed his eyes and sent out some godless prayer of thanks as the car drove on through the mythic godless American night.

His next awareness was of an automatic door sliding open, and the small car plunged into the chthonic realm of the parking garage, dark and circling down and down through several levels, and Will felt that there was something significant in this underground journey; perhaps it ushered in a darker phase of his American experience, he wasn't sure, but when he scrambled from his seat he saw that the car—a low beautiful Porsche—was golden, a fallen star or gilt chariot, and not the pale greenish gold of ordinary powder-coated cars but solid gold, though this may have been where he departed from reality and hadn't someone given him a glass back at the gallery that contained some drug dissolved in champagne that he had drunk eagerly out of *yes*? . . . In either case he had lost the thread of his narrative and before long they were in a capsule shooting upwards like a parcel of cash in a pneumatic tube not just to a higher floor but into the darkened sky, the nightly hold of the sun god Marcus. The capsule had a window in its wood-panelled inner wall and at once they broke through buildings and ascended to a zone of light suspended between the city and the stars and arrived.

There were people from the gallery waiting at the big double doors and Marcus unlocked them and went ahead. Immediately inside was a kind of antechamber created by a floating wall that functioned to delay the moment of entry into the glories it so charmingly concealed, and on this wall hung a painting, in shades of blue and deep indigo and plum, and Will was struck to statue and stood looking up at it, seeping into the colours that were a communion, while Paul and the others continued on into the apartment.

Marcus put his head around the wall and smiled.

'Ah, the Rothko,' he said in that soft, indistinct accent.

'It's incredible.'

'Yes. He was a friend of my mother's.' He lingered for a moment, fingers on the edge of the wall. 'I'll leave you with it.'

Will laughed. 'It's okay, I'm coming.'

Already there were knocks at the door and Daisy came in with Kim and Darla and other young and wonderful specimens: a woman with a blonde buzz cut, very slender but with enormous breasts, undeniable under a white t-shirt; the man wearing the red cowboy boots; another man who looked like a Japanese rock star. Will was swept along with them as they milled in like splendid cattle and it took him a moment to move his eyes from the throng to the apartment itself, but when he did he felt his face do a cartoonish jaw drop and a *whoa* escaped his lips and he saw Marcus laugh at him once again—he seemed to find

Will quite amusing—but in a pleased way, and so he didn't feel so bad about his antipodean lameness.

'What floor are we on?' he asked.

'Thirty.'

More knocks at the door and Marcus made a face that said *excuse me* and slipped off and Will made his way past the long sofa and coffee table where Paul was already racking up, and pressed his hands against the cold glass and looked out at the spectacle of light that seemed this city's gift to him: the dazzling plenitude that had become his first premature and optimistic symbol of America.

Once he had drunk his fill he turned back to the room. There were a great many icons and Mexican crosses arrayed on the wall that was not glass, woven rugs and modernist leather furniture. A deep red floor-to-ceiling curtain framed the window, for those moments when Marcus might inconceivably tire of the view. The long kitchen bench was made of pink marble, like the basin in the gallery bathroom from which not long ago he and Paul had been snorting up drugs. A large part of the glorious blunt impact was produced by the sheer size of the room, which was vast enough to temper the excesses of colour and texture, the kitsch irreverence of the wall of icons, and to enable such elements as balance and negative space. Between the kitchen and the living area there was room for a full-length cricket pitch. A car could make a lap between the sofas and the coffee table.

Everyone else appeared unimpressed, standing or sitting in small clusters as if they too had been arranged by the master curator, while Marcus himself wrestled with the cork of a champagne bottle.

Overwhelmed, Will went to find the bathroom. It too was palatial, the floor paved with Spanish tiles, the shower on an unscreened raised dais. The toilet was in its own room, and Will was glad to be alone and in a small private space. He heard the music start up in the lounge room, the bass and drums audible through his feet. He pissed and flushed and sat down on the lid.

Without volition, it seemed, he pulled out his phone and opened Laura's Facebook page, and at once he felt the cold tip of the knife enter his chest and knew how successful, how blessedly successful and temporary had been his campaign of obliteration through this drug-winged end-times tourist trip. But just as that unthought phrase—*end times*—revealed the defiant and staunch continued influence of religion on our poor downtrodden traveller's way of seeing, so did this brief glimpse reveal the unvanquished snarling form of grief that would not be killed so easily.

She had changed her profile picture. It had never been of the two of them; she was too cool for that. But her hair was different, cut short in a move that told him she was suffering too, or at least was playing out, through that pathos of symbolic change whose violent form for him had been this blind paroxysm flight, her riddance of him. And Maddie had posted a photo on Laura's timeline, taken in his own familiar now former home—the same ironic op-shop horse painting on the wall, the same blue sofa (*his* sofa! the sofa Maddie later admitted was the reason they'd chosen him to move in)—and in the image the cast of his former life sat smiling and holding tumblers full of red wine: Laura and Jack and Maddie and Tristan, and there was something in the eyes of Jack, which were fixed without decency on Laura, that caused a hot surge to rise within him.

He was still shocked by the brutal and direct connection between his brain and body, how he had run to the bathroom and puked in mute response when he heard Laura say the words *break up*, and as he looked at the image now he gagged a little in dry-mouthed despair.

And yet he was too reasonable, his nature not impulsive enough, to hurl the phone. Instead he pressed the button at the side and made the screen go dark and he drank some water from the hand basin and then pulled out his tin and extracted the tiny ziplock bag printed with yellow smiley faces, and with hands atremble tipped out a substantial mound of powder onto yet more pink marble and bent to the calm engrossing ritual of his willed return to oblivion and the bargain of delay, the silent whisper of *please, I don't care about later; just please not now.*

The woman with the blonde buzz cut was sitting on a stool at the kitchen bench and smiled at Will as he picked up a glass of champagne from a pre-poured row.

'Hi,' he said with effort, for he had lingered in the bathroom for some minutes and now the antidote, as he had begun privately to call it, was surging like a swat team through his body. 'I'm Will.'

'I'm Veronique.' The voice was deep and undeniably masculine and he hoped he hadn't done another of his naive cartoon double takes.

While he floundered for a period that may or may not have been evident, Veronique took practised charge, whether kind or oblivious he likewise could not tell.

'How do you know Marcus?' she asked.

'Um, well . . . I don't really, to be honest. I'm here with a guy called Paul, whose girlfriend is Justine Patton, who's part of the show. At the gallery.'

'Oh, Justine. Her work is *fantastic*.'

Will nodded.

'What's your accent? Are you from England?

'No, Australia.'

'Austraaaaaalia.' She stretched out the word with ambiguous emphasis. 'I've always wanted to go there.'

Here we go, thought Will. Something about kangaroos . . .

'Actually, you know what?' she said. 'That's a complete lie. I've never wanted to go to Australia. I don't know the first thing about Australia. Tell me something.'

Will laughed. 'Not a whole lot to tell, really. I live in Melbourne, which is just a big city—a way less exciting version of here. I used to live in a horrible small country town, which there's even less to say about. Though there are lots of kangaroos there.'

'Oh my god!' Veronique said. 'I come from a hideous small town too!'

'Where?'

'I call it Bumfuck, Ohio. I refuse to speak its name.'

Will could see that there was pain there, far worse than his own narrative of basic unbelonging and imposter syndrome.

'The main thing is we escaped, right?' She raised her glass. 'Cheers to that!'

'Cheers!' Will was peaking, his heart beating palpably in his chest, and he wondered if it was obvious. 'What did you think of the opening?' he asked.

'I didn't make it. I was on the way there, but I had to deal with a situation with a client. Story of my life.' She reached for a fresh glass of champagne. She was perfectly put together in her tight white t-shirt, black jeans, mauve point-toed stilettos perched on the rung of the stool, a double strand of very white pearls at her throat. A Chanel handbag rested on the floor beside her. Her make-up was subtle and flawless. The word *immaculate* came to mind.

'Do you mind me asking what you do?'

'You're so *polite*!' said Veronique. 'Is that an Australian thing? Like Canadians? They're always so *nice*.'

'Maybe.'

'Although I've met your friend Paul before, and let me tell you he was *not* polite like you.'

'Well, he has lived here for seven years now.'

'Touché. He certainly does a passable impression of an arrogant New York prick.'

'Yeah, although I've known him since I was a kid, and he was a prick back then, too. Much worse, actually.'

They both laughed, and Veronique tipped her head back and drank.

'So how do *you* know Marcus?' he asked.

'Oh god . . . Marcus and I go *waaay* back. We were both just kids on the scene together back in the day. These days I bring him a lot of sales . . .' She paused, sipped again. 'So to answer your oh-so-polite question, I'm a personal stylist. I work with very high-end clients.'

Her fingers twisted the pearls at her throat, tightening and loosening, tightening and loosening. Perhaps she was not quite as self-contained as she appeared.

'Wow!' said Will. 'Personal stylist. What does that involve?'

'I do basically everything for my clients. Except run their billion-dollar companies.' She winked, set down her champagne with the wealthy sound of fine crystal against marble, and leaned in. 'I'm literally on call twenty-four seven. For example, the client I missed the opening for . . . I'm on my way to the gallery, and he messages me, saying he needs me urgently. I message him back saying I'll skype with him in ten and just stay calm. I go home again, pour myself a vodka, because I know I'll need it, and then skype him. He's all in a panic because he's going on a date and he's stressed out about his cufflinks and if they're the right choice. So I tell him, *They're fine, but change your shoes.*' She set the tip of her tongue against the point of a canine incisor in a pose of coy impertinence. 'So, we pick out some shoes, and then we talk through his date and where he's going to take her for a drink after the dinner reservation. Which I made for him. And then we hang up. That took one and a half hours. I had to tell him to hang the fuck up or he was going to miss his date. I was like, how's it going to look: *Oh, I'm sorry I'm late, I was skyping with my personal stylist . . .*'

'Fucking hell. That sounds like torture.'

'And,' said Veronique, '*and* . . . this man owns a Fortune 500 company!'

Will raised his eyebrows, pretending to know what that meant exactly. That he was fucking rich, basically. 'No one speaks truth to these people,' she continued. 'One client said to me recently, *Do you know who I am*? And you know what I said to him? I said, *I don't care who you are, honey; when I met you, you were wearing pleated pants and they were two sizes too small for you*. And he was like, *You're right. I'm sorry. I don't know what I'd do without you*.'

'So how much do you get paid?' he asked, and then, 'Shit, is it okay to ask that? I'm sorry, that's totally not okay, is it?'

'Look, I probably wouldn't tell you if you lived here, but since you'll be taking my secrets back to Bumfuck, *Australia* . . .' She leaned in again. 'I get paid around five hundred an hour, depending on the client, plus twenty per cent of spending. I'm no Marcus, but I came to New York City thirteen years ago with nothing, and I sure don't need no man to pay my bills. Although, mind you, I wouldn't mind a man to pay my bills.' She sat back up and clutched her pearls again. 'I do alright for myself.'

'What do you mean, twenty per cent of spending?'

'I mean, whatever I spend, I get paid twenty per cent on top of that.'

'So you actually get paid *more* the more of their money you spend? That makes no sense! Don't they want to *save* money?'

She laughed a short, scathing laugh. 'Oh, honey . . .'

Before Will could ask anything else, Paul was beside them. He held up a clear capsule between thumb and forefinger, inside which clustered three or four dirty-looking crystals. He didn't speak, just raised his eyebrows and smiled dumbly.

'Ooh, is that Molly?' said Veronique. 'Yes please!'

Paul held out the cap and Veronique stuck out her clean pink tongue to receive it.

She crossed herself, picked up her champagne and drained the glass. 'For what we are about to receive . . .'

'Bless you, my child,' said Paul. He turned to Will, produced another cap from his jeans.

'Oh, fuck it. Sure, why not?'

Paul tried to repeat the ritual, holding out the pill towards Will's mouth, but he took it from Paul's fingers and placed it on his own tongue.

'What is this gorgeous woman telling you? Don't believe a word of it,' said Paul, in a tone that frankly, Will thought, made him seem like a bit of a dick.

'Nothing about you,' he said. 'Don't flatter yourself. We were actually having a lovely time before you interrupted.'

'Well, I imagine you'll be having an even lovelier time soon, thanks to me.'

'Thank you, sugar,' said Veronique, in that sweet, irreverent tone she had so perfectly mastered.

Paul offered a small wave and an addled grin and returned to the couch.

'God, he really is a bit of a prick,' said Will.

Veronique laughed loudly, and Paul glanced over at them, making Will feel guilty.

'Wow, it's such a different world here,' he said. 'New York is pretty wild.'

'It's not all like this, believe me.' She nodded at the room.

'Seems to be from what I've seen so far,' said Will.

'Maybe you're just seeing what you want to. I can tell you there are plenty of people doing it tough here. Marcus and I are the lucky ones among our friends. Many of them are still living on nothing. Some of them are dead. But that's not just New York, I guess, that's capitalism. I work for the one per cent—well, maybe the five per cent—so I see how crazy it is. They have more money than they could ever possibly spend. It's disgusting, if I'm perfectly honest . . . Hey, top me up, would you, sweetie?'

Will pulled the champagne bottle from the ice bucket and filled her glass messily. The bubbles overflowed and ran over the pink marble. Veronique bent and kissed up the spilled liquid from the benchtop with a giggle. She almost toppled off her stool and had to grab Will's arm to right herself.

They chatted on until Will began to feel a tremor through his system, that unavoidable malignant quarter-hour when the coming euphoria sends in its missives of agitation and jaw-clench unease.

'That's what these protests are about,' Veronique was saying.

'Which protests?' he asked, trying to stay focused.

'Occupy Wall Street. It's this movement that's just gaining traction. I know some activists who are involved. The first protest is coming up in a couple of days.'

'And what's it about?'

'About the level of inequality that exists in this country, basically. I'd go, but I'd lose my job if my clients found out. They pretty much all work on Wall Street, so . . .' Will looked up at her and saw that her throat had flushed. She caught his eye and smiled brilliantly. 'Here we go,' she said. 'Forget politics—let's get high.' She got down from her stool with a small jump and held out a hand. 'It's time to dance now.'

'I don't dance,' he said.

'Oh, honey, please!' said Veronique, and because he was so far from home and everything he had been, because of Laura, because of *yes*, he let her take hold of his fingers and make a little pirouette under his raised arm and she led him across the room to where the dancing was being done, like some strange earnest ritual being performed, each dancer separate and serious in her own small sphere of pleasure and forgetting. To his surprise, it felt amazing to dance. He had to move; the energy of the drug was so intense as it came on.

This feeling: it wasn't like sex; it was love, benign and warm and impervious to any bleak facile selfish isolation or future angst. The island was dissolving into the sea. He was not quite a dolphin—would never be capable of that—but a wave perhaps, with its mathematical rise and fall, a single contraction of the earth's green liquid heart. He looked around him at the bodies moving in a complex polyrhythmic choreography. They were mostly women, and he felt the energy coming off them—knew with certainty that he had the power to perceive the precise valency of every person's soul—and it was good: benevolent and flowing and communal. There were perhaps twenty people dancing, and Will felt that if he could just make a colony of souls with these shining fellow beings, the future would be one of love. This is how to stave off the apocalypse, he thought. He saw with diamond clarity the falseness and ignorance of the self he had thought he was until this pure epiphany, and he saw the bad faith of his isolation, the self-protective shell with its armature of false cool. He was a raw, soft homunculus of love inside the machine of fear and pretence. So careful, so guarded was he against judgement that he hadn't noticed the world loved him.

He looked over at Paul, still sitting on the couch, backlit by the universe of stars but like a dark planet himself. Will could not rest his gaze upon him: he was anathema, a fissure in this new state of being. *Oh, Paul.* He had taught Will so much. It had been so long that he had forgotten the seminal influence of those lessons: close like a fist; dread humiliation; expect unkindness; stockpile your weapons; the future is dark. Passed down from the hand of the father, the mouth of the patriarch. Paul had probably shaped him more than his own father had, spineless semi-blank as that man was and scant indeed as role model. What had his father taught him? The future is disappointment; a family is a net; hold tight to freedom, for if you lose it, the only agency—the only pleasure—left is the indulgence of nostalgia and complaint and refusal to do other than arrest ungainful and ungrown as your offspring surpass you and you remain the sole and stubborn son of your still-young wife, her martyrdom her own salt consolation.

Look away, he thought, the future is love.

He danced and danced, found himself contemplating how purely noble it was that humans contained within themselves the urge to climb mountains, an act of no advantage except the spiritual. He must go, after this metropolis-dream, to the Rocky Mountains, and there wed his soul to the American metaphysics. To the redwood forests and the canyon rapids of that America that knew wild harmony and transcendence. The Rocky Mountain Hymnal; the lonesome howl of the wolf;

the pure concourse of the shared trail. Oh lord, oh American goddess, he was soaring like an eagle!

—

Later still, sweaty and sated, just before the second crystal pill, he found himself in conversation with Marcus, the two of them leaning side by side with their spines against the marble bench. Most of the lights had been extinguished and there were thick red candles burning around the room, bleeding slow wax tears that ran down carved wooden candlesticks. Marcus had asked him with seeming genuine interest about himself; about Australia; about what had brought him to America. And Will had blurted it all out, incapable, in his current state, of holding back.

'Do you know that you speak very negatively about your own country?' Marcus said.

Will was surprised. Was it that obvious? Did it make him look like even more of a philistine, because he had succumbed to that most quintessentially Australian malady, the cultural cringe?

'Still, what you have done is quite bold,' Marcus continued. 'I have always harboured fantasies of sudden flight. The passport snatched from the drawer. Everything else left behind. No goodbyes. But you have done it. No turning back. I admire it.'

'Well,' said Will, 'the no-turning-back part may prove problematic. I don't have a Green Card or anything. I'll probably end up having to slink back after ninety days with my tail between my legs.'

'Can't you find a way? I know it's not like when I came here, when all you had to do was marry your female friend, pretend both of you were straight, and get a Green Card. Moving around the world has never been so hard. It's the same everywhere. But at least Obama's in now. Clinton's immigration reform bill . . .' He sighed. 'That was not good news for people wanting to come here. Could you get a study visa?'

'Don't think so. Uni was another thing I left behind. That was probably really stupid. I'll fail a bunch of subjects.'

'It must have been a grand romance,' said Marcus.

'I don't know if it was, to be honest. I thought it was. I mean, to *me* it was, but clearly not to her.'

'Then it was. Reciprocity has nothing to do with it. You should consider yourself fortunate just to have loved with such intensity. Whether or not you are beloved in return . . . that's secondary. That you have the capacity to burn with passion, that is a gift. *Your* gift. That is not a gift for the object of your love.' He paused. 'I have never had that gift.'

'Really? You've never been in love?'

'I don't think so, no. I am too divided. I discovered desire too young. *That* I have certainly felt. But love I reserved for my mother. I split the two.'

'Wow. I've never thought about it like that before.'

'And you were brought up religious. You should understand, surely.' Marcus showed his perfect teeth.

'Yeah, I guess. But isn't that more a Catholic thing? My religion was more the kind where people hook up at Bible camp at sixteen and get married two years later.'

Marcus shook his head. 'And did you meet your love at Bible camp?'

'Hell, no! I never went to Bible camp. I sort of excommunicated myself at about thirteen. Never went to church again. I don't think my mother will ever forgive me, but hey . . .'

'Did you? You *are* a dark horse.'

Will looked down, embarrassed. Was Marcus going to hit on him? Fuck, he hoped not. He didn't want to have to have that awkward interaction.

'Are you still religious?' he asked, in a desperate tactic of diversion.

'I would say I'm religious, yes,' said Marcus. He was so damned calm; the way Will imagined a serial killer might always remain calm. Every move unhurried, even the final kill. 'But no longer Catholic. My religion is of my own alchemical fashioning. It's syncretic. What I retain from the Catholicism of my childhood is a love of ritual and excess. The objects of worship. The recognition that transgression and taboo are absolutely essential to desire. That becomes tricky once there are no real prohibitions . . . And mother worship. The three Madonnas: Madonna, my mother; Madonna the Virgin; Madonna's "Like a Virgin". That is my triumvirate.'

'Your what?'

'The holy trinity.'

'Oh. Yeah.' Will chuckled, thinking that this was obviously something Marcus had said before; a catchphrase. Mother worship? The idea was as foreign to Will as this luxury.

There was a long silence, both men looking over at the remnants of the night, the sprawled and still-dancing bodies, and the aquarium of light behind them. The music was the only thing that wasn't cool about this party, Will thought. It was too techno. Too Euro. Though it did suit Marcus. For Will, it was associated with the hedonism of a former generation, the heady '80s of the century passed. Pretty soon, Will thought, no one would be able to countenance such excess as this. The baby boomers had almost eaten it up already and now they were working on the scraps. The skyscraper had had its day. It signalled only high-density living; the rising panic of population; fire risk. Nine-eleven, of course now too. The skyscraper? What a cold dead symbol of phallic power. And cocaine? Will hadn't had much of it back home because it cost at least three hundred dollars a gram. In his circle, the definition of a night of debauchery was more likely to involve taking cheap acid and giving each other stick-and-poke tattoos. Marcus's erotics of prohibition . . . it was as vacant from his own fantasy life as the sexual symbols of the aristocracy—corsets and riding crops and other such laughable things. The champagne bottle, the luxury car, the mirror and the razor blade, the sexual sociopathy of Wall Street and Bret Easton Ellis: it was all gone now. Only here, tonight, might he taste it this once. In America.

Marcus sighed and looked around the room and wished that all these people would leave. Even the boy. He was not so intriguing as he had hoped. Watching him dancing, so messily trashed . . . He was straight as a post, too, and wallowing in self-pity. *Dios*, was there nothing left in this world that could interest him? Even the days-long binges of chem-sex had lost their appeal. Even art. Where was Veronique?

'Hey, thanks for inviting me to your party,' said Will.

'Thank you for being here,' said Marcus. 'Are you having a good time?'

'Amazing! New York is so amazing! I can't believe it's actually better than what I expected.'

'I despise it,' said Marcus.

He said it so softly that it took Will a moment to register the sting.

'Really? You *despise* New York? Why?'

'I'm so profoundly bored by it. And depressed by what it's become. When I first arrived here, when I was seventeen . . . back *then* it was amazing. Back then it actually stood for something. It was different from the rest of America. It was transgressive—everything I was talking about. It was free and dangerous and full of young people hustling and barely surviving and living the kind of life that was . . . I hesitate to use the word, but it was *real.* Capitalism had not won completely, I don't think.'

Will looked away as Marcus spoke on. He felt as if someone had taken a pin and punctured his taut and air-filled happiness. He wanted to shout at Marcus to shut up. All he wanted was just to be able to go home and say how incredible New York was; to actually be surely and unashamedly *enthusiastic* about something and know that he wasn't making a fool of himself. Was that too much to ask? He did not want to be burdened with this knowledge that the real, the *authentic* New York was gone, long-vanished, and that what he had visited was a theme park built upon the ashes.

Fortunately, there was soon the second pill, fed to him again by Paul, to whom he had barely spoken all night, and he quickly ascended to a different altitude of intoxication. I have never been this high before, he thought at some point, touching his own face. And then he was in another room, the door closed behind him, and in there was a girl he had danced with earlier but had not spoken to—very short and thin, and clearly very high herself; she kept rubbing her hands over her body as she danced—which was okay . . . which was wonderful, but also Justine, which was bad, which he had to stop, but his teeth were writhing so in his poor dry mouth. The two women were making out now and he thought how Paul would be pissed at Justine, and then that of course he would be more pissed at him, and somehow that had only just occurred to him but he was so munted that he thought if he only touched the other girl, whose tits—he felt them now—were really small, barely there in fact, but oh, her ass felt great . . . what the guys at his school would have called a bubble butt: two round firm handfuls; but she was taking his hands and putting them back on her tits, putting his fingers on her small nipples that were like the erasers on the end of those yellow pencils, and he felt the blood in his body doing strange things to his brain as it shifted. His hands felt a very long way from his head, like in those dreams he'd had as a child. It was not a sexy feeling, and he was dizzy kneeling on the bed with somehow no shirt on and where was Justine? Oh, there she was, and he noticed that the inside of her mouth was very cool . . . she must have been drinking something with ice cubes in it. She was really taking charge, the other girl, and time-lapse images of stars going around in a circle, bright rings on the sky's vinyl playing what Eurotrash? If you ate pineapple it made your jizz taste better, Jack had told him that, and she was laying him down now like a child, and the stars . . . *Not this one, baby* . . . but she bent over him—cradled him almost, her tits at the level of his mouth, and he wondered whether he might get to suck on them, suckle up all that feminine energy . . . maybe that was the formula—prick shrink away to become a hollow tube, but not a lack. Never lack, he had learned *that* at uni, the thorough take-down of Freud and Lacan. Oh, but these were not thoughts to sustain a hard-on . . .

WILL WOKE FROM ABSURDIST AUGURIES. Some kind of Cassandra narrative. He knew about the impending apocalypse, but not how or when it would begin. He was in one of those mega-stores—Walmart or Costco or Aldi—paeans to cheap offshore mass production and easy repression. In the electrical section, multiple televisions were tuned to the same channel, each with a slightly different colour balance and level of reflectivity. A newsflash appeared across the screens: animals the world over had begun to turn on people, as if at some signal broadcast beyond the range of human hearing. There was footage of a tiger mauling someone in a village and, pitifully, a koala in a wildlife sanctuary tearing at the face of the woman holding it for a photo. This was it; it had begun. The shoppers were frozen, watching the screens, and Will began a desperate search for his family. Then he saw a man who was oblivious to what was happening, wearing headphones and pushing a trolley. Will was overcome with rage towards this man. He ran over and wrenched the headphones from his ears. And then, the bizarre dream punchline: he could hear, as in movies, the music coming out of the headphones, tinny but audible as it never is in real life. It was Madonna's 'La Isla Bonita', the too-perfect soundtrack for such an apocalypse, with its imagery of paradise and wild, free nature. And then he woke.

What the fuck was *that* about? he thought, the question preceding necessarily but only slightly the awareness of torment and consequence that seemed to fade up with his waking, like someone turning the volume on the stereo from zero to eleven. The blood in his head was replicating the bass drops from last night's techno, casting even his hangover in the same mode of '80s debauchery as the night itself. He was cold, lying face down on a mattress with one arm hanging off the edge. When he tried to sit up, the arm wouldn't move. It had become prosthetic, and soon the pins and needles began to tingle, probably a mere warning of the suffering to come. He was shirtless, shoeless, but had his boxers on, at least, as well as his filthy socks. Beside him was a guy Will had seen but hadn't spoken to last night, an older guy, maybe fifty, with salt-and-pepper hair in a floppy Richard Gere cut, also shirtless, and with disconcertingly buff pecs. There were two other people in the bed too: the Japanese rock star, totally naked, his long hair tangled in his open mouth, his cheeks baby pink; and a girl, topless, covered partly by a sheet, her face squashed and ugly with sleep . . . Oh fuck, what had happened here? Will got up and began in quiet panic to search for his shoes and clothes. Through the uncurtained window the sky was still textureless and dim, but cars flowed unabated far below, their lights flashy and horrible in the existential grey of almost-dawn.

—

Will traversed the city among the joggers and street sweepers with their obvious unwanted symbolism, the suits just emerging like vampires in reverse, clutching their newspapers and coffees and fitted with the medical white earbuds that were so ubiquitous they looked as though they must connect to some life-sustaining source of whatever-it-was, housed within tailored pockets.

Oh, wretched morning! Will hoped he was invisible to the city. Somewhere in Midtown his phone died and he had to get a cab because he didn't think he could find his way back to Paul's on foot. At least he still had his wallet, the key to Paul's apartment in the coin pocket.

He unlocked the heavy glass door and scraped his sorry arse up the stairs, which seemed endless.

He could hear the shouting before he reached the apartment. He would have turned around immediately and fled, but he had needed to shit since he started walking. He opened the front door just wide enough to see that Paul's bedroom door was closed.

As he crept inside, he heard Justine shout: 'Oh my god, you'd think you'd paid a fucking *dowry* for me. I. Am. Not. Your. Property!'

'You are such a fucking hypocrite. I cannot believe the utter bullshit that is coming out of your mouth right now,' Paul yelled back. 'It's okay for you to fuck whoever you like in the name of fucking feminism, but if I so much as look at another woman then it's the fucking patriarchal apocalypse!'

'No, Paul, you moron . . .' Her voice fell to a level at which Will could not make out what she was saying; only the absolute disdain of her tone transmitted through the door, making him think inevitably of his parents.

He slunk to the bathroom. On the toilet, he bent forward and covered his ears with his forearms, hands clasped behind his head, and tried to concentrate on letting his body carry out its loyal and ceaseless cycle of waste evacuation. He saw his toothbrush lying on the edge of the basin beside him, and he sat up and reached for the toothpaste and began to brush while he was sitting there, the fresh mint and the easy shit like the swift miracle of penance. He spat between his legs into the bowl.

The pipes hammered as he washed his hands and he listened for a ceasefire, but the hard angry murmuring continued, as fitting a soundtrack to the morning as Marcus's techno had been to the night before. He wanted a shower, badly, but the more urgent need was not to be observed here, and so he rolled Paul's deodorant into the wisps of his stale pits and moved his rubber face about with his hands in the mirror, giving his cheeks a soft double slap.

His hand was on the front doorknob when he heard the crash of some part of someone's body colliding with the wall, and Paul's shout: *You fucking bitch!* He felt his maxed-out body begin another of its automated cycles, felt the adrenaline wash out of some weary raised gate within him and flood the inner tunnels of his veins like those walls of water that chase fleeing action heroes as if in churning slow-mo.

He heard Justine begin to cry. He kept his shaking hand on the knob, listening for further violence, but Paul was silent now. Perhaps he had punched the wall. Small comfort, but at least it did not necessitate intervention. He hoped to god that

Paul would not emerge from the bedroom and discover him, frozen to the doorknob. He wished he had not stepped inside the apartment, had gone across the street and taken a dump in the coffee shop bathroom and thus been innocent of this filthy knowledge and shameful implication.

Fuck you, Paul, he thought. And then, like an elevator falling ten floors inside him, he realised that *he* may in fact have fucked Justine last night, or as least been seen by Paul in a passed-out vogue of compromised intent. And so he opened the door and literally tiptoed, cowed and coward-wise, back out into the street that may have become his home, his phone still dead and his meek belongings abandoned as if in escape from a fire.

Oh god, this was too much for him. This was not what he wanted, this patched reverse of the stage-set New York, all bits of duct tape and frayed pine planks staple-gunned into place and measurements drawn on in pencil. Unhomed and made enemy by his own dumb mechanics. He was too afraid even to go to the coffee shop in case Paul or Justine appeared, and so he walked to the bagel place across from Tompkins Square and got a cream cheese bagel and a coffee and took them to the park, where he sat on a bench in the reproachful Friday morning sunshine and watched the dogs chase each other, their faces streaked with bliss and innocence, all that he longed to dig back for in the loamy non-linguistic past of his own life or his species' as far as it was necessary.

He sat a long time on the bench, bludgeoning his self-esteem with this poorly fashioned instrument—regret—until the sun was shining onto the gravel of the path and the stink of dog pee vaporising in the heat became too strong and then he found another bench beside a gingko tree and fell asleep with his knees drawn up and his head on his elbow.

He woke up chilled and went back to the bagel place and got another coffee and asked if he could charge his phone, which he could. The girl smiled at him, and it was warm in there and smelled of yeast and toasted sesame and he felt a little better. He picked up a newspaper and took it to a corner table. The front page featured stories about war and money: the threat of Europe's debt crisis to global financial markets, and how five central banks were pumping US dollars into the European system—he pictured a long pipeline with money flowing out into a depleted reservoir—and another about the arrest of a rogue trader who had come from Ghana via Israel and the UK and a Quaker boarding school to hold a post in a major Swiss bank, where he was accused of causing two billion in losses, though how it was an actual crime to lose money Will didn't know. There was a picture of Obama standing with a Marine called Dakota Meyer who had been awarded the Medal of Honour for helping rescue comrades in Afghanistan, and a story on the question of 'how much latitude the United States has to kill Islamist militants in Yemen and Somalia', and it seemed surreal to Will that these questions of the rules of war were somewhere being debated and decided as they came up, like a card game with several variants.

The girl who had served him came over, holding out his phone. 'Hey, you got a message,' she said. She smiled at him again, a plain, ponytailed smile.

The message was from Paul:

Hey where u at? Sorry I left u at the party.
Hope u ok . . . I'm gonna head to spotted pig for a burger b4 work. Wanna join?

So Paul didn't know. Or maybe nothing had happened. He entertained the image of Paul luring him to meet and king-hitting him outside the Spotted Pig, whatever that was, his face smacking the pavement and his teeth bouncing out across the ground like thrown dice.

Paul was talking to one of the bar staff when Will walked in to the pig-themed establishment. It was like the home of his aunty Sue, which was bedecked on every surface with ceramic cat figurines. Except here it was pigs. There was even a string of plastic pig-shaped fairy lights above the door between rooms.

'Hey,' said Paul.

'Hey.'

'This is Gav. Gav, this is Will.'

'Good to meet you,' said Gav, a tall ginger with a British accent and odd little juvenile teeth like a row of Tic-Tacs.

'Hey, we're gonna grab a couple of burgers and beers if that's okay,' said Paul. 'I'm on soon and I am coming down like a motherfucker.'

'Thought you had a bit of a case of the Hollywood sniffles,' said Gav.

'That and the rest.'

'Yeah, no worries. I'll sort you out. Grab a table and I'll bring your beers over. Pints?'

'Just a pot for me,' said Will.

Instead of calling him a pussy or trying to convince him to go large, Paul said, 'Yeah, okay, make it a pot for me too.'

As they sat, Will tried to glance at Paul's knuckles for evidence of violence, but he'd tucked his hands into his jeans pockets. He cracked his neck and made one of those horsey puffing sounds, blowing air through his loose lips.

'Good night, hey?' he said. 'You have fun?'

'Yeah, great night,' said Will, scrambling to make his face a mask for his bewilderment. Paul obviously had no idea he'd returned to the apartment and heard the fight, but why was he acting so cheerful? Was this some kind of trap?

'Sorry I bailed on you,' said Paul. 'I went to look for Jus at some point and saw you passed out in bed. You looked pretty asleep so I figured I wouldn't wake you.'

'What time was that?'

'About quarter to five. Justine fucking disappeared on me.'

'Really? Did you find her?'

'Yeah, I found her.'

Guys in chef's whites were walking past shouldering, like small transparent coffins, gigantic plastic tubs full of shredded potatoes and brioche buns. There must have been a hundred litres of uncooked fries balanced on the shoulders of the men who were about to cook them.

Gav approached the table with their drinks.

'Cheers, Gav.'

'Cheers.'

Paul sipped his beer and stared at the table. 'This shift is gonna be a *bitch*,' he said.

That word. Will felt the discomfort of his position building.

'Luckily . . .' said Paul. He pulled the edge of the Altoids tin from his shirt pocket and wiggled it.

'Oh, man. I can't even look at that,' said Will.

'Yeah, well. Some of us poor cunts have gotta work.'

Will shook his head. 'I don't know how you do it, to be honest.'

'Practice. Years of practice. It's practically the first thing they teach you in chef school.' He sipped his beer again.

Will hadn't touched his yet. He looked around for a water station.

Their burgers arrived. Brown meat on a tanned leather bun with some pale melted cheese and a mound of very thin French fries, like the straw that nestles expensive bottles of wine. There was not a hint of green, not even a token leaf of cos inside the bun.

'Fuck, yeah,' said Paul, taking the plate from Gav. 'Get in mah belly!' he addressed the burger in an appalling Scottish accent.

Will slid out of his seat and went over to the water jug on the bar. He poured two glasses and returned with them to the table.

'Cheers,' said Paul with his mouth full.

Will saw that the knuckles of his right hand did look slightly red, but not incontrovertibly so.

'So, when I woke up this morning,' said Will, picking up a brittle chip, 'I was in bed with naked people. Freaked me right out! There was a topless girl, and that Asian rock star–looking guy you were talking to for most of the night . . .'

'Oh good, he got some. Good for him. He was so fucking uptight.'

Will glanced at Paul, studying him for signs of dissimulation. Maybe he really hadn't seen anything.

'And then there was another guy in the bed too. Did you see that weird buff older guy? Do you know who I mean?'

'Oh yeah—looked like some kind of cowboy crossed with a dental surgeon.'

'Yes!' Will laughed. It came out sounding strained and slightly hysterical. 'That's the one. That's exactly what he looked like. Well, he was lying next to me. He was so freaking ripped. You know when someone's chest actually looks like moulded plastic?'

'Gross,' said Paul. 'Yeah, he was passed out next to you when I came in. God knows what the two of you got up to.' He winked at Will.

'Ew, no! Man, I have literally no memory of anything after you gave me that second pill,' he lied. 'I must have blacked out.'

Paul chuckled. 'I told you it'd get pretty loose. You're not in Melbourne anymore, sweet pea!'

In the time it took Will to swallow the first two bites of his burger, Paul had already finished and was standing, wiping his hands on his jeans.

'Sorry, bro. I've got to get to work.' He finished his beer and burped. 'And you know I've gotta leave early tomorrow, too? I've got that gig out in Martha's Vineyard. The rich cunts. I'm getting picked up at seven and helicoptered out there, so I probably won't see you till I get back. Sorry to leave you for most of the weekend, but that's the job. Justine said she'd take care of you, though.'

'Yeah, no stress,' said Will, his bewilderment multiplying. 'She doesn't have to babysit me. But that's nice of her.'

'I think she'll be hanging out with the girls. It's Darla's going-away drinks. So you can tag along if you're keen. Or you don't have to, obviously.' Paul took a final pinch of his remaining fries. 'Okay,' he said. 'I'm off.'

After Paul had gone and Will had eaten his burger at an invalid pace and drunk half his beer, he realised that he had been left with the bill, or the check, and he began to think in earnest for the first time since he had arrived about that sad necessity called money and to wonder how big a hit his bank account had taken so far. The burgers were twenty-six dollars each, plus maybe six dollars each for the beers. That made sixty-four dollars, divided by point six for the exchange rate and it was just over a hundred Aussie dollars for this brief greasy futile fix.

He'd had close to five thousand dollars saved up before he'd booked the flight here, the remainder of the seven-something from his nan, his portion of a small inheritance divided among nine grandkids. He'd used some of it when he moved to Melbourne, some during the fortnight he'd taken off work during exams last year, and some on a week at the snow with Jack and Tristan and Laura and Maddie before he and Laura got together. The plane fare had slurped up close to two grand. He'd be lucky if he had two grand left now to last him the rest of the trip.

The trip. It was certainly beginning to feel like one: a world on acid whose disconcerting imagery reminded him of those children's stories around which clustered smug theories of narcotic allegory: *Alice in Wonderland*; *The Wizard of Oz* . . . What this city was tripping on, though, was money. That was fine, but the fact was that he could not afford to buy into this mythology of Rome-before-the-fall decadence. For some reason he thought again of his dream, its surreal apocalypse comedy epitomised by the attacking koala.

Back out on the street, the black-humoured hearty comedown threw its weighty arm around Will's shoulder and began to tease him cruelly, diddling him under the chin as if to say, *Buck up, son . . . oh, hold on, you can't. You've got no serotonin left!*

It was a grey day but mild, the tails of ivy on the expensive West Village houses twitching in sleep. Wealthy-looking people passed by, with shiny hair and visibly muscled upper arms, pushing strollers or being led by smiling dogs on leather leashes.

Will looked around him, no idea what to do next. What in truth was he doing—seeking—on this knee-jerk caper? A fair enough question. What *was* he? Brave explorer of the new cultural motherland? Lame desperate escapee and shirker of the debts of his various bankruptcies: material, spiritual, amorous? Or mere touristic dandy, mass-produced surveyor of the mass-produced sites laid out for his predictable ocular and fiscal consumption, nourishing as orange soda and significant as plastic bottle tops? Or was he, worst of all, his father's son?

He recalled the first time that his father had told him about Europe. It was just the two of them, in the garage. Will must have been twelve or thirteen, old enough to ask his father if he could start using his weights. He remembered lying on his back on the black vinyl bench, his scrawny shaking arms extended, his father standing over him, ready to catch the bar if he failed. He remembered the smells of the garage den: the old gym scent of the blue foam mats where his father practised his aikido and the damp of the concrete floor and the cat-piss smell of his own pubescent feet. The dirty hollow feeling when his father told him about the women he'd slept with in London ('Free love,' his father had said. 'I was just a country boy. I didn't know what had hit me!'); about how he'd got a job working in a pub in Camden, and how all the English girls thought he was so exotic with his tan and his muscles and his accent; about how he'd tried acid for the first and only time at a music festival ('I could literally *see* the music') and been altered forever; how he'd planned to drive to Spain in a kombi van with some guys and girls he'd met in the pub—among them a beautiful blonde folk singer who'd become his almost-girlfriend—and then head down into Morocco, but instead had got the call from his father, Colonel Richard Free, to tell him that he was to become a father himself, and so, said that caged resentful father-boy, 'I got dragged back home, and two months later I was married. And a month after that, Grace was born.'

It had been a classic father–son moment—the initiation by complicity and secret knowledge; the forced guilty pact that usurped the mother—and his father had picked the moment well: Will was at the age when he longed to be a man, couldn't wait for his body to be grown, to be able to start shaving. At the time, he'd taken his father's side in an agonising self-enforced unnecessary act of choosing. His mother was the law against which man and boy were joined in shared resentment. It was only later that he came to hate the repeat performance of confessional bragging that his father put him through whenever they were alone, though he did not return allegiance to his mother but instead removed it from them both, and so began his lonely years of scorn and high-and-mighty distance from family and church and town and country that had brought him here at last.

—

On the evening of the following loose-end lonesome day, Will received a benign and innocuous message from Justine:

> Hi Will, it's Justine here. I'm meeting the girls for a drink
> at 8 if you'd like to join us.
> Same place as last time. We might
> go for a dance later too. No probs
> if you have plans but I told P I'd
> keep an eye on you while he's away ;)

And so our low protagonist walked out again unwise into the sleepless city, descending more slowly this time the seven sets of stairs, having aged already past that giddy clattering boyish bounding down, the touching only with his boot tips of every second stair tread.

It was close to 9 pm when he arrived. The women were sitting much as he'd seen them the first day, except that Daisy was with them, making them seem even more like a Benetton ad and himself like the shrivelled symptom of something almost overcome. As he approached, they all looked up and smiled at him and he felt it as a benediction, but when he leaned down to kiss Justine on the cheek, the way she twisted her mouth away and presented the side of her face, closer to her ear than her lips, made him think that there were weird vibes there and he started to panic, to urge his blank resisting mind back to the night of the opening and to assume he'd made an arse of himself. He sat down, diminished, in the empty seat between Daisy and Darla.

'How was Thursday night?' Daisy asked him. He didn't know what to reply, whether he would seem like a jerk if he said he'd had a good time.

'Um, yeah, good, I think,' he said. 'To be honest I don't remember a whole lot of what happened at Marcus's place. Paul gave me a couple of pills and I think I may have exceeded my threshold.'

'Oh dear,' said Daisy. 'Too much excitement?'

He nodded.

'Would you like some bubbles?' Kim asked. There was a bottle of champagne in the middle of the table. 'I can ask for an extra glass.'

'Um, that's okay. But thank you. I might just start with a beer.' He got up.

When he returned, there were two conversations happening, and he didn't know which one to join.

'I've started to notice it a lot lately,' Daisy was saying to Justine. 'It's men of a certain age. They're basically older rich white guys, who've all of a sudden hit, what, sixty-five? Like, they're officially old, and they fucking *cannot* handle it. And they are *so* goddamn needy it is ridiculous.'

Justine shook her head and poured more champagne into Daisy's glass.

'It's killing me, seriously.' Daisy rolled her eyes. 'This regular came in the other morning. We weren't even open. Like, the sign clearly said closed. And I hadn't even put the chairs down. I was dialling in on the coffee machine and this guy—Rob—comes in. He's one of those regulars who always calls me by my name, really loudly, to show everyone that he comes in all the time and knows the staff. You know?'

'Yup,' said Justine. 'I know the type.'

'He always has to have a *conversation.* Always has to reference some detail I mentioned last time, like, *So, how was your sister's baby shower?* And that's exactly part of what I'm saying, what I'm seeing is this aggressive need to, like, assert their presence. Not go unnoticed.'

'And it's always with younger female staff, too, don't you think?' said Justine.

'Yes. And I don't think it's a sexual thing, either. They're not hitting on us. It's like, for the first time they're in a situation where they have zero relevance. They're basically invisible to this person—this twenty-something woman—and they don't know what to do about it. It's the first time they've experienced it and . . .'

'And it *terrifies* them.'

'It terrifies the *shit* out of them.'

They laughed.

'Yeah, so,' Daisy continued, 'the other morning, I was like, I'm really sorry, Rob, but we're not open yet. You'll have to come back at seven thirty. And he was like, Oh, that's only a few minutes away, I'll just sit here and wait. And I said, I'm sorry, no. I've got to set up the space. I was there by myself, and it was only, like, ten past seven, so I didn't want him just sitting there watching me for twenty minutes. So I said, Look, I'm very sorry, but we're not open yet, so unfortunately you can't be in here. If you could please just come back at seven thirty when we're open. And then he's like, *Daisy*—really emphasising that he knows my name—I come here all the time. You *know* me.'

Justine made a disgusted face.

'I know, right,' said Daisy. 'So *then* . . . he starts taking the chairs down, and says he'll help me.'

'What?' said Justine. 'No!'

'It was *so* weird. I started to get really uncomfortable. He's just this older corporate type, but he was just being *so* insistent. In the end I had to actually tell him he was making me feel uncomfortable and that he was being full-on. And then he got all offended and indignant and left. And he'll probably never come back again.'

'Good riddance,' said Justine, leaning back in her seat and crossing her legs. 'Yeah, I get that shit all the time.'

Will began to feel awkward, listening in to this conversation. Justine wasn't trying to include him as she had the other day. Was he being paranoid, or was there a hostile energy coming from her?

He drank from his beer and looked around the courtyard. Then he got up and went to the bathroom, and when he returned he tuned in to Kim and Darla's conversation instead, or at least partly tuned in. He was thinking about what Daisy had been saying and whether these old men were really just going to leave the building, so to speak. Were these women actually going to get the future they desired: the seat at the table, the corner office, the gold watch, the confidence of the board, the final word? Or was that even what they wanted? Maybe they wanted something different that he couldn't even guess at.

Darla was off on her wolf project the next day, and after a second bottle followed the first and both sat upside down in melted ice buckets, they went to dance at a gay club nearby. A friend of Darla's was playing at midnight and they were all on the door list except Will, who had to pay a twenty-dollar entry fee.

From the outside, the club looked industrial and depressing, but inside, Will was surprised to find it fitted out in the style of an old church, with a raised, balustraded section of wooden pews to the side of the dance floor and stained-glass windows high up in the raftered ceiling.

There was hardly anyone on the dance floor, but in the raised side section stood the celebrities, figures of sartorial and cosmetic perfection: a fantastically tall drag queen in a spangled G-string leotard that revealed the tightest butt cheeks Will had ever seen; another less androgynous queen, dressed in swirling white crinolines and snowscapes of white tulle like a doll atop a roll of toilet paper, gloves white and wrist-length, and hair set in the gelatine waves of a 1930s starlet.

Will was becoming accustomed to feeling out of his depth, and looked around him with interest.

'What do you want to drink?' Justine asked him.

'Whatever. I'm easy.'

'I think we're having a round of Fernet shots and then we'll probably sit on gin and sodas for the rest of the night.'

'Sounds good.'

He followed her to the bar, his eyes returning helplessly to Daisy, to her bare neck and the profile that he glimpsed in stills as she turned from the light to speak to Kim or Darla. She clasped five shot glasses between the fingers of her deft long hands. She held them out to Will and he took one and they all tossed down the bracing medicine.

'Do you come here a lot?' he asked Daisy.

'Not a lot. But when we all feel like a dance we come here. Most women I know prefer to go to gay clubs so they don't get hassled.'

The girls piled their handbags in a corner by the stage and began to dance. It was 11 pm and people were just starting to arrive, mostly groups of guys, with an occasional girl or two. The tulle-clad queen sashayed out to the floor and made a neat, arch turn or two and then returned to the bleachers.

Kim left at midnight after several parting hugs from Darla and promises of regular contact.

Frayed and neurologically depleted as Will was from the opening, the night took its smooth inevitable course, and he found himself in the crowded bathroom where a prim young man in hotpants handed out luxe paper towel for tips while all around him people spilled their drinks on the glitter-slick floor, shouting to one another above the music as they sniffed bottles of what Will assumed must be amyl nitrate and applied make-up in the single overpopulated mirror.

In the cubicle, there was a small mirrored shelf above the toilet cistern, and Will wiped it down and put it to its intended use. Then, before he had even had a chance to offer the tin around, he accepted a pill from Darla and after a jagged forty minutes in which he decided he'd had too much cocaine and had maybe developed an allergy, the symptoms of which included a twitching distant pain somewhere in the back left quadrant of his brain and a feeling of agitation that flashed like a string of ice-blue LEDs, the Molly delivered him from that perjury and once more into heaven.

Pretty soon the club was heaving and the wet packed crowd was shirtless all around him and the music was better than at any club he'd ever been to before, of course, because this was a club in New York City.

'I love this place,' he shouted to Justine, and she returned him a golden backlit smile, her hands moving in her hair and down across her breasts.

At 4 am, they were tumbling through the door of Justine's apartment, Justine and Will and Darla—Daisy had made a French exit at some stage but Will was too full up with the milk of human kindness to be sad about it—and were all at once set upon by the lissom chamois tongue of a body-wagging Weimaraner who was so happy to see them that she seemed to have grown a multitude of deer-coloured giant dancing paws. After greeting them all and licking their faces, which Will had to admit felt amazing, the dog made a series of galloping tours of the tiny apartment. Justine spoke to it in the adoring coos and nonsense language reserved for animals and infants, and the dog sat before her and gazed into her face, its tail making thunks of happiness against the floorboards.

'This is Uma Furman,' she said. 'Shake, Uma.' And the dog put up her big soft-rough paw and Will took it, feeling the catch of the pads against his fingers and the strong tendons of each clawed toe and the way they each moved, segmented, under the pressure of his hand like the fleshy soft keys of a piano. He crouched and stroked her loose neck and the prow of her chest and felt true comfort pass through her and into his hand, for he was a dog lover and deeply susceptible to the pathos of noble submissive adoration that has been cultivated in the canine species, like the deep scarlet colour in the rose's bloom, because it is rich and wondrous beyond value.

Justine was rolling a cigarette, a bag of coke sitting like small change beside the pouch of tobacco on the coffee table. Darla had the window open and was smoking a tailor, her elbows on the sill.

Will was still incredibly high; in fact, being in an apartment rather than the club—where the external sensory excesses of light and volume and the proximity to hot damp pungent bodies matched the inner excesses of heart rate and blood flow and dilation and release of those sweet neurochemicals—was somehow exaggerating the feeling. He sat down on the worn leather couch that seemed to take up most of the apartment and Uma Furman bounded up beside him and flopped out all her long limbs, her head coming to rest on his knee, and he patted her ribby side, while Justine began to bustle about, so small and full of furious propulsive energy, the muscles in her arms standing out as she reached for glasses from a high cupboard, her unlit cigarette behind an ear and lighter in one hand, and it was only in the sloppy pouring of the gin into the glasses—almost a third full each—that he could tell she was pretty tanked. She plonked in some ice cubes that cracked like knuckles, making the dog lift its head, and she cut a lime and put a thick slice into each glass and set them on the coffee table and went about lighting candles and he had to stop watching her, she was too quicksilver frenetic. She went to the stereo and put on The xx.

'Help yourself to a line,' she said. She lit her cigarette, inhaled, picked up a glass and was leaning on the windowsill by the outward breath.

Darla had slumped onto her elbow, the fading cigarette held out the window and her eyes closed.

Justine moved a strand of hair from Darla's face.

'Wake up, Darla, honey.'

'Need to pee,' said Darla without opening her eyes.

'Okay, you go pee and then come sit with us and have a drink. I've poured you a gin.' She swirled her glass in front of the closed eyes of Darla. 'Mmm, gin.'

Darla coaxed open her lids and pushed herself up. She took a drag of the cigarette, left it on the windowsill, and staggered behind a Japanese paper screen that partitioned off the rest of the room, behind which Will thought he could see the edge of a bed.

Justine stabbed out her cigarette and came over to the sofa. She pushed Uma Furman's bony hindquarters into the corner and squirmed sidewards into the gap. Uma's head was still on Will's leg, her pale shining eyes now flicking away towards a sound, now returning to his face as he ran his hand down the glorious smooth pelt of her side. He was intensely aware of the movement and the hot dense pooling of his blood in his thighs and his cock and the thickness of his liver and kidneys and in his heavy chanting heart.

'How are you doing?' asked Justine.

'Ugh, I am still so fucking high,' he said.

She laughed at him, put her hand on the dog's flank, rested her cheek against the wall.

'Mmm,' she said. 'I probably am too, come to think of it. It's nice, though, isn't it?'

'Yeah, it's nice. As long as I'm not the only one.'

'You're not the only one.'

Justine's gaze travelled over the gorgeous greedy body of her darling dog, along Will's pale-haired arm and up to where his chest broadened at the shoulders, and if it lingered there, it was only because she was high, wasn't it? What was she doing, though—seriously? High again, two nights after the epic literal and figurative high of her opening. Hanging out with this random friend of Paul's. Actually, he wasn't as tedious as she'd expected; he'd even asked her some fairly intelligent questions about her creative practice earlier. And it was nice to be asked to actually *speak* about her own work for a change, rather than offered some self-aggrandising critical analysis. Especially by a guy. He clearly had zero memory of the other night, which made her feel like some kind of deviant, because she could recall it all in crisp excruciating detail. She really had to become a better person. She had literally no self-discipline. She'd stop drinking tomorrow. Two weeks. Back to yoga and in the studio whenever she didn't have a shift. The problem was it wasn't enough to be *productive* in the art world; you had to be out all the time, networking and going to openings and partying with curators and potential buyers. Not that she had any of those excuses tonight. Oh well, she was here now, and she felt great, of course . . . And there was something about hanging out with this younger, sweeter, less-damaged friend of Paul's that was helping her to understand Paul more. Something about the particular brand of insecurity and aggressive self-denunciation they both displayed. As if daring you to agree with them when they called themselves a loser. It was only meeting Will that had helped her put her finger on it, though what on earth she could do about it in relation to Paul she had no idea. But she didn't want to think about Paul right now. That was probably why she was high . . . Monday! She would spend the whole day in the studio. She *had* to be better.

Will watched Justine as she twisted her dark hair with one hand, dangling the glass in the other, fingers clasped around it, palm covering the top. He wished he could think of something to say to her, but he was trapped within the various intensities of his deep and shallow body, which were both blissful and slightly anxious, now that the comedown was close by. After a while she pulled her head upright.

'Where the fuck is Darla?' She got up noisily and Uma made a little irritated sound and rolled onto her side so that she took up the whole of the sofa, her front legs sticking straight off the edge.

'She's asleep!' said Justine, returning from behind the screen. 'She just lay down in my bed and passed out. How rude! Oh well. I guess I'll have her drink then.'

Will had barely touched his gin, but Justine drained the last inch of liquid from her glass and picked up Darla's. She sat down on the floor against the sofa, between the front and hind paws of the dog.

'You want a line?'

'Nah, I think I'm good.'

'Cool.'

'Hey, Justine,' he said with decisive effort and ambivalent intent.

She looked sideways at him from the level of his thighs. He knew he sounded way too serious and felt the flush of blood to his face.

'Mmm?'

'What actually happened the other night? I was too munted to know what I was doing and I don't actually remember . . . but I think maybe it was something'—he paused—'not good?'

'Oh gawd,' said Justine. 'I thought you seemed pretty wasted but I wasn't sure.'

'Shit,' said Will, panic beginning to beset his already woebegone and homeless lovesick soul. 'What did I do? I didn't hit on you, did I?'

This, though, was disingenuous. He remembered enough to know that so trite and anachronistic phrase as that could never fit within even the general outlines of the night.

'No. Well . . .' Justine put down her glass and began to roll another cigarette, the paper pliant and the skinny thing tight and even and licked and done in a matter of seconds. 'Fuck,' she continued. 'I've been feeling like *I* did a really bad thing. I mean, you're just a kid . . .'

'Fuck off,' he said, pushing her shoulder in what could only be described as a kid-like move. 'Just tell me what happened.'

'Ugh, okay,' she said. 'Hang on, I need to smoke. Come to the window with me.'

She got up and Will extricated his legs from beneath the warm brick of the dog's head. Uma thumped her tail against the sofa and stayed where she was, stretched out to her full soft-muscled length and so beautiful, her eyes twitching closed again at once, the lashes moist.

There was a low wooden bench under the window with cushions made from scarlet pieces of Afghan rugs. They sat at opposite ends and Justine picked a dot of tobacco from her tongue and flicked it out into the darkness.

'I can't believe I have to recount your night to you,' she said.

'Oh, come on.'

She looked at him, tilt-head and grinning and as embarrassed as he was, and blew out a full mouth of smoke.

'So basically my ex, Leah, was there, at Marcus's. I didn't introduce you, but I thought Paul might have told you who she was.' Will shook his head. 'Okay, well, that answers one of my questions.'

'I don't understand. What do you mean?'

'Nothing. Just, I wasn't sure what your motives were. But I think you were just completely out of it.'

Will rubbed his eyes and grimaced. 'That doesn't sound good . . .'

'I'm just sick of the whole thing, to be honest. When she started dancing with you—'

'Oh, that was *her*?'

'Yeah, that was her. She's sort of really manipulative in some ways. When I think about it, she probably would have known from your accent that you were Paul's friend.'

'But why would that even be a thing?'

'I don't know. She's just one of those people who likes to create drama.'

Will found himself thinking, Like you; like Paul. But he just nodded.

'And she hates Paul. Anyway, then you and she disappeared and I freaked out and came to find you, and you were already pretty into it, and then when I tried to drag Leah off, you . . . you sort of tried to pull me in too.'

'Oh, man, did I do that? I'm sorry.' He said the words, but he wasn't convinced that Justine's version of the story was entirely correct; it didn't accord with the snippets of churning memory, or with the feeling in his belly for the truth of what had happened. 'Does Paul know?'

'Well, no,' she said, cagey now and the pissed-off energy coming from her again. 'But he knows what happened *after* that, which was that I got Leah away from you but then she and I ended up going to another room together . . . Paul found us in there.'

'Jeez,' said Will. 'This is all pretty messy.'

'I know . . . Can you reach my drink?'

'Sure.' He leaned over and grabbed the glasses. The ice had melted away and the lime lay in its own haze on the bottom. He sat down again and began to pick at a hangnail on his thumb. 'Hey, I have to tell you something.'

'What?' She looked worried.

'I came back to the apartment the morning after the party. And I heard you and Paul fighting.'

Now Justine flushed, it seemed to Will with anger, but who knew. 'I didn't listen in or anything. But it made me kind of worried for you.'

A proud fixed defiance came over her face. Her eyes flicked to him and then away. 'Look,' she said, getting up, 'I don't need your *concern*. I did choose to fuck my ex-girlfriend while Paul was in the next room.'

'Yeah, okay,' he said. 'But, like . . . I dunno, is Paul, like, violent? Because you know his dad was.'

'I know,' she said quietly. She was just standing there next to him. Outside the window he heard a bird call. He put out a hand and took hers and was shocked when she began to cry.

'Fuck,' she said. 'I was just about to have a line. Now I'll be all snotty.' She draped her arms over her head like a desolate child, and he could smell her armpits. 'I don't know what I'm doing,' she said. There was mascara running down her cheeks, and he looked for a box of tissues but couldn't see one.

'You know you can just break up with him.'

'I know,' she said, sniffing. And then, firmly, 'I know that. It's not that. He's actually not violent. He's never hit me. It's just, he's so fucking vulnerable I don't know what to do with him. He's so hurt and sad and angry, and I find it completely repulsive. Does that make me a horrible person?'

'No. It doesn't. I know him, remember.'

With bamboozling speed, Justine sat down on the bench beside him and put her wet mouth on his. He felt how puffy her lips were, and the slick of tears and snot that cleaved to his stubbly upper lip. It felt so good and he wondered why he and Laura had never had sex on drugs and then remembered that he'd only taken ecstasy a couple of times before this trip and he'd hated it, a violent sexual chewing feeling that wouldn't end and was nothing like this, and he felt himself turning on with his whole body, with his earlobes which her fingers were brushing and with his eyes, dilating beyond anything he had felt before, giving him a kind of X-ray vision and linking up with the almost painful sensitivity of his fingers and it made the whole thing feel autoerotic somehow, like her cunt was part of his own body, his own handful squelch of his mother's pump-pack Sorbolene, and as he took a breath and wiped her hair from his face he looked out the window behind her and saw the sun, rising over the water towers like a red full stop.

In the shower back at Paul's he watched the water drops run together into the shapes of birds and stingrays. He thought about Steve Irwin, and what it would have felt like to be stung in the heart.

He didn't know what time Paul was getting in but it wasn't even 9 am yet so he felt safe for now to let his mind drift or flatline or make the shrill pain-sound of a finger on the rim of a crystal glass that seemed to be the voice of his dying brain cells.

After a while, when the bathroom was dense with mist, he stepped out and dried his corrupt pink-clean body.

Then he dressed and packed his things into his backpack, left the key on the table, and walked out of the apartment.

2
America

WHEN WILL DROVE OFF THE I-70 and into the town of Littleproud, Ohio, he recognised in the air and in the buildings themselves something mixed and contradictory, both gloomy—probably the dominant impression to most visitors—and intimate, to him in particular, because it was an ether he had breathed all his childhood, and it was this: a town in decline. An atmosphere of spruceness covered ineffectually the evident slow decay that could not afford to be mended, like termite-ruined beams puttied over and given a cheerful coat of paint. But more than this, the town wore a dual visage that displayed concurrent its Janus aspects of embattled decorous dignity and a soft languorous beckoning towards the sweet repose of resignation, though this impression was less than half intuited and more perhaps a product and projection of the viewer himself, for our hero had felt it too—that sweet beckoning—but not succumbed. At least not yet, the task of not succumbing still the slog of many days and the sleep-denying effort of many nights.

If the town evoked these phantoms for Will, what he also saw, or equally projected, was a visible authentic American heyday. The streets were wide and ancient traffic lights hung swaying on wires mid-intersection. There was not a mote of trash or debris on the pavements, which were decorated with painted cement baskets of flowering plants and with green fire hydrants. Three or four quaint antique stores clustered optimistically on a single block, though many other shopfronts were papered over. The town hall, the clear centrepiece of this neat uncanny vacant tableau, was properly grand, built of pale sand-coloured stone, wide and three storeys tall, with pillars flanking the entranceway and a high clock tower. It rested in immaculate grounds of lawn and hedge and small clipped trees. There were several memorials to served and fallen troops set in the lawn on either side of the building, and a polished red granite plaque nestled in the grass, etched into its front the words, *My stone is red for the blood they shed. The medal I bear is my country's way to show they care. If I could be seen by all mankind maybe peace would come in my lifetime.*

Will grimaced at the clumsy rhyme, and then felt like a prick. He could imagine this building as it would have been—identical but for these more recent self-made scars of the past century's distress—with horses hitched to the railings and carriages drawn up in the street, and he stood before this apparition of the old Midwest, bogged in his despair. It was a sign in the wilderness that had brought him here (not unambivalent, but a sign nonetheless, and the wilderness his own creation: the adrenal havoc and the unassuageable tremors and bleak delirium of yesterday), but it looked now as though it might come to nothing, and perhaps that—the coming to nothing—and not the brief false optimism would be the true enduring nature of his relation with the world.

—

After leaving Paul's apartment the day before, he had looked up car hire places on his phone and was surprised to find one not far from where he stood on East 9th Street, and he waited until 9.01 am and then called ahead as he set off walking. He had fantasised some American dream of a car—some sleek-bodied beauty—to speed him on his way across the land; it was laughable now, but in his mind it was a vintage model, even a convertible. Instead, he took possession of the metallic beige sedan with as little emotion or analysis as possible (in this the lack of sleep was helpful) and authorised with his signature the exorbitant fee to hire it for a month and return it down the line in Santa Monica, the terminus of that post-ironic pilgrim path—Route 66—the traversal of which he hoped would gestate in his boyish soul (if gestation was the natural metaphor, he would endure it) the state of manhood he had often felt he would never attain, as the pilgrimage to an ancient shrine or grotto to bow before the cool and touch-smoothed statue of a virgin saint might lead to actual pregnancy. He wished he could take longer, stopping as he pleased along the way, but he could not justify the cost, and the thing was now to keep moving: to leave this city, with its personal stylists and art world bigwigs and cheap cocaine and its actual fucking lack of disappointment as a site of culture that discriminates (or so it seemed) not on lines of race or gender or sexual proclivity but on the brute simple basis of capital and one's ability to stand within the winnowing eye of its ceaseless light-spangled storm; to flee his brief and possibly botched experiment in decadence and blasé betrayal; to embrace the anonymity of travel and the grand American ideal of self-determination. And yet he sat stalled a slow while in the clean-smelling car, after the first short petrifying drive of not many blocks and the first authentic New York City horn blast directed at his person, his shaking hands the only parts of him to heed the call to motion. He could not believe it had only been a week since he'd arrived. Outside, it was Sunday again, and he could see a small crowd of people lined up outside some innocent brunching place. He felt . . . oh god, he had no idea how he felt, and he didn't want to know. He imagined Paul walking past and seeing him, and how his face would loom in fury before the windscreen shattered.

He was recipient of many further horn blasts in the halting journey south-east through lower Manhattan towards the Holland Tunnel, his phone propped up against the dash and announcing each frightening turn and merge in its quaint Australian accent. Still, as he picked up speed and the highway dispensed with traffic lights and he passed the city limits, he experienced a brief interval in which his ego rallied. He did not feel like feeling guilty. He would probably never see Paul again, and certainly never Justine or Daisy or Marcus or Darla. They had been extras in the film of his life, and perhaps even Laura had only been a bit part, and the real story was yet to come, and he hoped more than anything that it wouldn't be boring.

He wanted to write this down as the third act of breezy heartless lonerism—the first being the move from the town of his birth to the (now shrunken) metropolis of Melbourne and the second his fool romantic leap into the heart of New York—and to believe that perhaps such acts, brave and invigorating as base-jumping, might come to define his very nature. He would not be like his father and fail after take-off and relent back home defeated—this would be who he was now. Of course, his romance of fuck-and-run was Kerouacian in both its generals and particulars, and he even began to imagine himself stopping for a week or two here and there along his route to work picking fruit or vegetables alongside other illegal workers, and so enacting again and yet again the thrilling ever-onward ritual of moving on and moving on and moving on. He was really getting good at deciding which of his many sets of thoughts and feelings to bury or postpone, almost beyond the need for conscious volition.

But this little peak could not compete with so much trough. He had been up all night, and by 3 pm he had been driving for four hours and fighting sleep for two, and so many rest-stop coffees had only made his hands shake harder, and he could not keep going.

He pulled into a brown low-roofed and cheap-looking roadside motel and parked the car. Inside, there was a stained sofa and a coffee percolator, a stack of polystyrene cups and a carton of creamer in a puddle of its own spillage. Behind the desk sat a woman about his mother's age, and like his mother she appeared to be a woman who had no truck with vanity, who sported no make-up over her sun-worn skin, whose hair was lank at the root and frizzy at the shoulder, and whose chlorine-blue t-shirt and elastic-waisted jeans bespoke a semiotics of frugality, though where his mother's plainness was ideological in nature—flaunting the godliness of renunciation and unbeauty—this woman's was under no illusion, and therefore bore a nobility that was lacking in his mother. Her name—Marie—was printed on a narrow badge pinned above her breast, and she smiled at him unstintingly. He asked her for a room and she clacked a while upon a chunky grey keyboard and took the credit card he slid towards her. He hadn't even asked the price; whatever it was, it was that or road-toll oblivion five hours outside of New York City and he preferred not knowing.

'Unfortunately that's come back declined, hon,' said Marie, looking at him with a frankness that made him think this must happen pretty often.

'Um . . . it shouldn't have but it's an Australian card. Maybe your machine won't accept it. Do you have an ATM here?'

She took a hasty gulp from a mug of coffee. 'There's one at the gas station just up the road, hon.'

'Okay. Can you hold the room? I'll be straight back.'

Marie watched him as he pushed out the door and peered around. She wondered what his story was, as she often wondered about the hordes of scrap migratory and mostly doomed humanity who passed across her property, their broken pasts hitched to them, obvious as trailers. This one was young, though, and far from home, and he didn't look like a junkie or a felon, had an innocence about him that was crying out for mothering. But you couldn't get involved. That only led to a world of pain, didn't she know it. She sighed for the struggles of the world, her own included, and got up to refill her mug.

*

Furnished finally with a key, Will walked the concrete strip along the row of conjoined brick boxes and ascending numbered brown doors and brownish-cream curtains, drawn across whatever depravity or modest daily wretchedness, and he opened his own door and disappeared into the brown and overwarm deodorised interior. The instant he removed his shoes he began to execute one of those clothed slow-motion crashes onto the bed and was asleep before the first creaking upthrust of its coiled metal springs.

He woke abrupt in darkness and checked his watch. It was 6 am, and he had rarely felt worse in his life. He was sick and shaking with the bends of waking; could feel the pressure of the rope that hauled him slack and foetal through that heavy element still tight around his chest. And this was just the briefest and least persistent of his woes, which numbered both the foolish and profound: the enormity of his comedown; the dire insufficiency of his savings; his heartbreak and the weight and truth of his solitude here, now that he had removed himself some thousands of miles from home and then set fire to his only source of welcome.

He sat up and flicked the switch beside the bed and the short fluorescent tube stuttered awake and revealed the room, the dark rectangle of the bathroom like the doorway to hell itself. There was not a blessed thing to ease his eye or spirit, no dime store picture on the wall nor plastic flower on the table.

'Well,' he said, slapping his thighs to rouse in himself some masculine stoicism and immunity to ambiance. He scrambled from the sagging bed and checked his phone.

There were a great many messages from Paul, the first a kindly 'where you at?' and the last so vile that he could barely read it to the end. He deleted them all and showered under scalding water, a futile clichéd purgative, and then he stumbled out again into the ceaseless self-renewing world.

The reception and the parked cars were still dark grey paper cut-outs, but the sky was paling minimally above the silhouetted scrub horizon, and he walked along the highway, past a buzzing streetlight around which moths were clustered like rough sleepers around a drum fire, past the whoosh and flash of early cars with their damned certainty of destination and past the hulked enormous shapes of trucks, and entered the dependable searing brightness of the petrol station. With an egg-and-sausage roll in its skirt of greasy paper, he wandered to the rear of the building, where he straddled the damp bench of a cement picnic table and ate his lonesome breakfast or deferred dinner and watched the sun rise once more above the flat blacktop and the clouds turn from ember to white as the day came on.

There was the sound of birds calling out from nearby woods and the road was rinsed clean and the breeze carried no scent except that of cloud-held water. He saw movement: a clutch of deer a short way off among some ragged saplings. He stood quietly and watched them in their soft shifting congregation. He had never seen them in the wild before (or what passed here for such: the weed-sown fringes of this vagrant junk landscape), and they bore for him a kind of old world northern magic in their archetypal poses of alert tranquillity, the strength of their hind legs, and the clarity and depth of their dark eyes, which seemed to contain so much sadness and understanding, as if they saw the world as it was, and loved it still. As Will observed them, he felt minutely blessed, and almost believed that he might expect a sign.

It was not the sign he would have chosen, but when he checked his phone back at the motel, slumped on the sagging bed edge with his toothbrush in his mouth, he found a days-old Facebook message from his one remaining contact in America: a girl from his own home town and therefore someone he had hoped to avoid (though Paul was from there too, he supposed, and it was only his association with New York that made him more appealing and maybe Tamsyn would turn out also to be thus changed).

Tamsyn Bruce had been in the class below him at school; their mothers were still friends and almost-neighbours and attended the same church. He recalled her as loud and laughing and clearly sad beneath it in a painful, obvious way that was uncomfortable to witness. She was what people called 'bubbly' and also what they called a 'bigger girl'. He remembered with a wince how one of the popular guys had described her as 'almost too ugly to fuck, but not quite'. He himself had not been kind to her, though not mean either. He had been too busy saving himself to think of helping others. She had found a guy online while they were still in high school and got engaged to him before they'd even met, and now she lived out here, whether with the same man or not, Will had no clue.

She had seen his check-in at Dante and sent him a private message:

Hey Will, are you in New York?!!

You *have to* come visit me!!!
I mean I'm nowhere near NY—haha. But if you happen to come past Littleproud, Ohio then come say hi! If I wasn't so damn pregnant I'd come meet you there. About to pop any day now. How are you anyway? I hear your living in Melbourne now. Anywayz if you've got a cell number here lmk and I'll give you a buzz—be nice to catch up on old times.
Luv, Tamsyn

Two days before he would have ignored her message or pretended not to see it until he was at some long-gone remove, but the intervening hours had knocked a bit of snob out of him and he felt just oh so utter and enormously alone.

And it was weird, wasn't it, that her message coincided with his deer-hallowed moment of superstitious semi-blessing, and stranger still that when he put the name of her town into his phone it was on the alternative route to Chicago offered him by Maps, and would add only an hour thirty-eight onto his trip. Of course he thought of Veronique and 'Bumfuck', Ohio, and chuckled smugly to himself, but he could be there in four hours and might at least get a free meal or even a free night's accommodation. Maybe she would know of some work he could pick up for a week or so to keep him going, and then perhaps he could extend his car hire . . . All this he thought in clear and self-protecting logic, but underneath it, too, was the lonesome homeless boy to whom the prospect of a familiar face and smiling welcome was relief as well as shame, and he replied to Tamsyn Bruce to say that he would be passing by *today*—wasn't that crazy timing? Would she be at home?—and then he got back on the road.

—

Here he was, now, in her hometown, and it had been hours and he hadn't heard back from her and his sense of fortuity was fading. Out of the air conditioning it was hot and terribly still. It was almost four o'clock but it felt as if the sun were at its zenith, for the magnified light and heat seemed to come from no one quadrant of the cloudless sky.

Perhaps he should just get back on the highway and keep going. But he knew he couldn't afford another motel. He should probably buy a tent. At the thought, he experienced an involuntary montage flash: the deserted trailer park; the hard unwelcoming ground; the shameful fear of the dark. *Wolf Creek*. Strung up and gutted by some backwoods nutjob. He had to literally shake his head to get the images out. Man, he was coming down like a motherfucker. Oh well, he'd be back on track tomorrow and reach Chicago, get his shit together and find the start point of that long highway down which he planned to careen himself into a whole new purity of movement.

He looked along the street and was overtaken by a sense of unreality, of not knowing where in the latitude of his life's geography he found himself, cast into that state of proprioceptive confusion that is common to waking in unfamiliar rooms. Perhaps the drugs had wrought some insidious permanent damage that was only just beginning to announce itself. It was a figure from the past who had led him to this decorous and familiar and plainly dying town, and it made him bitterly aware that he could not uncouple from his own history and still more aware that even his performance of decisive freedom-taking was a product of that history, enacted in honour of the very ghosts the town invoked, and that he would always be accompanied by them and never be rid of them.

He stood in the pooled static light and thought about what to do. Walk, he told himself, from a practical and unperturbed place somewhere deep within him, and this plain and good advice was comforting, and made him feel he may yet have reserves of strength, until now untapped, that this period of trial would open up; that this might be what he found here: something he had possessed all along but, in the way of such quests, had by necessity to ride out to the tip of whatever metaphorical headland to recognise. And so he walked, feeling purposive action in the movement of his legs in their too-warm black jeans and his feet in their sweltering boots down the wide unlittered pavement.

There was not a soul afoot. A faded brown pickup truck stopped at the intersection and he felt eyes on him. No traffic passed while the light was red and the truck idled in purposeless compliance and then revved off on the green instant. There were American flags mounted everywhere, at the corners of buildings, hanging like washing in the late afternoon heat. A barber's shop, either temporarily or permanently closed, displayed a printed fabric sign tacked lengthways over its side window that read, *Support Our Troops.* Further on, two austere and utterly unwelcoming churches faced one another across the street, one old and tall and grand, with dark stained-glass windows, the other low and new and defiant in its red-brick plainness, with a flat roof and a white-painted wooden cross affixed to its windowless street aspect, the only adornment, it seemed to say, necessary or proper. He knew of which his mother would approve, and thought that the visible bearing of that particular showy self-denial must take the form of ugliness the whole world over.

At last, he checked his phone again and there was a message from Tamsyn:

> Omg I am SO sorry! Been in a birthing class all day and only just saw ur message. Are you still around?

Tamsyn's house was a neat small bungalow on a flat hot treeless street, white with green trim and a sweet little porch with a wrought-iron railing. He pressed the bell and a dog began to bark. There was a sense of failure in just being here. Or maybe it was humility and growth, he wasn't altogether sure.

And then Tamsyn opened the door, smile-ready and bountiful in every way, and she hugged him as if he had been a better friend to her, and it was so female, the press of soft breasts and hard enormous belly and a smell all warm and yeasty risen.

'Will Free,' she said, holding his arms and looking him in the face.

'Tamsyn Bruce.'

'Not anymore. It's Mrs Tamsyn Nash now.'

'Congratulations. And congratulations!' He looked down at her belly, the popped-out navel showing like a nipple through her stretched t-shirt. She was wearing leggings and fuzzy pink sport socks, her curly hair was up and her face shiny. There was an asthmatic sound to her breathing as she laughed and thanked him and led him into her home.

'My husband's at work. He manages a bar across town. Basically the American equivalent of a pub, except they don't have those here. I thought we could go out and have dinner there and I can introduce you to my baby daddy.'

'Great,' said Will, wondering if he should ask whether he could stay the night, or see if she offered. 'What's his name?'

'J.T. So American, hey?'

'Is that the same guy you met online?'

'Sure is.'

The barking intensified as they got to the kitchen, and Tamsyn opened the back door and let in a squat brindle staffy who hurtled at Will and began to leap at his legs.

'Down, Delilah!' said Tamsyn. 'Down! This is J.T.'s dog. I secretly want to get rid of her before the baby's born, but there's no way J.T. would agree to that.'

Will crouched down and rubbed Delilah's chest and she smiled that staffy smile and wagged her whole rump, and he missed Rosie with a deep and guilty pang.

'You must have only been, what, sixteen when you met J.T., yeah? Well, met online . . .'

'Uh-huh. We met on a fan site for that show *Supernatural*. Do you remember? About the two hot brothers who hunt vampires and stuff?' She laughed, embarrassed and proud. 'Would you like a cup of tea?'

'Cup of tea? I haven't been offered one of those in a while. A cup of tea would be nice.'

Will looked around at the kitchen, with its wood-grain laminate benchtop and its row of painted chipboard cupboards at face height and its ancient-looking stove. Tamsyn filled the kettle and stood smiling at him.

'It's so nice to see someone from back home!' she said. 'I shouldn't say that; this is home now. J.T. says I need to stop calling back home *home*.'

'I can't believe you moved over the other side of the world and ended up in a small town kind of pretty much like ours.'

'You know me,' said Tamsyn. 'I'm a country girl. There's no way I'd live in the city.'

She pulled out a jumbo pack of Tynee Tips teabags and waved it at him. 'I get Mum to mail these to me. Can't go without my Tynee Tips. It's my addiction!'

He followed her to the lounge room, where there was more evidence of care and careworn struggle in the mishmash of cheap new and likely passed-down furniture—the pale brown microsuede sofa with its square chrome legs, the glass-topped coffee table and the two big '70s armchairs with orange vinyl arms and brown wool seat cushions that ruined any consistency of style. On the wall above the gas fire hung a big framed studio print of Tamsyn and the man who must be J.T., the two of them sitting on grass, their legs intertwined, gazing into each other's wholesome boring faces. The soft lens blur that signifies romance.

It was airless in the room and by the time he'd drunk his tea Will was sweating. Tamsyn pinched the neck of her t-shirt and flapped it in and out and blew on her top lip. She chatted happily about her husband and her pregnancy and how much she missed her mum and sisters, while Will swung back and forth between judgement and guilt.

Tamsyn's father had died of asbestosis when they were still in primary school, leaving behind a wife and four daughters.

Will remembered his mother cooking endlessly for them—in his mind it seemed like for years, and it may well have been. The widow and her gaggle of teen and pre-teen girls, of whom Tamsyn was the youngest, were taken in by the community of Newshepton, or the community of Will's mother's church, and cradled until their tears subsided, and they emerged the tightest little bundle of sisters that Will had encountered, before he met Laura and her own two sisters.

He realised he'd tuned out—he was still sleep deprived and fuzzy from driving—and that Tamsyn was offering to show him the baby's room, and he tried to look enthusiastic. Once that tedium was endured, she suggested they go to The Shack, where J.T. worked and Will found himself desperate for a beer and nodding perhaps a little too eagerly. He felt like a dick for not getting excited about the baby, for his snide hidden scorn that he knew said more about himself than her, but he couldn't seem to help it. Although he knew he would never hang out with her back home, he did like Tamsyn and the way she spoke to him as if it was only last week that they'd sat right here and shared their minor daily news, and how she talked in trivialities and didn't ask him the big questions about why he was here or if he had a girlfriend or how he'd changed since they were at school together.

There was a baby capsule already installed in the back of Tamsyn's car, and Will had to move a *Baby On Board* sign from the passenger seat before he sat down.

'I can't wait to put that up!' said Tamsyn. 'I wanted to do it as soon as I bought it, but J.T. said that was weird.'

They drove back through the town centre, over a broad slow river and past a clutch of fast-food restaurants with their signs up on high poles like the handles of gigantic souvenir teaspoons, and turned onto a road marked Buckeye Drive. On the left were some tiny rundown houses of peeling weatherboard set very close to the road. The struggle was undisguisable here, though the rows of shoes on the porches were lined up in a pathos of determination.

The world was falling into that deep blue elongated lull of crepuscular timespace in which the hours seem to pass more slowly than those of other colours. The town began to show signs of petering out. There were car lots and a leisure centre and a sign for a drive-in cinema and then Tamsyn slowed beside a line of cars pulled up every which way among the prominent roots of some large trees, most half or quarter mounted onto the grass verge so that the whole row looked like the aftermath of a mild earthquake. Tamsyn humped the right-hand wheels up onto the verge to join the rest.

The Shack was exactly as he had expected: the bland ubiquitous sports bar interior with the rows of screens above the interchangeable backdrop of vinyl and laminate and carpet tile, in which men sat with necks up-craned in the absorbed docility of spectatorship and families crowded around burgers and ribs and wings and colourful plastic baskets of fries and onion rings. The air was humid with fry oil and rowdy with clatter and talk.

Tamsyn ignored the *Please wait to be seated* sign and walked towards the bar section, in the swaying and footsore manner of very pregnant women.

A waitress came up and kissed her on the cheek. 'You're about to pop!'

The waitress had a hot body and was dressed in short denim shorts, green Chuck Taylors and a tight black t-shirt. She had on a tiny black apron, tied low around her hips, with an order pad and pen protruding from a pocket at exactly crotch height. She was young and firm, but her face was plain, with thin pale lips, over-plucked eyebrows, and eyes full of the kind of commercial-grade fatigue that only the service industry can impart. She wore glasses, which almost elevated her plainness to a sexy *Ghost World* geek-girl look, but the frames weren't quite right, not thick and black as they should have been, but thin, trying to be unobtrusive and so failing to make her appear to *own* the look. All this our cynical protagonist registered with the smooth unconscious fluency of the twenty-two-year-old native of late capitalism.

J.T. walked out from behind the bar and kissed Tamsyn and then bent and kissed her stomach.

'Hey, babe,' he said. 'I didn't know you were coming in.'

'This is my friend Will from back home, who I was telling you about,' said Tamsyn.

'Heya, Will,' said J.T., holding out his hand. He was a tall, slightly pudgy white guy with a goofy smile, perhaps around thirty. To Will, he was entirely unremarkable, and he wondered whether Tamsyn had been disappointed when she finally met him.

J.T. went to serve a customer, and Tamsyn trundled off to the ladies' room, leaving Will to take a seat at the bar and fiddle with his coaster.

'Sorry 'bout that,' said J.T. when he returned. 'Where's Tam? Gone to pee, right?'

'Yep.'

'Can I get you a bev-er-age?'

'Um, maybe a beer?' He looked down the bar at the bank of taps. 'What have you got?'

'Usual suspects: Bud, Heineken. If you're after something craft, we've got a local IPA I can highly recommend.'

'Oh, great. Made here?'

'Right here in Littleproud.'

'I'll try that. Thanks.'

J.T. poured him a pint and set it down. It was cold and deep and delicious and without doubt the best thing that had happened to him all day. It made him feel instantly grateful and full of good cheer, reinvesting the randomness of his being here with a level of mild promise.

'*Damn*, that's good,' he said.

J.T. grinned. 'Not bad, hey? My buddy Luke works in the brewery.'

J.T. poured a Sprite and set it waiting for Tamsyn. 'So you're just passing through? Where you headed?'

'No idea,' said Will.

J.T. laughed and gave him a quizzical look.

'I'm kind of on a mission to get lost. I had to get away from Melbourne and I've always wanted to come here. Like, not *here*, but the States. I've been in New York for a week, but now I'm just kind of driving. No plan, really.'

'Seriously? That's *awesome*.'

Will took another gulp of beer, glad that his frankly bizarre actions had been received positively.

'How long you staying? I assume you're crashing with us?' said J.T.

'Oh, actually Tamsyn and I hadn't really talked about it. I totally don't have to . . .'

'Of course! You're so welcome.'

'Are you sure?' he said, the relief immense. 'It'd just be tonight. I'll probably head for Chicago tomorrow morning. Unless there's anything you think I should see before I go.'

'Not a whole lot to see in little old Littleproud. Although my band's playing tomorrow night. Ha!' J.T. looked instantly embarrassed, which endeared him still more to Will.

'Really? Cool. I haven't been to a gig in a while. What kind of music?'

A guy further down the bar raised a finger and J.T. gave Will a 'just a sec' look and slid over to him.

Will sipped his beer and wondered if maybe it was really this simple, the easy interchange of the traveller, the global equivalence of craft beer culture, the shared codes of non-mainstream masculinity. He imagined himself at J.T.'s gig the following night, tried to guess what precise genre taxonomy J.T.'s music would fit into. Could be anything, really. Hardcore, psychedelic, alt-country, Americana—or did that genre only exist *outside* America? He wondered what the girls would look like, and he glanced over at the waitress again. She was wiping down a table with a competence of movement that he found a turn-on, displaying a no-fuss ease in her own body that was unselfconscious and cool, not like other kinds of girls who had the same ease and coordination—dancers, for example, who did everything as if they were being watched.

Tamsyn came back from the bathroom and climbed up beside him, breathing heavily.

'J.T. seems great,' he said.

'He is. He treats me real good.' She began rubbing her belly in a circular motion.

'Sorry,' said J.T., returning to them once again.

'What about you?' said Tamsyn, making a cheeky face. 'You got a girlfriend back home?'

'Nah. I actually just had a pretty bad breakup. That's kind of why I'm here.'

'Ah, I get it now,' said J.T. 'Damn! That must have been one hell of a breakup.'

'It wasn't great.'

Even now, though he knew he would stay in control, he could feel the heaving slosh of sadness, as if he were a bucket of water that had only just stilled and then been picked up roughly and swung by the handle.

'I've only had one of those myself,' said J.T. 'Back in high school. And it *sucked*! But all *I* did was get a shitty tattoo.'

As they were all laughing, a new customer approached and pulled out the stool one over from Will.

'Wayne!' said J.T. Will could hear the affection in his voice, and he turned to look at the newcomer.

He was a big man, probably in his early fifties, not especially tall, but aptly fitting the description *barrel-chested*, with the pasty skin of someone who hasn't eaten a vegetable in a while. He was wearing a red cap that said *Makita* on the front, and he pulled it off and ran a hand through thinning brown hair and set the cap on his knee under the bar. He smelled strongly, though not unpleasantly; a grassy, outside smell, like the sweat of horses.

'Hi, Wayne,' said Tamsyn, peering around Will.

J.T. introduced them and told Wayne about Will's mission to get lost. 'Probably the best reason I've heard for visiting Littleproud, wouldn't you say?'

Wayne laughed and nodded.

'Wayne's an incredible guitarist,' said J.T. 'He taught me to play. I was just inviting Will to my gig tomorrow night, in a shameless act of self-promotion. Hey . . .' He turned to Will. 'If you *really* want to see something interesting while you're in town, you should go out to Wayne's place. Wayne's Wild Kingdom.'

Will looked between Wayne and J.T., trying to ascertain whether this was an in-joke or serious.

'It's a private zoo—although you hate that word, hey, Wayne?'

'Correct. Those are my children.' He winked at Will.

J.T. poured a Budweiser and handed it to Wayne.

'Those are some demanding children,' said Tamsyn.

Will continued looking between the three of them, smiling clueless and uncertain.

'Did I tell you Zorro took a swipe at me on Sunday?' said Wayne.

'No. Fuck!' said J.T. 'That's teenagers for you, though, right?'

'Right.'

'Don't you go getting the father of my child killed now, Wayne!' said Tamsyn.

'Most of the time they're good as gold. Total sweethearts. But you do need to remember they're wild animals, and when they're hungry, they might love you, but you're still meat.'

Tamsyn was stabbing her straw down on the ice cubes in her glass in a way that made Will think there was some tension there.

'I don't get it,' he said. 'Zorro? What kind of animal is that?'

'Tiger,' said Wayne.

'No way!'

'Yup. Naming them's getting kind of tricky now, there's so many of them. Our first exotic we named Simba. Not exactly original, I know. I think *The Lion King* had just come out.'

Will must have looked as baffled as he felt.

'So,' said J.T., 'Wayne owns a bunch of wild animals. *Exotics* is the technical term. Licensing laws in Ohio mean it's fine here to have pet lions and tigers. Anything you want, really.' He turned back to Wayne. 'Forty-nine all up, now, yeah?'

'No way!' said Will again.

'Eighteen lions, fifteen tigers, a couple of brown bears and a grizzly, wolves, leopards, primates,' said Wayne.

'Are you *serious*?'

'And a panther. Uh-huh. Most of them we've had from babies. They're all tame. Except you can never *completely* tame a tiger. We've got a couple of cubs at the moment, though, that are beautiful. Like giant kittens.'

'It's pretty amazing,' said J.T. 'I help out there pretty regularly. I love being around the animals. And Wayne, of course. Probably the wildest animal of them all.'

Wayne laughed and looked pleased by this description.

'Actually, Wayne . . .' J.T. cleared his throat and glanced at Tamsyn. 'I need to talk to you about what happens when the baby comes. I've got exams coming up, too. And Pa . . . It's just tough right now.'

'I hear you,' said Wayne. 'It's tough for me too, as you know. And you're about the only person I can trust these days.'

J.T. was wiping the same patch of bar over and over, and Tamsyn took a breath as if she was about to speak.

'Let's talk about it tomorrow, J.T.,' said Wayne. 'We'll work it out.'

'Thanks,' said J.T. He looked at Tamsyn, and she nodded, her face stern. 'So, Wayne, what do you think? Can we give Will a tour? I could bring him out Wednesday.'

'Sure,' said Wayne. 'If J.T.'s vouching for you, then you're welcome.'

'Wayne sometimes gets grief from these animal activist types who think it's cruel to have them as pets,' said J.T. 'But he just invites them to come and stay and get to know the animals and then decide if they still think it's cruel.'

'Used to, anyway,' said Wayne. 'I'm less trusting these days.'

'And do they?' Will asked. 'Change their minds?'

'A few came,' said Wayne. 'And a couple did change their minds, too. You just fall in love with them. Can't help it.'

'There was one guy who came who was real intense,' said J.T. 'Ended up in the psych ward, I think.'

'That he did,' said Wayne.

'He tried to let one of the tigers out and got himself mauled in the process. Wayne had to take him to hospital.'

'Oh my god, don't tell me this stuff,' said Tamsyn.

'Yeah, but he was an imbecile,' said Wayne. 'Thought he could just step into the cage of an animal who doesn't know him from squat. That's just asking for it, pure and simple. As soon as I got there, Snow let go of him straight away. But I let him lie there a little while, just to teach him a lesson. Snow was prowling around and the guy was crying like a baby.' Wayne chuckled.

'Jesus,' said Tamsyn under her breath.

'He was totally safe by then, don't worry. But like I said, no one's taking my babies away.'

'Still up for a tour?' J.T. asked, laughing.

'Um,' said Will, uncertain, but recalling his vow. 'Okay. It sounds pretty wild. Like, literally!'

'Hey, babe,' said Tamsyn. 'Can we get some food, please? Your foetus is hungry.'

'Sorry,' said J.T. 'I'm not being a great host here, am I? But let's lock in Wednesday, okay, Wayne?'

Driving home along the river in the leafed darkness Will saw the swift-turning tails of deer among the banks of saplings that deepened in the high beams into a cold-lit density of trunk and branch and foliage and then returned to flat black as the car drew level, as if everything was turning away from their approach.

Tamsyn was quiet and yawning as she drove. 'Sorry,' she said. 'It's past my bedtime.' She began to tap the steering wheel with an agitation that made Will look over at her. She was biting her lower lip as she stared ahead at the rushing centre-line that spooled out before them. 'That man,' she said. 'He really gets to me.'

'Wayne?'

She nodded.

'Why?'

'He takes advantage of J.T. I've barely seen him lately because he's always out helping Wayne when he's not at work or studying. I just think he needs to tell Wayne to find someone else to help him out, but I know he won't.'

'Why not?'

'He's got a lot of loyalty, J.T. Which I love about him, obviously, but . . . and Wayne *has* been a father figure to him. J.T.'s dad is pretty unwell, mentally. He's a veteran.'

'Vietnam?'

'Yep. Wayne is too. But yeah, he did a lot for J.T. when he was a teenager. Taught him guitar, yada yada yada.'

Will laughed.

They pulled up in front of the house and Tamsyn turned off the engine. 'Wayne's not in a good place right now,' she said. 'His wife's left him. And he's probably about to go to prison.'

'Prison?!'

'Yeah. I mean, even *I* think that's bullshit. Some trumped-up gun charges. He reckons they just want to take his animals away. But then, so they should, if you ask me. It's out of control out there!'

'Hmm,' said Will, starting to question whether his visit to Wayne's Wild Kingdom was a good idea.

—

He woke breathless in sunshine in the stultifying non-suspiration of the house's lungs and lay staring up at the mobile above the cot as it swayed minutely in no breeze he could feel. Tamsyn had laid down the sofa cushions for him on the floor of the baby's room, and they had slipped apart as he'd slept, and now his hip was pressing on the hard floor and he was sore in body and spirit alike and unready to meet the bright new small-town day.

Some kind of loud appliance began revving in the kitchen, and he pulled on clothes and opened the door.

Tamsyn was pouring a thick berry-coloured smoothie from a blender into a chunky adult version of a plastic sippy cup.

'Yay, you're awake!' she said. 'I was about to leave you a note. I've got the second day of my birthing course today so I won't be able to hang out with you, I'm sorry.'

She went to all the womanly and imminent-maternal lengths to show him where the coffee and the mugs were and to list for him the local attractions by which he might divert himself in her absence—a waterfall and a shopping mall and a 'famous' dogleg bridge—and then she gathered up her keys and smoothie and stocked her bag with snacks.

'J.T.'s still asleep,' she said. 'He's got the day off but he'll be setting up and sound-checking for tonight.'

Will followed her to the door, where she seemed to hesitate.

'Will . . .' she said.

'Mmm?'

'I spoke to my mum this morning. I told her you were here and she said she'd seen your mum at church on Sunday and that she was worried 'cause she hadn't heard from you.'

Will half turned in an obvious involuntary display of irritation.

'I don't mean to get involved,' Tamsyn continued. 'But maybe you should call her? Just let her know you're okay.'

'Ah . . . yeah, maybe,' said Will to the doorframe beside Tamsyn's foot.

'I know it's none of my business . . . it's just, as a soon-to-be mum, I know I'd want to know that my kid is safe, that's all.'

Well, now *your* mum can tell mine that I'm fine, he thought. Problem solved.

'Okay, that's all, I'm off.' She blew him an ingratiating kiss that only pissed him off more, and was gone.

While he was showering, Will realised how hungry he was. He didn't want to wake J.T., so he set off back to town, finding a diner and allowing himself an unholy breakfast of two glazed donuts, out of sight or judgement in this mint-green-laminated all-American space with its squat cream mugs and thin hot bottomless coffee and bleached synthetic oil-based creamer.

This simple act of indulgence restored in him a sense of vacation. Wasn't he here, after all, at last? In *America*? And here he would remain, goddamn it, until he had reached the destination, had gone below and tasted the ashen fruit, had been imperilled and escaped and could return a man; *America*, where, he must remember, his psychopomp would likely take the guise of animal collector or barman or guitarist in a hardcore band.

What Will desired more at this moment than any other thing, so keenly it could have erupted in a cry, was *experience*. He wanted to imbue his current predicament with the tough and simple purity of the journey, which achieves by solitude and material deprivation a slow annealing of the spirit to adamantine.

He wanted, from the unglimpsed vantage future, to see this voyage stretching out behind him like a freight train, laden with primal significance, a quest culminating somehow in the state of wisdom, though that destination seemed as reachable as Hyperborea from this bolted-down length of the endless forward track.

After his holiday repast and lapse into self-indulgence, both gustatory and emotional, Will drove back to confront again that homely spectre of the old centre, where he touristed himself for an hour or so, snapping pictures on his phone, aestheticising this ordinary authentic Midwestern town, with its neat civic buildings of red and brown brick and its empty lots of cracked asphalt where weeds insisted along the borders and corroded water tanks despaired on rotting wooden platforms. Forcing down the cringe, he allowed himself to upload a few careful photos to Facebook, to create an album under the heading *USA Road Trip 2011*. There was another message from Paul, but he deleted it without reading.

Later, thinking that some air would do him good, he drove to the falls that Tamsyn had suggested, through stands of woodland, thick and green in a way that was wholly foreign and wholly beautiful. There was a bunch of guys, who looked like they should be in school, smoking a joint on the rocks by the disappointing cascades, and they eyed him with hostility and he did not stay long. He tramped back along the muddy trail to the picnic ground where his car sat alone, performing an obvious metaphor of forlorn solitude.

Close among the trees he saw more deer, and again he stood and watched them graze. He saw himself through local eyes, comical, like tourists in Australia encountering kangaroos for the first time when, for him, they were as unremarkable as crows, moving in mobs across the golf course behind his parents' house each dusk, or splay-legged rigid on the roadside, as he had seen deer here, too. Eventually he broke the moment and stepped forward and the deer sniffed and tremored, turning their heads towards him in a single motion, though their bodies were angled every which way, creating an eerie still frame that burned into his memory, and then as one they dispersed and ran, leaving the patch of lawn bereft.

Driving back to town, circuitous thoughts of wildlife recalled him to his brief hopeful period of father worship, when he and his dad would walk out in the evenings to the golf course where kangaroos trailed in their daily migration as leisurely as the absent golfers, pausing in the green and gold light in their emblem-stance of static soft eternal vigilance before bounding off across the grass. He had the sharpest image of it in his mind: the light all boiled-down golden and the smooth green turf always looking so velour until you tried to lie down on it; the tick and chug of the big sprinklers that he liked to run through in that summer moment, which must have been season-short—the moment of liking his father.

He saw his father in his tracksuit of the crumpled parachute fabric that had been popular for an equally short interval—black with a fluorescent orange band across the chest that glowed, too, in that dying light—his greasy black hair in the long bowl cut he had kept all Will's life in outdated deference to his youth.

By then, Will's brother and sister had long grown into the disillusion and disdain that Will would soon reach, like a pencil height-mark on the doorframe, as if that period of father love could be measured in inches and all his children would grow through it and out of it at a certain height, never to return. It was after the time his father had initiated him into the mythology of his trip to London and after Will had stopped going to church, and for that brief span Will shared with his father a conspiracy of sullenness and petty rebellion against Will's mother, which Will later joked was because they were both for that moment the same mental and emotional age.

Together they would walk the greens and flop down within the close-mown circle of hole ten, which sat atop a small rise, and there survey the kangaroos as they paused and let their joeys out to practise their gangly hopping on the bouncy cropped grass. Sometimes his father would make him wrestle or practise aikido moves, toppling the boy without mercy on the lawn. Sometimes they would look over at the smeared clouds and talk about whether aliens were real (his father had a great many books with grainy over-enlarged black-and-white photos of supposed UFOs, which Will examined endlessly on the dog-smelling couch in the garage while his father did bench presses, Led Zeppelin or Hendrix or Santana on the stereo). It had been a time when the kangaroos had held, for Will, the same self-evident magic as the deer evoked for him now, and which must be the inborn correct and open-hearted response until familiarity, or the judgement of others, habituated him to that state of cultivated and tragic bored indifference. How much of joy and openness had he lost to that same enculturated false ennui? Had he lost Laura to it, too?

He parked outside Tamsyn's house and sat listening to the ticking of the engine as it cooled. Tamsyn's car was there, but she hadn't called him, so he didn't know if he should go and knock. She had told him she would call after her class. He thought with irritation of her lame migration to this small-town home-away-from-home, and he judged her narrowness and envied her contentment in equal measure.

He pulled out his phone and looked at his Facebook album. His niece and Jack and fifteen other people had liked the album; his mother had liked every photo individually and Tristan had liked just one image, a low-angle of an abandoned lot with weeds breaking through a crack in the pavement, a water tank up on a high wooden platform in the background. It was one Will had worried was a cliché of American rust belt decay, and it amused him that uber-cool Tristan had lapped it up.

His mother had commented on several photos. 'Lovely picture, darling,' she had written below one of the town hall and, 'What a great history lesson!' below the one he had ironically posted of all the miniature US flags stuck into the grass around the nationalistic grandeur of the memorial statue. He would have been embarrassed by her comments normally, but he felt nothing at this moment other than the resistance and responsibility associated with calling her.

He flicked to the world clock on his phone. It was 5.13 pm here; 9.13 am at home. Spurring himself like a reluctant horse, he called his mother's mobile.

'Hello, Jo speaking,' she answered, her voice metal and vicious distant.

'Mum, it's Will.' He could hear his voice come back to him in cruel echo as it bounced off some dark or sunlit satellite.

'Will,' said his mother, and he heard in the singular utterance of his name all the frequencies of maternal history that he had striven to remain undetermined by. 'I've been so worried about you!'

'Sorry,' he said. 'I just haven't gotten around to calling. It's all been quite busy.'

'I spoke to Leslie. She said you're visiting Tamsyn and her husband.'

'Yeah, I'm here now.'

'That's great, darling. Send her my love, won't you?'

'Okay.'

'Did you give Paul my regards? How was he? Did he look after you? Show you around?'

'Um, yep. Yep, he's good.'

'That's good, darling. I'm glad you've got some friends over there to look out for you. You don't want to be just arriving in another country like that without knowing anyone. And I hear parts of New York are quite dangerous still.'

'No they're not! It's perfectly safe,' said Will, hearing the impatience in his voice and hating himself for reverting within seconds to this pattern that he could not seem to outgrow. He knew he acted like a petulant teenager towards her, and that part of why she still treated him like a child was because he still behaved like one in her presence. 'Anyway, I'm fine. I'm in Ohio now. Just for a couple of days. I really need to find some work, though.'

'Is that allowed? With your visa?'

'Well, it'd have to be cash in hand, but I'm sure people do it all the time.'

'Oh, Will, are you sure? I wouldn't, darling. If you get caught, you could get deported, couldn't you?'

'It's *fine*, Mum. Don't worry.'

'Do you need money? We can send you some.'

'No, Mum.' He put his head down on the steering wheel. 'Please, can we just drop it? How are you? What's been happening?'

'Oh, nothing much. The usual. I've been on night shift the last week so I'm exhausted. We might go down to Melbourne next week. Your father needs some new slacks, and I need new shoes. I like the ones I can get in that shop in the city there. They're very comfy.'

'Mm-hmm.'

'That's about it. No special news. I'm doing a lot of sewing for the church car boot sale in a couple of weeks. Mostly baby things, which sold very well last year.'

'That's good.' He banged his head softly against the wheel.

'Should I put Dad on?'

He straightened at this. 'No, that's okay. I should probably go.'

'Really? I'm sure he'd love to say hello . . . *Gary!*' she called out. '*Gary! Will's on the phone* . . . I think he's in the garage. I'll take the phone in.'

'Mum!' Will said. 'Mum, listen to me. I don't feel like talking to Dad.'

'Why not?'

He made a sound of frustration. 'I'm just still really pissed off at him after the Melbourne trip. How he acted in front of Laura. He's pretty much the reason she broke up with me!'

'Oh, darling! I don't think that's what would have done it. I know your father can be a bit . . . well, you know. But if she couldn't take one dinner with him, then maybe . . . How would she go being part of this family for the rest of her life?'

'Well, exactly!' said Will. 'I'm sure that's what she saw in the future and thought, no thanks! I don't blame her, frankly.'

'Look, darling, I know you're hurt and upset right now, but I don't think that's entirely fair, do you?'

That patronising, parental tone!

'Probably not,' he said. 'But that's where I'm at, so I might go.'

'You were just as rude that night as your father was,' she continued over him.

'For fuck's sake, Mum! He's the *parent*, not me! I mean, is *anyone ever* going to expect him to just act like an adult?'

'Will . . .' he heard her begin to protest, but he cut her off.

'I have to go. I'll call you back another time.'

He hung up and threw his phone onto the passenger seat. He leaned back and ran his trembling fingers along the upholstered ceiling, feeling its spongy texture. The space of the car was soothing, signifying independence, freedom, adulthood, agency. He could start the motor and drive through the night, lose himself, never call home again. He imagined throwing his phone from a bridge over a river, driving and driving, past the expiry of his visa and on into pure anonymity.

When he picked up the phone again, he saw that there was a message from Tamsyn:

> Hey Will soz—fell asleep after my class lol. Wanna come here 4 dinner b4 the gig? I've got pizza x

Instead of going up to the door as soon as he'd got the message, which would look weird and might reveal he'd been waiting outside, he started the car again and drove around a bit, stopping off at a corner store to buy a sixpack of beer. His card was accepted this time, and he tried not to think about what that meant: that he had enough money for beer but not enough for one night's accommodation in a roadside motel. He felt sick at the thought of how he was going to pay for a month's petrol. Maybe he could call the bank and get his credit limit increased.

He went back to Tamsyn's and they shared a soggy microwave pizza. He drank a beer, and she swigged heartburn liquid from the bottle. She told him in detail about the birthing course, about her birth plan and all the scary things that could go wrong.

'Hey, Tamsyn . . .' he said. 'I know this is pretty unlikely, but you wouldn't happen to know of any work going around here, would you? I think I'm gonna have to find a way to make a bit more cash to last out this whole trip.'

'Hmm . . . dunno,' she said. 'But I'll ask J.T. There might be shifts going at the bar. They're always short-staffed. You've got hospo experience, yeah?'

'Just from working at the Royal Oak back home after high school.' He laughed, embarrassed. 'I've been working at Officeworks in Melbourne, so no real recent experience.'

'Oh my god, the Royal Oak!' said Tamsyn. 'I miss it! No one even knows what a shandy is here.'

Will could tell that Tamsyn had moved on already, back to her habitual theme of stunted nostalgia. She clearly hadn't understood the severity of the situation, but he didn't really want to make it any clearer. Fuck! What was he going to do?

Tamsyn watched Will as he took the plates to the kitchen. She thought how serious he still was, though in other ways—his clothes and way of speaking and whole vibe—he was pretty different. He was really at pains to make it clear how much he'd hated their home town and their high school years, which in some ways had been the happiest of her life—not so much school itself, because the girls were mostly horrible, but living with her mum and sisters, and the thrill of meeting J.T. online and their hours-long chats and all the things he said to her in those early first-flush days. She didn't mind, though; Will still reminded her of home, and she liked having him around. She smiled to herself, remembering the long-ago image that would always be her clearest memory of him. She'd been looking out her bedroom window after school one day and seen him walking past. He'd stopped in the street, believing himself unobserved, and staged a clumsy elaborate kung fu battle with an invisible opponent. They must have been eleven or twelve years old; old enough that she'd well and truly outgrown such blissful unselfconsciousness, and it had shocked her to witness it. Then he'd looked up and seen her in the window and flushed in that way he still flushed now, and literally run away down the street. She wondered if he remembered it; if the memory still stung like some of hers still stung. She'd never teased him about it. She knew even then what that kind of cruelty could do to a person.

Poor Will. He was clearly broken by this chick who'd dumped him, and that could make people pretty self-involved for a while. And he was a boy, after all—they grew up so much slower. She kind of secretly hoped she was going to have a girl. No, that was terrible. She'd love a boy just as much; it would just be more work with a boy. Jeepers, look how Will had just dumped the plates in the sink and walked away, leaving them for her to wash up.

WILL WOKE FACE DOWN ON the couch. He was thick and frayed and ruined, a cardboard man left out in the weather. Through one eye he could see the coffee table in front of him, on it an empty bottle of Jim Beam and an orange plastic bong. He peeled up all his edges and scraped himself from the sofa, leaving a dark patch of drool on the light brown microsuede. Cam, the drummer from J.T.'s band, was asleep in the corner, lying on the cushions Will had slept on the previous night, which were only big enough for his torso, leaving his legs draped across the carpet.

On the way to the bathroom, Will passed J.T. and Tamsyn's open bedroom door. They were still asleep, Tamsyn's head on J.T.'s chest and her body angled across the bed to leave space for her belly. He felt sorry for Tamsyn, who'd come out all sleepy at some point after they got home from the gig and hung out with them for a bit while they got even more drunk and stoned and played loud music. She'd sat on J.T.'s lap and he'd put his arm around her but kept moving to highlight some bit of whatever hardcore music was playing with exaggerated air guitar or drumming, and she kept slipping off and then shuffling back on again and trying to snuggle up to his sweaty lurching oblivious body.

The gig had been okay; about as good as he'd expected. He'd felt awkward about going on his own, but he couldn't exactly beg Tamsyn to come out late because he was too shy to rock up alone. She'd disappeared after dinner and returned to the kitchen wearing a pink dressing-gown and said she was too tired and pregnant and was going to bed.

So Will had ventured out into the unlit industrial fringes of Littleproud, crawling his car along the centre of the street where the venue was meant to be, trying to locate a number on any of the dark warehouses until a low door opened under an awning and the aquatic light from within revealed a bunch of people standing out front who he hadn't even noticed.

'Which band are you here for?' the door girl shouted at him.

'Um, I don't know their name. J.T.'s band.'

'Blooter.'

Oh god, he thought. This is going to suck.

The room was big, mostly empty, with some couches along one wall and a couple of rugs on the floor in front of the box stage. There were freestanding lights with blue cellophane taped over them, and a PA was cranking out some kind of terrible fast bass-heavy music that sounded like Mr. Bungle. Will hoped it was not indicative of what was to come. A massive steer of a guy, a big white twenty-year-old meat-eater, manned the bar.

Bud was all they served, but it was only three dollars a bottle. Will bought one and went and stood against the wall.

Then, movement: four men, one of them J.T., walked from the darkness behind the stage, three carrying guitars, and they heaved onto the stairless platform and the empty-handed one sat down at the drum kit while the others plugged in. One struck a chord that was very loud and then the background music was subjected to a harsh fade-out, the band nodded to each other, and with no further ceremony they began to shred the air with sound.

The music wasn't that bad, though heavier than anything he would listen to by choice. There were no vocals, and a great many complex tempo changes that were not always precisely synchronous. The bass player seemed to be the weak link, but J.T. was clearly a great guitarist. The dudes at the front of the crowd began to thrash around and jostle each other in a bent collective epilepsy.

Will found his mind removing itself, returning like a carrion-feeder to the tender corpse of Laura, thinking of the many gigs they'd gone to together as he'd tried to make a minor name for himself in the sceney and prohibitive world of Melbourne music reviewing. He knew already that this was not the kind of experience he was seeking; it was too easily accessible, too similar to what was already available for him at home, making his being here seem like simple dumb defiance. He felt a dark glimmer of suspicion that he had pinned too much on this trip.

The band finished their short irritant set, unplugged, and climbed back into the darkness, reappearing with towels before the brief applause had stopped, wiping their faces and the backs of their heads and grinning—except J.T., Will noticed, who was scowling—as they merged into the dispersing crowd.

J.T. stepped behind the table, patted the bullocky barman on the shoulder, and helped himself to a beer from the fridge, flinging the cap against the roller door with a ping and chugging half the bottle on the spot. The stereo was turned up again, playing the same music as before.

J.T. saw Will and smiled. 'Hey, you made it.' He pulled another beer from the fridge and handed it to Will, waving away his attempt to pay.

'That was awesome, man,' said Will, inclining his head towards the stage.

'No. It wasn't. It fucking sucked. Fucking Brad.' He looked around. 'We need to fire that no-rhythm motherfucker.'

'Is that the bass player?'

J.T. lifted his hands and then let them drop. 'See?' he said. 'Fuck. Is it that obvious? It's really obvious, isn't it? Fuck!'

'No, no,' said Will, wondering why the hell he'd said anything. 'It was still great. Seriously. You're an awesome guitarist.'

J.T. growled and wiped his face with the towel. 'Fuck it,' he said. 'Let's get drank!'

—

After a long piss with his head against the wall, Will went to the kitchen and slurped water from the tap. He found a slice of pizza left in one of the stack of cheese-scribbled boxes they'd ordered in last night. The pepperoni was brittle and snapped into pieces under his teeth.

He was thankful at least that he'd passed on the bong, although he'd definitely had a few decent drags on a fat joint back at the gig, and another on the walk back to J.T.'s. He wasn't sure what to do, with everyone still asleep. He drank some more water and looked out at the yard—single-treed, recently mown—where Delilah the staffy lay in the grass chewing a rubber bone.

Eventually, he decided to walk back to the venue—he thought he could find his way—pick up his car and maybe get coffees for everyone on the way back. He needed a coffee like a shot man needs whiskey. He put on his shoes and went out the front door as quietly as he could.

It was mild outside with a soft breeze, the day lambent pale, as if taking pity on him. He checked his phone. It was only 8.45 am and he realised he had roused himself from what was only the first painful bout of wakefulness, that he should have slept again for another couple of hours at least. Too late now.

He would leave tomorrow, he thought, after today's apex of random tourist acquiescence—the visit to the private zoo of some outlandish Midwestern character—which, in its sheer strangeness, in its poetics of gung-ho masculinity and excess need to prove dominion and no-fear in the face of the wildest animal nature, might be the most Australian thing he had encountered in America so far. It had been a lapse, relenting to the comfort of familiarity represented by Tamsyn. Even in New York he had not been truly anonymous, and that was what he wanted; how else was he to reinvent himself? Yes, tomorrow he would push off again into the current, and the thought made him lighter, and if he grew a little smug, momentarily, we can forgive him, because he is twenty-two and ego-bruised by heartbreak, and the world will beat it out of him soon enough.

Already, in fact. He returned to the house heavily laden: four coffees on a cardboard tray were no match for the strife and worry he hoisted in his empty other hand. There had been no money in his wallet and he'd gone to find an ATM and got out a fifty. The ATM would not give him his account balance, but at last he braved the act of logging in to net banking on his phone while he waited for the coffees, and he felt the sick invisible change of pressure like the plug being pulled from a full bath, the gurgle and suck from below that the gambler must feel when the card is turned and hope revealed as fallacy.

The others were still asleep, their bodies carrying out their disparate unconscious tasks of baby-making or the processing of alcohol and THC, stoic and unmutinous as draught horses, while their minds floated serene and unaware.

Will left the coffees on the bench and opened the door to the yard. The staffy dashed up to him, wagging like mad, and he sat in the sun on a fibrous doormat that poked through his jeans and sipped his latte and rubbed the dog's back, thumping her firm side with a hollow, familiar, infinitely comforting sound.

He felt once again how much he missed Rosie. More, without doubt, than his family. Laura and Rosie: the only two beings whom he truly loved. At least Rosie's devotion was unwavering and loyal. He vowed that she would again be part of whatever life he resumed or metamorphosed into on his return. He hadn't heard from Jack or Tristan or Maddie since he'd left. Perhaps he really would have to make a whole new life for himself. The idea was hard to face head-on, and he wrenched his mind away and thought only of Rosie.

He drank his coffee slowly, and by the time it was finished his headache had receded.

He got up and opened the door, and before he could stop her, Delilah had muscled in and bounded down the hallway towards Tamsyn and J.T.'s room. He heard the clacking of her claws on the floorboards cease and then a shout and splutter from J.T. When he got to the doorway, J.T. was propped up on one elbow, wrestling the dog, his chin held up to avoid her lunging kisses, and she was uttering plaintive whimpering sentences of adoration as Tamsyn turned away, groaning and covering her face with her arm.

'Sorry!' said Will. 'I didn't mean to let her in.'

'It's fine,' said J.T., sitting up and sliding the dog backwards across the bed. 'It's the best way to wake up, isn't it, furball? So much love. So much slobbery love.'

'I went out and grabbed some coffees,' said Will. 'They're in the kitchen.'

'Oh, man, lifesaver!' J.T. struggled up off the bed, sniffed his armpit and grimaced, pulled his t-shirt off and threw it into a corner, revealing his hairy white chest and belly and his strangely wide navel. He slapped his stomach and clicked his fingers and Delilah leaped off the bed and followed them to the kitchen.

J.T. seemed to wake from both hangover and sleep with the single relaxed masculine stretch and shake and exaggerated yawn he carried out in the kitchen, one of those people who greet each day with indefatigable optimism, not self-willed or stubborn but expectant, even passive, as if already given a glimpse into their own future and satisfied that it is good and now released from the hectic futile agitation of the vessels of their lives that others engage in to reassure themselves through movement alone that they are in control of their course.

'Let's go see some fucking lions!' J.T. said, gulping his lukewarm coffee and crumpling up the cup in his big hand and shooting it into the bin. Soon they were showered and pop-tarted and the still-sleeping Tamsyn had been kissed goodbye and Cam prodded with a boot toe until he offered up a grunt and poor loyal Delilah returned to her rubber bone.

Then they were off in J.T.'s old black pickup, driving down Main Street with the windows down, Will catching a glimpse of his own two-day-old phantom walking this same quaint decorous path by the Antique Arcade where now no soul walked on foot, his present or future self sailing by, companioned by this cheerful, welcome and welcoming guide, who was tuning the radio to some travesty of commercial country music and declaring it his guilty pleasure with a confidence that made it so easy.

They crossed over the river and under the highway and through the outskirts and when they were out of town they passed a behemoth of piled and shining indistinguishable metal that stretched beyond view, traversed and turned over by three gigantic yellow excavators, this apocalyptic installation advertised in peeling red letters on the side of a shipping container office as Folk's Scrap Metal.

'Whoa,' said Will. 'That's a lot of metal.'

'Yeah. It's the town's main industry. That and the chicken factory out the other side of Wayne's. We supply a lot of steel back to the industry for smelter. My pa was in the business. I was heading that way myself.'

'What happened?'

'Actually, Wayne, pretty much. He's been a huge influence on me. I started taking guitar lessons off of him when I was fifteen. Probably one of the biggest turning points of my life.'

'Really? How come he was such a big influence?'

'He's just . . . different. It's hard to explain. See, I met him through my dad. They're both Vietnam vets. And my dad is really messed up from it, you know. PTSD they call it now, but back then there was no label and no support. Anyway, Wayne became a father figure to me. Not that he's not kind of fucked up too. I mean, what he saw and did was probably worse than my dad. But there's something about him that nothing can kill. He's got more energy and passion for life than just about anyone I've ever met.'

'Huh.'

'Like, even before the war he was different from most people in this dead-end town. He got his pilot's licence when he was sixteen. He loves his motorbikes, fast cars; anything dangerous, pretty much.' J.T. laughed with affectionate indulgence. 'He used to own a gun shop, but then at the same time he's actually a total pacifist. *Loves* animals, obviously. Been married twenty-five years. Well . . .' J.T. paused. 'That's a bit of a sore point at the moment. They're separated. Valerie walked out on him, and he's pretty devastated. That's why I've been helping out with the animals a lot more lately, 'cause you're really meant to have two people there when you feed them, for safety.' J.T. paused again and seemed to have lost his train of thought. 'Anyway, my point is he's hard to categorise. You'll see.'

'He sounds intriguing,' said Will, though his focus was snagged on the gun shop.

They made a left turn over a quaint girdered bridge that spanned a slim creek and abruptly left behind the zone of heavy industry, the road, with the practical name of Ridge Road, climbing through green woods and emerging into a pastoral idyll of fields and barns and horses, belied only by the shabbiness of the small farmhouses and the visible ribs of some of the horses that announced shameful hardship. The way ahead was all aflicker with tree-shadow; the windows were open and the air smelled of hay and sweet grass and Will's hangover had faded to a faint nausea. J.T. took the bends fast but steady, his left arm out the window, patting the door of the pickup like a good dog, and Will felt almost at peace.

'Hey,' said J.T., turning the volume down. 'Tamsyn had a word with me last night . . . She mentioned that you might be looking for some work.'

'Yeah, I think I'll have to. I checked my bank balance this morning and nearly had a stroke. I spent so much freaking money in New York, hey. And the exchange rate is a bitch.'

'Well, Tamsyn had an idea, which is that I could ask Wayne if he'd hire you to help out for a few weeks to give me a break when the baby's born. It's due any day now, and Tam's been freaking out about how busy I've been with work and study and looking after my dad, and then helping Wayne on top of it. She's pretty pissed about it, to be honest. I mean, I get it—she doesn't have her family here and I need to be there for her.'

He glanced at Will, trying to gauge his response. 'Anyway, I think it's a good solution, if you're up for it. I could even speak to Wayne today . . .'

'Umm, yeah . . .' said Will. 'I mean, I do really need the money . . . don't take this the wrong way, 'cause I know Wayne's your friend, but Tamsyn did mention that he's maybe, um . . . going to prison soon?'

'Oh, yeah, she mentioned that?' J.T. looked displeased. 'It's not clear yet. It's a total bullshit charge, though, if you're worried about the kind of guy he is. Like I said, he used to have a gun shop, and he closed it down but hung on to a lot of the stock, which the local sheriff wasn't too happy about. They hate him keeping all the animals, too, but there's not a thing they can do about it, it's a hundred per cent legal. So anyway, the cops came to his place and they found a couple of guns that weren't licensed, and that's why he's potentially going away. But we don't know yet. Hopefully he'll get off with just a fine.'

'Wow.'

'Yeah. I know it sounds bad but he's not, like, some kind of scary guy.'

'Okay. That's comforting, I guess.'

'So you think you might be interested? In the work? You'd be saving my ass, man.'

'Yeah. I mean, I *was* planning to get on the road again, but . . .'

But money. He certainly wasn't going to be able to just show up anywhere, no work visa or CV, little experience, and get short-term illegal work.

'Yes,' he said, decisive now. 'I'm interested. If Wayne's into the idea, of course.'

They lapsed into silence again, Will wondering what zones of danger his vow of wild abandon might be leading him into. He really didn't have a whole lot of options, though—that was the truth of it—and an act of brave or even unwise assent was better than the alternative, which was essentially just to go home. And he did really like J.T., too, and didn't hate the idea of spending more time with him. Of course, he wasn't the kind of guy he'd be hanging out with by choice, but he wasn't a total dud, either. Something in his body language conveyed a pre-emptive deferral, as if saying, *You're the alpha male, we don't need to fight about it*, even though he was a big guy and in other ways came across as confident. There was something childlike about him, an unguardedness that Will had to check himself to avoid assuming was indicative of a kind of simplicity. Will might have guessed that he'd been bullied in childhood, and had long ago learned to avoid confrontation.

They descended the ridge, breaking out of trees to a more expansive view of the same shabby pastoral, a red barn with a silver capsule grain silo redeeming the image to cross-stitch dignity. At the foot of the hill, a driveway led off to the left and disappeared over a rise. There was a painted sign at the entrance that proclaimed the place as *Wayne's Wild Kingdom*.

'Is this open to the public?' Will asked.

'No, not officially. You need a different permit for that. But that's Wayne's dream eventually.'

J.T. opened the gate and the car juddered over a metal grille and hit the unsealed road, clouding up dust.

It was close to 1 pm and the day was clear and warm as they rumbled up the gravelled rise and it all came into view: the driveway dipping and then making a slow climb to a big house at the top of a grassy hill. Will's gaze did not linger there; his attention was taken by the long double row of enclosures that sat up ahead on the left-hand side. There must have been twenty of them, racked up like Monopoly houses, the same identical box shape in serial repetition and presumably containing such inconceivable tenants as full-grown lions and tigers. On their right, they passed a decrepitude of rusting vehicles: two sunk-wheeled Winnebagos, a couple of cars, a horse float and trailer and a small red tractor.

J.T. slowed the pickup. The smell of dust curled in, as well, now, as the sharp ferrous scent of caged animals, which Will had encountered in zoos in his childhood and which brought back an amygdala-flush of memory: concrete-floored enclosures containing baboons with startling red-swollen bums; the loping downcast automaton path traversed by a Tassie devil; the disappointing glimpses of lions from his father's shoulders, resting in a clump among lion-coloured grasses and unable to be wished closer; the later, thrilling sound of their dusk roaring when he was elsewhere in the zoo.

They drew level with the first cage, and Will saw a tiger, gigantic, prone and bored-looking on a log. The next three cages also contained tigers, one with its back end immersed in a cut-down blue plastic tub of water. The fifth contained a full-grown male lion, dark-maned and close to the bars, its enormous golden face turned towards them, gold eyes deep and calm above the huge paws. The sight of it aroused in Will some deep inevitable jolt of biology that made his heart rate spike. He was shocked at the blunt power of this animal over his corporeal self, the manifest endurance of species memory that dwelled like an eyeless fish in the evolutionary dark.

'There's Wayne,' said J.T.

With an effort, Will transferred his gaze from the lion and saw Wayne standing at the front door, waving, dressed in the same red Makita cap and blue t-shirt, excessively pocketed khaki shorts and black work boots he had been wearing at The Shack. He had the kind of top-heavy figure of some older men, carrying all his weight around his chest and belly and upper arms while his legs and forearms stayed thin. Will noticed the almost scrawny ankles sticking out of his boots.

They pulled up by another pickup, presumably Wayne's, and got out. The scent of animals was stronger out of the car; it felt almost physically invasive in the warming day and with his hangover still lingering.

'Phwoah,' said J.T., stepping over to Wayne and exchanging a backslapping half-hug.

'Yeah, a bit stinky today, sorry.' Wayne turned to Will. 'It's not usually this bad. I've been hosing out the cages.' He held out his hand. 'Anyway, welcome.'

'Thanks. Thanks for letting me visit.'

'Hey, I never turn away visitors. Come on in.'

Unlike most of the other houses Will had seen in Littleproud, this one was cream brick and far more recent-built. It would have been at home in the flat-packed estates of Melbourne's outer west, but the associated symbolism was clearly undermined in the current circumstances by everything that surrounded the chagrined modern mansion.

'Beware,' said Wayne, leading the way, 'apes on the loose. Actually, they're a bit scared of strangers, so give me a second to get them back in their cage.' He disappeared into the house. From inside came a loud screeching that sounded to Will more like seagulls than monkeys.

Will looked at J.T. 'This place is insane,' he whispered.

After a minute, Wayne returned. 'They're having too much fun. If you come inside they'll get scared and hopefully go into their cage and I can secure them.'

Will hesitated and J.T. laughed. 'They won't come anywhere near you, I promise.'

They followed Wayne into a tiled hallway. To the right, a doorway opened onto a huge lounge room, where a blue leather sofa faced an enormous wall-mounted television playing American football with the sound down.

'Just come in slowly,' said Wayne.

They paused, and Will caught sight of two black monkeys, about the size of tomcats, sitting in the opposite corner. They looked up and Will saw their strange beautiful faces, so human, full of expression and yet alien: the features elongated, as if drawn by Modigliani, the noses very long and narrow, the skin pigment-black, and eyes visored and orange-brown. They were both females, and their ridiculous names, Wayne informed him, were Cissy and Tootsie.

Both began a raucous hooting and leaped into their open cage, revealing as they turned the bare pink patches on their behinds.

Wayne stepped forward and closed the cage. 'Gotcha!' He turned back to the door. 'Come in,' he said, ignoring the continued hullaballoo. 'I was just about to have some lunch, if you're hungry. It's just some leftovers I found in the freezer, but there's way too much for me. Hey!' He pulled off his cap and flicked the side of the cage with it. The sound continued unabated. 'They'll quiet down eventually.'

'Lunch sounds awesome,' said J.T. 'We're a bit rough after the gig last night and all we've had is Pop-Tarts.'

'Thought you might be. Let's head into the kitchen. Maybe that'll be far enough away to calm them down.'

At the far end of the room, past the cage, was a rustic stone-paved feature wall containing a large open fireplace. The whole place seemed to be a mash-up of housing estate and ranch-chic, the common denominator being sheer square-metreage. The space between one set of leather sofas grouped around the fireplace and the other around the TV was vast and slate-tiled. The ceiling was sloped with thick exposed beams. Two electric guitars lay on the sofas by the fireplace, one plugged into a Fender amp on the floor.

'I told you Wayne taught me guitar, yeah?' J.T. said. 'I'm actually studying music therapy now, so I have him to thank for that. Finally decided it's time to follow my dreams. Well, a grown-up version of my dreams anyway.'

Will was struggling to listen over the noise. Wayne yelled out to the monkeys again and then beckoned the men to the kitchen, which opened to the left of a dining table at the rear of the room. The table sat in front of glass sliding doors that looked out onto an undercover deck and an empty inground pool. On the deck was a child's wooden playpen and inside it were two lion cubs.

'Whoa!' said Will, going up to the door.

'Oh, the lions,' said Wayne, chuckling. 'I forget it's not a usual sight for most people. You can go pet them, they're tame. Bottle-fed them both myself. The bigger one's Nate and the little one's Nala. Spaghetti and meat sauce okay for everyone?'

The cubs were wrestling in their rickety pen, swiping each other with their paws, which were too big for their bodies, and making the pen creak and jolt about on the pavers.

Will stopped and looked back at J.T., who laughed at him again.

'They're fine. They're normally out of the cage.'

'I've just got them penned 'cause the monkeys were out,' said Wayne. 'You want me to let them in?'

'They're pretty cute, but I think I'm fine like this,' said Will.

The microwave beeped, and Will could smell fried mince-meat and garlic. The monkeys had finally quietened down, and he avoided looking at them for fear of starting them up again.

They sat at an outdoor table overlooking the fetid brown water at the bottom of the pool while the cubs pushed their short muzzles through the bars of the pen and sniffed the food smells and made funny little high-pitched yelps. The pasta was average, the meat sauce grey and bland and lacking salt, and Will found it hard to eat with the air so thick with the reek of animals, but he felt the carbs and protein staving off the hang-over and so he shovelled it down like the other two.

He glanced over at Wayne. The man's face was a series of convex curves, starting with the visible arc of his balding head, the two heavy eyebrows, the grey-blue eyes, and his mouth, thin and turned down at the corners. Then he began to speak, and everything changed: the eyes lit, the line of the mouth lifted into enthusiasm. He seemed to Will a man divided, as though his natural exuberance had been battered by some huge suffering that rose up in even the seconds between impassioned sentences.

'Hey, Wayne,' said J.T. 'I have to get to work early today, so we should probably get going on the feeding asap, if that's okay.'

'Sure,' said Wayne. 'Not a problem. Although I was hoping you could help me do some work on the tractor. But that can wait until tomorrow, I guess.'

'Sorry, Wayne,' said J.T. 'Tomorrow for sure.'

'Fine,' said Wayne, meat and chewed-up pasta visible on his tongue. 'You know I need you out here as much as you can spare. There's so much to do.' Wayne turned to Will. 'If this was a public sanctuary, they'd probably have a staff of a dozen people to look after the animals. But it's just the two of us here. I'm working day and night to stay on top of it all.'

Wayne stood up as he closed his mouth over his last forkful and slid his chair back with a screech.

'How long does it take to feed them all?' Will asked.

'A couple hours at least,' said Wayne. 'That's just feeding. Then there's watering, and we check the cages morning and night. And then cleaning and all the rest. But feeding is where you really need two people.'

From down the hill, Will heard a noise like a two-stroke motor turning over, and then another joined it, and the first became a full roar that roused again that rush of chemical fear and elation which seemed to originate in the space between his shoulders, causing, he assumed, his hackles to rise.

Wayne led them to where a capacious wheelbarrow leaned beside an enormous pair of fridges plugged in at the end of the pergola under the eaves of the house. Then, without warning, he opened the door on a shambles—bloody, temperature-controlled and horrific—such as might be found by a team dressed in sealed plastic coveralls in the basement of a serial killer: shelves of bulging plastic bags of formless gore suspended in a watery red liquid of diluted blood, like that which collects at the bottom of a meat tray. On the top shelf lay the hacked-off limbs, still furred and hooved, of what appeared to be a small deer.

Will reeled back. 'Jesus Christ!' he said. 'Is that a deer?'

'Roadkill,' said Wayne, beginning to heft the weeping bags into the wheelbarrow.

'What's in the bags?'

'Chicken guts. We get 'em from a factory out of town. Drive out there in the van every few days and load up. Yeah, it's a full-time job keeping forty-plus carnivores fed.'

Will could smell the stink of dirty meat, muted only by its chilling, competing now with the animal piss and whatever else composed the hot stench that filled the air entire.

When the barrow was full, Wayne grabbed a deer leg and passed it to Will, laughing at his obvious reluctance to touch the thing in its still lifelike refrigerated rictus.

The leg was cold, but the hair on it was smooth and felt alive, like that on a taxidermy deer. Will grasped it just above the hoof and examined the crude raw jag of meat and bone where it must have been sawn from the body.

Wayne passed the other leg to J.T. and pulled on a pair of stiff work gloves and then was off, pushing the heaped and wobbling barrow towards the side of the house. Will followed with the deer leg hanging like some Neanderthal club formed from one animal to be wielded against another while J.T. walked ahead of him with the other leg. Clouds had blown in from the west and lay massed and low and grey as if in opposition. There were black birds of some large variety circling above.

And then the blunted day honed itself to a point. For at the rows of cages set along the flank of the driveway Will stood before living predators of enormous size and physical power, creatures that once again set off some deep-dwelling response of recognition and fear and ambivalent euphoria, some reawakened blink of the sleeping senses in an animal who has long forgotten what it is to be prey, warm thrumming human meat that contains within its dormant species destiny the potential and even lust to be taken and absorbed into and merged with the material being of these dream-exquisite beasts. And as the creatures caught sight or scent of Wayne with his barrow, a fearful roaring broke out and spread, gathering resonance as it multiplied like bass feedback until Will could feel it in his feet and in his chest, as if his own heart was vibrating, whether in fear or sympathy or reverence he would not have been able to guess, for in this uncharted zone of experience he was able only to observe his own animal responses and extrapolate from them some new set of facts about what kind of man he was or might become.

At the cages, the smell intensified—the men's urinal in an Aussie pub to the power of one thousand. Wayne set down the barrow by the first cage, which held a frankly humungous white tiger, prone and impassive, its death-commanding paws lined up in prim parallel and its body curved so that the long close-striped tail wrapped around to lie beside a front leg.

'This is Snow,' said Wayne. 'He's a white Siberian tiger. Weighs in at almost six hundred pounds.'

J.T. glanced at Will, who was standing back, the deer leg hanging against his calf. Will felt it drip from its hacked end into his boot.

'You look like you might be wigging out a little,' J.T. said.

Will laughed, tried to make the laugh full of ease. 'I kind of think I might be. This is pretty wild.'

Wayne smiled at him. 'When you actually get to know each and every one of them, and see that they all have their own personalities . . . it's the most incredible thing in the world.'

The tiger was so close to the bars that Will could hear his huffing out-breaths and discern each long white whisker sprouting from the plump muzzle-cheeks each side of his pink nose. He lifted his gigantic head and opened his mouth, revealing curved canine incisors that looked like they could punch straight through Will's skull.

And then the tiger stood and leaped up sudden and full height, his tufted paws pressing the bars. The three grown men reached barely to his chest. He nuzzled his head against the wire, and Wayne put his hand through and sunk it to the wrist in the deep white shag of the tiger's fur.

Will stopped breathing; he couldn't help it. His hands were shaking. This was *crazy*. The word 'majestic' came into his mind, but he was immediately embarrassed by the cliché and struck by the utter inadequacy of language to represent this creature, this experience. He remembered the theory of the sublime, which he'd read in philosophy class, and thought that this was what it meant. The zoomed-out microscopic self; the protective carapace of culture rupturing and falling away. He rebuked himself for retreating into theory, undoubtedly a protective mechanism in the face of that which he could not assimilate. And there he went again, when he should be simply and profoundly *looking*, encountering this animal being and remembering that he was an animal himself. Fuck, no wonder he had no girlfriend; he was so far inside his own head that the sight of a tiger had sent him into some kind of existential crisis.

'Okay, big guy,' said Wayne, and he gave the tiger a shove. 'Dinnertime. Get in the back.'

The tiger dropped onto his four paws and paced into the covered rear section of the cage with the same bisected rolling gait as a lazy cat, the origin point of movement first one shoulder and then the other, the proceeding ripple travelling all the way along each side of the body.

'We feed in a particular order,' Wayne was explaining. 'To avoid competition. The male tigers first. Then the female tigers. Then the male and female lions. Lions hunt in packs, so they're used to sharing. Tigers, now . . .' He shook his head. 'Uh-uh.'

A galvanised ladder and a long metal pole with a hook on the end leaned against Snow's cage. Wayne walked over and opened the ladder.

Will suddenly remembered that he might soon be employed here, subjecting himself to this fear and irrefutable sheer mad risk on a daily basis, and he hoped that Wayne would not go for the plan, letting him off without humiliation.

J.T. walked around to the other side where a long sheet of chain-link wire, almost the height of the cage and attached at both ends to tall wooden planks, rested along the wall. The wire was threaded through a slit in the side of the cage, and the wooden end-post prevented it from pulling through.

'I designed and built these cages myself,' said Wayne.

'Like I said, Wayne can make or fix just about anything,' said J.T.

'With J.T.'s help,' Wayne corrected himself. 'We designed them together. There's a wire partition that we need to pull across and lock before we open the door.'

'Okay, phew,' said Will. 'I was hoping we weren't just going to head on in. I was about to be, like, *Okay, thanks for the tour, I gotta go now.*'

J.T. chuckled. 'When I first started coming out here and helping Wayne, that's exactly what we did do. But there were a lot less animals back then, and we trusted them more, I guess. With only a few, you spend much more time with them. There's too many now, if you ask me.'

Wayne shook his head. 'No one is ever going to convince me I've got too many children,' he said.

'I mean, they've all been hand-reared,' J.T. continued. 'But not all by us. There's quite a few rescues now. But even the ones that know us from babies, they still need the regular contact.'

There looked to be about twenty-five cages in all, each built from tall metal poles with solid square wire mesh welded onto them. Each had a covered section and a kennel-like shelter and an open section, and a big water tub for drinking from or bathing in. However you looked at it, there were a hell of a lot of wild animals here, or *exotics*, as Wayne and J.T. called them in some specialised parlance of the collector of living creatures.

Wayne began to explain how he and J.T. had built the cages by hand after the county had said the previous enclosures were inadequate and after the issuing of several hefty fines. He laughed as he told Will how a couple of the feisty young lions kept getting loose from the old chicken run where they'd formerly kept the juveniles, and how they'd jump the fence and get into the neighbour's paddock, chase his horses and scare the bejesus out of his elderly mother.

'I remember one day we'd been jamming, J.T. and I, and we were a little stoned when we got the call that Tyson was out and over at Deever's place.' He looked at Will with his grey eyes sparkling. 'Well, actually we were more than a little stoned, to tell the truth. It was raining and it was getting near dark, and we hauled ass down the hill with the horse trailer and a hunk of meat to try and coax Tyson with, and I remember we were running the horses out into the other paddocks, but he kept chasing after them, and we kept tripping over in our rubber boots in the mud and in the end we were laughing so hard we had to sit down. Old man Deever found us and gave us a lecture like we were a couple of schoolboys and it just made us laugh even harder.'

'What the hell?' said Will, laughing himself in disbelief. 'Did the lion get any of the horses?'

'No! No way. He never wanted to hurt them. He was just playing. He was barely out of diapers at that point. We got him in the end, but things got a little sour with the neighbours after that.'

Wayne was standing with one boot on the bottom rung of the ladder. Inside the cage, Snow paced forward again, and he gave a low growl as resonant and rattling as a snare drum.

'Okay, buddy. I know, you're hungry,' said Wayne. 'Better get on with it.'

'Sorry, I'll stop asking questions,' said Will.

Wayne climbed to the top of the ladder with the metal pole. 'So, how it works is I pull the partition across and J.T. feeds it through so it doesn't get caught on the wire. Snow,' he addressed the tiger, 'get back. Food's comin', big guy.'

He poked the end of the pole through the wire and prodded the flank of the beast. Snow returned to the rear of the enclosure and waited, panting with a low rasping sound. Wayne thrust the pole across the cage and hooked it into a metal ring in the wooden end-post. He began drawing the fence across and J.T. folded it out and stopped it sagging so that it could pass through the slit. It caught a couple of times and J.T. had to unhook the links from the cut edges of the wire. Once it was across, Wayne opened a padlock hanging from the side of the cage with the key in the lock, and used it to fasten the metal ring to the cage wall.

The partition that now separated the enclosure into two sections did not fill Will with a sense of safety and confidence. It was slightly too long, so the wire bowed at the top, and the whole thing looked like it would simply tear away if Snow decided to take a lunge at it.

With his shaking hands clenched into fists at his thighs, Will watched as Wayne unlocked the small door, picked up a wet sack of guts and ducked inside. He pulled out a crusty flip-knife from his back pocket, held the tight bulging bag over Snow's food trough, and stuck it with the knife, pulling the blade downwards in an expert movement. The chicken guts poured out with a slopping sound like a load of fish being dumped out of a net.

The filthy stench of the offal reached Will over the base smell of piss and shit and sweat and the other pheromonal secretions these wild predators pumped out into the atmosphere. He retched slightly; imperceptibly, he hoped. It was the hottest part of the day, the light intense as the sun began its slide towards the ground, and the smell evaporating out of the dirt of the animal pens was almost visible in its fetid intensity, and Will's hangover was ramping up again.

Wayne stepped out, locked the door and tucked the slick limp bag down the edge of the loaded barrow. He unlocked the partition, and he and J.T. began to draw it back again through the side of the enclosure. As soon as a gap wide enough opened up in the cage, Snow padded forward, unhurried and full of massive muscled grace, and bent his great shaggy head with its easy-killing bared incisors and began to lick up like an ordinary house cat the pounds of heaped glistening guts.

There was only one other experience in Will's life that had felt as oddly myth-significant as this: when he had been hiking with his father, as a teenager, and they'd seen an albino echidna. It was an experience that had marked him, as he knew this day would, too, and had become a mental touchstone when he needed to believe in some sort of magic.

He remembered the day so clearly: cold and richly damp; just him and his father on a two-day hike that he had resisted with an almost spiritual vehemence; the hiking boots that caused a heel spur which plagued him for months afterwards; the colours of the tree trunks with their kelp-like bark hanging in ragged strips, the patches of green exposed like new skin beneath a scab, showing that the blood of the tree was as vulnerable and thin-covered as our own. There was the climb they had just endured, his dad responding to Will's new teenage surliness and steep-declining father worship with a punitive patient sulking of his own.

And then they saw it: so utterly unreal, with its ghost-white spines and pink proboscis and fanned back-facing hind claws. It stopped when it felt them move and cinched into a ball of translucent pale quills like something transported by sorcery from the depths of the ocean into this place of green and brown and grey.

The man and the boy halted without speaking and took a seat on a fallen log and stayed very still. After a long time the echidna half uncurled and flicked its blind pink sparkling gaze across them, tonguing the air for traces, and then unrolled itself the rest of the way and went about its business, snuffling the leaf litter, while Will held his breath, trying to extend this momentary encounter with the strange and rare and wild, feeling deep within his being the natural veneration due to the beautiful anomaly.

The son and father sat unmoving, touched now and then by the wind that stirred up out of nowhere, smelling of eucalyptus and lichen and the moisture hanging there in the thin low clouds, and making the dry bark and the living leaves chime against each other. Each was aware in the other of the same feeling of gratitude and pagan reverence, knew that they might secretly believe, from this moment on, in signs and blessings and in the clear bright unsought portents of the natural world.

The ghost-white creature foraged for ten minutes in the humus, and when it moved on, it walked so close to them that

Will thought it might clamber over his foot and was not sure what to do if it did, if it would feel the living pulse right through his boot toe. But it did not touch him, and merely shuffled by, its quills rippling as if caressed by a current, and eventually it was out of sight.

The experience had marked another shift in the relationship between father and son, a reopening in the everyday that the awkward scornful boy and boyish bitter man reached through towards each other and which took months to narrow once more from gateway to fontanelle to hairline fissure and then at last to knit like bone. Today, Will felt in the presence of these wild and dangerous creatures the same door-opening potential, the chance to grasp that albino-rare and miraculous gift: the subtle life-altering change accomplished in the passage of a single moment.

At the next cage, they repeated the same clumsy process and Will felt even more intensely the true danger of the act as Kahn, a seven-hundred-pound male tiger, sat snarling just behind the partition, showing his teeth, his tongue the size of a baseball mitt, as Wayne hoisted the next bag and stepped through the door into that paced and scented maddening small territory of dirt. He released the bloody rush into the bowl and ducked back out, and the tiger rose and roared full-chested and dream-haunting and pawed the wire, and the men without speaking unlocked and pulled back the barrier.

'This guy was a rescue,' said J.T. 'He was surrendered by a woman over near Stovertown who couldn't handle him anymore. So he didn't grow up here.'

'He was nowhere near this big when we got him,' said Wayne. 'He trusts us now, but it's not the same as when you've reared them yourself.'

Will was sweating, and they were only two feeds in to, what, forty-something? Jesus Christ! When he wafted the neck of his t-shirt he could smell his own sweat, even over the reek of the animals, and it was acrid and unlike his usual odour and he knew that what he was smelling was fear in its chemical components.

After they had fed the rest of the male and female tigers, they took the deer leg to Mustafa, a male lion in his self-evident prime, with a glossy hide and the wide powerful shoulders and sleek hips that his human visitor recognised and bowed to as the essence of peak male virility. When Mustafa slumped down and bent his mouth to the deer leg, Will felt as never before the full significance of this flesh reality of one animal using its mouth and teeth to tear away the body of another, whose life had been extinguished, its quickening—that whatever irreligious spark that makes the worm move through the dark soil—tamped out and dispersed across the infinite muddy field of the universe: gone.

Will felt himself not far from that deer, his empathy and imagination stretched as never before, and he felt an exquisite sadness for the animal being consumed before him, a sadness resulting from a shamed immediate and practical concomitance of his own fear of death by animal attack and the image of the rough-hacked still-furred haunch in the mouth of the lion, as well as the memory of watching the congregation of wild deer in their quiet seeming-wisdom, which allowed his mind to cross the gap and nest itself within the body of a non-human creature.

'Shit,' said J.T. suddenly, as Will watched the intimate destruction of the deer. 'I need to get going. I'm gonna be late for work.'

'Crap, I totally forgot,' said Wayne. 'When do you have to be there?'

'Like, soon. I'm really sorry, Wayne, but you might have to do the rest alone. I know it's not ideal.'

'Damn,' said Wayne. 'You can't get there later?'

'I mean . . . I've already arranged this with Justin. He's coming in to train me on pays before my shift.'

'Couldn't he show you tomorrow?'

J.T. made a face that showed his frustration. 'It's a bit late now.'

'I could stay and help with the rest of the feed, if you think I can do it,' Will offered. As he said it, he was already picturing a montage of maulings and escaped tigers and chaos.

J.T. looked at Wayne.

'That could work,' Wayne said. 'He can just help with the partitions.'

'The only thing is, I'd need a lift back to town.'

'That's not a problem. I'll probably head in to The Shack for dinner anyway.'

'Yeah?' said J.T., looking relieved. 'If you're okay with it, Wayne, that would be awesome. Thanks, man,' he said to Will. 'I owe you.'

J.T. slapped Will on the shoulder and hugged Wayne, and Will noticed the deferential way he lowered his head as he leaned forward, though he was the larger man, and Will thought again that he liked J.T., this guileless open friend who spent all of his available hours feeding and caring for the outrageous Old Testament-proportioned menagerie of a man who must surely be suffering from some Ahab-esque monomania of the spirit, inbred or instilled, perhaps, by some early insult that it had become his mission to dispute, though the one who had cast the blow would never witness its rebuke or, if he did, would doubtless not recognise it as such, so much a non sequitur was this undertaking and so deeply peculiar a means to assert one's power in the world, the literal Adamic dominion over all the beasts of the jungle.

After J.T. had left, they fed the remaining lions, the leopards, wolves and bears, and the single splendid black panther, and then did one more lap of the cages. The now-sated beasts approached the cage fronts and pushed their furred faces against the wire as Wayne rubbed their heads and called them gorgeous and beautiful and precious and described them to Will in all their particular biographies of temperament and history, while Will stood back, sealed and silent in his awe. He watched as Wayne kissed the whiskered muzzle of a lioness where it sheathed the ivory daggers of her teeth. A male tiger extended his long tail vertically like a monkey and shot a jet of spray from beneath it against the bars of the cage, the scent strangely like coriander. Will felt that he could do this for days, just being close to these animals in their hot irrepressible aliveness. He thought of Darla and her wolf project, and it seemed now clear that such an encounter could be nothing but transformative.

The sun was in its final quadrant when they returned to the house. Back on the patio, Wayne fastened leads to the collars of the lion cubs and led them like frisky puppies up the hill to their compound, made from wooden fenceposts strung together top and bottom with wire and pegged around what appeared to have been a landscaped garden, set into a slope of grass and terraced with river stones to form a kind of amphitheatre, with saplings growing among the stones within the shallow basin of dirt. Penned in this ramble were two tiger cubs and another lion cub, still quite small and YouTube cute. When the leashed and even smaller cubs saw their siblings and interspecies cousins, they bounded and tumbled to the rickety fence and licked the others through the feeble barricade, which apparently nonetheless held some symbolic authority to prevent them from knocking it down.

Wayne led the leashed cubs in and unclipped them and the rest tumbled them joyously back into the dusty smelly pack.

'Back in a minute,' Wayne said. 'You can stay here and watch them.'

Will nodded, grinning at the rumble in the dirt, at the sweet mock growling and the flailing of soft too-big paws. Here it was shaded, though still warm, and a trellis of flowering purple wisteria over one side of the pen smelled sun-warmed and almost sickly, and beneath this perfume still the emanation of animals.

'Man, I'm shattered,' Will said when Wayne returned carrying another bag of chicken parts and two bottles of milk with teats attached.

'Welcome to my life!' said Wayne. There was no resentment in his voice, though, Will thought, as Wayne left the bottles on the grass and walked in again and at once the fray turned on him, with his bounty of the scrap parts of countless chickens. He pushed his way to a long metal trough, the five young lions and tigers massing around him like giant pigeons, and he slit the bag and dumped the meat and liquid in. 'Dinnertime,' he called and stepped back laughing as the horde descended and became a patchwork of soft greedy moving backs.

'Who are the bottles for?' asked Will.

'The littlest ones. They're pretty much weaned but I give them one a day still, just to supplement the solids. And to keep up the contact. Only for the next few weeks, so you lucked out. Ever bottle-fed a lion before?'

Soon, Will was sitting on the grass with a warm lion cub draped over him, one front paw pressed warm and rough on the hand that held the bottle, the other resting familiar on his thigh, sucking with strong noisy lunges of its head the way he'd seen poddy calves do on his friend Duncan's farm when he was a kid. Wayne was beside him with the other cub, and Will was overcome by what felt like a drug rush, a surge through his veins of some maternal endorphin triggered by this warm animal infancy, never mind that he was the wrong species, the wrong gender. He felt afloat in soft milk-fur bliss as the lion cub—Nala was her name—gurgled and nuzzled and whimpered with satisfaction. Milk leaked from her mouth and beaded her cat-like nub of a chin. A tear of white hung from one of her sewing-needle whiskers.

I'm feeding a lion, Will kept thinking, I'm feeding a lion.

She was a milk-passive baby and he had all the time in the world to study her teddy-bear face, with its half-biscuit ears and wet black nose flaring and snuffling and her coarse eyelashes and the flickering delicate membranes of her lax eyelids. He felt how easy it would be to love her, to come to know her nature, and perhaps be loved in return, the way he loved his dog, and maybe even more.

Overhead, the sky was all spatula-streaks of pink and lilac cloud. A flock of birds—wild ducks or geese perhaps—flew in a V formation.

'This is pretty great,' Will said, beaming stupidly.

'Incredible, isn't it? Nothing else like it. At least you'll be able to go home now and tell your friends you hand-fed a lion cub.'

When the bottles were empty and the cubs were drowsing in protein dreams, their mouths moving gently, their bodies heavy and splayed in a melt of satiety, Will looked at his watch. It was almost 5.30 pm.

'Yeah, we'd better get these giant kittens off of us,' said Wayne. 'I've just got to feed the horses before we go, but that'll only take a minute.'

They rolled the cubs onto the ground, where they sprang into boisterous wakefulness in a matter of seconds, and put them back in the pen.

In the house, Wayne grabbed two beers from the fridge and handed one to Will, who took it gratefully. He felt the post-adrenaline flatline coupled with the shaky, empty-bodied nerve hum that follows a big night, and beer was the salve for all of it. He sat in the twilight and gazed at the empty swimming pool and thought of nothing while Wayne went to feed the horses.

·

Soon they were rolling down the driveway in Wayne's faded red pickup. The green of the hills was dulled as if someone had spread over them a thin gauze shroud, and the full clouds that had gathered earlier had rolled themselves out to cover every region of the sky. The animals were all hushed now, their bellies filled with industrial meat-farm waste and roadkill, and the dusk calls of birds was the loudest sound. A duck flew low and made a long water landing on the dam, leaving a gouge of silver behind it as if the pond were made of mud-soft metal.

They passed the wheelbarrow sitting between the verge and the cages. Five big ravens were perched in the bowl and on the handles, drawn by the rumours of blood. One had an empty plastic bag in its beak. They turned their carrion gaze on the car and then with an unhurried flapping hauled themselves into the air.

'Ah, crap,' said Wayne. 'Forgot to hose out the barrow.'

As they passed, the ravens returned to their perches and bent together in a slick of black feathers. Will shivered, his body shaking free of the gruesome thrilling dream of today, and he drew his gaze to the road as Wayne opened and shut the gate and they humped over the grille and made a right, heading uphill towards a tunnel of darkening trees.

Wayne drove with confidence, taking the turns with one hand on the chin of the wheel and the other around his beer. Some crackly twelve-bar blues played on cassette and Will looked out at the innocuous rural picturesque and wondered what might be hidden up other driveways. He thanked Wayne again for today, saying how incredible the animals were, and he saw that this pleased Wayne, that he had noted and approved Will's awed reverence towards the wild children in his besotted care.

Wayne thanked him in return for helping with the feed and explained that he felt much guilt about his reliance on J.T., who had enough on his plate, but without whom he simply could not cope.

Will thought about mentioning Tamsyn's plan, but decided it was better left to J.T. He hoped his old and small-town association with Tamsyn would work in his favour. Not that he was unambivalent about the prospect of working for Wayne: there were more sources of potential threat in the man's *wild kingdom* than he had probably encountered across his lifetime so far, and Wayne himself was not the least of them. He recalled Wayne's mirth about the guy who'd been mauled by Snow.

'Indulge an old man's nosy curiosity,' said Wayne, 'and please don't take it as condescension, but what are you looking for on this journey of yours? J.T. said that you're on a mission to get lost. Was that his phrase or yours?'

'Mine, I think,' said Will.

'That intrigued me,' said Wayne.

Despite his sense that he could trust this man to understand at least some part of what had motivated him in his quest or anti-quest, Will prevaricated and said to Wayne that he wished to see America.

'This *is* America,' said Wayne.

Will laughed and said he knew it was, but Wayne did not laugh and looked at him with grave seriousness and then returned his gaze to the way ahead. He told Will that if what he sought was the road, then that was one thing, but the road was the road and it was not America. He said that the road was the same everywhere, and those who loved the road were like those who loved the sea and they would never know America nor Littleproud nor any other place and they would never know peace. He said that Will should think carefully before he started out on that journey, that there are many wonderful places on this earth that are worth knowing, and this was one of them, whereas the road was no place at all.

'I lived that life for a while,' he said. 'When I came back from Nam. I thought it would heal my pain. But it didn't. Only coming home did that.' He said that Will would do better to simply stay in Littleproud and come to know the essence of this place than to waste his journey on the road, which was just another name for the inside of his own head.

Will nodded, not annoyed exactly but not especially willing to be told by this stranger what the solution to his problems was sure to be. He was certain that this close variant of his own home town could not provide whatever he was seeking. And yet he was impressed by this monologue and what it revealed about his interlocutor. Perhaps J.T.'s rapturous description of Wayne might in fact be near to accurate, he thought; perhaps he might have found in Wayne, sudden and unexpected, a man who understood and spoke the language of his own unrestful soul, and he laid his eyes on Wayne's averted cheek and rested them there to show that he recognised him.

Wayne's expression was smiling, and yet immediately he ceased his monologue, his face changed and he appeared crestfallen and beset by woes. Will noted once again how divided this man seemed, invested with more than average enthusiasms, but these levelled perhaps by the weight of his soul's peculiar burdens.

As they ascended Ridge Road, Wayne said to Will that the animals were the most important thing in his life other than his wife, Valerie. He confessed that he and Valerie were separated and, though he hoped they would reconcile, right now his animals were all he had.

Wayne began to speak again after a short lapse of silence. He said that he hoped Will would not take offence at his lecturing him like the old man that he was, though he still felt exactly like Will in some essential part of himself, still a lost young man in search of something else beside the facile sham of meaning presented by society, which most people lapped up like sweet sedatives mixed with chocolate milk, and at this Will couldn't help but laugh and say he agreed.

Wayne looked over, and Will thought he could see behind the man's gaze to its origin: a mind that suffered and sought no solace in the ordinary soft and softly beckoning means of mitigation for that ordinary pain with which Will himself was also grappling, and which may in fact be the desolating simple nature of living.

The second thing he had to say, Wayne went on, emboldened now and growing self-indulgent in his dispensing of wisdom, was that self-sufficiency was a lie. 'We're pack animals,' he said, as they passed again the melodrama of apocalyptic symbolism that was Folk's Scrap Metal, the stilled diggers silhouetted now against the acid sky and the mountains of reflective metal waste blinding in their eerie futuristic grandeur. The metal hills seemed to toss among them a quick bright ball of moving light or to conceal within their jagged forms a series of flashbulbs that flared in a succession of dazzling brilliance as the car swung in an arc around the perimeter of this vast region of sky-lit scrap.

Will was reminded, oddly, of the pile of dust in the gallery in New York, and of the strange nature of beauty, and was pleased with himself for thinking so.

Wayne was talking on, telling him that all the evidence of evolution pointed to humans as social creatures. 'We're not lone hunters like the tigers. We don't rear our young and then let them go out on their own and never see them again.' He said that even though he was living an unconventional life and had not been able to conceive children with his wife, he knew the necessity of the pack.

He took up his beer by the neck and his eyes were firmly on the road, by which signs Will perceived that what he was about to say was difficult for him.

He told Will that because of his experiences in Vietnam he struggled sometimes to be around people, but that that did not mean he was above the need for companionship, and he truly believed his animals were his family and that it was possible to find love and community beyond our own species. He had his people, too: his wife, of course, and J.T. and Doc Hazel, the vet who'd been treating his animals for almost twenty years now. 'You don't need many,' he said. 'But you do need some.' He said that the impulse or attempt to be a world unto oneself was one he knew—knew deeply and had explored up to its very limit—and had come to see was false.

Will felt at once condescended to and understood and perhaps too clearly seen, and he struggled to know how to respond, but Wayne appeared to sense this, too, and said with a mood-lightening chuckle, 'Okay, I'll shut up now.'

*

As the two men crossed the road to The Shack, Will's mind turned swift and heartless as biology to the *Ghost World* waitress—as if confirming him to be the very epitome of foolish youth and the appropriate needy recipient of Wayne's advice—hoping that she, perhaps, was clustered among the offerings held out on the world's open palm. He thought of her pale waxed thighs and short shorts, her high-tops and hurried grace of movement and her sharp determined chin. He imagined her naked, wearing a G-string and glasses, her breasts bigger than they probably were in real life, and he shook his head a little to remove the image, knowing he would probably see her in about five seconds.

And then, of course, rose up the unvanquished thoughts of Laura, with a force that took him off guard, a rushing wave of longing, aroused, perhaps, because at this very moment he was on the point of assuming a temporary but wholly fleshed new life, with work and companions whose faces he had never seen three days previous but that were growing already familiar, and even with an object of new lust, most unsettling of all because of its implication of the inevitable unwilled and faithless forward movement of the heart and the blood and the mean self-satisfying cock, and one day, though he knew it was not today, he would in fact occupy some fully formed new life with a cast whose faces were unimaginable to him now, some of whom may even be his wife and children, but would not, he knew, be Laura.

'HOW DID HE DO?' J.T. asked as they took a seat at the bar.

'Great!' said Wayne. 'Didn't get mauled. Didn't poop his pants. I'd say that's a good start.'

'I'm pretty shattered, though,' said Will. 'I really don't know how you do that every single day.'

'Yeah, well, they gotta eat, like we all do. Speaking of which . . .'

'The usual?' said J.T.

Will glanced around as the *Ghost World* waitress burst through the saloon doors of the kitchen carrying a tray laden with a cornucopia of burgers.

'Actually,' said Wayne, 'I hope you don't mind, Will, but I'm beat. I think I'll take a burger to go and eat it on the way home and hit the hay.'

'Of course,' said Will. 'No worries.'

'Perhaps we can share a meal together another time. I can see we've got some things in common.'

J.T. typed in Wayne's order and then came around the bar.

'Hey, Wayne?' he said. 'Can I speak to you about something real quick?'

'Sure,' said Wayne. 'What's up?'

'Could we maybe step out the front? It's nothing; I just wanna run something by you is all.'

'Okay, J.T.'

'Hey, Erin,' J.T. called to the waitress as she passed. 'Can you keep an eye on the bar for a minute? I just need a word with Wayne.'

She nodded, doubled back.

'Hey, this is Will, by the way,' said J.T. 'He's an old friend of Tamsyn's. From Australia.'

'Hey, Will,' said Erin. She stepped over to him, shifted the tray she was holding to the flat of one hand, wiped the other on her hip and held it out to him. It was small and thin and cold and he could feel the bird bones squeeze together as he clasped it. 'I'll just drop these orders off and I'll be back,' she said.

Wayne farewelled Will with a malodorous hug and followed J.T. out, and Will sat and looked at the plastic menu.

'Drink, Will?' Erin asked, hustling behind the bar.

'Please. I'll have a pint of that IPA. The local one?'

She nodded and poured it and set it in front of him, and then she turned and began putting away glasses with her back to him, and he watched her reaching up to the shelves with arm extended and the opposite foot lifted off the floor. She had great legs. He drank his beer and felt shy and wished he could think of something to say to her.

'Do you want food?' she asked when she was done with the glasses.

'Um, yeah, thanks. What do you recommend?'

'We're famous for the ribs. I wouldn't know, though. Never tried them.'

'Really?'

'Vegan,' she said, without a smile.

But of course she was a vegan. There was something both sexy and predictable about this new detail of her character.

Will wanted to try the ribs now, but he also wanted Erin to like him. He looked back at the menu in painful indecision.

'What's the vegie burger like?'

'Shit.'

'Okay. Not the vegie burger then.' He tried to laugh, but her seriousness was intimidating. Can't you at least smile? he thought miserably. He decided finally on the mac and cheese with a side of breaded pickles. By the time she'd punched in his order and set him up with cutlery, while he struggled for a topic of conversation, J.T. was back.

'Well, that was easier than I thought,' he said. 'You really made an impression on Wayne. He said you reminded him of himself when he was your age. Not sure that's a great compliment to be honest.' He laughed. 'But anyway, he's up for it. Said you could stay out at his place, too.'

'Oh, really?' said Will, uncertain about this part of the plan, and then remembering that J.T. and Tamsyn were about to have a baby.

'He's pretty lonely, I think,' said J.T. 'Poor old Wayne. I wish I could do more for him. I love the guy, but I've got my own problems right now.'

'Wow, so that's it? All sorted? When would I start?'

'Could be straight away. I could do with a bit of extra time before the baby comes. Wayne said he'd call you tomorrow. I can pass on your number, if you're okay with that.'

And so our hopeful adventurer sat at the bar and drank too many beers and chatted easy and aimless to J.T., this provident innocuous and kindly figure of easy welcome and blessed simple shallow friendship, and he marvelled at the haphazard fate of the traveller, whose authentic ranks he may finally have joined. He wondered whether Wayne's act of hospitality was frequent and habitual and indiscriminate or long held in store for just such a figure of young and desperate searching as himself, a fertile anonymous outline on which to project the image of the younger self or son or double still able to receive and act upon the future man's impassioned impotent and soon-to-be-familiar advice. But hadn't he vowed, after all, to say yes to everything? To the world? Well, this was what the world was offering: wild animals; the depths and secrets of small-town America; housing and employment with a random, quite likely troubled and possibly even dangerous ageing veteran, creator of his own rogue Midwestern Xanadu and dispenser of philosophy, of what utility to his own vague cause Will was not yet sure.

At 11.30 pm, J.T. called last drinks, and the waitresses began sanitising tables and putting up chairs in the empty dining section. Will was mesmerised by Erin's vicious methodical sweeping. She worked fast, blowing at a loose strand of hair that kept falling over her face. Once the place was empty, she carried off the broom and returned with a mop and bucket and began to mop just as she had swept and Will remembered, from his short-lived hometown summer of pub work, the odd contagious pride that hospo people took in these menial tasks—the fast efficient cleaning of a floor; the ability to clear a whole table in one load—and the enjoyment he had also felt in the process of doing something well and vigorously and in as little time as possible. As she mopped, the kitchen crew tiptoed over the wet floor in their rubber clogs and pulled the chairs down from a table near the bar and slumped down into them.

J.T. had changed the music to Eminem, and soon Erin was done and pulling off her apron and slapping it down on the table next to the kitchen staff, and J.T. was removing his apron too and motioning Will to come over to join them. He introduced Will, and ran through everybody's names too fast, and they all nodded and said, 'Hey,' and, 'Hi, Will.'

J.T. brought over a tray of pints and shots of a brown spirit and passed them out. J.T. raised his shot and Will did the same and they all threw them back and made the usual noises and wiped their mouths on their arms. The shot was sweet and strong and Will guessed it was bourbon.

'I'm gonna do the tills,' said J.T., picking up a stack of cash drawers, trailing the white ribbons of credit card settlements.

'Tonight was fucked,' said one of the waitresses, who had blue hair and who Will thought was called Beck, though already he couldn't be sure.

'Tell me about it,' said a woman from the kitchen, whose name he had definitely forgotten. 'We got *zero* prep done.'

'So,' said probably-Beck, turning to Will, 'what's your story?'

Erin snorted. 'Don't be an asshole, Beck.'

Phew, thought Will. *Beck*.

'*What?*' said Beck. 'I wasn't! I was just asking what his story is.'

'How the fuck is anyone meant to answer that question, seriously?' said Erin.

Will smiled diffusely, not knowing what was expected of him.

After a while, J.T. reappeared with the now-empty cash drawers and he carried them over and set them down near the window, all their hinges up to signify the obvious lie that there was no money in the place.

'We're gonna go to The Beat, if anyone's up for it,' said one of the chefs.

'Hell, no. That place is the worst,' said Erin.

'I've gotta go pick up Ashleigh from my mom's,' said Beck. 'That's my kid,' she said to Will. 'Or my drunken mistake, as I like to call her.'

The others left—the kitchen staff shuffling in a line in their clogs like the walking dead—and J.T. got up and fetched more beers.

'Will has been feeding lions and tigers and bears today,' he said. 'I took him out to Wayne's place.'

'Oh my god, really?' said Erin. 'I've never been out there. Isn't he some kind of total psychopath?'

'Wayne? No! I've known him all my life.'

'Okay,' said Erin. 'But why would anybody want to collect all those wild animals and keep them in cages? I remember when I was a kid hearing that he used to cut people up and feed them to the lions—to dispose of the bodies.'

'For fuck's sake!' said J.T. 'That stuff makes me angry. Wayne is such a nice guy.'

'Maybe,' said Erin. 'But still, it's cruel to keep animals caged like that. I'm sorry, but it just is.'

'He's had them all since they were babies,' said J.T. 'They don't know any different. And they actually love Wayne. You should see it. He's their family.'

'I don't buy that,' said Erin, pulling another chair around to face her and putting her feet up. 'Imagine *you* were born in a cage and lived your whole life in it. Just because you don't know anything else doesn't mean it's not torture.'

'Since when are you the animal rights expert?' said J.T.

Erin looked hurt. 'I just care about animals, that's all. I did actually go through a really hardcore animal rights phase in high school. I started this letter-writing group. It was mainly against animal testing, though.'

'Yeah, that's horrible,' said J.T. 'That should be stopped for sure. But this is completely different. I'm sorry, but I'm out there pretty much every day, and I know for certain that they are not tortured. They're safe and well fed and happy.'

'What do you think, Will?' said Erin. 'Did they seem happy to you?'

'Oh, look, I don't know,' said Will, desperate not to get caught in the middle of this argument in which his desire to impress Erin and not to upset J.T. were equal and pressing. 'They all seemed healthy and well looked after, but I get what you're saying about just the basic idea of keeping animals in cages.'

'Do you know the chicken factory we've got right here, just out of town, is one of the worst in the country as far as standards go?' said Erin, thankfully redirecting her fury away from J.T. and Wayne. 'PETA released a secret video they made there a while ago. It was so, *so* awful. They take the eggs and this machine breaks them open—that's the chicken's experience of being born: being broken out of its egg before it's ready, onto a conveyor belt. And some of them fall off onto the floor and they're just wandering around cheeping, looking for their moms, until they pretty much just get stepped on. They don't even bother to bend down and pick them up off the floor.'

'Stop,' said J.T., covering his ears.

'What, so you'd rather just not know?'

'But chicken is so *tasty*!'

'Why do I bother even talking to you, J.T.?' said Erin.

'That does sound pretty bad,' said Will, cringing at his obsequiousness.

'It is. And that's just the start. Do you know what they do with the male chicks?'

He shook his head.

'They separate them, and then they just toss them straight into this big mincer. Alive. Feathers and beaks and everything. They become this pink paste that then becomes chicken nuggets. Well, the ten per cent or whatever it is that actually *has* to be chicken. The rest is just synthetic meat.'

'Wow,' said J.T. 'I really wish you hadn't told me that. Wayne pretty much lives on chicken nuggets, so I eat a lot of them too, by default.'

Erin fell silent. Her hands were so small, and she fidgeted incessantly, with her empty shot glass, her lighter, picking at her nails and the dry skin of her lips. 'I need another shot. A shot and a cigarette,' she said. 'Who's gonna join me? I think I might leave my car here. It's my weekend anyway.'

Will was torn; he wanted to go along with this night, to keep hanging out with J.T. and Erin, but he felt strung out from lack of sleep and booze, and knew he couldn't afford another night of drinking, either, so he was half relieved when J.T. said that he had to get home.

—

Will spent the next morning with Tamsyn. She made them waffles with syrup and spray-on cream, and after Will had cleared the plates she fetched a tub of body butter and sat gouging out handfuls and rubbing it into her belly, her t-shirt tucked into her bra, and she finally began to grill him about Laura. She was incredulous, then incensed, when he told his story of rejection in the wake of Laura meeting his family.

'What do you mean?' she asked, clutching her belly as if her own child had been maligned. 'I'm sorry, I don't get it. You're saying that not only did she *not like your family*, but she didn't like them so much that she *broke up* with you?!'

Will sighed. There was no chance Tamsyn was going to understand.

'I'm sorry, Will—I know you loved this woman—but seriously, if J.T. didn't like my family, that would've been a deal-breaker for me. He *had* to come over and meet my mum and sisters before I'd even *think* about moving back here with him.'

Loved, Will thought. That sure despicable past tense.

'And, I mean, your family are the *nicest* people you could ever meet,' Tamsyn continued. 'Your *mum*!' Her voice rose to an almost-shriek. 'The way she looked after us after Dad died . . .'

Her eyes pooled and she fanned her hand in front of them. 'Sorry,' she said. 'It's the hormones. I can cry at an effing ad for life insurance at the moment.' She huffed out through inflated cheeks and took a gulp from her mug, from which hung the tags of two Tynee Tips teabags.

Thank Christ, at that precise moment the doorbell rang and Will was spared.

Tamsyn hurried off in her fluffy socks and Will wondered when he might be able to move out to Wayne's and away from the blinkered oestrogen nostalgia of Tamsyn for the loathsome town where they had both grown up, in which it seemed they'd been living on different sides of some partition of smoke or perceptual acuity or perhaps, he admitted, temperament, his own so miserly from birth in its meting out of both joy and fellow feeling.

'Hey, it's Wayne here for you,' said Tamsyn, coming back alone into the kitchen.

'What? Really?' Will was legitimately startled. 'Where?'

'Waiting at the door,' said Tamsyn with an exasperated expression. 'I invited him in but he said to send you out.'

Wayne was standing at the lip of the stairs in an attitude of deference and he pitched forward as Will appeared.

'Hey,' he said, shaking Will's hand. 'I thought you might like to come for a drive.'

He was so strange and date-like in his approach that Will couldn't help feeling nervous, even though he knew he was only going to be offered work.

After not much small talk, Wayne launched right in as they drove and said that J.T. had had a chat with him last night.

'Truth is, I do need the help real bad right now,' said Wayne. 'And there's no one in this goddamn town, aside from J.T., who I can turn to.'

He laid out his offer: he would pay Will fifty bucks a day, bar Sundays, on which he fasted the animals and Will could have the day off. He could stay out at the house—free food and board—either inside or in one of the broken-down RVs which, he said, was where some volunteers had slept back in the early days. Wayne could afford to hire him for a month, which should give J.T. some time to settle into fatherhood, and after that he'd have to see.

Will wondered when Wayne's court date was, and whether he'd even be able to keep the animals if he was in prison, but he just nodded and said a month was a bit long for him, he'd only have just over a month-and-a-half left on his visa if he stayed till then, and he had the hire car to return, too, in California.

Wayne said he could give Will a car at the end of the month—they could fix up one of the old bombs on the property; there were some in close-to-working order in the big shed—and he could return the hire car now and get some of his money back. He could drive Wayne's truck or the van while he was here.

This seemed to Will like the only feasible option he had, and he felt the sweet relief of knowing he could surely stay until the very end of his visa now, and wasn't that the most important thing? No one back home would know he'd stalled a month in this nowhere town, and anyway, working for a madman with a private zoo and feeding fuck-off giant lions and tigers every day would be a great story, and he was pleased, overall, and acknowledged the unlikely providence of his circumstances.

'Should we check with your wife?' Will asked. 'Make sure she's okay with a random stranger staying in her house? I mean, I know she's not living there, but—'

'She's fine,' Wayne cut in. 'Don't worry.'

'You've spoken to her?'

'Yes. I've spoken to her.'

The way he said it made Will question just how happy Wayne's wife had been with the idea.

'We settled then?' said Wayne, holding out a hand.

'Okay. Deal,' said Will. 'Thanks, Wayne!'

'No, thank *you*! I was getting a bit desperate to tell the truth. I sincerely believe this may be the work of providence or fate!'

'When should I start?' Will asked.

'You can start today, if you've got no other plans,' said Wayne as he dropped Will back at the house. 'Follow me out now and we can do the feed together this afternoon and set up your living quarters and whatever else. I was going to have to feed by myself today because J.T.'s on a double.'

And so Will went inside and told Tamsyn what was happening and got his few possessions from the baby's room. She told him to come in for a meal or a cuppa whenever he liked, and said she was happy he was going to be here for a while, and that he'd get to meet the baby, too—he'd be the first person from home to meet it. He succumbed again to the overpowering femaleness of her embrace, which was greasy this time and smelled strongly of chocolate, and then he started his car and set off after Wayne towards his new outlandish temporary home.

*

That very afternoon, the two men fetched a heavy chain from the sheds behind the house, where lurked other vehicles in various states of death and decay, and in which was also housed a workshop of tools and materials for cage building, and they hitched the largest of the grass-sunk RVs to a tractor and towed it up the hill on the westward side of the house, away from the enclosures, with their likely sleep-prohibitive sounds and smells and the excitatory sheer hot being of wild animals.

Will gave the flimsy and slant-floored home a quick sweep out and banged the dust from the bench seat cushions which, laid together over the fold-down table, formed what would be his bed for the next month, and Wayne brought out sheets and pillows and a couple of rough grey blankets.

'You won't have power out here,' he said. 'But you can spend as much time in the house as you like, have dinner and watch TV or whatever, and then just come out here to sleep. You'll have to make friends with Cissy and Tootsie, though.'

'Who?'

'The monkeys.'

'Oh, shit, yeah. That should be interesting.' Will flung open one of the sheets and draped it over the bed.

'Don't worry, they'll get used to you pretty quick.'

They began the long and fearful work of feeding that was to be Will's daily employment: the lions and tigers, the bears and wolves and leopards, and the mythic beautiful frightening black panther. Wayne stressed the importance of routine: feeding should happen at the same time each day or they get anxious, he said. Each enclosure needed replenishing with water, and this was easiest done simultaneously with feeding, but required concentration and timing so as not to cause a flood. And the cages had to be checked morning and night—especially those housing the tigers, who were strong diggers and would try to get out by tunnelling—and any holes filled with stones and cement. Will thought of the conversation with Erin. It wasn't a great sign that the animals were trying to escape.

After the feeding, they returned to the cage of the enormous white Siberian tiger, Snow, and again the gigantic muscled beast lurched up massive on his hind legs, flanks bunched with stored power and hide smooth-grained like a horse's, finer than velvet and tight-stitched to the flesh so that his pelt revealed all the contours of muscle and bone, shining or shadowed depending where the light fell and crisscrossed by the black markings like the jagged dark seams within a glacier. He pressed his chest and throat, where the skin was thick-furred and loose, against the wire for rubbing, and stood at least seven foot high and all smoochy soporific as Wayne cooed and caressed and called him his beautiful, beautiful boy.

Next, Wayne showed Will how to measure out and heat the formula for the two still-suckling lion cubs, and Will luxuriated once again in the floppy milk-sated embrace of Nala, who he could see would fast become his own little darling, and then, in the state of pleasant torpor that follows hard work and a hot shower, the two men reconvened in the kitchen as the monkeys screeched from their cage.

'They'll quiet down eventually,' said Wayne as he handed Will a cold beer. 'We'll eat and then we'll bring the cubs in with us for a bit.'

He opened a low cupboard in the kitchen and pulled out the kind of square freestanding plug-in frypan that Will had not seen outside his grandmother's house. Wayne was soap-smelling and dressed in what were evidently his house clothes: a pair of black boardshorts with an orange flame print on the side of the legs and a black dollar-store t-shirt emblazoned with a tacky image of a lion. His feet were bare; thick-ridged nails overhung the toes in bad need of clipping. He fetched a five-litre bottle of oil from the pantry and chugged a good half-litre into the frypan, then opened the freezer and pulled out a capacious plastic sack of small crumbed items.

'Chicken nuggets okay for you? They're just about all I eat. Can't get enough for some reason.'

'Sure.' Again, Will thought of Erin, and recalled her description of the whole-minced baby roosters. 'Can I help?'

'Nothing to it. I don't usually cook, to be honest. Mostly I just drive out and buy a family pack from McDonald's, but Liam at the chicken factory gave me this bag because they were past their best-before date. Best-before dates are a conspiracy anyway.'

Will nodded, hoping the nuggets weren't going to kill him or give him the squirts.

Wayne scooped out several fistfuls and put them on a plate. The air began to smell like heating oil and he turned down the pan. He put the plate into the microwave and paused with his finger on a button.

'How long to defrost these do you think? A minute? Five minutes?'

'Dunno,' said Will. 'Maybe start with a minute? You don't want them to dry out.'

'Wise counsel,' said Wayne. 'You can see I'm no MasterChef. Valerie used to do most of the cooking. It's a pitiful thing to be a bachelor again at sixty-one.'

'Nah, it's not pitiful,' said Will. 'It's pretty common I think. A lot of my parents' friends have split up in the last few years. I think my folks probably would've too, except that my mum's religious and doesn't believe in divorce, or, you know, sees it as a massive failure. And my dad's just too lazy, pretty much.'

'Yeah,' said Wayne. He stood looking at the plate of nuggets as they turned haltingly on the lit screen of the microwave. 'Well, life has a way of forcing you to keep on changing even when you don't want to. *Particularly* when you don't want to.'

The microwave dinged and Wayne pulled out the plate and began prodding and turning the nuggets. He stuck his finger into one, leaving a shallow pinkish navel in the brown crumb. 'Still frozen in the middle,' he said.

At the table, a plate of fifteen unadorned and uniform-shaped lumps of deep-fried breaded chicken paste before each man and bottles of ketchup, barbecue and hot sauce between them like a row of candles, Wayne asked Will about Australia.

'I've always wanted to visit,' he said. 'You've got some crazy animals down there! The platypus! And the kangaroo! Who could dream up an animal like that? I've seen them here, in the Amish sales. But I'd love to see a flock of them in the wild. Is that what it's called? A flock? A pack?'

'A mob, I think,' said Will. 'Did you say the *Amish* sales?'

'Yeah, the Amish are the main dealers of exotics in Ohio. Something about their faith endorses it. The dominion of humans over all other creatures of the earth or some other religious mumbo jumbo; I don't really bother to look into it too deeply. Like all religion, it's built on trading in your freedom for the comfort of never having to make another decision in your life. But a kangaroo fetches up to about three grand.'

'Holy shit.'

'Yup. Lion cubs are only about five hundred bucks.'

Wayne pulled another two bottles of beer from the sixpack at his feet and handed one to Will. 'You know what I was saying in the car yesterday,' he said, 'about your trip?'

'Yeah,' said Will. 'I've been thinking about that.'

'Well, I wanted to apologise.'

'Oh. No, don't. You're totally right. I mean, I've probably got this totally ridiculous romantic idea about America and, you know, Route 66 and all that. It's like my dad going to London when he finished school; he had this grand romantic idea about it—still can't shut up about it, actually. For me, America's been the place I've always wanted to see . . . But I think you're right about, like, getting to know a specific place and not just seeing the road.'

'Well, I have to confess that J.T. may have whispered in my ear that you've had a recent heartbreak.'

'Oh. Yeah. He told you?'

'And that makes sense of everything. You had your heart broken by a woman and your instinct was to run. It's natural, I guess, to run here if, as you say, you've got an interest in America. But the main thing was to make a break. And I understand that completely.'

'Really?'

'Hell, yeah! You were probably on the verge of settling down and marrying this woman, and that's fine—that's one kind of life, and it's a beautiful thing. But now, since you've had that option taken away, you want to try out the opposite: the loner thing.'

'Well, I don't know if I was exactly on the verge of settling down . . .' Or was he? Perhaps in his heart he had been. 'I'm kind of embarrassed now, though, about running away. I'll have to go home eventually. Tail between my legs and all.'

'Why tail between your legs? Why not go home a hero? You know, I did pretty much the same thing as you when I was . . . maybe a bit younger. How old are you?'

'Twenty-two.'

'Hey, you gonna finish those?'

There were three nuggets on Will's plate that he couldn't eat.

'Nah, I'm done. Thank you, though.'

'Pass them over, then.' Wayne tipped the nuggets onto his own plate and bit into one. 'Yeah, I had my heart broken at eighteen. Just smashed to pieces. The girl still lives here in Littleproud. Woman, now. She's about two hundred pounds and lost a foot to diabetes a couple years back, so I guess I'm finally over it, but I was a *mess* back then. After she ended it, I used to fly over her house every day. I got my pilot's licence at sixteen. I buzzed her house every damn day—thought that was the way to win her back, for some reason I can't fathom now. Eventually her father came out with a shotgun and aimed it at the plane and I stopped after that. Then I signed up to go to Nam. I flew helicopters over there. And I came back a decorated pilot; a hero.

And *then* she wanted to get back together. Ha! By that time I was over the idea of settling down. Until I met Valerie.'

'That's crazy.' Will leaned back in his seat. 'Hey, I'd love to hear more about your experience in Vietnam.'

Wayne went through another of his liquid shifts of expression. 'Mmm . . . Maybe another time.' He began to gather up the plates and cutlery and condiments and took them to the kitchen, and Will followed, flustered and abashed, with the hot sauce and the empty beer bottles.

'I might hit the sack,' said Wayne. 'I get tired pretty early these days. Gettin' old.'

'You're not old!' said Will in obsequious tangential apology for bringing up the war.

Wayne just shook his head. 'I'll do these in the morning,' he said, stacking the plates in the sink. 'Dishwasher's busted.'

'I'll do them.'

'Don't bother.' Wayne put his hand on Will's shoulder. 'Goodnight,' he said, and walked off down the corridor, his shoulders curved and making a sad figure in Will's eyes, in his boardshorts and cap and bare feet and with those oddly scrawny ankles, leaving Will alone with the monkeys and the pan full of cold brown oil and the fluoro-lit kitchen silence. He wasn't sure if it was his probing about the war that had made Wayne abrupt off to bed like that, or if it was just his way. He didn't know this man at all, in fact. He might come out in the night with a shotgun, for all Will knew. Wayne had said they would bring in the cubs after dinner, though, so it must have been the war.

He looked at his watch. It was only 8 pm.

As he was filling the sink, his phone rang in his back pocket. It was his brother Tom. He wondered if Paul had spoken to him and he silenced the call and let it ring out. A short while later a message came through:

> Seriously disappointed in you little bro!
> I know you're hurting n going thru that post-breakup destructiveness—I've been there and I know how it is.
> But Paul is family. How could you do that?!
> Anyway call me. Hope ur ok mate. Tom

With Wayne gone from the room, the monkeys began to hoot and screech again in agitation. Will stood helpless and on the brink of despair. He came out of the kitchen with sudsy hands and whispered an ineffectual *shhhh* in the direction of the cage. After a minute, Wayne returned, wearing only Y-fronts and carrying a blanket. His head was bare and the thin hair stood out all wispy around his ears.

'Quiet down, ladies,' he said to the monkeys. He latched the cage door and threw the blanket over it. 'That should settle them.'

Will thanked him and he gave a nod and then walked back down the hall, a figure of even greater pathos now, with the seat of his underpants hanging low and the patches of hair visible across his pale shoulders and in the dimples where the buttocks began their subsiding former swell.

Will didn't know what to do; he found himself inhabiting such a moment as those in which we look around ourselves and see not one object that is friendly or familiar, in circumstances that as little as a week ago we would have been incapable of imagining, let alone believing would be our own in so brief a span of lithe and thwart and mocking implacable time, and in the taut-stretched and overdue silence, with the pressure of the wordless night against the window, his dark burdened soul at last could run no more, and down it crumpled on the blue leather sofa. After a week's blind running through a self-willed blinding myth-created fog that obscured whatever reality of New York City landscape through which he in fact moved, passing whatever spectres who stepped aside to let this blinkered hurly-burly go on its fool somnambulant way, and after the past four days' still-blind gravel-sounding skidding to a halt, Will saw that he was stationary now, here in this foreign port of forbearance and slight welcome, and that the reckoning he had been chasing off had paused at the horizon and turned back, and was advancing now towards him at speeds exceeding even those he had been travelling at since taking off from home.

From his place upon the sofa, he looked outside. The clouds that had been gathering all afternoon above the hills did not like him: through the glass they displayed their hostility in dry flashes. And as if on cue, another vile message arrived from Paul to prove that it was not just pathetic fallacy, that he was disliked by sky and clouds and people too.

What was there to do but turn on the television? There, on the news, a report of protests in Zuccotti Park. The scene looked strangely cheerful, with vigorous and scant-clad young people chanting slogans about the necessary death of capitalism and twirling hula hoops and putting up tents. There was a sign that said *This is Day Five*, and another, *We are the 99%*. There were people wearing Anonymous masks and the black-and-white

Palestinian scarves that for some unaccountable reason had become part of the uniform of the young white radical left. People were making signs from cut-up cardboard boxes. One declared that fifty million Americans had no health care; another that the top three richest men owned more than the debt of the fifty states combined.

Will recalled his conversation with Veronique, and it was as if, in this moment of darkest self-involvement, even the television, most indiscriminate of all acquaintances, disliked him too, insisting that all he had seen and done in New York City had been a mere perverse fantasy created by his provincial ego and that his smug and drug-fuelled decadence was nothing but a blaring advertisement of his shameful naivety. And in the face of such diffuse immanent hostility he began, in humiliation and despair and as quietly as he could, to cry.

But he must not be seen like this. He struggled up and with his phone as torch he crunched across the driveway to the dusty hutch of his RV home and lay down in the thick and total darkness.

He lay awake a long adversity of time. Now that he was no longer in New York, no longer crashing into oblivion at 3 or 4 or 6 am, he was returned to the eternal sleeplessness that was his cross to bear, a phrase befitting such nightly private trial, which felt biblical, at times, it wracked his spirit so. Alone in his childhood bed, then his Melbourne share house bed, he had charted whole archipelagos of unsleeping, frightening tropics zoned only by dream logic, which is no logic at all, and where the mind's hull cannot be trusted.

Laura had been an insomniac too, and being with her had made him aware of certain consequent similarities between them: a frayed near-manic mental energy; a feeling of existential isolation; the tendency to ruminate; a preference for depressants rather than stimulants; the development and practised repetition of techniques, self-designed in desperation and undoubtedly idiosyncratic, yet sharing a common methodical character, with which to wheedle the intractable brain towards that sweet warm bier of sleep, where it might be eased at last of unendurable consciousness. His own practice involved making increasingly obtuse alphabetised lists in his head: the name of a country beginning with each letter of the alphabet; the name of a film; a city or town; a disease or malady; a city or town he himself had visited; a girl's name; a girl's name with three syllables. Laura's trick had been to imagine herself sweeping her house, to place herself within each room and feel herself spatially orientated in relation to every chair and bookshelf, starting in one corner and working her way around each obstacle, the sensation of the broom handle against her palm.

Some of their best times, for him, had been in those grey soft-lit sleepless star-fade hours in her plant-full room. *Are you awake?* one would whisper, very quiet, so as not to disturb the other if they were blessedly asleep, though they had perceived already the signs of hateful consciousness. *Yes, are you?* would come back the reply. Then Will would tickle his fingertips over her naked back, which was her favourite thing in the world, or they would share a pair of headphones and listen to music, or, most often and most effective, they would fuck each other towards a slumber that was like valium, so limb-loosed and core-stilled.

There had been a morning when he had said to himself, *Remember this moment*, feeling drowsy and temperate and perfectly happy, their legs intertwined, listening to the harsh repeated call of the 'native rooster', as Laura called the red wattlebird that came each dawn to the grevillea outside her window to usher in the day with its abrasive crowing. He regretted so that love-dumb act of indelible archiving, and knew that he *would* remember it now, always, and could never let it go.

Oh, some nights Will felt that simple darkness and three hours' silence in its company might be enough to send him mad.

Arthritis
Bubonic plague
Chlamydia
Dengue fever
Emphysema
F . . . F . . . Skip
Gallstones
Hepatitis
Irritable bowel syndrome
Jaundice
K . . . K . . . Skip
Legionnaire's disease . . .

It was no good. He scrabbled upright again and returned as quietly as he could to the house. In the pantry he found a half-full bottle of Jim Beam. He told himself that he would replace it tomorrow, and he took it to the window and faced the reckoning that flashed and menaced at the horizon, and he answered aloud its thunder-call of threat: *Bring it on, then. Bring it on.*

WHAT FORM THAT SOUL'S RECKONING took as he faced it down in the long night we will never know—perhaps he did not know himself, for he seemed to pat himself down on waking to check that he was unscathed and found that he was whole in body at least. The bottle was empty on the couch beside him; thank god Wayne hadn't come out and found him here like this, on the first morning of his official employment.

He set the bottle on the floor, pulled on his boots and went to the door. It was only just first light, and he stood there looking at the long slope of the driveway and the small silver dam, listening to the bird calls that flashed from each dawning hill. Then he stepped outside and walked, tentative and expectant, towards the enclosures.

Just to be near them—six feet, then four, and at last just a foot away—felt fearsome and bold. Will stood, a slight and anxious human animal, before the cage of Mustafa the lion, who returned his gaze with incurious cool intensity. The lion's head was of incredible proportion, the mane composed of two tiers, each a different shade, the inner the colour of sandstone and the outer almost brown, and it fanned out thick around the broad velvet face and fell midway to the lion's deadly velvet paws, the claws sheathed like a house cat's but visible, curved sickle and dirty-pale and ready, and the animal was so alive and sentient, standing there looking at him from out of its lion consciousness through pale orange keen inhuman eyes. The taut tendons of the back legs were each as thick as Will's wrist, containing all the stored displayed strength to propel the muscled chest and brutal front paws as easy as a bow-loosed arrow at any blood-hot living target, and every part of this calm impassive being that was right now looking straight at him was element, precise and perfect, of a killing machine of epic grace and power.

Will stepped right up to the wire so that he could hear the rasping of the lion's breath and smell its scat-spray scent, and the lion turned its eyes away to the horizon as if in deference, though surely it was not that.

After a time, Will moved off and continued down the row. Some of the lions approached him as they had done with Wayne, and a lioness stood full height like a golden grizzly, her pink nose and white-whiskered muzzle pressing through the wire, making her appear to smile. The black spongy pads of her paws pushed against the fence, spread and showing the pale tufts of fur between them. Will wanted to touch her, but kept back. He spoke to the lioness, whose name—Lindy—was written on a metal plate attached to her enclosure, as were the names of every one of Wayne's wild children, greeting her as Wayne had done, and telling her she was beautiful. She huffed and swivelled her flocked subtle ears, and when he did not pat her she landed lightly back on her paws and stood flicking her tail.

Past the numerous lions were the miscellaneous specimens—the wolves and big lumbering bears, the two exquisite spotted leopards with their flat shy faces, the black panther—and then the tiger cages started. How those tremendous living tigers made him feel! To stand alone in such proximity in the early morning light where, if he had dragged his eyes away from the reverie of gilt-pelted muscle he would have seen bright bugs helicoptering everywhere in a sunburst like lively motes, was to Will a kind of worship, a feeling he had renounced long years ago in a new-built church and had neither sought nor expected since. That such beings existed . . . They seemed to him dream creatures conjured real. The improbable wonder of their stripes! Of course he knew like any doomed despairing passive modern man that in a human lifespan this already improbable wondrous species would extinct into the realm of image and he felt with new conscience how evil that future was, sacked of the distinct and bright-kindled life of such perfect living things, who would become mere pathetic legend, unicorn-magic with their startling hides, but seen here grooming and lounging and alive in their humble right of existence, or some cruel parody of such.

Having offered up his surreal Midwestern matins, he returned across the shade-wet grass to the house. He took off his boots and went to the kitchen, where he found a box of Cheerios and these he consumed with half-and-half, because there was no milk, and then felt ill. He was just examining the coffee percolator to see how it worked when he heard tyres on the drive and went to the door to see Wayne's van pull up.

'I thought you were asleep,' he said as Wayne climbed out.

'Nope. Been up for hours already.' Wayne went around to the van's sliding door and pulled out a cardboard box and set it on the roof, and then another.

Will hopped barefoot over the gravel to help him. The boxes were full of fruit.

'Saw you tapped out on the couch, so I snuck out real quiet,' Wayne said.

Shit; why had he let himself do that? And on his first night here. It was not a good start. Oh, but the tribulations he had endured.

'How did you sleep?' Wayne asked, no trace of displeasure in his voice.

'Okay, eventually,' he said in noble understatement.

They carried the boxes in and set them on the kitchen counter. Will thought he saw Wayne glance at the liquor bottle on the floor.

'I've been eating and drinking whatever I could find,' he said. 'But I'll go into town today and pick up some supplies and replace the stuff I've used.'

'Don't bother. *Mi casa su casa.*' Wayne flicked the blanket off the cage, and the monkeys caught sight of Will and began again their terrible screeching. 'Time for your monkey aversion training,' said Wayne. Perhaps this was his punishment.

'Okay,' said Will, attempting bravery for what felt like the millionth time in the past short span of days.

From one of the boxes, Wayne retrieved a plastic container wrapped in cling film. He removed the wrap and held the container out to Will. Inside was a writhing nest of pale brown segmented glossy worms, darker tipped at their claw-faced heads.

'Mealworms,' said Wayne. 'They love them.'

He poured about a quarter of the worms into a metal bowl and passed it to Will and put the rest into the fridge.

'If you want a snack later . . .'

'Yum!' Will looked down at the bowl but stayed where he was.

Wayne laughed. 'I promise they will not hurt you.'

Will moved hesitant towards the cage. The monkeys began to shriek even louder as he got close, and they bared their sharp incisors. He stopped and held out the bowl. The two small furred bodies fell silent. They edged forward, dipping and craning their necks towards the worms. Up close he could see their long deep-lined prehensile hands with their small black fingernails. Another step, and they fled screeching to the back of the cage, and Will was able to open the door, push in the bowl and retreat again. The monkeys continued their racket but stayed pressed into the corner, smelling of piss and fear.

'See? Total scaredy-cats,' said Wayne.

He held up a finger, and Will waited unmoving near the cage until Tootsie, the larger of the two, shuffled forward on her rear, like a toddler tired of standing, to where her thin fingers could just reach the rim of the bowl. She pulled it towards her and sat curved around it, considering and then consuming a single worm as daintily as if with chopsticks.

After cutting up the load of fruit and dividing it into portions, and after Will had made another timorous and shriek-protested delivery to the monkeys, the two men set off in Wayne's van, which they aimed to fill with scrap chicken parts from the factory a half-hour drive away. They clattered over the metal grille to a Springsteen soundtrack and turned left away from Littleproud into unvisited regions of dilapidated pastoral and the mesmerising flicker of tree-shadow and early sunshine, in a silence Will hoped was friendly or habitual. It was a day of such mild and dew-rinsed splendour that it could have been the first day of a fresh new world, the beginning of some actual intended life here, and only mild were the effects of last night's sleeplessness and drink, and he did not even think of Laura as they shot through smooth green tunnels and over a succession of small hills that made the stomach and the spirit leap up glad, as on the first gentle dips and rises of a rollercoaster.

The windows were down and the hair on his bare arms was caressed against the grain, and they had left behind the smell of caged animals and he could breathe in deep the green and golden scents of fields and woods. He felt the child's desire to hold out his hand and let it dip and ride dolphin-like astride the silky texture of the air stream, but resisted because he would look foolish in front of Wayne.

A sign for MacIvor's Chickens loomed ahead and there was a long compound fence and a boom gate with a swipe card reader and an intercom. The place looked more like a juvenile detention facility than a chicken factory.

Wayne pressed a red button and waited for a response.

'Yeah,' came a crackled voice.

'Two Big Macs and a large fries,' said Wayne. He grinned at Will.

'That you, Wayne?' said the tin-can voice.

'Hey, Terrell.'

The gate opened and the van moved through into that industrial prison farm and deep-hidden gated id-place of the unslakable consumer psyche. They drove over speed humps and past a car park big enough to service a small airport as they approached the factory, squat and grey under the blue sky with its tinted windows and its docking bays. They passed a line of semitrailers bearing the MacIvor's logo, a bizarre image of an apron-wearing cartoon chook and three smiling yellow chicks grouped around a dinner table on which sat a steaming brown roast chicken. They were back within the odour of caged animals, but here it was different, a smell that mingled horribly the supermarket scent of raw pink hormone-plump chicken and the reek of dirty birds.

Finally they drew up at an unmanned counter window under a petrol station-style awning. Wayne jumped out and pressed a buzzer and then opened the rear doors of the van. A pale white guy, wearing an elasticised hair cover of the kind worn by surgeons and with terrible red acne on his cheeks, came to the window.

'Hey, Liam,' said Wayne.

Will got out of the van.

'Liam, this is Will. He's Australian.'

Liam waved a rubber-gloved hand. 'How much you after today, Wayne?'

'Just the usual. Ton of hearts and sixty pounds of necks.'

'A ton?!' Will half shouted.

'That's right. And you'll see how quick that goes. That's not even a week's feeding, if we don't find any roadkill.'

'No way!'

'Back shortly,' said Liam, and disappeared again through a plastic strip curtain.

'A male lion eats around ten pounds of meat a day, five days a week, then bones one of those other days, which I get from a butcher in town. Females less, but still.'

'That's insane.'

'Yup. And we don't have fridge space—or a big enough van, for that matter—to stock up less often. So I do this run every week, roundabout, depending on the season. They eat even more in winter.'

The coolroom door eventually slid open and Liam appeared with a flatbed trolley stacked with boxes.

'You okay to start loading these while I pay?' said Wayne.

The boxes were heavy and there were a lot of them. There was a tarpaulin laid over the floor in the back of the van, which made it hard to slide them in very far. Will climbed inside and crouched and lifted the first few boxes, stacking them flush against the metal cage behind the cabin.

'You stay in there and I'll hand the rest in to you,' said Wayne, when his big torso appeared in the doorway.

Together they stacked the cold, heavy boxes until the whole of the van was full.

On the way home, Wayne pulled in to a drive-thru and ordered a family pack of chicken nuggets and Will ordered a burger because he couldn't stomach chicken and they sat and ate in the van, the engine running with its hollow diesel stutter. Will tried not to think about what portion of bone and hide and eyeball he was now ingesting with its necessary excessive complement of salt and sweet soft bread and ketchup and yellow cheese poured and set to a bendable tile, and he ate in quick dog-like chomps as the juice dripped onto the paper wrapping laid open on his lap.

Halfway back to Wayne's they passed the stick-legged carcass of a deer and Wayne slowed and churned up onto the verge.

'Looks fresh,' he said. 'We'd better collect it. Saves a lot of money. It's technically illegal, unless you call the sheriff to issue you a collection slip, but I don't bother with that. Sheriff's department aren't likely to do me any favours anyway. But we'll need to work quick. Cut it up enough to fit in the van here and then do the rest back home.'

Will nodded, queasy and sad, and put his hand to the door.

'Hold up,' said Wayne. 'I'll back up a ways so the van hides us a bit.'

He waited for a car to pass and made a veering reverse course towards the dead animal.

'If you jump out and pull it a bit further off the road, I can stop right next to it.'

It was like he was in a Tarantino film, Will thought, pulled up on some Midwestern verge in a van full of chicken guts and being told by his possibly batshit-crazy boss to get out and haul a dead deer further off the road so that they could get to work hacking it to pieces. Next thing, the van would be hijacked or they'd be kidnapped by drug lords and would have to use the meat saw to brutally slaughter them before bagging them up with the deer parts and feeding them to the tigers.

He tried his best to lose himself in the absurd fucked-up comedy of the scene as he gripped the dry hooves of the deer and dragged it towards the sapling edge of woods while Wayne reversed over the flattened patch of grass where the deer had lain in bloodless demise. At least the deer didn't stink. That was a first.

Wayne opened the van and surveyed the stack of boxes. 'Not a whole lot of room,' he said. 'We could dump these home and come back, but that'll add another hour to the whole trip. And someone else may take the deer. We might have to carry some of it up front with us.'

'Won't it, like, bleed all over us?'

'I've got garbage bags. Never travel without them.' Wayne reached into a compartment over the rear wheel and pulled out a roll of black bags, a tomahawk and a short hacksaw with a yellow plastic handle.

Will felt his stomach lurch. 'Um, alright,' he said.

'Okay, great, 'cause we've got a lot of work to do still today.'

Will held a hind leg and looked away into the trees while Wayne sawed. He tried not to focus on the vibration that travelled up the braced struts of his arms as the saw ground its widening track through the deer's body, catching frequently on the bone and then jerked back into its groove.

A massive tip truck loaded with scrap metal passed them, heading towards Littleproud. Wayne stood and put his hands in the small of his back and swayed from side to side, the saw still embedded in the haunch of the deer.

Will glanced down helpless at the face—the rigid pink tip of tongue sticking out the side of the mouth, the soft brown eye open but no longer wet with life. He saw a rib protruding through the pale brown fur, but other than that there was no sign of violence. That was all occurring now, as Wayne worked at the final vellum tear of the finishing cut and pulled the leg free.

'You're really not letting me ease in to this job, Wayne!' Will said, attempting lightness. 'Where's my gentle handover period?'

Wayne chuckled. 'Open up a bag for me,' he said.

He heaved the leg in and they turned the animal and began on the other side, and soon enough they were driving again, the air buffeting in through the open windows and drying their rank remorseful sweat.

Will held a weighty black bag on his lap; another rested between his knees, and there was an empty feeling in his guts. The CD had looped back again and Springsteen was crooning the creepy opening lyrics of 'I'm On Fire', and from the woods the homesick sound of cicadas sprouted and bloomed, sudden and huge, seeming as always to originate not in a single voice but to be signalled and initiated across the whole species by a green omniscient conductor.

Wayne told him that J.T. was coming for dinner, and after they unloaded the van, he left for town to pick up groceries, accepting the last twenty dollars in Will's wallet for a replacement bottle of whiskey.

Will sat down on the couch, took off his boots and popped a beer. The monkeys began to hoot at him, but more half-hearted now.

Again with apparent unvolition he opened Laura's Facebook page, but there were no new updates. There she was on Maddie's page, though, with her cropped hair, drinking with the gang in Edinburgh Gardens, wearing a cotton dress with sunflowers on it, for fuck's sake, and he had to check himself from reading into this blatant springtime imagery of new blossoming a cruel and badly coded message just for him. He examined his poor heart for signs of resilience; perhaps the skin had callused some, for the pain seemed duller—did it?—like screams heard through a closed door, and he found that the exercising of his grief through this compulsion of looking and remembering was, if not yet unenthusiastic, at least a little less engrossing in its performance, and at length he put down the phone and fell asleep in his filthy socks and didn't wake until Wayne and J.T. came noisy and laughing and laden through the door.

The men spread out across the counter the bounty of their bloodless modern hunt (the first bloodless action of the day, it seemed to Will): whiskey; laundry liquid; powdered mashed potato; supermarket coleslaw; sliced white bread and peanut butter and whole milk for Will; ground coffee in a jumbo-sized tin; a tub of peanut choc fudge ice cream; and two kinds of beer.

'J.T. insisted on the fancy beer,' said Wayne. 'Said you'd be in agreeance, which disappointed me some.'

J.T. handed a pale ale to Will and opened one himself, while Wayne pulled the ring on a can of Bud. Next steps involved the rolling of a joint, in which Will shared, though less liberally than the others.

'Let's bring the babies inside,' said Wayne soon after, and the three of them retrieved the lion cubs from their wisteria creche:

little Nate and Nala and bigger Charlie, whose brother, Wayne said, had died. Wayne spread out toys for them—balls and rope rings and a couple of empty kegs from a water cooler—and they swiped and crashed around the slate floor, and as Will sat in their boisterous midst, Wayne and J.T. plugged in guitars and added to the din with an extended blues jam. Both were talented musicians and though Will did not love the blues he listened, buzzed and contented, while around him the small furred hurricane of unruly play raged and peaked and began to subside.

When lions and musicians had exhausted themselves, Will helped J.T. make up bottles and asked if he could feed Nala, and soon they were sitting, three nicely toasted men with warm and heavy suckling lions in their arms, all grinning stupid and afloat in the wonder that was apparently—to look at Wayne—unceasing, and Will gazed down at his new sweetheart and thought that this was just the balm for his still-hopeful spirit.

'Hey, thanks again, Will,' J.T. said. 'For helping out here so I can catch up. I've got assignments to do before the baby comes and my dad's not well just now.'

'How is Frank?' Wayne asked.

'Yeah, he's not real good. I went to the hospital today but he wasn't speaking. They say he'll be alright to go home soon, but I can't see how. How's Mom gonna cope?'

'How long has he been in hospital?' Will asked.

'He's in and out. Basically he's never been okay. My whole life, at least. He's physically real sick now. With diabetes and liver trouble. But he's unfortunately one of those who never really recovered from the war. And I'm pretty sure his experience wasn't even as bad as Wayne's, but . . .'

'Hey. Hey now,' said Wayne, shifting Charlie on his lap. 'You know better than that. It's not about who had it worse. People handle it differently. Me, I've never been the silent type, and I think that helps. And we don't really know, either. The worst stuff is often never told.'

'Yeah, you're probably right,' said J.T.

'Don't be mad at your old man. I know you don't want to hear this from me again, J.T., but he was ten years younger than you are now when those bastards sent him into that hellhole. It's them you should be mad at, not him.'

'You mean the government?' said Will.

'Hell, yes, I mean the government. I have never forgiven *the government* for what they did to us. I used to take my democratic right seriously—at the age of eighteen. I recited those presidential names, goddamn it. But I tell you I have not voted—not once—since I came back from service. I'm not going to be conned into thinking I'm participating in some kind of fair and transparent system. It's all rigged and controlled by powers much greater than us small men, just like the war, and in the end they will do precisely what serves themselves.'

Will thought it best to avoid a conversation about American democracy, but he gave a nod to signify solidarity, at least.

'We were spat at as we got off the plane, for Christ's sake,' Wayne continued. 'While we were being welcomed home by our families. For me . . . I was already completely disillusioned, so that was just the nail in the coffin. But for those guys who still believed in what they were fighting for, and thought they were coming back heroes . . . That was enough to break them.'

'I thought you said you did come home a hero,' said Will. 'You were telling *me* to go home a hero.'

'Yeah, well, I was *officially* a hero.' Wayne stared down at the lion in his lap. He ran his finger up the soft ridge of its nose and between its plump eyebrows, and then he looked back up at Will and grinned. 'Anyhow, you don't need to be a hero to any more than one woman, right?'

Charlie began to wriggle on Wayne's lap and he put the big cub down and began to tussle with him on the floor, the two batting each other with paws and hands. Wayne grabbed Charlie around the chest and rolled him over so that his flailing legs were in the air and the cub bent his face around to chew the side of Wayne's head. Wayne began to rub his fluffy belly and Charlie stopped kicking and relaxed and allowed himself to be petted, lying full-length along Wayne's body, a sight that made Will laugh in disbelief and pull out his phone. Nala had fallen asleep against his chest and he snapped Wayne and Charlie and then J.T. with Nate, and then turned the phone on himself and took a blurred shot of smiling human and somnolent lion faces pressed together.

The evening progressed as might a less surreal slumber party or gathering of teenagers. The three men worked together in the kitchen to assemble dinner, and because they were stoned, and because each in his own way was in extremis, and all possessed within them the shallow-buried boyhood urge to random behaviour, they began to deep-fry blobs of mashed potato and then mashed potato balls with a filling of coleslaw, with much laughter that verged towards the hysterical. Then Wayne made a ball of mashed potato with an ice cream centre that leaked in the hot pan and scalded his hand, and it was only then with the hand under cold and sober water that they calmed their hijinks. They returned the lion cubs to their pen and brought in the tigers and sat down to dinner while the small striped bodies pranced around the table as if for their entertainment.

Then, as the night grew late and the men more stoned, all those held-down-drowned emotions came bobbing and bloated back to the surface, and the gathering came still more to resemble a sleepover of teenage girls, for after bowls of ice cream on the couch they looked around and found that one of their number was dissolved in tears.

'Whoa, it's okay, buddy,' said J.T., his face full of kind concern and free of embarrassment or diminishing respect or even of surprise, all of which Will experienced as he watched the older man, guitar in hand and tears running down his rough cheeks, mouth bent in a twitching inverted grin.

'She's left me, J.T.,' Wayne cried. 'She's not coming back.'

J.T. put his hands on Wayne's shoulders. 'You don't know that, Wayne. You guys are the greatest couple I know. I'm sure you can sort it out. I have total faith in the two of you.'

'I spoke to her today.'

'You did?'

'Yeah. I asked her if she could come and stay for a couple of nights so I can go visit Mom. That's been approved, so I'd like to go.'

'That's great, Wayne.'

Wayne sighed hugely. 'Yeah. And she said she'd come. I told you she feels real bad about how hard it's been on you. How much you're helping out around here.'

'Wayne. You're my best friend and I'm so happy to—'

'I know, I know,' Wayne interrupted. 'I didn't mean that.'

J.T. lifted the strap over his friend's neck and took the guitar from him and laid it on the sofa.

Will sat remote in his native embarrassment and when Wayne's wet gaze fell on him he was not certain what his eyes conveyed, and was relieved when those of the other moved on with no sure sign of having registered even his simple blinking presence.

'I don't want to lose her, J.T.,' Wayne said. 'I can't.'

'You won't, buddy. You'll work it out.'

'I don't blame her. I asked too much of her, I know. I thought I was invincible. After what I've survived, I thought no one could touch me. But I should have known. Those bastards . . .' He stopped and looked down, the tears spilling again. 'They're trying to destroy me.'

'Wayne, buddy . . .' J.T. said. 'You need to stop going down this negative path. You know you've said the same to me before. None of this has happened yet. You need to stay strong. Focus on fixing things with Valerie. She still loves you, I know it.'

Wayne snorted up his body's liquid evidence of emotion. He took off his cap and wiped his eyes with the back of his hand and put the cap back on again and then he clasped J.T.'s arm.

'You're right,' he said. 'Thank you.'

When he had composed himself, he turned to Will. 'I'm sorry, Will. This must all be very strange to you—on top of my usual strangenesses, too, which you're probably still trying to assess.'

'It's totally fine, honestly,' said Will.

'This is a new challenge for me. When you love a woman with all your heart and she don't trust you enough after twenty-five years to just hold on . . .' He made a groaning sound and put his hands up to his eyes.

Will nodded with what he hoped was a look of commiseration.

Wayne mashed the palms of his hands into his sockets and screwed them around and then he stood up stiff and bowed on those thin legs, the knees swollen from hard work like the burls that grow around the limbs of trees.

'Sorry to ruin the party,' he said. 'I was having a real good time before I got a bit too high and embarrassed myself.'

J.T. walked Wayne down the corridor to bed like an overtired child, and Will began clearing up the mess. He wasn't sure what to make of it all.

J.T. returned and leaned against the kitchen bench. He scooped up Bubbles the tiger cub, though he was the size of a kelpie, and pressed his face into the soft stripes of his neck until he squirmed for freedom and tumbled off to pounce his brother awake.

'Sometimes when I'm feeling down, I come out here and go into the pen with the cubs and just sit there and let them kinda flow over me.' J.T. started filling the sink and piling in the dishes.

'Is he okay?' Will asked.

'He can get a bit emotional on the old green. But he's okay, I think. At least he doesn't drink much. My pa's an alcoholic and the booze just makes him violent. Weed's much gentler, if you ask me.'

Will nodded as he took a clean plate from J.T. and dried it.

'It's this fucking town,' J.T. continued. 'I mean, it's the war, obviously. But what Wayne was saying about coming home . . . I mean, no one got spat on here. They weren't anti-war here. They *were* officially heroes, like Wayne says. But coming home to a small town where everyone knows you, and you're a *totally* different person, just a complete shell of who you were. No one knew how to help them. And I see it happening again now, with the guys back from Iraq. That's partly why I wanna do this music therapy thing.'

Will dried the final plate and hung the tea towel and the two of them looked around the still-chaotic room, at the dented blue water kegs, at the guitars and empty beers and, strangest of all, the two tumbling small tigers.

'You want another drink?' said Will.

'I should get going,' said J.T. 'I never get Friday nights off and Tamsyn's not too happy about me spending it out here instead of with her. But I told her she'll have a month with me now, and Wayne needs the support too.'

J.T. walked over to the patio door and unhooked the leashes for the tigers. 'Shall we put these babies to bed?'

'Hey, J.T., what was Wayne saying about Valerie coming here?' Will asked, as they led the cubs across the damp grass.

'Oh yeah. He wants to go visit his mom interstate. She's in a nursing home in West Virginia. He had to apply to the court to go visit her, 'cause he's out on bail right now. And I guess he's asked Valerie to come and cover him here. He didn't need to—you and I could have made it work. Or, who knows, maybe it was just an excuse to contact her? Like I said, I think they'll get through this. They were so in love; you've never seen anything like it.'

'So when will she be here?'

'Not sure. I'll find out. But you're fine. Nothing'll change for you. And she's great, Valerie. You'll love her. Everyone does.'

The sensor light on the patio flicked off and they were in darkness, cool and hill-smelling, and the sky opened up and the stars seeded themselves across it like bright scattered grain. Will hadn't seen a sky like this since whenever he'd last gone camping back home. The hills cupped the house in darkness like a handheld moth and there were no lights to be seen from the neighbour's farm he knew was over the western rise of paddock and oh, the swimming sky, the slow-swinging stars, burning there as though to guide this lost world, and him along with it, to some distant, perhaps unreachable home.

—

Lying awake at dawn, Will heard the first bird—the Venus bird, Laura called it, aural equivalent of the first star—and then the roaring of a lion, and he wondered if that noise could ever become familiar enough to be unnoticed, like the passing of the trams outside his window back home, which had seemed at first impossible to ignore or sleep through.

He looked out and saw Wayne standing down by the cages in the grey particulate light and he pulled on clothes and walked down towards the ambivalent figure of, he supposed, his employer.

'You're up early,' said Wayne.

'Been awake half the night. But that's pretty normal for me. I'm a terrible sleeper.'

'Ah,' said Wayne. 'You too.'

'Yep. I hate it. It kinda rules my life at times.'

'That it does.'

'Have you always had it?'

'Just since the war. Before then I slept as soundly as America itself.'

Will couldn't help but chuckle at this piece of hyperbole. 'You checking the fences?'

'No, just visiting with my friends.'

They were standing near the cage of Simba, the oldest of the lions, and Wayne stepped forward and called the lion's name and up he came, with his ambling shoulder-rolling leisurely gait, and Wayne bent his face and the lion appeared for all the world to kiss his friend or master through the wire. The creature turned side-on and leaned his long body against the fence, and Wayne put his hand through and scratched the old lion's ear and then his lower back above the tail where the fur was tufty and moulted under Wayne's fingers.

'Is that nice? Do you like that?' Wayne cooed. 'Yeah you do. You love a good scratch.' And then, without warning, he unlocked the door and stood there patting his leg as Simba ambled out.

'Ahh . . .' said Will, stepping back a couple of paces.

Wayne laughed. 'It's okay. We let this guy out a lot of the time. He's lived with us all his life, haven't you, old man?' He rubbed the lion's jaw and the lion pushed against his hand all domestic meek, lifting his lip in pleasure to show his brown-stained teeth. 'He's about ninety in human years. Probably doesn't have long to go now. But you don't know that, do you?' He put his hands over the lion's ears. 'He loves to tag along with me, whatever I'm doing around the place. Sometimes I let him ride up front with me in the van. Went through the drive-thru with him once, but that didn't go down too well.'

Wayne moved from cage to cage with Simba at his side and received at each the same affection and gave back the same sweet talk, and Will slunk after them in awed witness. There were a few that even Wayne stood back from: Kahn the rescue tiger, and King, a splendid full-maned lion, who stood in the far corner of his cage, twitch-tailed and horizon-gazing at their approach.

'I guess I got a reputation for never saying no,' said Wayne. 'So now and then we get someone asking us to take an animal. Not often, mind you. Exotic owners would normally rather die than give up their babies. But King here . . . his owner couldn't afford to keep him. Her husband died of cancer. Friend of mine. We used to race boats together. Brain tumour; just tragic. Anyway, June couldn't keep the farm and she begged us to take King. She comes to see him from time to time. Always breaks down crying when she has to leave.'

'Does he recognise her?'

'Of course! Runs right over, soon as he sees her. She goes into the cage with him and he jumps up and puts his arms around her shoulders. Practically knocks her over. She's not a large woman.'

He held his hand at the height of his chest. 'Once you've raised them from a cub they'll never forget you. No way.'

As they walked back towards the house, leaving Simba free to roam, Wayne broached the subject that walked silent between them.

'I'd like to apologise about last night.'

'Oh, no, please,' said Will. 'There's nothing to apologise for. Seriously.'

'Like I said last night,' Wayne continued, his eyes dogged on the approaching door, 'I know you know the feeling. Probably pretty close to it yourself, I'd guess.'

'Yep,' said Will. 'I've certainly shed a few tears over it. Over Laura.'

'That's her name?' said Wayne. 'That's my mother's name. You know,' he continued, after a pause, 'I think you've come here for a reason. I know you probably think that kind of talk is crazy, but I've had so many improbable experiences that it would be crazy for me *not* to believe in some kind of fate.'

'Really?' said Will. 'What do you think I'd be here for?'

'I don't know. But I'm guessing it'll become clear. I do know that I recognise some of my younger self in you. And we're both going through this tedious heartbreak, also.'

Will nodded.

'This'll sound even more crazy,' Wayne said, 'but there have been times when I've been able to influence the outcome of events by my own thinking.'

'Really?' said Will again, and silently: yep; sounds crazy to me. He did not ask for examples, and Wayne thankfully let the subject rest.

*

Wayne set Will up weighing and portioning chicken meat into bags—eight-pound bags for the big male lions and twelve-pound bags for the male Siberian tigers and so on down the line—while he got to work brush-hogging, which meant cutting tall weeds and unwanted sapling sprouts with an industrial mower hooked up to the tractor. Will stood by the fridges, scooping guts onto a scale with rubber-gloved hands, tipping them into plastic bags, sealing them and marking their weight with a permanent marker.

After lunch he called the rental company and arranged to return the car to Columbus for a partial but acceptable refund, and after feeding the animals he and Wayne took a tour of the property and selected an old grey pickup with a missing fender to get Will back on his journey at the end of the month. It had been protected from the weather in the barn and at least turned over when Wayne opened the door with a creak and tried to start the ignition.

'I know a guy we can get a fender from,' said Wayne. 'Shouldn't take much to get her running.'

The next day was Sunday—the day of worship, Wayne said, which turned out to mean that J.T. appeared with religious regularity for a long blues jam. It was fasting day for the big cats, so there wasn't much feeding to do.

After J.T. had left, Wayne offered to drive with Will to Columbus the following morning to return the car. The two of them were sitting on the sofa, eating dinner and watching the news. Will had declared he couldn't eat chicken nuggets again and had driven to town to pick up supplies. He'd made tacos, which was about the only meal he could cook.

'This is fancy,' said Wayne, scraping up mince with a shard of corn shell. He ate sitting hunched forward at the edge of the couch, his plate on his knees and his mouth directly above it.

On the television, the protests in Zuccotti Park continued. Eighty had been arrested now; that was sixty in just three days.

Wayne waved his beer at the screen. 'If it wasn't for the animals, I'd probably drive up there'n join them.'

'Nah,' said Will. 'I'm done with New York.'

'You don't care about the fact that our government is letting this country turn into a tax haven for about ten guys while the rest of us suffer? I mean, don't get me wrong, I don't identify with the *majority* either. They just want their two-car garage and their three kids and their secure office job, and they think as long as they keep their head down and keep on working till they're sixty-five, the government will look out for them. If they choose to drink that Kool Aid, they deserve to get poisoned.'

Will smiled, uneasy. 'That's a bit harsh,' he said.

'I disagree. But that's not my point, anyway. My point is that the government is corrupt. Bankrupt. Out of options. I mean, nine-eleven: just a big show put on by the CIA to start another war or two. To get at all that sweet black gold.'

Oh dear, Will thought.

Wayne set his plate down on the seat beside him. He appeared to be getting warmed up. 'This country has been at war somewhere—doesn't matter where, as long as it's off home soil—continuously since World War One, bar a year or two here and there. And you know why? To keep the weapons industry afloat. Most of Congress are shareholders in the big munitions companies. They profit. *Directly.* From sending young men off to die.'

'Okay, but surely Obama's better than, like, Bush, right? Or than whoever was president when you got sent to Vietnam?'

'That would be Mr Lyndon B. Johnson, when I got signed up. But he was following in the footsteps of Kennedy. Ah, look . . .' Wayne paused with a piece of tomato at the end of his fork. 'They are all the same,' he said slowly, brandishing the fork with lunatic ebullience and dull menace.

Will couldn't be bothered to disagree with him. He was pretty sure that Obama was a better option than Nixon, for example, and who knew what might come next? Some Bush the Third in all probability.

'I was a door gunner on a Huey helicopter in Nam,' Wayne continued. 'And I would've fired more rounds from my M60 in a single hour than all the cops in Littleproud will go through in their whole lifetimes—hell, all the cops in the whole of Ohio. And that was just one gun. Imagine the amount of ammunition that was getting produced!'

Will was curious about the war and Wayne's experiences there, but he was getting worried about Wayne's agitation level and, after the last time, he didn't want to push it. The news was over, replaced by a documentary about the Fukushima meltdown back in March, featuring talking heads and slow-motion archival footage of mushroom clouds.

Will managed to wind the conversation down by staring at the screen and eventually Wayne said goodnight and swayed off down the hall.

It was only his fourth night here, but Will was beginning to understand the erratic graph of Wayne's routine, the short spikes of intense vigour and subsequent dips, and the longer-range downward curve of each day's energy, starting higher than most people's and so declining with greater speed towards the final spike that jolted the attenuated day to an end just after sunset.

—

The following morning began for Will in balmy onanistic RV comfort. His body felt used and tightened by these days of labour and he played out in the frugal afterglow a fantasy of returning home strong and tanned and transformed, his outer form representative not just of his increased virility but of his mind's suddening into the masculinity of experience. He had been thinking, unexpectedly, and with pleasure and too-small guilt, of Justine. He wondered if he would tell anyone about her back home. It was the worst thing he'd ever done, and maybe too bad to brag about—he didn't want to look like a plain jerk—but he couldn't help feeling somewhat proud that he had done something genuinely impulsive and fucked up and complicated.

Lying there in his prone damp droop, he allowed himself to approach in lenient daylight the roiling composite bewilderment of his week in New York City, knowing in some deep and only half-acknowledged part of himself that it had been exactly what he sought in this both hasty and long-dreamed-of quest or flight or tourism: a surfeit of action, event, sense-impression; the trying out of new ways of being, away from those real and imagined observers who thought they had the measure of his far-from-definitive self; the compression of incident and adventure into time with a density offered only by travel or mania; the performance of some deep intensity, which he had long suspected was an element of who he was; the not giving a fuck. The emblems of his days there were almost comic in their clichéd end-times symbolism: the greed and lust and avarice and the coveting of another man's wife; the drugs and sex and food culture and the art that was not for sale and the bright-lit never-ending night-times and the beauty and the money. No, he would not become his father, harping on about this trip until the end of days, but it was okay—wasn't it? or understandable at least—to be satisfied with its shameless brash success. And in his position, would we not tell ourselves the same?

Through the rhomboid window he watched the Canada geese—he knew their name now—flying pennant across the pale blue sky. He heard a car on the stones and thought, Wayne's been out early, and he raised his head, wave and smile held at the ready, but it was a sheriff's car, black with a yellow decal that looked like racing stripes.

The cop looked about Will's age. He stood well back, polite and power-stance-perfected, legs spread and gun butt square and arms crossed at the wrists behind him. Will dressed in a panic and hobbled towards the house with his heels out of his boots, rowing the air with his elbows and with fantasies of masculinity shed behind like his footprints in the wet grass.

He reached the house as Wayne opened the door.

'Mr Gage?' asked the buzz-cut baby cop. He heard Will come up behind him and he swivelled in momentary fright.

'That's me,' said Wayne. He looked grizzled and diminished in the doorframe, barefoot and bare-headed, his hair all askew and his face turned down jowly like an old dog's.

'Sir,' said the cop, righting himself, 'there's been a report of a wild animal sighted loose on your property. A *tiger*, I think they said. So I've been sent out to see if you've had any animals escaped.'

'Oh, hell!' said Wayne. 'I haven't checked the cages yet today. But if it's on my property I'd guess it's likely to be one of mine. Where was it?'

'Not too sure, sir. It was a woman driving past who made the call, so it must have been down by Ridge Road. I didn't see anything myself, though, driving in here.'

'Better check the cages first,' said Wayne. 'I'll get my boots.'

It was Zoya, a juvenile Bengal tiger, who'd dug out of her cage overnight.

'Crap!' said Wayne. 'One goddamn night I don't check the cages. One goddamn Sunday when I'm too damn tired is all it takes.'

'Oh, shit, I didn't even think of it,' said Will.

'We'll have to get the horse float and hitch it to the truck. And get some chicken. She'll be hungry after fasting yesterday.'

The cop had been trailing after them, silent, looking into the rows of cages in frank and wholly understandable amazement. But now he asserted his presence again.

'Sir, you do realise that if a wild animal strays outside of your property I will have to shoot it.'

Wayne riled up, instant as a gas fire. 'Look, officer, I know you're just doing your job, but this is a tame animal. She's basically still a cub. I was bottle-feeding her myself only six months ago. So, I hear you, but if you shoot my tiger . . .'

'Alright, sir, watch yourself. Let's focus on finding the tiger. I'm just letting you know what my orders are.'

'Orders?' said Wayne. 'Whose orders are those?'

'Sheriff's. He said to tell you to bear in mind your situation and don't make it any worse for yourself.'

Wayne seemed at this to pull back from some inner precipice. He beckoned Will to the truck and they drove up to the big shed, where they connected the horse float and Wayne piled into the back a roll of wire with fencing posts attached with which, he said, they could recapture the escapee.

'Not that she can't jump right over it. It's more psychological. Stops her bolting.'

The cop waited, leaning against his car, with his thumb tucked faux-casual into his gun belt.

Wayne stopped the truck by the house and Will ran to grab a bag of chicken from the fridge, and they rolled down the driveway as if on a flat battery, scanning the field.

'Lucky I've been good with mowing lately. If the grass was long we'd be in trouble.'

As they pulled over the rise they saw her by the fence, all fantastic russet-barred against the green. She was sitting longways against the fence line, close to the road, her face turned away towards the paddock opposite in which grazed a big hunk of brown bull, a glorious guy whom Will had admired before, standing statue always, his face an intent comical frown. Tiger versus bull, he thought in dumb internal self-amusement to quell his nervy state.

'There you are,' said Wayne. 'Good girl. You just stay right there.'

They crept on and Wayne stopped and reversed so that the horse float jackknifed across the driveway, its rear facing the tiger. The cop's cruiser perched on the rise, seeming to rock there on the fulcrum.

'I just don't want that son of a bitch to shoot my tiger,' said Wayne. 'He's young, and that worries me. I've seen it too many times in combat. People get scared and they're all keyed up and something startles them and they just shoot—sometimes their own guys.'

He picked up the bag of guts off the floor. 'So. The plan is to make a trail of meat leading up to the float. And set up a perimeter we can close once she gets close.'

The tiger sat peaceful in the pale thin air of the morning. Small white moths or butterflies flittered in the grass like airborne petals.

'You take the chicken and I'll set up the fence,' said Wayne.

'Really? You want me to lay out a trail of chicken towards a humungous tiger?'

Wayne laughed despite the situation. 'She's not going to attack you. But okay, I'll take chicken duty.'

Zoya looked over at them as they set to work. Her tail swept the grass, releasing more of the white moths, but otherwise she did not move. The air was still and Will could hear the bull's soft bellowing across the road. The tiger watched them haul the bale of fencing wire off the lowered tray of the truck and then, with no hurry in her, she raised herself, stretched out from her front paws in the classic yoga pose, and began to make her way along the fence.

'Uh-oh. She's on the move.' Wayne dropped the wire and tore open the bag of chicken parts. 'Zoya!' he called. He grabbed a handful of chicken and began to follow her, crouched and crabwise, making kissing sounds and calling her name, but she did not look at him and broke into a lope across the driveway.

'Shit!' said Wayne. He stood and watched the slow streak of her path along the far border of the property, and then he dropped the fistful of chicken and wiped his hand on the grass.

'What now?' said Will.

'I guess just go after her.'

They drove past the cages again, peering between them to catch sight of Zoya, and then Will saw her further up the hill, moving low and fast, her shoulders the highest point and her head tucked down, the sight of her putting all sleek and powerful human machinery to shame.

'I see her,' said Wayne. 'She's heading up back.'

Will half wished he'd seen her clear the fence to the horse paddock, but was relieved, too, that he hadn't witnessed the death-play power of that leap.

The horses were shying in a clump, ears back and whinnying, and the gold-striped form sloped after them, picking up her front paws one by one like some incarnation of old and antic demonry, and Will experienced again that responding writhe of fear, originating somewhere deep in his low brainstem.

'Is she going to kill the horses?' he asked.

'No. No way,' said Wayne. 'She's just playing tag.'

The cop car crunched up behind them and stopped. Will felt the impatient threat of violence hedging him on both sides, these diametric forces of authority pitted against each other: the new against the ancient; the social against the wild; the learned and costumed and performative against the effortless and oblivious.

Wayne sat watching a moment before he reached for the doorhandle. 'Okay, here's what we'll do. You tip the chicken into the horse trough and then open the gate to the feeding pen. I'll try to drive the horses in there and hope she follows. Once she's in and eating she should calm down and I can get the lead rope on her.'

Will was scared truly shitless, his rectum crawling back up inside itself like a collapsible telescope. He shuffled to the edge of the car seat, scrunching closed the torn bag of chicken guts as best he could. The liquid poured out in a thin bloody stream onto his boot as he slid out of the cab. He mimicked Wayne's hunkered knee-bent haste towards the feeding pen, which was constructed of long wooden poles. There was a good two feet between the first pole and the ground and the same between the next two poles, and he was pretty sure it was a bad idea to drive the tiger in here. Still, he tipped his parcel of clotted viscera into the concrete trough, opened the gate, and ran back to the truck.

Wayne couldn't herd the horses because Zoya was herding them herself, happy as a kelpie whose work is play disguised. She ran the poor creatures in a tight circuit of fear, while she was pure frolic. Wayne trailed hopelessly with the dangling rope, turning and holding out his arms as the little band was urged from corner to corner by the gleeful beast.

Will had to admit that Zoya did not look intent on killing; she frisked after the horses for all the world like a kitten increased a thousandfold in size. This was certainly one of the more eventful days of his life. He thought how sorry Laura would be if he died out here, and this lessened his fear slightly.

As he watched the strange parade, Will had an idea. He would wrap the perimeter wire around the feeding pen so that if Wayne did succeed in running Zoya in there, or she decided to go in of her own accord, which frankly seemed more likely at this point, she couldn't just slip beneath the fence, as uncatchable as if she were greased in butter. He dragged the wire off the truck and rolled it to the pen and tried to push the first post into the hard dirt where the hooves of horses had acted as a compressor. He couldn't get it in more than scratch-deep but he began to unroll the wire anyway.

Wayne saw what he was doing and called out to him, 'Good thinking! There's a toolbox in the back of the truck. Should be a hammer in there.'

Zoya was over the other side of the paddock, far enough away that Will felt safe to turn his back and bend to open the clasp on the metal toolbox and rummage inside for a hammer.

He grabbed a hatchet too and he called out to the cop, sitting smug or coward in his car, 'Help me, would you?' But the cop shook his head, and Will threw the hatchet hard into the dirt and turned back to his task, hammering the first post crooked into the ground as far as it would go, and moving on to the next.

He saw the horses driven by that stripe of living fire towards the fence and saw them panic and divide, some halting, back-stepping, turning to the centre of the field as the others bolted down the boundary, galloping now as Wayne yelped out feeble curses, no longer even trying to follow but simply turning in the centre to watch the passing carousel.

Now two of the horses came towards Wayne and he began to run ahead of them, waving his arms as if to guide them, and he sprinted for the pen, glancing back like a boy running a kite. Behind them was Zoya, giddy with freedom, and the adrenaline rose up in Will, but he kept on unravelling the fence, though it was likely as tiger-proof as a barricade of tissue paper. He was only two-thirds around and he dropped the hammer and continued, not thinking, just dragging open the heavy scroll of wire as waving man and bolting horses advanced.

The horses overtook Wayne, and Zoya bounded up to him and in a quick romp pounced him flat and kept coming. Wayne sat up and began to yell and wave his arms, and Will looked to the destination of his desperate gaze and saw the cop leaning on the shield of his open door, a rifle held up and looking like a boy playing soldier.

The horses ran tempest into the pen and they stalled near Will with a clashing of hooves and a swirl of dust. Will couldn't see past them and he crouched behind the flimsy barrier he had failed to complete and then they reared and whinnied and broke away again, and when Will looked up there was just the tiger standing in the centre of the pen a mere two metres from him, and Wayne was shouting, 'Don't shoot! Don't shoot!'

She had seen the food, and just like that she threw off the chase and padded swish-tailed and shining in the sunlight like a goddess approaching the offering laid out for her, the candles and the flowers and the moon-shaped cakes or the cup of blood cooled to a skin upon the stone altar. She kept her tail neatly held up off the dirt in a soft curve as if it was fashioned out of wire wrapped around with fine velvet fabric. Will crouched still and listened to her eating.

Wayne approached, first fast and then slow, and he unhitched and swung shut the gate, lifting it each time it scraped against the hard ground. Will swivelled on his heels in the dust and looked up at Wayne to see by the cast of his face if they were doomed, but Wayne's eyes were pinned to the cop in fierce defiance. While Zoya lapped from the trough, Wayne squatted down beside her, speaking to her low and loving, and clipped the lead rope to her collar, and only then did the cop lower his weapon.

Still the crisis was not averted. Wayne instructed Will to drive the float around and back it up to the pen so they could coax Zoya in, but the sated tiger would not move, only sat there licking her paws and brushing the blood traces from her whiskers, and it was very clear to Will that the leash was pure symbolism—that if she so desired, she could drag Wayne at the end of it to the edge of the known world. The sun was halfway up the sky and the only effort she would go to now was to twitch away with her long expressive whiskers the big black flies drawn by the gore.

Wayne performed a series of mimed postures of attempted dragging and pushing and levering, but the single outcome was that Zoya added the irritated switching of her tail to the small movements of her contented stubborn basking.

'Look, I don't know what we can do right now,' said Wayne. 'We might have to just wait it out until she gets hungry again.'

'You can't tranquillise her or something?' asked the cop.

'Be my guest,' said Wayne. 'It'll take ten minutes to kick in. We can take bets on which way she bolts.'

As they were debating, Will's phone rang in his pocket.

'It's J.T.'

'Answer it. He might have an idea what to do,' said Wayne.

'Hey, J.T.,' said Will.

'Hey, how's it going? I tried Wayne but no answer. I'm just calling to let you know that Tamsyn gave birth last night.'

'Oh my god, really?' said Will. 'Wayne, Tamsyn had the baby!'

'She did? Congratulations, J.T.!' Wayne shouted towards the phone.

'Mr Gage!' said the cop, lurching up from his false relaxed leaning against the cruiser.

'Um, J.T.,' said Will, 'we've actually got a bit of a situation here . . .'

They waited an eternal-seeming interval, during which Wayne stood half bent, sweating and pale with his hands on his knees, and Zoya rolled onto her side in the dirt, her mouth open in sunlit pleasure, and the cop sat in his car writing out some kind of report or fine. At last, J.T.'s pickup struck the driveway like a match. Will could see the trail of dust and hear the suspension bumping over the ruts, and then he was out and into the makeshift pen with Wayne and Zoya, and Will felt like a coward. But though Zoya clasped J.T.'s outstretched arm in her awesome loving paws and he palmed and roughed her skull with his other hand, their situation was essentially unchanged.

It would have been funny, the one man hauling on the rope and the other pushing the tiger's rump like a mud-bogged car, but the cop was growing tetchy with all his authority unheeded, and he slammed his car door and glanced in quick fear at Zoya and then righted his gaze and told them he was calling an animal handler to come and tranquillise her, and that if she bolted he *would* shoot her.

Wayne's face went dark and he muttered beneath his breath.

'If only Valerie was here,' said J.T. 'This is her baby. She does whatever Valerie tells her. She's probably playing up in the first place because she misses her.'

Wayne produced a bitter scrap of a smile.

'Hey, wait,' said J.T. 'What if we get her on the phone? Maybe if Zoya hears her voice she might cooperate.'

Wayne gave a cowed shrug.

J.T. pulled out his phone. 'Just give us a minute, officer, please,' he said.

And then J.T. turned his phone to speaker and a woman's voice was summoned forth, as full of tender coaxing as any mother's, and as he walked backwards up the ramp, the voice called out, sweet as all the bells and sunrays befitting such a miracle, *Zoya, Zoya honey, come to Momma*, and the tiger rolled upright and padded after the sound like the lamb following the shepherd. Wayne held up his arms to the sky and they were saved, man and beast alike.

As the cop set about issuing his petulant paperwork, Will thought that Valerie must be a pretty incredible woman.

THE FOLLOWING DAY, WAYNE WAS sullen and brooding in his boots. In glum near silence, he convoyed Will to Columbus to return the hire car, cheering only when he spied a drive-thru and pulled in for nuggets. Back home they hurried through the feed and showered and then drove to town to visit Tamsyn and the baby, a little girl whose name was Kaylee.

Mother and baby were still in the hospital, and they waited in the bluish light of the entranceway, where Wayne's pacing repeatedly triggered the automatic doors, until J.T. appeared and showed them up.

Tamsyn sat propped against mountainous pillows, looking drained and purple around the eyes, cradling the little pink and scrunch-faced baby. They bent and kissed her in turn and offered up their *oohs* and *aahs* in awkward feigned appreciation of the generic creature's beauty and perfection. Wayne presented J.T. with a cigar, and J.T. took the baby from Tamsyn and passed her to Wayne. The big man shied visibly as he held her in the stiff cradle of his arms.

'Don't know how to handle a *human* baby,' he said.

J.T. laughed. 'I guess they're all pretty much the same. Just this one's got a little less fur.'

'J.T.,' said Tamsyn. 'Don't compare your daughter to an animal!'

The baby began to fuss, and Tamsyn held out her hands.

'We should leave you to it,' said Wayne. 'Pleasure to meet you, Kaylee.' He pointed to the cigar in J.T.'s shirt pocket. 'Hey, you wanna come smoke that outside for a minute?'

'Sure; why not?'

'Gross. I hope you've got gum,' said Tamsyn. She turned to Will. 'You want a quick cuddle with Kaylee, first?'

'Um, okay. You guys head down, if you like. I'll come meet you.'

Wayne kissed Tamsyn again and steered J.T. paternally to the door with a hand on his shoulder, and Will sat down in the clammy vinyl chair by the bed and received the milk-scented and sweetly grunting Kaylee.

'I can't believe you're a mother!' he said, trying by tone of voice to alter the implicit subtext.

But when he looked up at the new young mother she was quietly weeping, and it was the second time in a week he'd been ambushed into discomposure by the inability of others to keep their emotions properly contained.

'I miss my mum,' Tamsyn wailed.

'Is she coming over to visit?' he asked uselessly.

'She wants to. But she can't afford the ticket right now. Or get time off work . . . Not till after Christmas.'

'That's not that far off.'

'I know. I just want her here *now*.'

Her face was blatant uncomposed in its wet pink childlike need of comfort, and now her own hours-old child began to squall too, its croaky amphibious lungs swelling under Will's incompetent hand, and he tried to hide his dismay while Tamsyn's crying simmered down in necessary if not natural response to her child's. She wiped her eyes and nose and took Kaylee back and began her inevitable apologising.

'I think I've been holding it all in because I don't want J.T. to think I'm not happy,' she said. 'Of course I am! I just always thought my mum would be with me when I gave birth, you know?'

Thank god I am not a woman, was all Will could think.

And yet, alone in the elevator, the smell of newborn baby still palpable upon him, he rode a-roil in mixed unwanted and intractable emotions of his own. She took him back there every time—it was practically all she talked about; the very breath she exhaled was contaminated with nostalgia for that small-town state of maternal and changeless symbiosis. He wondered not for the first time if there was something wrong with him, that he could not look back with fond serene distance on that provincial childhood that he felt as one long stultifying summer afternoon, home from school and not bothering to change out of his uniform, the air unmoving except to carry from the yard the heavy bounce of the ball and the hollow wooden thunk of the backboard and the attenuated springing echo of the metal hoop, and the whoops of his brother and Paul, and from the garage the sound of his father's old indistinguishable kung fu movies played ceaselessly on their stretched loops of tape. For hadn't it been a good childhood—innocuous and free of any real suffering outside the mild too-deeply-felt humiliations of younger brotherhood and the still-nauseating sense of un-belonging that dogged him to his dreams? Why was he flailing still as though webbed in the sticky clinging hostile past that in reality was gone (if not dead, at least neutered passive and inert), engrossed in that frantic clawing dance like a man who has walked in the dark through an orb spider's net of thick and clasping panic-silk? And why did poor Tamsyn repel him so in her happy repetition of the ordinary animal pattern of young incautious fecund reproduction? Why could he not be more like her and happy?

He emerged surly from the cool-lit foyer, shoulders tense and fingertips jammed into the too-tight pockets of his jeans. He looked around for Wayne and J.T. and found them by the red cigar-end that kindled into view across the parking lot. They were standing together, making an unconvincing show of rolling smoke around their puffed-out mouths.

'Congratulations again, J.T.,' he said as he approached.

'Beautiful, isn't she?'

Will nodded, and Wayne thumped J.T. on the back and said, 'You'll be a great dad.'

'Thanks, Wayne. That means a lot.'

'Hell of a time to be bringing a person into the world, though,' said Wayne. 'This country is in deep trouble. I'm talking real Rome-before-the-fall type stuff. And then there's the melting ice caps, if you believe in that kind of thing. Genetic mutation of crops . . .'

Oh my god, dude, shut up, Will thought to himself. The guy has literally just become a father.

'Uh-huh,' said J.T., rolling his eyes at Will. 'You really know how to pick your moment, don't you, Wayne? *Hey J.T., your daughter is going to have a terrible life. Here, have a cigar!*'

'You're right—I'm sorry, J.T.,' said Wayne. 'Normally Valerie would be giving me a swift kick in the shins to shut me up.'

They milled about in silence for a while and Will took a turn of the rank cigar.

'Anyway, I don't think not having kids is the answer, personally,' J.T. said in belated response. 'I think we *need* good people to have kids, to make the world a better place. Who knows? Maybe Kaylee'll be the one to save us.'

Of course she will, thought Will. He'd heard this argument before. Every new parent thought that their child was going to save the planet, while they themselves just sat back and carried on as usual, buying cute outfits and plastic crap for the future Messiah.

Then, out of the darkness itself, it seemed to Will, a man approached them. He was furtive and clearly high. 'Got a cigarette?' he asked.

'Sorry, no,' said Wayne. 'Just this cigar. My friend here has just become a father.'

'Congratulations,' said the guy. He half turned as if to leave, and then turned back. 'Hey, you wanna buy some Oxy?'

'No thanks,' said Wayne. The guy slunk off, and Wayne shook his head and chuckled and held out his hand for the cigar. 'There you go,' he said. 'Welcome to Littleproud, Kaylee.'

—

Will woke the next morning to find Wayne gone. He was glad to have a bit of time to himself; it had been hard work from morning to night since he got here and he figured his pay was sitting at around five dollars an hour—and on top of that, Wayne talked pretty much constantly.

He went over to the house and made coffee with real milk, and toast with quick hot-spread and glistening peanut butter, and then he went back to his trailer and collected all his filthy clothes and put them on to wash, keeping out and pulling on just a pair of shorts that were still unworn since his arrival.

He went and fetched Nala, the soft little biscuit-eared darling he'd by now fallen utterly in love with, and played with her while his clothes washed. She was perfect: her downy fur; her stomach still ghosted with the leopard spots that Wayne had told him all lions were born with; the black tip of her tail and little black-licked ears; the way she tore around the room with her mouth open pink and making sweet involuntary squeaks. He lay on his back on the rug and she dashed at him and raised her front paws and retreated, and he rolled over and grabbed and tussled her, all warm and strong. At last they tired each other out and he gave her a bone to chew in the pen on the patio and he sat and watched her, full of love.

Half an hour later, his bare chest crisscrossed with red scratches, he was hanging out his washing with a great degree of effort, accompanied now by Bubbles the tiger cub, who was pulling at the leash he had looped around his ankle inside Wayne's gumboot.

There was a day moon still in the sky, just an unswept shard in the blue, and the geese flew over making the chattering calls that Will was beginning to recognise. Wayne had told him that Canada geese used to be rare in these parts, all but hunted to extinction, but now they were so common that the state issued permits to blow them up with explosives and to addle their eggs, and the Littleproud Golf Club used a tractor-sized vacuum cleaner to suck up the goose shit from the greens. The order of things was out, Wayne said.

Will heard the sound of a car approaching, and he looked up expecting to see the van, but instead a small red hatchback came into view, driven by a woman. He was at the eastern side of the house, where the clothesline sagged between two weathered T's of wood, and this aspect was in full sight of the driveway, and he realised he looked altogether too eccentrically at home for a tenant of just six days. He hopped his foot out of its too-big rubber boot and slipped the leash from his ankle, pulling Bubbles to heel.

The woman got out; she was small and unsmiling, dressed in jodhpurs, a white collared shirt and brown riding boots. It was an upper-class country look he was familiar with from back home. It reminded him of the prim sadistic mother of his primary school best friend, who had ridden dressage and had featured heavily in his early masturbation fantasies.

The woman leaned against the car and shaded her eyes as she looked up the lawn at him.

He began to walk towards her, pulling Bubbles, who was gnawing at the leash.

'Hi,' he said.

'Who are you?' she replied. 'Where's Wayne?'

'Uh, I'm Will . . . I'm staying here . . . I'm not sure where Wayne is, but . . .' He was all a-panic in his toplessness and his appropriated gumboots and with the small and energetic tiger making sallies for freedom at the leash end. He stopped a few feet away from the woman.

'Well, that's interesting. I'm Valerie. Wayne's wife.'

'Oh my god, *Valerie*?! Shit. Sorry. I thought . . . Wayne said he asked you if it was okay for me to stay here and you were fine with it.'

'This is the first I've heard of your existence.'

'What?! What the hell?'

Valerie looked down and pinched the bridge of her nose in a pained manner.

'I'm just here helping out for a month so J.T. can get a break,' Will said. 'I was there the other day, when you were on the phone. With Zoya . . . I am *so* sorry. I can leave—now, if you like . . . I just don't get why Wayne would say he'd told you if he hadn't.' Will could feel his face reddening with the old familiar flush of humiliation.

Valerie pushed her hips off the car. 'Who in the hell knows why that man does what he does,' she said. 'I really should have stopped being surprised by now. It's fine. I'm only here to ride my horse, anyway. Are you staying in the house?'

'In the trailer over there.'

'Okay, well that's something. I suppose that means you'll be here next week. Wayne's asked me to come out while he visits his mother. I assumed J.T. would be helping with the feeding.'

'No, it'll be me I'm afraid. J.T.'s baby was born on Sunday night.'

'Really?' She softened minutely at this news. 'I'll have to call him. Boy or girl?'

'Girl. Kaylee.'

She made a face. 'Terrible name.'

'I'm really sorry about this,' Will said again, casting his gaze around at the tiger and the washing basket. 'I was just doing some badly needed laundry.'

'It's not a problem.' He caught her glancing at Wayne's gumboots.

On an impulse, he walked forward and stuck out his hand. She shook it, but remained unsmiling. Up close she appeared older, perhaps in her late forties, her face powdered and softly lined. She was tiny but strong-looking, as those horsey women seemed to be. Her eyes were green and shrewd and forthright, and he was intimidated and in response began to think he was not going to like her.

Bubbles was rolling on his back on the ground, clasping the leash in his four paws as a cat clasps a bird, and Valerie leaned down and examined the tag on his collar.

'Bubbles!' she said, smiling for the first time. 'You've grown so big!'

She went off to the barn to fetch her riding gear, leaving Will uncertain and uninstructed, once more reminded that he had no freehold here nor anywhere upon the earth.

He returned the sweet young tiger to his pen and skulked off back to his own, where he folded up his bed and sat at the table and thought that he did not want to be here anymore under these altered and inexplicable conditions. He spent an hour he would never get back staring at his phone, and when he looked out his window he saw her on the ridge of the hill behind the house, a small erect figure on a tall horse, her hips rising and falling from the lap of the saddle, opening and closing a sliver of sky. Of course it brought to mind sex. Then she slipped over the hill as though fleeing from his gaze.

She was gone again by the time Wayne's van rumbled up the driveway, and Will was all jittery with anger and embarrassment. He watched from his trailer as Wayne climbed from the van, and was aggravated further when his employer looked over and saw him and beckoned for him to come out.

When Will reached him, Wayne was unloading some big black garbage bags.

'Bones,' he said. 'Give me a hand, would you?'

Will found he could not act normal, and he blurted out, all sulky petulant: 'So, Valerie was here! She just left. Why the hell didn't you tell her about me? It was really bloody awkward.'

'I did tell her,' said Wayne.

'You can't have. She had no idea who I was when she arrived. She was *clearly* surprised.'

'Well, I don't know why she'd go and act surprised; I certainly told her,' Wayne replied. And yet he looked down as he spoke, like a child caught out in bad behaviour.

Will shook his head and gave the slumped man a baffled frown. What else was he to do?

—

Over the following week his anger dried out and he ceased his analysis of Wayne's strange unnecessary lie; it was something between Wayne and Valerie, and he knew about the petty games played out between couples, for hadn't he observed them all his life?

On Thursday, which marked two weeks at Wayne's Wild Kingdom, Will was woken by polite persistent knocking on his RV door and found Wayne with one boot on the metal step, wearing jeans, a plaid shirt and brown leather jacket, and his mandatory cap.

'Sorry to wake you,' said Wayne. 'I forgot to tell you I'm off to visit my mom today, and I need a ride to the airstrip.'

Will had been dug up out of a deep ditch of sleep and he was dirty with it. He roughed his bed-numb face with his palms, tried to rub away the irritation.

'A bit of notice would've been nice,' he said to Wayne, who nodded in a way that conceded the point while implying that Will was humorous in his rumpled morning temper.

In the truck, Will leaned his head against the jolting strut beside the window and bleared a while until they halted at a drive-thru and Wayne bought them coffee and donuts, and then he sat up and shed his grumps, feeling glad at least that after just two weeks he and Wayne had slipped into a strange familiar intimacy that authorised such displays of unmastered mood.

They drove through Littleproud and out to a small airstrip where windsocks punched the air with a nautical sound.

Wayne pulled the truck into the parking bay, laid down like an asphalt mat upon the cropped grass.

'I could take you for a quick spin before I go,' said Wayne.

'What do you mean?'

'In my plane. This is where I hangar her. I come out most weeks and fly.'

Will knew his face registered surprise, but he hoped it wasn't obvious that the last thing he wanted this morning was to go up in a light aircraft with his volatile new friend.

'We don't have to do it today,' Wayne said. 'I should get going, anyway. It's a hell of a lot of fun, though.'

'I'm not much of a daredevil,' Will said.

'Who said anything about daredevil? Daredevil is landing a Huey in a hot zone in the jungles of Vietnam using the rotor as a tree lopper. This is just a joyride. But I swear I won't pull any stunts. You do know I've been flying for forty-six years? I still do charter flights every now and then. My flight hours probably add up to more than you've been alive.'

Will laughed and asked Wayne how long he would be gone.

'Just three nights.'

'And when will Valerie get here?'

'This afternoon. I hope she remembers how it all works.'

Will watched Wayne walk into a demountable building and then along the asphalt path towards the hangars, and he kept watching as the little plane trundled out and wobbled in place, its engine climbing through decibels to a deafening shrill that buffeted the air in waves. It fumbled forward to the runway, made a short desperate dash and hunkered into the sky. He caught sight of Wayne's face through the cockpit window, looking relaxed and in control, a headset microphone at his chin.

*

Back at the house, Will killed time until he heard Valerie's car arrive. He was nervous after their unfortunate first meeting. She hauled a red suitcase from the boot and he shook her hand, took the bag and trailed her flat beige ass through the doorway.

She was already across the room at the cage when he entered the lounge room. The monkeys were making a noise he hadn't heard before, smacking their lips with a kissing sound, and Valerie was saying over and over again, 'My babies, oh, my babies, I've missed you,' and then there was a leap and skirmish of black fur and they were in her arms and she was crying and their fragile limbs were all about her, their fingers worrying at her like those of anxious children, reassuring themselves that she was solid and the same in all her parts, hair, shoulders, ears and face, and she leaned back and examined their strange and loving faces while Will stood forgotten and moved by the certain mutual love between the forbidding Valerie and her animal children.

'I've got some treats for them in the car,' she said. 'Would you mind getting the box in the front? I'm a little encumbered.' She gestured with her chin to the living monkey cloak that enrobed her torso, and she pulled the key from her pocket and tossed it over.

Will was put out, even mildly incensed, but nevertheless complied.

When he returned to the house, the suitcase was gone and she had vanished, but he could hear the monkeys chattering somewhere deep in the section of the house where he had never been.

He put the box of fruit on the bench, and she reappeared and thanked him and said that she would take a shower and retreated down the hallway once again, surreal in silhouette with her dark animal freight like a woman set upon by demons, like something from Goya's black paintings.

The place smelled different, marked like scat by the scent of her perfume. It seemed more homey, he could admit that, but he felt both shy and resentful nonetheless. He had been made intruder, and he rattled around useless and irritant like the one-cent coins this country inexplicably retained. What was he doing, stalled here against his resolution like a stilled shark? It was not good for his head, and neither was the hour he'd spent on Facebook like a window-haunting pervert.

And then, like the very saviour, J.T. arrived. 'Is she here already?' he asked.

'Yeah.' Will grimaced. 'She's having a shower. You know, she came here the other day while Wayne was out, and it turns out he hadn't told her about me at all. She had no fucking idea who I was. And she was clearly pissed off about me being here. It was *fucked*.'

J.T. bent his forehead into his hand. 'Oh, Wayne!' he said. 'What was he thinking?'

Will shrugged.

'Look,' said J.T., taking in Will's distress in his quiet way. 'I need to talk to her about some stuff, and I wanted to help out with the feed today 'cause it's been a few months since she's been here. Just to make sure everything goes okay, and you're not put in a shitty situation or anything. And check the cages, too. That escape last week got me worried. It's not like Wayne to slip up like that.'

'Okay, thanks, that sounds good,' said Will, relieved.

'So, I was thinking,' J.T. continued. 'Why don't you take the afternoon off? Go have a couple of beers at The Shack or whatever.'

'Really?' said Will, not wanting to sound too eager.

'Absolutely.'

'Should I wait till she's out and let her know?'

'No need. I'll talk to her.'

Will spent an aimless afternoon at The Shack, drinking slowly and trying not to feel like a freak as he watched Erin work.

'How's the Wild Kingdom?' she asked him as she passed.

'Pretty strange, I have to say.'

She raised her eyebrows but didn't stop to talk.

He sat there formulating the stories he could tell her—the dramatic escape of Zoya and the trip to the evil chicken factory for a *literal ton* of guts, and the sawing up and carrying on his lap of the roadside deer—but he didn't get a chance; she was moving constantly like a bee among the table-flowers, and then it was getting close to dinner service and the place was almost full, so he gave up and left, picked up some more beer, and headed back to Wayne's—or Valerie's, as he supposed he should think of it for now.

There was an open bottle beside him as he drove through the Klein blue dusk and there were deer about so he took it gently and was thankful not to collide with any of these creatures of such mixed metaphor, symbol of exalted nature and the saw-hacked violence of meat in one heartbreaking package—like we all are, he philosophised as he swept along the shadowed buckeye corridors of Ohio.

*

The first thing to greet him through the knock-and-call front door was the smell of home cooking, and it brought with it all the simple consolations of the world and it had been so long since he had felt consoled.

Valerie was in the kitchen, wearing blue jeans and a white singlet, her hair wet, her small square feet bare, their nails painted red. The half-circle of her upper chest was flat and sun-speckled and the top ribs visible where they met at the centre-line. She had a beer open on the counter.

'Hey,' she said, and her tone was so different: relaxed and even welcoming. 'I was wondering when you'd be home. Dinner's almost ready.'

There was a pot of red sauce on the stove and one of boiling water, and spaghetti waited upright in a tumbler like a bunch of dried grass.

'Do you need a shower or anything?' she asked.

'Maybe.'

'You go for it. Dinner'll be ready in fifteen.'

'Okay. Thanks for cooking. I've had enough chicken nuggets the past two weeks to last a lifetime.'

Valerie laughed. 'It's a pleasure. It's nice to be home. Beer?'

'Thanks,' he said, looking down at her feet as they moved across the slate floor.

The monkeys were back in their cage, sleeping in a huddle, and didn't make a sound as he passed.

Under the shower, he saw lightning through the open window and the thunder was right behind it and explosion-loud, and he heard the monkeys cry out. The clouds had been piled up between the hills all afternoon like apples in a bowl, and they must be right above them now. The window blew wide with a crash and Will felt the gust through the heat of the water. It was a luscious sensation, the heat and the cool, and he put his face under the shower and through his water-closed lids perceived another flash of lightning. Before the rend of thunder, he heard the sliding door growl open and bang against the frame, and as he looked out the window he saw Valerie dash past with the laundry basket. He shut off the water and that was when the lights went out.

He fumbled himself back into his jeans and down the hallway to the open door, colliding with Valerie, who was rushing basket-first inside.

'Did we lose the lights?' she asked.

'Looks like it.'

The only glow was from the gas rings in the kitchen. Her phone screen lit up and she turned on the torch.

There was another clatter from the timpani clouds and the monkeys screeched again in the dark. Rain began to splat on the patio bricks.

'Phew, got to the sheets just in time,' said Valerie. 'I wonder if we should bring the cubs inside? Their pen turns into a mud bath when there's a big storm and then we'll have to wash them all. They get a bit spooked by the thunder too, bless them.'

She looked at him, screen-lit from beneath her sharp chin.

They pulled the leashes from the hook by the door and ran barefoot across the patio and up the grassy slope as the clouds lit up again, crouched alien there above the roof, another flash illuminating the dam as if the earth's pale eye were flickering open in sleep.

They leashed Nate and Nala and led them to the house as the smell of rain stirred up all around them. They had just leashed Bubbles and Bam-Bam when it came in a line like machine-gun fire and they ran, leaving Charlie bedraggled and butting at the gate, and by the time Will returned with him grappled in his arms, both were drenched.

Inside the house there was a crowd of dark timid cubs waiting for their brother and a clamour of monkeys. He could see the flashing beam as Valerie came with a proper torch down the hallway carrying a pile of towels.

They bundled up the final soaked docile cub and rubbed him dry, and then the tigers, while Will's hair dripped into his eyes. The cubs began to tear about the room like dogs after a bath, wrestling on the rugs in the yellow circle of the torch.

Will pulled off his t-shirt and wiped his head and chest with a towel that smelled of animals.

'Shit, the pasta,' said Valerie, the torch beam flashing over the wall.

Valerie lit candles and produced a bottle of red wine and they sat down to their dinner while the cubs churned around them, and the chaos and excitement of the night permitted a certain intimacy to glimmer between them.

'I'm sorry about the other day,' said Valerie.

'No, *I'm* sorry!' said Will.

And so by midnight they were somehow friends, this beleaguered boy and woman, and Valerie was tipsy and talkative, telling stories about the early days and how they kept the first animals with them in the house and how after a year they had to get the floors completely redone and then they put the lions out in an old chicken run from which they escaped constantly. She told Will she planned to move back to her family's ranch in Wyoming and train horses and maybe start a riding school.

Will realised that the company of this woman was something completely new to him. She must be only ten years or so younger than his mother, but she seemed so much younger, and so obviously not maternal. Not to human children, at least. She was still at the centre of her own life, still living vibrant and engaged in her continuing story, interested in it, and in herself. There was nothing she had put aside as no longer relevant or seemly. She even flirted with him a little, or was habitually flirty in her manner, perhaps. She was like the friend of an older sister, though he had not had any such interaction with his older sister's friends, who had all become mothers young and were somehow lost to their own selves, their eyes trained on their babies.

'I wonder if Wayne's got any weed stashed around the place,' she said.

'Yeah, he would. We smoked some on Sunday.'

She went and found it and rolled an expert joint, and they stood in the patio doorway, their thin smoke battered away by the rain, and then returned to the table.

They had put the cubs into the toddler pen, where they were jumbled in a heap, and the monkeys too were quiet, preening each other lovingly on the sofa. Valerie leaned back in her chair, her calves resting on the corner of the table, her bare feet crossed at the edge of their little circle of warm light.

The way she asked him questions and listened, nodding as he spoke, was flattering, he had to admit. She seemed to take him seriously as an equal partner in exchange, and it made him proud and shy and then, as the weed worked on him, simply proud, and he began to talk with an ease and earnestness he hadn't felt since his last New York coke high.

He talked about Laura, of course. But more than that. He told her about his family; about his unwilling infantile father, who had nonetheless passed on to Will certain traits that were central to who he was, chief among them the scornful terror of being conventional, but also a reverence for foreign and 'superior' cultures, though he saw his father's worship of Europe, and of the Aquarian hippydom of the late '60s and early '70s, as helplessly naive. And about the strange random pattern of his parents' procreation, how they'd had his sister Grace when his father was nineteen and his mother just eighteen, after his father was recalled ignominiously from his one and only overseas adventure to make an honest woman of literally the girl next door, and how they'd had his brother Tom eleven years later, and then, five years after that, when they were in their mid-thirties and Grace was sixteen and they should have ceased making their lives more difficult with such grit tenacity, they had Will, the last mistake, as he secretly and cruelly referred to himself.

'That certainly is a strange way to go about making a family,' said Valerie.

'Yeah, it sure is,' Will replied. He remembered the time his father had told him, so offhanded, about the stillborn baby girl that came after Grace, and how his mother hadn't wanted to try again for years and years; how she—his mother—had never once spoken of it. He decided not to mention it to Valerie; some things are buried just too shameful deep and will not consent to the air. He hadn't even told Laura about it.

Valerie was standing again at the screen door with a cigarette in her hand and a monkey on her hip, while outside the commotion of clouds had abated and the rain fell without haste but still with no sign of quitting. The lights had not so much as flickered.

'I feel like both my parents were seekers, in some way,' Will went on with woozy sudden insight. 'But it's like they were looking for totally opposite things and it was only the seeking itself that they had in common, and I've inherited that from them, but in a really confused and mixed-up combination of the two of them.'

'How so?'

'I dunno . . . My mum's super religious. More and more she just lives her whole life according to what the Bible says, or what her priest tells her to do. She wants that structure, so she doesn't have to make any decisions herself, you know? And then Dad . . . he used to be really into reading all this philosophy and Eastern religious stuff when I was younger. I mean, it was a total mishmash of stuff that made no sense—aliens and shit, even.' He paused, laughed, looked at Valerie, but she was just nodding still, intent and apparently absorbed by his doped intense discoursing. 'Yeah, Dad claims he saw a UFO when he was a teenager and it changed his life. He, like, *firmly* believes they exist. But it's like, he's got all these beliefs that he dabbles in, but really he's just pretty much given up on actually *doing* anything at all. He never travelled after that one time, never had a career. He's been unemployed for *years*. So it's like they both had this drive to . . . to find some kind of *meaning*, I guess. But I think the uncertainty was too much for them both. Mum decided she needed someone else to make all her decisions for her, and Dad just sat down on the couch and . . . stayed there . . .' He raised his hands as if to say, *What can you do?* and brought them down on his thighs with a slap.

'How fascinating,' said Valerie. 'I'm impressed that you've thought about it so deeply. And what about you? You said you've inherited some of that?'

'I guess I feel like I've inherited that *seeking* thing from them. I don't know what else to call it. I think a lot. Way too much. But when I look at them . . . I don't know . . . what am I trying to say? I feel like it's important to be able to acknowledge the ultimate meaninglessness, or lack of answers. Kind of look it in the face, you know? Not just run away from it however you can. I guess that's why I admire Wayne . . . He seems like he really thinks for himself and actually takes some kind of responsibility for making his life . . . different. Or just his own, I guess.'

'Mmm,' said Valerie. At the mention of her husband, she picked up the bottle and found it was empty. 'Come to the basement with me,' she said. 'I want to keep talking, but we need more wine and I don't want to go by myself.'

She swayed a little as she led the way down the hall. Will was expecting to be taken into some new unglimpsed section of the house, but she took him to the laundry and, passing him the torch, pulled up the rag rug to reveal a trapdoor, which she raised and propped with a wooden strut.

'Come around,' she said. The conical torch beam lit a staircase of untreated pine that led down for all Will knew into some kind of dungeon or gimp room.

She went first in the dramatic re-enactment lighting, all scalpel chiaroscuro, and he thought, I'm glad it's her I'm following down here, or this would be actually terrifying.

'Okay, I'm down,' Valerie called.

Will held the torch in one hand and the plank railing in the other and descended. Valerie's serious face was waiting for him, and if he thought briefly in that moment of kissing her it was only because he was twenty-two and sex was as present to him as oxygen.

She held out her hand for the torch, but he was already and instinctively minesweeping with the yellow beam, and what it showed as it broke into particles at its furthest reach made him utter a hushed syllable of shock as the light moved first over a survivalist paradise of tinned goods and gasmasks and plastic flagons of water and then onto the guns, a whole wall of them lined up on racks: rifles and pistols and what looked like machine guns, though he knew nothing at all about firearms.

'Uh-huh,' said Valerie from the darkness. 'Those are the guns.'

'Jesus Christ!'

His idea of Wayne shuffled and reordered itself, and Will felt real fear gust through him.

'Uh-huh,' said Valerie again. 'And those are just the ones he could show licences for. The rest got seized in the raid. I tried to tell him to get rid of them, but do you think he would listen to me? And then he expects me to stick by him while he goes to prison? For no good reason—just pig-headed dumb ego.'

Valerie took the torch from him and swung it away to a shelf of wine in the other corner of the room.

'There was a raid?' said Will to the darkness, and in the midst of his shock, he felt like a total idiot, too, confessing his admiration of Wayne when he clearly knew shit about the guy. This was not just a mildly troubled veteran. Not just a man going through a tough divorce. This was someone preparing for Armageddon, though whether to survive or initiate it was currently unclear.

Valerie turned back to him. 'It was the most terrifying thing I've ever experienced. I will *never* forgive Wayne for putting me through that.'

'God, I can't even imagine . . . When's his trial? He hasn't told me anything. I only know about it from J.T. and Tamsyn.'

'Seriously?' She let the light drop and made a noise of frustration. 'I honestly can't keep up with his lies,' she said. 'What does he think is going to happen? Hold on, let's get out of here.'

She crouched and picked out a dusty bottle and Will climbed back out of the thick darkness and held out a hand for Valerie, who stumbled a bit as she stepped into the lesser darkness of the laundry, where the light from the candles in the kitchen wavered dully in the doorway and the monkeys waited, chittering, for the object of their adoration.

'I'm out of practice,' she said. 'Haven't smoked in months.'

Back at the table with their glasses very full, she told him the story of the terrifying raid. There had been an informant, she said, who was sent by the FBI and who befriended Wayne, pretending to be a veteran too, and an animal lover, and he had eventually convinced Wayne to sell him a gun illegally.

'I told him if he kept selling guns I was going to leave him, but he didn't listen,' she said. 'You can't *imagine* how frightening it was. They broke the door down at five am.'

The FBI had seized a few unlicensed guns, one of which was a machine gun Wayne's father had brought back from World War II, and which had never been fired, but they did him for it anyway, and for selling the gun to the informant, because his arms dealer licence had expired. He was currently on bail and he was going to take a plea so that Valerie was not charged as co-owner of the property. His sentencing was coming up at the end of the month, and he was likely to go away for up to a year.

'A year?!' Will said. 'J.T. said he might not even go to jail at all.'

'Yeah, that's probably what Wayne told him. He's in complete denial. His lawyer thinks he's likely to get twelve months.'

'What will happen to the animals?'

'I don't know,' she said, looking down. 'We'll probably have to give most of them up. There's no way I can look after them by myself.'

'Oh no!'

'I know. And Wayne has absolutely no plan, of course. He'll probably leave it up to me to find homes for them once he's inside. I hate him for that.'

Valerie explained to Will that Wayne had been exposed to Agent Orange in Vietnam, and that the military would not acknowledge it; that was probably why they couldn't have children, she said. Over time, he had become increasingly bitter and vocal in his criticism of government and the military because of being drafted and what the war had done to him.

'Wait,' said Will. 'He was drafted? He told me he signed up to go to Vietnam. After a bad breakup.'

'Well, I don't know why he'd tell you that. He was drafted. Nineteen years old. Twenty when he got there.'

'Why on earth would he lie about something like that?'

Valerie raised her hands. 'You've seen it; he can be free with the truth. Or sometimes just confused. Like how he said he'd spoken to me about you staying here. It could be he thought he did and then forgot.'

She told him that Wayne had started sending crazy letters to the governor and to his former commanders and to journalists and had got himself on various watchlists—unless that was another one of his paranoias. Still, no one liked a decorated veteran speaking out against the military, and then there was some minor tax fraud, so the IRS was after him too, and the animals, which local law enforcement couldn't stand, but could do jackshit about, and *then*, on top of it all, the illegal sale of guns, which Valerie said he'd done more than once, even sometimes trading them for animals.

Will shook his head.

'It's just all so insane!' he said. 'It's like something out of a movie!'

Valerie watched his face across the candle-flicker and the dirty plates and she thought, this kind of life is utterly unknown to him; he is a sweet boy from a good and law-abiding family and these purlieus of lawlessness and the kinds of men drawn to guns and fast machines and racing down the periphery of suicidal speed are as foreign to him as danger, and she felt a pang of something like envy and the keening loss of the years she had spent in the company of fear, a kind of counterweight or ballast, until she could no longer stand to be the living symbol of simultaneous ambivalent stifling and solace. And she thought that if her stillborn son had come into the world, he would not have turned out sweet like this boy, and that it was probably lucky, after all.

The next morning Will and Valerie were shy around each other, two strangers who had shared the intimacy authorised only by dark or drink or crisis—in this case all three. Will had woken on the sofa at 2 am when all the lights had blared back on. He couldn't remember falling asleep. He'd dragged himself out to his trailer to find his bed still folded away and so had gone back to the sofa and woke again in daylight with a terrible mouth to see Valerie in the kitchen, wearing a white robe of the kind found in hotel closets, and he could tell that she had been looking at him while he slept. He sat up and stretched his arms above his head and smelled the wine-sweet odour coming off his skin.

Valerie walked over and handed him a mug of black coffee and set the half-and-half on the table. 'Storm's passed, at least,' she said.

She left the room and returned dressed in riding gear, and she leaned against the fireplace and eyed him over the rim of her mug where he sat crouched over his own.

'We don't have to discuss it right now,' she said, 'but we should talk about what I told you last night.' She began to pick at a dried paint drip on the lip of the mantelpiece, chipping it away with her nail. 'I'm just not sure if you should let Wayne know that you know. I mean, he really should have warned me if he didn't want me to say anything. I just assumed . . .'

'I'm not planning to say anything,' said Will. 'To be honest, I'm a little bit terrified of him after last night.'

'*Don't be!*' said Valerie. 'Please. There's absolutely no reason to be scared of Wayne. I know the guns are . . . confronting, shall we say? But he is *absolutely* not a violent person. Completely the opposite. He's an adrenaline junkie, sure. A narcissist, maybe. But not violent. In fact, when he came back from the war he swore he'd never hurt another living thing again for the rest of his life.'

'Okay, well that's good to hear.'

Valerie pushed off from the wall. 'Like I said, we don't have to discuss it now. I just wanted to flag it. I'm going for a ride.'

—

Will wasn't sure where they would go from the intensity of the previous night, and if that strange easy closeness between them had been an illusion, but it seemed over the following days that they had indeed become friends. Will liked to watch Valerie riding around the property, so calm and competent on the back of a tall horse, to see her with her monkey children clustered about her, the three of them taking so much loving comfort in one another. She brushed them with a wire cat brush that made them sink their heads down with pleasure, and she sang them quiet songs that made them calm, or loud songs that made them screech and leap about. She was some kind of celestial centre to whatever was about her, and Will could see how Wayne—perhaps the most untamed of all the animals who inhabited this troubled home—would float away without her like so much space junk.

They shared a more sober dinner on Friday night, and on Saturday morning Will drove to the chicken factory while Valerie looked for a house in town. She had spent the past months at her family's ranch in Wyoming, and now she was staying with a friend in Littleproud and looking for a short-term rental while she waited for the outcome of Wayne's trial and worked out what her next steps might be. She was forty-nine and she wanted to make a break from her old life. Will admired her for it.

Valerie said she would be out that night; she didn't say where. Will thought it might be nice to have the place to himself, and it was, for a brief half-hour, as he sat with a beer after the day's long, rough and still astounding story-worthy work of feeding the menagerie. It was dusk, and he sat by the creche, where the warm air smelled of grubby young animals and the rank dust they stirred about in their noisy play. He rested on his elbow on the slope of grass and caught the first star at the very moment it appeared to switch on, there, against the depthless pale. But soon, alone, he felt the haunting presence of Laura, and though he knew that it was all on his part, that she was far away and not even thinking of him, still it unsettled the twilight and the peace like any haunting, and he shivered and stood and went inside for a jumper.

He had been thinking of her more since the conversation with Valerie, her sisterly presence allowing him to approach such thoughts within a zone of female safety and comfort. It had been almost a month exactly since the breakup, and though he felt himself still within the epicentre of the crisis, in truth his heart and body were beginning the rescue or betrayal of healing against his mind's stubborn holding on. Part of what he clung to was a version of himself, a twin shadow wholly unglimpsed till Laura had kissed it awake like some fairy tale prince: a part or double who had done and said and felt things in the wild privacy of love, where the mind ceased its cruel self-surveillance with a feeling of unutterable relief; things that the tight and serious boy he had been before would never have done or said or felt and would have scorned as sentimental (the very worst thing to be accused of being). He could not even recall them now without that swift clamping down of sneering protective contempt, and they brought with them a hushed sad yearning because he had never thought he could let himself go like that and it had been the nearest thing to freedom he had known—far nearer than the indiscriminate yea-saying and release of his New York bender. Yet he recalled them nonetheless: the way he'd cupped her face with such unguarded ardour as they kissed; how he'd looked so bold and unwavering into her eyes; the words he'd written in her birthday card; all the times he'd said to her, *I'm so happy right now*, keeping nothing aside for safety—and the images were scalding in their humiliation, for he had shown her all he had, and she had judged it insufficient.

Aardvark

Baboon

Cat

Dog

Elephant

Fox

Giraffe

Hyena

I . . . I . . . Iguana

Jaguar

Kangaroo

Lion

. . .

When he fell asleep at last, he dreamed not of Laura, nor of this dream-weird place in which he had washed up, random stranger or fated guest, but of his childhood home. He approached the door and turned the unlocked handle and entered, only to find it dark and abandoned, the living room just as it had always been, in its disjunction of ugly pragmatism and minor floral indulgence—the wheeled plastic computer table still in the corner beneath the flouncy curtain, the wood veneer shelf beside it still filled with the black ring binders with date-marked spines in which his mother recorded the household budgets, bills and taxes. He wandered through the empty rooms and found the back door open and he knew that he had missed some terrible exodus; that he would never see his family again.

ON SUNDAY MORNING THE SKY was newborn blue and without cloud and Valerie went around to all the cages and Will went with her, and he watched her as she spoke to every creature and they hurried forth to greet her. She told them she was leaving again but that she would see them soon, and in his new knowledge of the likely fate of this broken animal family, Will found her leave-taking unutterably sad. She opened the cage of her baby Zoya and the almost-grown tiger sprang up and embraced her, its paws draped heavy across her shoulders and Valerie's face reaching only to the soft curve of the tiger's chest, and he saw the animal's confusion and loss when she stepped back out, crying silently, and locked the cage once more.

Valerie exchanged numbers with Will and told him to stay in touch, to call her any time and to let her know how Wayne was doing, if he didn't mind. And then, with her red suitcase and a box of items she was taking from the house, she left. All morning the monkeys clung together and made a quiet bereft cooing like doves.

*

After lunch, Will drove back out to the airstrip to collect the master of this blighted realm. By the time they swept back down the final swoop of the hill, where the gentle plunge of the road coincided in such a satisfying way with the clearing of the hilltop woods, the view spreading itself like hands, the sky was covered in small clouds, the blue mere negative space between them, and Will observed that the firmament of Wayne's soul seemed likewise clouded. He had not smiled as he walked towards his own chauffeured van from the field where he had lately landed with the appearance of being sucked gradually towards the earth, and his face was once again all convex arches and his hair beneath his cap a slick that made Will think of armpit hair after a shower.

Will felt an agitation of the guts, the shift in energy like a barometric change, but he told himself it was more than partly his own anxiety and new awareness of Wayne's impending fate.

'How was your mother?' he asked, and as he uttered the question he appreciated anew the poignancy of the visit.

Wayne sighed mightily and did not reply for a full-felt minute. 'She's not real well,' he said at last. 'Not sure just how many more visits I'll get with her.'

'I'm so sorry,' said Will.

After another interval of silence, Wayne spoke again. 'How did you enjoy your time with my wife?'

Will glanced over, realising that he had stumbled unprepared upon some new impediment of suspicion or jealousy, which he had omitted entire from his inner list of anticipated obstacles in the converse between himself and his chicaning friend.

'Um, it was fine,' he said. 'She's nice.'

Wayne narrowed his eyes at Will, nodded, and did not pursue the subject.

When they pulled up to the gate, Wayne got out and walked back towards the road. Will turned a startled shoulder, but he was only checking the mailbox. He opened and shut the gate and sat back in the van, all the while peering at and turning and holding up to the light a letter in a yellowed envelope that must have sat in some drawer somewhere until the lick-and-seal adhesive had hardened to varnish, for it was stuck down at the back by two strips of masking tape that were torn off too long and overlapped the front side of the envelope with their ragged ends. Between these two torn ends of tape was handwritten the name of the addressee: *Wayne Gage*.

'What's this?' said Wayne, leaning back in his seat but leaving the door open.

'No idea,' said Will.

'Did you see anyone deliver it?'

'No. But there's no way I could see from the house . . . Wayne, the door.'

'Did you check the mail while I was away?'

'No. I actually didn't even notice the mailbox until just now.'

'What about Valerie?'

'I don't know. Wayne, the door.'

Wayne pulled his legs in and slammed the door and sat picking at the end of one of the strips of tape with his stubby nails until he got the envelope open. He drew out a piece of blue-lined paper, marked red along its top edge where it had been torn from one of those flimsy wax-bound notepads. He unfolded it and held it in his lap and read.

Will kept glancing over as he steered; he could see that it was handwritten and short, but he was only able to read again Wayne's name, printed at the top in squareish capitals, and then he veered onto the grass in shock as Wayne punched his fist into the metal door of the glove compartment.

'Whoa, what the . . .'

'Son of a bitch!' Wayne shouted. He crumpled the letter into a ball in his other hand and shook his fist in pain. Blood was beading up across his knuckles, and he pressed the clenched ridge to his mouth.

'Did you write this?' Wayne said, looking down at the crushed paper in his hand.

'What?' said Will. 'No! What?!'

'Are you sure?'

'Of course I'm sure! What does it even say?'

'It says . . .' Wayne stopped short and his face contorted for an alarming moment and then righted itself. He opened his thin lips and a strange inhuman squeak came out, like that emitted by a rusty hinge. He lifted his undamaged hand, large and haired to the wrist, and he pressed it flat against the roof of the van as a drunk man palms a wall to halt the nauseating gyre of the earth. There was a slight performative edge to this gesture, and Will was aware that his sympathies were elsewhere at present than with this man absorbed entirely by his pain. On the heels of this thought came a clear and ugly image of his own staged paltry demonstration of heartbreak and self-involvement, which had brought him to this place.

'It says,' repeated Wayne, his voice reclaimed from rust, 'that my wife has been unfaithful to me.'

'What? With who?'

'Doesn't say. Do you have any idea? You're the one who's just spent three days with her.'

'Wayne . . .' Will recognised the significance of the moment and he brought his voice to a spirit-level calm. 'I *promise* you, I have no idea about any of this.'

Back in the house, Wayne made Will produce a sample of his handwriting in both capitals and cursive, to which the young man submitted out of some complex of embarrassment and the indignation of the wrong-maligned, before Wayne would be satisfied that he was not the author of the letter.

Then, even worse, Wayne sighted the neat half-dozen empty wine bottles set beside the bin as if waiting for a bowling ball to fell them.

'You two obviously had a good time,' he said. He picked up a bottle and scrutinised the label. 'Are you sure that nothing out of order happened here?'

'Wayne!' said Will. 'Dude. No offence. Valerie is an attractive lady, but I'm twenty-two. She's literally old enough to be my mother. So, *no.* Nothing *out of order* happened. And I swear to you she didn't mention anyone else being in the picture either, so if that's your next question . . .'

He wondered then about the 'friend' whose house Valerie said she would be staying in until she found a rental. But fuck it, who cared anyway? She had left Wayne, and he had to accept it.

Wayne put the bottle back down on the slate floor with a thunk.

'Look,' said Will, taking a single step towards the wretched man, who seemed caught in a frothing stationary tug between rage and grief, a piece of flotsam bobbing at the point at which two currents meet and churn. 'I swear. I don't know anything about this letter. Or about Valerie.'

'Alright,' said the ghost of Wayne at last. 'I believe you.' He looked again at the letter, spread out crumpled on the table beside the smooth document of Will's writing for paranoiac comparison. 'I need a plan,' he said.

'What kind of plan?'

'To find out the truth.'

Will scrunched his face at Wayne. 'I know it's super upsetting,' he said. 'But—'

'*Super upsetting*?'

'What I'm saying is, you don't *know* if it's even true. What if it's just someone trying to mess with you, for some reason? *And*, I just think that if you actually want to patch things up with her, then getting all hardcore and possessive is probably not going to be the best strategy, you know?'

Wayne looked away. He removed his leather jacket and draped it over the back of a chair and then he simply nodded and turned and lumbered off down the hallway like a tired old bear.

—

Despite the darkening of Wayne's soul, the days went on as usual: check and clean and repair the cages; replenish the water; cruise for roadkill; fetch and bag the chicken; feed the menagerie; play with the babies. Then, one night as they were sitting after dinner, picking corn from their teeth and drinking whiskey and watching the nature channel at Wayne's insistence because, he declared with showy gloom, he no longer cared to stay informed about the world's sad and interminable problems, there came the sound of a car approaching up the driveway and a brief attenuated sweep of headlights that shone in through the front window and then extinguished.

'That'll be Colton,' said Wayne.

'Who's Colton?'

'A guy I'm buying something off of.' Wayne pushed himself up from the sofa and muted the television, but he waited where he was through the sound of the car door slamming and only moved when the knocking started.

Will collected the dinner plates from the coffee table and took them to the kitchen, unsure whether he was expected to depart for his trailer.

Wayne returned, followed by a tall, terribly thin man, holding a carrying crate such as might be used to transport a pet cat.

'This is Will,' said Wayne. 'He's staying here at the moment. Helping me out around the place.'

Seeing the stranger, Cissy and Tootsie took up their old scared racket-making, and Will felt a bit of an old hand, no longer the newcomer.

'I'll get a blanket,' said Wayne. 'Drink, Colton?'

'Sure,' said Colton. He ran his fingers through his greasy, impressively long black hair. It was very *metal*, Will thought, though maybe, in the context of the checked shirt and blue jeans cinched in at the waist with a big-buckled leather belt, it was simply redneck.

Wayne disappeared to fetch a blanket and Colton looked around in obvious jittery unease. Will wondered if he was afraid of Wayne.

'Would you like a beer? Whiskey?' Will said, feeling like the wife.

'Beer'd be great,' said Colton. 'Damn, those apes are loud.'

Wayne returned and flung the blanket over the cage and the sound faded out.

'Should I go?' said Will. 'I can head out to the trailer if . . .'

'No, no need,' said Wayne. 'I trust you.'

Trust me? thought Will. What's actually happening here?

'Let's take a look at her, then,' said Wayne.

Colton picked up the carrying case and opened the door and Wayne leaned forward, his face restored to the boyish enthusiasm that had been lacking since the day of the letter. Colton reached in and pulled out a tiny black creature, not much bigger than a kitten.

'Awwww,' Wayne sighed. He held out his hands and Colton deposited the cowering thing into them and Wayne drew it to his chest. Then he opened his hands, and Will saw the face of a baby monkey, its little eyes wide and terrified.

'Oh my god,' said Will. 'It's tiny!'

'Isn't she beautiful?' Wayne beamed up at him as full of soft maternal pride as Tamsyn with her own baby girl. 'Here,' he said, 'you take her,' and he lifted the monkey up towards Will.

Will took the monkey as gently as he could and brought it close to his body as Wayne had done. It was warm and spindly-thin. He could feel its loose fine skin through the downy fur, its spine under his fingers and its heart beating very fast, and he was overcome by a great sadness.

Wayne left the room again and Will heard a door slam somewhere. He didn't speak to Colton, just gazed down at the little monkey, which was the same kind as Cissy and Tootsie, and he held it up to his face and spoke to it, as he did to all the creatures now, whispering the soft probable lie that it was safe, and everything was going to be okay.

Wayne reappeared, holding a gun.

'Whoa!' said Will.

Colton stood up from the sofa, and Will saw that he was smiling.

Wayne made a show of ejecting the clip from the gun and checking it and then he passed the gun to Colton.

'It's empty,' he said. 'And I'm not giving you any ammo, either.'

'Okay,' said Colton, turning the gun in his long pale hands. 'No sweat.'

'You know I don't do this anymore,' said Wayne. 'This is just for you, so don't go telling anyone. I don't want people rocking up here in the middle of the night with baby lions in cardboard boxes like in the old days.'

Colton shook his head. Will couldn't help thinking of Valerie, and how that must have been for her. When Colton had finished his beer, he wiped his hands on his jeans and picked up the carrying case. 'You need this?' he said. 'It's my mom's, so if you've got one I'll give it back to her.'

After Colton had gone, Wayne prepared a bottle and took the monkey back from Will and suckled it on the sofa.

'It's a surprise for Valerie,' he said. 'What do you think?'

'Oh,' said Will.

'How could she resist you?' Wayne cooed at the monkey. 'There's just no way . . .' He turned back to Will. 'I've asked her to come out tomorrow night, so maybe you can go visit with J.T. or something.'

'Okay, sure, no worries,' said Will, feeling in fact that there were several.

Wayne took the baby monkey off to bed with him, and Will went to his trailer with a sinking apprehension in his guts.

—

The next day Wayne was full of energy and good cheer. He showed the baby to Cissy and Tootsie through the bars of their cage and they craned forward and reached out with their frog-like arms, but Wayne did not get too close, and withdrew with the baby down the hallway once again.

After the day's tasks, Will showered and changed, wished Wayne good luck, and headed in to The Shack.

'How's it going out there?' J.T. asked across the bar, pouring Will an IPA without asking, which made him feel like a local.

'It's going okay,' he said. 'It *was* going really well, and I really like Wayne, hey, but . . .'

'I knew you would,' said J.T.

'Yeah, he's a pretty great guy, like you said. Some of the stories he's been telling me are pretty crazy.'

'Yeah, I know. Like the boat racing and stuff.'

'Like the boat racing. And all the different crazy jobs he's had. And he's been telling me a bit about the years after he came back from the war, before he met Valerie, when he just travelled all over the place. I mean, he's just done so much *stuff.*'

'Impressive, hey?'

'So impressive. He's like the complete opposite of my old man, who's done literally nothing his whole life except for one fucking trip to London. I mean, I'll never be like Wayne, but it does make you think about how to get the most out of life.'

'So why did you say it *was* going well?'

'He's been pretty different since he came back from his mum's, hey. I'm actually kind of worried about him. He's got this baby monkey that he's trying to give Valerie tonight, and—'

'What?!' J.T. cut him off. 'What baby monkey?'

'Some dodgy guy called Colton brought it out last night.' Will thought it best not to mention the gun in public.

'Oh, dude,' said J.T., shaking his head. 'I'll try to come out there tomorrow. I feel real bad I haven't been out for a jam the last couple of Sundays, but it's been real tough with Kaylee. I'm on, like, *zero* sleep. But I'll try to get out and see him.'

Will experienced such relief at this that he realised just how fretful he had been. He felt like getting drunk, but it was a longish drive back to Wayne's and he sure as hell didn't want to get busted by the cops. Still, he pushed it slightly, drinking three pints in just under three hours, which he thought would be fine on top of a burger and fries.

At 10 pm Erin sat down beside him and slapped her apron on the bar.

'Done?' asked J.T.

'Done!' she replied. 'Can I have a knock-off, please?'

J.T. put a shot down in front of her, and one in front of Will.

Erin turned to him. 'I'm sorry, I've forgotten your name.'

'Will.'

'Will, that's right. Sorry. Cheers, Will.'

He cheersed and drank, thinking, Oh well, I'm doing it now. He was in that state of restless energy that demands some outlet. He imagined what that release might be, in the best-case scenario, then tried to sanitise the images from his mind. He felt himself flushing; his old curse. This was already going badly. What the fuck was wrong with him?

Erin was untying her hair and forking through it with her small fingers. He caught a waft of cigarette smoke and apple-scented shampoo.

'How was your shift?' he asked dumbly.

'Fucked. As usual. Hardly worth the seven bucks an hour.'

'Seven?!'

'Yup. Plus tips, but they're bullshit . . . Hey J.T., can I get a beer, please?'

He thought again of the artwork he'd seen in New York. That short tidy stack of bills, like the stack he himself was collecting in the broken microwave of his RV.

J.T. gave him a questioning look. 'Another beer?'

'Sure. Fuck it,' he said.

He noticed he was jiggling his knee under the bar and stopped himself. He remembered Paul teasing him about the habit years ago, telling him it was a sign of sexual frustration, even though he was only twelve or thirteen at the time.

'Do you smoke?' Erin asked.

'Nah. But I can keep you company if you're going outside.'

'Sure.' She smiled knowingly. Was he that obvious? She went to grab her bag from the lockers and he followed her to the rear of the building, where they sat on some empty beer kegs beside a buzzing coolroom. The kegs were too high and the cold metal pressed painfully into the shallow flesh between his thighs and bum. The air was chilly and he could see the goosebumps prickle up on Erin's thin bare arms.

'Aren't you cold?' he asked, sounding parental and uncool.

'I'm okay.' She shook a cigarette from her crumpled pack and lit it. 'So, what's it like out there at the zoo?'

'It's not really a zoo, as such . . . but it's pretty nuts, actually.'

She looked at him, interested, drawing her lips to the side and blowing the smoke away through the corner of her mouth.

He wanted to impress her, but he didn't know what tone to take. He knew she disapproved of the animals being in cages.

'One of the tigers got out the other day,' he ventured, smiling to show it wasn't going to be a bad story. 'She was chasing the horses around and we had to put out meat to try and lure her into the horse float. In the end, we had to get Wayne's wife to call up and talk to her on the phone before we could get her in. It was crazy.'

'Oh my god!'

'Yeah. Like, I know you think it's bad keeping them in cages, but seeing that really made me realise how tame they actually are, and how much they do love Wayne and Valerie.'

'That's his wife?'

'Yeah. She's awesome. Such a nice lady.'

'This is kinda weird, but I've been thinking so much about those animals since the last time we spoke, and I started asking round about Wayne . . .'

Uh-oh, Will was thinking, where's she going with this? He felt himself frowning.

'My uncle's a cop,' she continued. 'Total fucking prick, but anyway . . . He said Wayne's wife left him and he's about to go to jail and all the animals will probably be put down.'

'Nah, no way,' said Will.

'No way what? He's not going to jail? Or his animals won't get killed? 'Cause that's what my uncle said.'

Will thought about what Valerie had told him, that Wayne might get a year.

'I dunno,' he said. 'It's not really my business. Wayne doesn't talk to me about that stuff. But I'm sure Valerie'll look after them if—'

'You should make it your business.' Erin dropped her cigarette butt and swivelled her toe on it. 'Honestly, I can't stop thinking about those poor animals. You should talk to him. Make sure he's got a plan.'

'Yeah,' he said weakly. 'Wayne's . . . he's not that easy to talk to.'

'But, like, the animals . . .' She looked at him again, full into his eyes. She seemed so genuinely worried, it made him feel like a jerk.

'I'll try.'

'Really?' She smiled at him, her face softer than he'd seen it. Her glasses were misting up in the cold and she took them off and breathed on them and wiped them on the edge of her t-shirt, showing him a piece of her flat, very pale stomach.

Back inside they finished their beers and Erin chatted about how she was planning to move to New York at the end of the year, and Will told her a version of his week there. He listed the bars he'd been to and she knew some of them and seemed impressed, and he was glad they'd moved on from the subject of Wayne and the animals, which was not the kind of talk he wanted to have with the scrawny hot vegan. Why had he said he'd talk to Wayne? Because he wanted her to like him, of course; but did he actually have to *do* it now?

When J.T. was off somewhere, he turned to her and with the dulled bravery of booze he asked her if she'd be up for going for a drink with him sometime.

'Sure,' she said, but there was something automatic in her response, as if she had taken the same indiscriminate yea-saying vow as he himself had taken on this trip. Even worse, as soon as she agreed, which had caught him by surprise, he felt a deep and undeniable knowledge that he didn't actually want to go on a date with her, that asking her had had the very opposite of the anticipated effect of this performance of moving on, and had filled him with a desperate sudden and full-bodied longing for Laura. He thought only of Laura as he drove back to Wayne's and his grief was cruelly new, as if he'd peeled back the dressing, hoping to see the healed pink skin, but had seen instead a festering wound.

*

Valerie's car wasn't there and the lights were out in the house. Will was glad that Wayne had gone to bed and he wouldn't have to hear about the inevitable disaster until tomorrow. He opened the door and walked towards the kitchen for a glass of water and was startled half to death when Wayne spoke from the blackness.

'Oh my god, you scared the shit out of me!' Will said. 'What are you doing sitting in the dark?'

'I think better in the dark.'

Wayne picked up a glass that clinked with the sound of ice cubes and took a loud gulp.

'Well, do you mind if I turn on the kitchen light for a sec?' said Will.

'Go ahead. Get yourself a glass. I could use the company.'

The lion cubs were in their pen by the fireplace, asleep in an adorable pile that contracted and expanded with their synchronised breathing.

Will gave himself a large pour of whiskey and topped Wayne up. He sat down and dragged off each of his boots with the toe of the opposite foot and looked around.

'Did she take the monkey, then?'

'Nope,' said Wayne. 'Monkey's in the laundry.'

'Oh,' said Will, and then, 'Oh. I'm sorry, Wayne.'

'Yep. So am I.'

The two of them—both heartsore and full of hurt—proceeded to get very drunk. It began to rain heavily, and the sound was comforting on the roof, and they left the lights off except in the kitchen, just so they could see to pour. When they finished the whiskey, Wayne went to a cupboard and pulled out a bottle without a label, and Will didn't even ask what it was, just held up his glass while Wayne sloshed the stuff into it and all over Will's hand.

'Hey,' he said, laughing, licking his thumb. Damn, it was strong, whatever it was. He wondered if it was the mythical American *moonshine*, and decided that's what he would call it anyway.

After Wayne had gone to bed, Will staggered out into the wet dark, his feet only half in his boots, and he tripped and fell onto the driveway, grazing his hands. It stung bad, and when he brushed the grit from his palms there was wetness there but it was too dark to see if it was blood or just rainwater. The jolt had set his head and stomach all a-churn and he felt with the drunk's amplified emotion intensely sorry for himself.

The booze had loosened him like a muscle, and like a muscle he felt in more pain than he had before the treatment. In his aching lack of inhibition and almost without thought he pulled out his phone and for the first time since the breakup he put aside logic and pride and protection and he pressed the screen at the place where Laura's name still shone at the top of his list of favourites. And then, with shocking lack of delay—as if time and geography were nothing but illusion—he heard her voice, and it was as if for a moment he could still lay claim to that now brazen-seeming right and privilege of longing for her and having her assuage that longing just like that with her simple, anything-but-simple, presence.

'Hello?' she said, and he could tell by the neutrality of her tone that she didn't know it was him.

'It's me.'

'Will? What number is this?'

'I'm in the States. I got a new SIM.'

'Oh, of course.'

Silence.

'Would you have answered if you knew it was me?'

'Of course,' she said again, reflexive quick.

'Yeah, right. You've probably blocked my number, haven't you?'

'Are you drunk? What time is it there? Where are you, anyway?'

'I don't know—about one am,' he said, picking the least problematic of her questions.

She didn't respond. He could hear the daytime sounds of traffic and people in the background.

'Will, I haven't blocked your number. I wouldn't do that. But I do think it's important to have a proper break, you know. Not be in contact for a while, so we can go back to being friends.'

'What if I don't want to be your friend?'

She paused as if to gather strength. 'Well, that's up to you, obviously. I can't make you. But I'd like to be friends still.' Her voice was so fucking calm it killed him.

'Why?' he asked.

'Why what?'

'Why do you want to be friends still?'

'Will . . . it's pretty obvious that you're really drunk. I don't think it's a good idea to talk right now.'

'No,' he said. 'Answer me! Why do you want to be friends? You clearly think I'm not good enough for you.'

'Oh my god,' she muttered. She breathed out with exaggerated patience. 'I do *not* think that. At all.'

'Then why did you dump me, huh?' He heard his voice slide out of conscious control.

'Will, I've told you why! We've been over and over it.'

'Well, I don't fucking buy it!' he shouted. 'Because I'm not *ready*?! I *was* ready!'

He started to cry, his hands shaking. He walked to his trailer in his socks over the wet grass, leaving his boots on the gravel. The flimsy pneumatic door hissed and clacked closed behind him and in the utter darkness he felt his way to the bed and sat down.

She listened to him crying.

'Will . . .' she said again, softer now and pitying and repulsed, he was sure.

'I just need to understand.'

'It's not the right time. I'll tell you when you're—'

'There!' he cut her off. 'I was right! You *were* lying. I *knew* it!' His tears vanished and he felt only fury and it was his turn to sound terribly calm. 'Tell me. Tell me right now. Was there someone else?'

'No!' she said, and her shock was convincing. 'I *promise* you, there was no one else.'

'Then *what*?'

Again, she uttered the short syllable of his name and fell silent.

'It doesn't matter,' he said. 'I *know* what it was. It *was* that you think you're too good for me, I could tell. You changed right after you met my parents. You saw who I really am and you decided you didn't like it.'

On the other side of the world, Laura laughed. 'You know what, Will?' she said, and her voice was angry now. 'Fine. You want to talk about it, let's talk about it. That—what you just said then—*is* part of why I broke up with you, but *totally* not how you think. You are so deep into this idea that I think you're not good enough, and it's total bullshit. It's in your own head, and it's completely paranoid and self-obsessed. And it actually makes you act like a dick. I *did* see a different side of you around your family. You were so embarrassed by them, and you were actually pretty mean to them. To your mum especially. And I could see how you could really easily become like that with me, if we stayed together.'

'I would never—'

'Hang on, Will,' she cut him off. 'Do you want to hear this or not?'

'Fine. Go ahead.'

She sighed again. 'You see? That tone you get . . .'

'Hey, that's not fair.'

'Look, I don't want to fight about it. I just think you need to . . . I dunno. Do what you're doing now. I could see you starting to resent me because you hadn't, you know . . . had enough experience or something.'

'You mean like my dad?'

'I mean, kind of. But you know what? Your dad actually did a pretty impressive thing in a way, coming home from overseas and fronting up and becoming a father at nineteen or whatever. It's actually more the way *you* think of that as pathetic, and think of him as pathetic for doing that, that worries me. I'm not worried you'll end up like him; I'm more worried about how you might *actually* end up, because of this complex you've got about being *cool*.'

'That is bullshit!'

'It's not, Will. And *you* actually started pulling away from *me* after I met your parents, not the other way round.'

'No, I didn't!' he said, but he knew he had. It wasn't what she thought, though. He'd just been so full of shame and self-loathing, after that dinner. After the exposure of his excruciating lie and after shouting at his father and storming out.

'Will! Can you please stop *arguing* and denying everything I say? Yes, I know it's just my perspective, and you disagree; you've made that very clear. But ultimately, I do have the right to break up with you, for whatever reason. And I don't *have to* explain it to you, either. I'm trying to explain because you asked me to. And it's not just about your parents' visit. The bottom line is it all just started feeling too hard. I don't want this to sound cruel, but you were pretty hard work sometimes, and I got tired of having to constantly reassure you all the time. And you didn't exactly give a whole lot of emotional support in return. Don't get me wrong—I love you, and you're a good person. But you need to sort some stuff out, because you've got real issues with self-esteem. The fact that you think I broke up with you after I met your parents, because I realised you were *uncool*? It's actually pretty insulting. And like, why on earth would you *lie* about never having been overseas before?'

And there it was, and it was all rushing up at him, that banshee flashback released from its dark well or locked-room place of deepest repression, and all his fervent self-deluding labour of the past month—the drugs and the yea-saying and the running ever running notlookingback—had been for naught.

He saw it all with terrible freshness: the too-fancy restaurant that Laura had booked for them and the table by the window where they'd sat waiting, drinking prosecco; his parents in the doorway—his father's red t-shirt and wide blue jeans and brown plastic belt and awful cheap black formal shoes. He saw the waiter's shock and sneer and Laura's mortification when his father asked if they could make him plain spaghetti and cheese, and he heard her saying, 'We can go somewhere else if there's nothing you like the sound of here, seriously,' and his mother saying, 'No, no, please. It's just Gary. He's a very fussy eater.' And he watched with the inevitability of fate as his father was sucked magnet-like towards his old excruciating ceaseless reminiscences.

'Will's probably told you but I went to London in 1972. Younger than Will is now. My only time overseas, but it was the best time of my life. I was meant to be there six months, at least, but then I found out Jo was pregnant with Grace.'

'Gary, I'm sure Laura doesn't want to hear about your old glory days,' said Will's mother with an awkward laugh.

'I keep telling Will he needs to go overseas before he settles down.'

'Do you mean by himself?' Laura asked. 'He said you've been overseas as a family when he was younger.'

He felt rather than saw his mother's eyes land on his face. She would understand at once. And Laura?

It was as though a sinkhole had opened in the very floor and the table with its white cloth and heavy cutlery and fine-stemmed glasses was scraping over the polished boards towards it and he was grasping, grasping at the cloth and the toppling bottle . . .

'I just don't want Will making the same mistake I did . . .'

'Gary!' his mother said again.

'As *we* did, I mean as *we* did.'

'For fuck's sake, Dad!'

'Will's never been overseas,' he heard his mother say over the sounds of breaking glass and the shrieks of other customers and the sliding of chairs towards the void. 'I've never been either. We never had the money.'

'But I'm sure he said . . .'

'All I'm saying,' said his father, 'is that the two of you should make sure you've seen the world a bit, before you become parents yourselves . . . I'm sure you're being careful, but just—'

'Dad! Shut the fuck up!' Will heard his voice come out a shout. He couldn't look at her. He stood in desperation on the earthquake floor. He saw his life's work crumbling. All the interminable care and effort. He felt the redness of his face; saw the people glancing over. How could he have been so dolt careless as not to anticipate this, not to steer away from this trap, as obvious in the path of conversation as a fallen fucking tree?

He launched a flare, by way of distraction: 'Can't you just for once shut up about bloody London!' he yelled. And then, in his humiliation and fury, he did the only thing he could to make it worse: he turned and walked briskly from the room.

'Will?' Laura was saying. 'Look, I'm gonna go, because you're clearly not ready to have this conversation and I'm walking home from work and people are looking at me.'

'Laura. Please . . .'

'And I think it's *my* turn for some self-protection,' she added, the harsh and final word before hanging up.

Will dropped his phone and left the trailer. Again, the instinct to run. He staggered back to the dark house in his wet socks and felt his way to the playpen where the baby lions were still sleeping and climbed inside. He lay his cheek on one of them, but it wriggled away, so he crooked an elbow under his head and spooned himself around the whole warm-breathing pile of them and then with blessed speed passed out.

—

He awoke to the first of several intensities of sensation: a young lion—his very own Nala—scouring his cheek with her rough tongue. Despite this miracle of circumstance, in a mere few eyeblinks the more tormenting sensations elsewhere in his body and spirit overwhelmed him. He made a sad performance of scraping by increments on to all fours and remaining there for some time with head hung down and guts pitching ship-wise, and then he clambered with an urgent burst of speed from the pen and stumbled out to vomit in the grass. He vomited again into the waterless sink of the RV and crashed onto the bed and slept again.

When he re-awoke, his dominant feeling was of resolute and palliative anger and close behind it a powerful desire not to face the truth of last night's conversation, and he didn't have a clue what to do with himself. He eyed the mess in the sink and left it there for later.

His phone was dead and he went inside to charge it, collecting his damp abandoned boots on the way. Wayne did not appear, and Will wondered if he had gone out, but the truck and van were parked as usual in the driveway. When he emerged from the bathroom, Wayne was on the couch in shorts and cap, no shirt, feet bare, feeding the baby monkey as the cubs pounced about the room.

'Morning,' said Will.

'Morning.'

That was all they said, and their shared wretchedness lay between them and neither felt inclined to meet the other's gaze over its considerable mass. At least there was the kindly scent of coffee in the air and it was the day of worship, in which to avoid one another and each repair his armour.

Will looked at his phone, plugged in above the kitchen bench, and saw a message from Valerie.

Hi Will how are you? Could we talk? You could come in and see me today if you can get away. Maybe don't tell W if that's okay.

He replied:

Of course. Where should I meet you?

He saw Wayne look over at him as he typed. Shit, he hadn't seen the message, had he? He tried to recall if it had been unopened on the screen or not. Either way, Wayne could have seen who it was from. Fuck it, he told himself. It's none of his business.

'Hey Wayne,' he said, 'I thought I'd head into town for a bit today. You don't need me, do you?'

'Only for a jam.'

Will laughed. 'Yeah, I'm not sure I'm up to jamming today. I'm appallingly bad at the best of times, as you know, and I've got one hell of a hangover.'

'What you up to in town?'

'Not much. Maybe pick up a few things. Might see how Tamsyn's going.'

Wayne nodded, sullen.

The address Valerie had given him was in a part of town he hadn't been to, an older part, and clearly where the money was, or at least had been. The houses were uniformly grand and pleasingly *American* in style—two storeys high, built of brown or dark red brick or cream weatherboard, with covered porches and dormer windows and slate-tiled roofs—and they had no fences around their thick-lawned front yards, as if to signify such absolute relaxed security and easy freedom from worry that they did not require even such decorative symbols of sovereignty and protection. Two grey squirrels hurried past him over fallen leaves. They leaped spread-limbed as if flying and circled a tree trunk and watched him, making quick movements with their heads and ears and shining intelligent eyes.

Valerie answered the door in the same outfit she'd worn on that first excruciating day: the beige jodhpurs and white shirt and riding boots. She looked stern and serious and Will felt the promise of comfort—a large part of why he'd come to see her—evaporate, and remembered that he barely knew this woman.

She took him through to the kitchen where a man was making coffee.

'This is my friend Bill. Bill, meet Will.'

The two men laughed and Bill showed his very white teeth. He was what Will might have called, in mocking tones, an *older gentleman*. He wore pressed jeans and a pressed checked shirt and shining leather boots with a pointed toe. His face was tanned, perhaps artificially, and handsome in a rugged, daytime soap kind of way.

'Coffee, Will?'

'Thanks. I'd love one.'

'You two go on out back and I'll bring it out to you.'

'Thanks, Bill,' said Valerie.

Will noticed her rest a hand on his arm.

She led Will to the screened back porch, which looked out over a garden as well maintained as Bill himself.

'Wow, nice place!'

'Gorgeous, isn't it? Bill's a lawyer. In fact, he's Wayne's lawyer. We've been friends for years. Bill's wife Mary passed two years ago. Cancer.'

'Oh no. That's terrible.'

Valerie nodded. 'Mary was the first friend I made here in Littleproud.'

The screen door creaked behind them and Bill appeared with a tray. Two mugs of coffee, a small jug of cream, a silver sugar bowl and a floral plate with an iced cinnamon scroll cut into quarters. Valerie smiled up at him as he unloaded the bounty. He tucked the tray beneath his arm, nodded to Will, and returned inside.

'So sweet! He even cut the bun for us,' said Valerie. She handed Will the plate. After his pre-dawn purge, he was grateful for the sugary offering. 'Thanks for coming in. I really appreciate it. You didn't tell Wayne, did you?'

'No, of course not.'

Valerie nodded and looked out at the garden. A bird landed just beyond the porch screen and produced a strange and complex succession of notes and then repeated them again exactly.

'I guess I wanted to talk to you because, after last night, I'm quite concerned about Wayne. You know he tried to offer me a baby monkey?'

'Yeah.' Will grimaced. 'I know. I was actually thinking I should talk to you too, but I didn't want to go behind Wayne's back or anything but, um . . . he got the monkey off this weird guy called Colton, I think . . .' He glanced at Valerie, but she made a face that said she didn't know who that was. 'Yeah, he came out to the house the other night with the monkey and . . .' He paused, feeling guilty for dobbing on Wayne. 'Well, Wayne gave him a gun. In exchange for the monkey, it seemed like.'

'What?! Are you kidding me?'

'Afraid not.'

Valerie put her hand up to her forehead. 'I should tell Bill . . . Should I?' She was clearly talking to herself, and Will cradled his coffee and waited. 'I'll think about that later.' She looked directly at him then, very grave. 'Look, Will. What I'm wondering is if you'd speak to Wayne. Try to talk some sense into him.'

'Me?'

'Yes. I tried to talk to him last night. *Again.* Same result, of course. But he talked a lot about you, and it made me think that you're someone he might listen to. He's got this whole fate thing going, as you probably know by now, and he's convinced that you've been sent here for some reason and . . . well, partly that makes me think he might listen to you. The voice of fate.' She gave a bitter short laugh, and Will shook his head. 'But also,' she continued, 'when I asked him what he was planning to do about the animals if he *does* get a year, he said he'd be fine, he's got you and J.T.'

'What the hell?'

'And I'm assuming that's not the case. That you're leaving at some point soon.'

'Yeah, I have to. I've only got a ninety-day visa. And we *agreed* on a month, which is almost up already. But also, he said he'd give me a car at the end of it, because I returned my hire car. And we haven't even started working on it yet.'

Valerie rubbed her palms across her face and made a sound of helpless frustration. 'Ugh! He's in complete denial. He's clearly got no plan for the animals. It's so upsetting . . . The fact that he's just gone and got a *new* one, for God's sake. I know that was his attempt to win me back, but . . . he won't accept that either, that it's over. I'm done . . . Anyway, I know they're my responsibility too, obviously, but there's no way I can look after that many by myself.'

'Can't J.T. talk to him? They're super close.'

Valerie nodded, chewing her lower lip. 'The thing is . . . I'm worried J.T. will just offer to look after them. He's so loyal. And I know that's not an option either, especially now he's just had a child. It's a full-time job for two people.'

'I know. It really is.'

She held her palms up. 'Right? You've seen it. And the thing is, we've got no money left to even feed them for the next year. So I guess I'm hoping you might get him to think about what to do. Realistically.'

'What *can* he do?'

'I don't know. Call on every contact we've got in the exotics world. Beg people to take them in for a year. I could stay and look after some of them. I don't love the idea but . . . But that'd be maybe ten at most. Plus the apes and cubs. I mean, half of them now aren't even *ours.* Wayne's taken them in from other people who couldn't handle them. Another thing I *begged* him to stop doing.'

She looked at Will again with that direct and serious, almost severe expression. 'Would you speak to him?'

Will thought of Erin and the dumb promise he'd made her, to talk to Wayne. Why did everyone think he was the one to have these fucking difficult conversations? Why did Wayne think he was some fate-sent surrogate son and not the simple, temporary traveller he was, moving through as swift and heartless as a bird?

'I guess I can try,' he said. 'But the thing is, he doesn't even know that I know he's going to prison. It's gonna be *pretty* awkward.'

'Mmm . . . Yes, that's tricky. But the trial's coming up so soon. He'll have to tell you at some point.' Valerie considered, gazing out at the garden again, her fingers smoothing her lips in an unconscious gesture of troubled and consequential thought. 'God, I wish I could just get on a plane to Wyoming and start over . . . But that's not the reality . . .' She looked back at Will. 'I think, if you tell him you need to leave, then he'll tell you about the trial. And then you can have the conversation.'

'Yeah, maybe . . .' Will hesitated. 'And what if he *doesn't* tell me about the trial?'

'Then maybe I tell him I'm going to tell you the truth. But that won't go down well. The thing is to catch him in the right frame of mind, and right now you're about the only one who's in his good books.'

'Am I, though? I don't know.'

'It can be hard to tell sometimes.' She laughed again, that brief embittered laugh, and gave Will a melancholy smile, showing at last the softness he was longing for. 'Hey, Will, are you okay? You seem a little . . . flat.'

'Yeah . . . I'm okay. Wayne and I drank a lot last night after I got home.'

'I'm glad he's got you there, Will. Really.'

Will nodded. He looked at this woman, this almost-stranger who had kindled such strange affection in him.

'Actually, I called Laura last night. I was really drunk. It was a terrible idea.'

'Oh, Will.' Valerie rested her hand on his, where it lay on the table. Her hand was cold but the weight of it was comforting and he allowed himself to accept this solace, as he had accepted it from Laura alone these unconsoled past years of spiteful distance from family and home and religion and his shameful former self.

'Yeah, it was rough. She said some stuff that was pretty hard to hear. About how I acted, and why she ended it.'

'Oh, honey.' She squeezed his hand in silence for a moment and then said, 'Will . . . can I say something?'

Afterwards, Valerie followed him to the door, not speaking.

'Will,' she said as he reached for the handle. 'Thank you.'

'For what?' He tried to smile but knew it looked fake.

'Just . . . I don't know . . . for being you. I've laid a lot on you today.'

Will opened the door and turned to reply and then he saw Valerie's face and swung back.

In front of the house, Wayne was standing beside his truck, his shoulders hunched and hands in his pockets, and on his face a seething mix of all the ungovernable shame and fury and intractable stubborn pride and self-protection that Will had felt unwitnessed upon his own face last night as he spoke to the woman who had caused such a wrack of feeling.

'Wayne?!' Will said. 'Did you *follow* me?'

Valerie pushed past him, shading her eyes with her hand. 'Wayne?'

'Hell, yes, I followed you,' said Wayne. 'And I'm glad I did, too.'

He looked at the message, Will thought. Bastard.

'Because now I see what's happening,' Wayne continued, looking at Valerie. 'You're having an affair with Bill.' Wayne advanced towards them. Will saw that he wasn't wearing any shoes. He must have grabbed a shirt and followed Will immediately. How had he not noticed?

'Wayne, stop,' said Valerie. He heard the same level and infinite calm that he had heard in Laura's voice last night, counterweight to such unmanaged passion. 'Let's just let Will leave. This is nothing to do with him. I only asked him to come and give me a report on how you are, because I'm worried about you. And then, after he's gone, you and I can talk.'

Wayne stood there churning on the path. 'Alright,' he said at last.

He let Will pass without a word, and Will looked back at Valerie to see if she was scared, but she nodded at him over Wayne's sad head as if he was a child and mouthed, *It's okay*, and waved him off.

Back at the house, Will roiled around the place, and could not settle. He went to his trailer, where the vomit lay congealed in the shallow sink and the whole warm closed room stank of it, bitter and sweet at once, like the bile and bourbon that were its main components. He gathered from the house a bucket and gloves, paper towel and bleach and he dealt with this most amenable of his messes. Then he lay down and stared at the ceiling, and by unknowing increments he worked his way from the bright threat of disintegration into the soft suckling dark of repudiation. What were these women trying to do to him? He really did not feel like having this kind of journey of fucking humility and self-examination. And what did Valerie know about it anyway? *Don't hold on to delusion*, she'd said. *Don't refuse to hear what Laura said to you.* That was her own shit. She'd basically admitted it herself; she was talking to Wayne, not him.

On the whole he preferred Wayne's idea that he might yet go home a hero. That the girl he had once loved would one day shrink (or grow) to just another woman, inciting zero desire or regret. How likely was it anyway that it was *all* his fault? Laura was dishonest and disloyal, unflinching in her certain judgement of him. She had broken up with him over something he *might* have become or some way he *might* have treated her in the future, and how bullshit was that?

Thus he eased himself to anger and he turned his thoughts to Erin, but found that she set off as much a nagging interior voice of demand as the others, and he brought Tamsyn in, too, to join the malevolent chorus: *Talk to Wayne; call your mother; let go of delusion; admit that you suck*. Well, fuck that, and fuck them!

He felt almost proud of himself for being so staunch unyielding in his refusal. Laura didn't know him and Valerie certainly didn't know him. In fact, if there was anyone who represented a counterpart and comprehending natural ally in all of this it was Wayne!

Still, he remained in his trailer for some time after the grumble of Wayne's tyres passed and ceased in an aggression of gravel and slamming doors, replaced once more by that terrible sublime of dusk roaring from a few sloped metres away, as the ravenous beasts endured their day of enforced starvation.

He floundered there in his quicksand bed, reluctant to face his untamed benefactor-double and struggling to master his own truculent emotion. Then: epiphany! He rifled in his backpack and touched there in the darkest lint-furred corner the Altoids tin, within it like a charm the little ziplock bag with what looked close to half a gram left, and he didn't even bother to close the curtains before he partook liberally of its rescue.

He found Wayne stalled morose and guitar-noodling and possibly stoned on the blue leather sofa and sat down beside him.

'Wayne,' he said, clenching his teeth, 'can I talk to you?'

Wayne unlooped the guitar strap from his neck and leaned the instrument against the sofa, and the monkey perched behind him on the sofa's back scuttled into his lap and began to sort the dark hairs of his forearm with careful concern.

'Sure. What's on your mind?' Wayne replied, bizarrely calm, as if the whole day's drama had been mere fireworks.

'Well . . . I will have been here a month on Thursday and I'm still keen to do this stupid road trip. But I realised that we haven't got around to fixing up the car yet, so . . . yeah, that's what I wanted to talk to you about; how long you think that'll take. Because I do need to get going.'

'Oh, not long. Not long.' Wayne waved the arm that was not encumbered by a monkey. 'But listen . . . I've been doing some thinking, and there's a conversation I've been wanting to have with you, too.'

'Okay.'

'I haven't been entirely upfront with you,' he began. He removed his arm from the loving ape and performed his habitual gesture of worry, lifting his cap by the peak with one hand and running the other over the sparse hair beneath it and then replacing the cap once more.

'Okay,' said Will again. Could it be that he was about to confess at last?

'The reason Valerie left me is because I fucked up. Royally.' He looked at Will, in apparent need to gauge his audience's attitude and readiness to hear what he had to tell, and he seemed to baulk and reverse and then start up again down a more accustomed path, or perhaps succumbed to his clear weakness for inhabiting the role of spiritual guide. 'Something I've learned, that you might learn from too . . . When a woman asks, or even begs you not to do something—to give up some grandiose plan you're set on—you had better listen. In my experience, women don't make idle threats. They hold their tongue and hold it until they reach the very end of their tether, and then they speak. And if you're hard-headed or distracted enough to miss that single clear command, or think you have time yet to test her patience a little more, then that will be your downfall.'

Will nodded in attempted sympathy, but really he was thinking, Get on with it, old man! And also, Why does every person desire to impart to me some wisdom or advice, to make me do or look at something I do not wish to look at? It wasn't healthy to expect so much of a weak fucked-up and heartbroke twenty-two-year-old, and it was frankly becoming pretty fucking annoying. He wanted to get this over with, to get back to the trailer and do another line.

'In a way,' Wayne went on, 'I blame Valerie. I do. She did such a convincing job of being on board with all my schemes, I thought we were of like mind in the kind of life we wanted.' Again, Wayne paused, lifted his cap, smoothed his skull. 'She's the love of my life, Will,' he said. 'I do know that. Whatever else I've got wrong, I know that to be true.'

After yet another pause and evident effort to rejig the mechanism of his thought, Wayne narrated at last the tragic final act of the story he had been circumambulating for a month now in his tales of high and noble daring and of ceaseless brave nonconformity: the downfall of the hero; the fulfilment of the fated curse. He told Will in humbled terms of the government informant and the raid and, yes, the impending trial and probable incarceration, and then he stopped and held out the callused and dirt-lined palms of his big hands.

There it was, and Will was impressed by the accuracy of Valerie's prediction: that if he were to tell Wayne that he was leaving, the man would offer him at last the truth.

Here then was his cue, as clear as if it had been written in as stage directions: WILL ATTEMPTS TO TALK TO WAYNE ABOUT THE ANIMALS.

But Will would not take the cue. That scene was written for him by others, to fulfil the needs of others, and he recalled with shimmering exquisite and undoubtedly narcotic clarity that his own story was one of heartless headlong motion, his map leading deep into the pure heart of solitude. He saw that he had been caught again in the cloying web of connection; of empathy and guilt and obligation. He liked these people—Wayne and Valerie and Erin and J.T.—but he must remember that, like Justine and Daisy and even Paul, they were only bit parts in his own consuming narrative.

Will felt woken from some brief deep slumber or enchantment. How had he let himself become so embroiled here? As soon as possible, he would leave these minor characters to their all-too-evident troubles and get back on the road, and he felt a peaking excitation at the rightness of this design, beyond, he thought, the effects of the coke.

Meanwhile, the fallen guide continued, mumbling out the unburdening of his odd-shaped riven soul. 'I've come up with a plan,' he said at last.

Will dragged himself back from his distant fantasising to hear what Wayne would say.

'I would like to ask you to consider staying on here. After I'm incarcerated. You could live here, have the place to yourself, and I'd find a way to keep paying you, and you'd just have to look after the animals. With J.T., of course—he'd help you out with everything you need, and—'

'But, Wayne,' Will interrupted him. 'My visa's only got a month and a half left now. I have to go home after ninety days.'

'Don't worry about that. Who's going to catch you out here? You'll be working for me. And Valerie. She'd withdraw your cash each week, or whenever you like, and that would cover all your expenses. You wouldn't have to use your own cards or anything. And then when you get to the airport, you just say, *Crap, sorry, I thought I had six months.* Ask for forgiveness, not permission, as they say. And I'm likely to be out in three months anyway.'

Will very nearly said, *Valerie told me you'd be in for a year*, but caught himself. He could feel his face and shoulder scrunching up on one side in a too-legible expression of hesitation and awkward demurment, and he saw on Wayne's own face the now-familiar play of fleet unwelcome feeling, the shadow of a cloud as it speeds across a hillside.

'Have I told you,' asked Wayne, changing tack again with surprising agility, 'that I have a certain ability to manifest a particular future into existence, if I desire it strongly enough, and with pure motives?'

'Yeah, you did mention that.'

'Of course, I'm focusing all my energy currently on winning my wife back. But I've had a strong feeling about you, Will. Ever since we first met.'

Will frowned in mild defiance. 'To be honest, I remember you seemed pretty suspicious of me when we first met.'

'Mmm . . . Maybe I was at first. I have many forces conspiring against me at present. It tends to interfere with the instinct. It's against my nature to be untrusting, but you did catch me at a low point. Still, I knew quite quickly.'

'Knew what?'

'That you'd been sent here for a purpose. You remind me of my younger self, Will.'

'Yeah, you said that.'

'You're lost and hurting and looking for answers. But there's something about you I recognised. You're out here, far from home, looking to make something of yourself.'

'Which is why I have to keep going, Wayne. There's other things I want to see and do, you know. You understand that, right?'

Wayne pretended not to hear. 'Valerie likes you too. Very much. She told me so herself. I know I was suspicious of your friendship with her at first, and I apologise for that. But if you stayed, I think Valerie might stay too, to help you. And then, once I'm out . . . Well, who knows?'

Will looked at Wayne from the apex of his high, and he felt a little shiver of brittle cold dispassionate distance and even cruelty. Why should *he* be made to face the hard and ego-bruising truth, while Wayne wallowed in such sweet delusion?

'Wayne, man,' he said, 'I'm sorry, but I really think you're gonna need to accept that it might be over with Valerie. Focus on moving forward, you know?'

'Did she tell you it was over?'

'Um, kind of, yeah. It's not that she's been talking to me about your relationship or anything. In fact she was giving *me* a bit of a lecture about moving on and accepting it's over with Laura, and . . . yeah, she might have mentioned that you should do the same.'

Wayne closed his eyes in pain, and Will watched as all his fate-sure bravado disintegrated to dust.

'Will,' he said, 'please, I'm begging you. I'm desperate here. I really need you to stay just a little while longer. I can make it happen, I know I can. I'll be out in a month. Two max. I promise.'

'You can't promise me that, Wayne! What if you're not? What if you get a year?'

Wayne turned his head sharp, his eyes shuttered. 'Why do you say a year? Valerie's been talking to you, hasn't she? You already knew! About all of it!' He picked the monkey up from his lap and set her on the sofa. 'Did Valerie tell you I was going to prison?'

'Well . . .' *Shit. Shit!* He took a breath, felt it catch on the white numbness at the back of his throat. 'Actually, Tamsyn told me. The first night we met.'

Wayne got up, shaking his head.

'Wayne, I'm sorry,' Will continued. 'I wasn't trying to be dishonest or anything. I just knew it wasn't any of my business, that's all. I was leaving it to you to tell me, when you were ready. If you wanted to.' He was babbling.

Wayne turned away and stood gazing at the empty fireplace. Then he turned back to Will in strange slow motion, like a cartoon villain. 'Maybe I've got it all wrong, here.'

No shit! Will thought. 'About what?'

'Maybe I've been wrong about everything. Maybe I *am* going to get a year.'

'Look, I think you should probably consider the possibility.'

'*Or* . . .' Wayne glared at Will again. 'Maybe it's you I've been wrong about. Maybe you've been sent to test me. Maybe *you're* just another of the spies and enemies impeding my path. Perhaps you're not the answer.'

Will couldn't help it; he laughed. 'I'm pretty sure I'm not the answer to anything, Wayne. I'm a fucking mess, can't you see that?'

Will watched the man before him as his face performed again the frantic movements of his injured mind, but Wayne had gone from him already, gazing past Will towards where the menagerie lay in all its hopeful and hubristic wild excess.

THE ENDS OF ALL KINGDOMS come at last, and lucky indeed are those generations who are born and die in the morning of a doomed civilisation, as each is doomed, equal and inevitable, and the earth's best hope is that our condemned, still-copulating mass might hover light and snuff out soft upon the terrain of the slower-dying cultures, the rocks and plants and mountains—just as we hope not to be overrun by the faster rise and fall of the kingdoms of germs upon our own vulnerable pink or brown bodylands—for to be a human creature born at the centre of concentric spheres of fall—the organism within the culture within the species—is to grapple with questions that trouble neither wolf nor abalone, peach nor composite rock, nor even the last tiger as it suns itself in the crosshairs of the vacationing dentist.

On a Tuesday morning in October, in the year 2011, Wayne sent Will out to do a solo run for chicken parts. It was a cool and cloudy day, though just the day before it had been a sunny sixty-eight degrees. Driving the hills was so different now from when Will had arrived four weeks ago, all shades of golden yellow and foxy brown with patches of dark scarlet like dried blood.

Will was glad to be alone, despite the time it took to load the ton of meat without help. He swung the heavy van around, light himself, or rather empty. He would stay another week, as he had agreed with Wayne, and then he would shake himself free—he thought he could do it—and drive away in the truck that waited, still fenderless but, Wayne promised, near ready, in the big shed.

Wayne had said that morning that they could go collect a fender from a buddy in Dayton any day, they just had to make time to fix the truck itself among all the thousand constant tasks of the Wild Kingdom. Then all that was left was to drive the truck to town and get it road-worthied and registered, and Will would be journey-set and free to go, and though he nursed some portion of guilt, leaving Wayne beclamoured all about by such loud-tolling miseries and no solution in sight, and J.T. weighted down by his responsibilities, and Valerie beside herself with worry, to delay was only to pretend that he could offer any kind of help for their troubles. His ninety days were dwindling as fast as meat for the menagerie, and since his talk with Laura he had anyway killed all feeling and told himself he cared for no one.

There was a storm predicted, and only a couple of good hours of daylight remaining in which to feed the always-hungry beasts, so he drove as Wayne did, the rearmost low-stacked boxes sliding and bumping against one side and then the other of the van as he took the hills for his not-long home, pressing his foot down smooth to crest the final rise and so create the now-familiar little stomach lift and rush of plain kinetic pleasure when the van tipped the peak and slid the convex towards the gate. Today, this childish thrill was notched up electric, for in the elbow of the dip sat two black sheriff's cruisers, flashing silently in alternating red and blue, and augurs of instant fear.

There stood beside the frontmost car the same baby cop who had visited the farm just three weeks before, and he stepped into the road in his black uniform and his neat buzz cut and extended his arm in a semaphore of halt. Will slowed the van and put it in neutral, pulled up the handbrake and rolled down the window.

'Hey, you work here, don't you?' said the cop. 'You were here when that tiger was out.'

'Yeah, I'm staying here,' Will replied. 'Why? What's going on?'

'We've had a call from the neighbour about a lion and a bear loose. We can't raise Mr Gage and the gate's locked.'

'I've got the gate key here,' said Will. 'But that's weird that it's locked. Wayne should be home. I'll drive up and find him.'

'No. You wait here, please, sir. Pull off the road and give me the gate key.'

The other officer was sitting in his car with the door open, talking into his radio.

Will's gaze followed the driveway where it disappeared over the first low hill and as he pulled the key from the ignition there was movement at the hilltop and a lioness came padding down the mown slope towards them. She was one of the smaller females—maybe Lindy or Sasha. She looked spooked. Her ears swivelled wildly and she ran low and glanced about her, picking up each pale front paw in quick succession.

The other cop got out of his car and went around to the trunk. He bent down, and when he became visible again he was holding a rifle in both hands and he stepped back out from behind the car and raised the gun.

'Wait!' Will called out, finding within him as he said it a desperate imperative: *Don't shoot!* He had not quite known that these sly feelings had crept up on him, soft-padded as this creature in his sight, and did not try to name them as love or friendship or any other thing, but he knew them from the horror panic that came in tandem with the image of her sleek furred body torn through and permanent stilled, that strange quickening of life sucked out through the clean or jagged hole like the air from a ruptured balloon.

He opened the door of the van but the baby cop called out to him, 'Sir, please remain in your vehicle.'

'Please,' Will called. 'Don't shoot. You saw the other day. They're not dangerous, they're tame! We just need to get Wayne and we can get her back in her cage.'

The baby cop was standing beside his car in the road with his gun in one hand and his radio in the other, calling into the crackle static some code to summarise the surely codeless situation; the other cop was crouched, fist resting on the hood of the second car and rifle aimed, and it was all so militaristic formal and TV familiar.

'Yes, sir,' said the baby cop into his radio, and he called out to his colleague that the captain had given the order to shoot any animal that left the property and the crouched and gun-eyed colleague nodded into his sights as the gorgeous streak of low-running lioness—close enough now to see the living pink of her nose and the scared back-tilt of her round ears—reached the fence, seven strands of heavy-gauge wire taut between the posts and her head the height of the second wire from the top, and Will heard for the first time an actual gun being cocked, a sound as pure American iconic as that clean-forgotten Empire State.

The lioness paused at the fence and Will pulled out his phone and scrolled for Wayne's number, his hands shaking. He did not want to raise his eyes from the screen, and yet he glanced back up and just then saw it: the lioness pushed her sleek heavy head between the strands of wire and the wire clasped and wrung her through like the belt-fed product of some machine and she was free. She stood up tall and looked around her and then came the sound, so loud that Will's whole body jolted and he hit his head on the doorframe as the body of the lioness was felled with impossible totality into the status of meat with not a twitch or bound or roar within her evermore. He cried out *No!*, and heard the noise, or felt it rush up his throat like a blast of air from some part of him that had broken off and dropped away.

The lioness lay there, dumb-slumped and slab, yet still awesome in her size and beauty and snuffed-out wildness—not wildness as ferocity, for she had been tame and gentle and once a bottle-fed baby like his Nala, but the wildness of all animal being, which makes a small boy dash and leap from place to place instead of plain and sensible walking.

Will looked down at Wayne's number on his phone. How would he tell the besotted human shepherd of this various flock: he who had repudiated violence these long years since the war? The cops stood too in attitudes of seeming shock and Will despised them and would not countenance their fear or the question of what he would have done in their place.

All was still for a long grey moment. Then, the crackle of the radio and the two-man synchronous return to movement. The baby cop sent through a report on their grim success with the lioness and said that a bear might still be at large. The shooter fiddled with his gun and his face showed the conflicted inner workings of his mind. His lips were two ropey pink clenched muscles and he steered his gaze in a high arc above the splayed exquisite corpse by the fence. The three men were given scant time, however, each to assimilate this unlikely event: the death of a lion in the heart of rural Ohio.

'Whoa, whoa, Steve!' the shooter called, and Will again stayed his hand above the phone as he watched a big grey wolf slip deft and sudden between the wires twenty metres to the right and lope off mid-line down the road.

'Sir, we have a sighting of what appears to be a wolf leaving the property and heading down Ridge Road,' Steve said into his radio.

Will heard the crackled reply.

'Get after it, Carter!' Steve shouted, and the shooter literally jumped into what would in other circumstances have been a laughable practised version of an action hero stance and then gave chase, running after the animal with his rifle upraised.

Steve spoke into his radio again. 'Deputy Carter is in pursuit of the wolf, sir. I'm thinking I should go up to the house and see what we're dealing with here. If there's a bear out, we don't want it getting off the property on the highway side. I've got an employee of Mr Gage's here and he's got the gate key.'

He nodded at the radio as the metal voice returned its order or permission and he clipped the device onto his belt and went around the car and pulled his rifle from the trunk. He laid the rifle inside the car along the dashboard and called out to Will.

'Hand me that key.'

Will got down from the van and tossed him the set of keys.

'Remain in your vehicle, please. Do not get out for any reason. But if you can reach Mr Gage on the phone, let him know I'm driving up to the house.'

Will offered a curt nod and got back in the van.

The cop drove a few metres into the property and then stepped out again with the motor running and came back down to shut the gate. As he walked, facing the road, Will saw movement in the wooded fenceline to his left, from where the wolf had recently emerged like some improbable emblem of the long-forgotten status of humans as prey, and now the yellow and russet foliage shook with false beguile and a dark form swayed forward into the dimming last light. It was a grizzly bear, and it raised up massive and came at the cop, rocking boulder-like in a heavy grunting charge, and it seemed that death galloped invisibly beside it.

'Hey!' Will shouted, and the cop turned and saw and ran full pelt back to his car around the driver's side, so that the vehicle was between him and the beast that barrelled huffing forward. He opened the door and reached in for the rifle he'd laid across the dash, and Will saw the brute fear come into his young face as the gun got caught on something and he jerked his arm once, twice inside the car with his eyes on the huge dark creature as it closed the grassy interval between them and came on like fate itself. The bear began to swing like the arc of the sun in its path around the hood of the car, whose lights still flashed in mute helpless alarm, and the baby cop bent in a momentary crouch of despair or weakness, unwilled and futile act of shelter or perhaps even of prayer, but he rallied upright once more and drew his pistol and Will could see him brace, draw breath, his training kicking in like instinct, and he shot the bear as it rounded the hood and began to rear up full to its craggy sheer and shocking size. The bolt entered its glorious head and like the lioness it was felled to earth with the same impossible swiftness that measured precise the speed of that fleet now-flown mysterious animate spark.

Will watched the awesome body drop. The sound was still caught in the chambers of his hearing, and it was the second gunshot he had heard, today and also in his lifetime. Then, from a further distance out of sight came the day's third rending shot, more like lightning than thunder in its brief and splitting nature, and then a fourth, and the baby cop stood up and walked towards the bear as Will began to make his own way towards the brave basic comprehension of what was happening.

'Call the motherfucking owner of these animals,' the cop yelled out to Will across the open gate, relieved of his civic manners by this crisis, and Will unlocked his phone and put his finger to the number still waiting there on screen, but there was no answer and after a long interval the message began to play in Wayne's recorded voice announcing his indisposition. When the tone sounded, Will paused a moment before he said simply, 'Wayne, it's Will. Call me. *Please*, it's an emergency.'

Back along the road the second cop, Carter, came running with his rifle by his side, the blond strip of longer hair that lay atop the buzz-cut side regions of his skull flopping as he ran, and he appeared as panicked himself as any creature under fire. He stopped near the van and Will saw him catch sight of the bear and heard him swear quietly to himself.

Beside the mammoth corpse the baby cop was speaking to his radio and his voice was taut and jagged with fear-provoked fury.

'Sheriff's on his way,' he called out to his colleague.

'I got the wolf. It went up the neighbour's driveway.'

'Good work.'

One bear, one lion, one wolf: a deformed postmodern suovetaurilia, failed attempt at ritual cleansing, in this profane temple of the pin-drop random twenty-first century, of the guilt of man. And where was the mad priest of this place? His creatures shot down into nothingness because dumb Wayne must have fucked up somehow, tried to do the feed himself and left the cages unsecured. Maybe he'd been attacked or mauled by one of the animals. Maybe he was lying up there bleeding without his phone.

'Fuck, that's a big fucking bear,' said Carter.

'Yep. That was probably the closest call I've had in my life,' said Steve.

'What now?'

'Like I said, sheriff's on the way. Should be here in twenty. He said go up to the house and try to locate the owner. Sir,' he commanded Will, 'I'm going to ask you to come with me up to the house to look for Mr Gage. As we both know, he can be uncooperative.'

Will got out of the van and clambered into the rear of the cop car, which smelled of chemical cleaning products, thinking as he shut the door that he had to get the chicken into the fridge soon or it would spoil, and with a soundtrack of insistent radio traffic they took slow leave of the fallen bear whose ridiculous and heartbreaking name, he now recalled, was Glen.

The range of Wayne's Wild Kingdom was hidden by the first hill up which the gravel driveway made its approach, but once the car broached the crest the whole property appeared, spread out across the long ascent past dam and cages and weed-bedded cars and Will's RV to the right of the incongruous cream-brick house crouched atop the second hill. The sky was crowded with a spectatorship of storm clouds and the dam was an unreflecting grey.

The first thing Will noticed was a male lion at rest on the reed-fringed dam bank. Steve stopped the car. 'Holy hell,' he said. 'Just what in bejesus is going on here?' He picked up the dashboard radio. 'This is LeRoy. I'm heading up to Mr Gage's house and there's another lion on the loose.'

The lion meanwhile did not move. He appeared to drowse like an old man after lunch. His mane was scruffy and he wore a purple collar.

'Actually,' said Will, 'I'm pretty sure that's Simba. He's often out of the cage, 'cause he's so old and he's got bung hips so he can't run.'

'Okay,' was all the deputy said. He relayed the information to his superior, who instructed him to stay inside his vehicle, but continue to try to locate Wayne.

It was when they neared the row of cages on the upward slope that they abrupted on the truth like an underwater snag. The foremost cage contained Sabrina, a white tiger who was heavy with her soon-due litter, but the door of her cage was open, as was the door of the empty cage adjacent up the hill, and the one beside it.

'What the . . .' said Will in soft-voiced horror. He had been gone perhaps four hours, if that, and all had been well at his departure, Wayne feeding the baby monkey and telling Will he was going to spend half an hour jamming with a joint between his lips before he got back to brush-hogging.

There was a full-grown tiger by the front door. It padded off around the side of the house as the car approached. Steve backed up and followed it. Up the hill towards the horse paddock stood a male and two female lions. Steve stopped again on the slope and turned the engine off.

'Do you know how many animals are kept here?'

'Around forty-five, I think. Maybe fifty.'

'Are you kidding me? This is a fucking full-scale disaster we've got on our hands.'

Steve conferred again with his superior officer, and was told again to remain in his vehicle. They drove back to the front of the house and Steve leaned a long loud minute on the horn. In the ticking silence that followed, they heard another gunshot from down the hill.

'We'd better get back,' said Steve. He tried the horn again and then they returned down the driveway, past the rows of cages. Every door in the front row at least was hanging open, though some of the animals were still inside. As they passed the wrecked and lawn-bedded cars on the left, Will saw a tiger move between the stalled forms of a boat trailer and an RV. Then, as they came level with the RV, he saw a brown bear on the other side, ambling away from them in the coming dusk. Simba was no longer by the dam. There were animals out everywhere.

Will looked at his watch. It was close to 5.30 pm. It would be dark soon and there was a storm front showing like spilled dark liquid above the hill that faced the house.

On the radio, a voice ordered Steve to return to the road. It said that they were setting up a perimeter, and that the guys from Narco had arrived.

'What's Narco?' Will asked.

'Narcotics.'

'Why are they here?'

'Better artillery.'

There were four police cars at the gate now. The bodies of the bear and lioness lay unreal on the verge and another corpse was laid out at the bottom of the slope, another lioness who must have been shot on the run; her legs were twisted and her head thrown back.

But she's inside the fence, Will thought. We could have caught her. But *who* could have? He thought of the struggle to capture the fugitive Zoya. Dread rumbled audibly in his guts.

'Should I call J.T.?' he asked.

'Good idea,' said Steve.

He made the call as they clattered over the pipe grille. Here it was all action. Men in uniform holding guns. A barricade up across the road.

J.T. picked up.

'J.T., it's Will.'

'Hey, Will, how are you?'

'Not good. I'm out at Wayne's and it looks like a lot of the animals are out. Like, maybe *all* of them. I went to get chicken and when I got back the cops were here. We can't find Wayne. It's really bad, hey. They've shot a couple of the animals.'

'Oh my god, no! Okay, I'm on my way. Just . . . don't let them shoot any more.'

Will was about to consult with Steve, but J.T. had hung up.

'J.T. said he's on his way.'

'Good. Hopefully he can tell us exactly how many there are. We need to know what we're dealing with here. You stay in the car.'

He got out and shut the door and Will slid up against the passenger window like a child to try to hear what was happening.

A man who might be the sheriff, an older guy with a red face and a thick white moustache, was issuing orders to a small group of men in uniform.

'Blake, Voss, you head to the neighbours' and make sure no animals get onto their property. Knox, Pelosi, head for the eastern perimeter. Don't let anything get through. We've got warning signs being set up on the I-70 and a team along Ridge Road. We've got about ninety minutes of daylight and we need to act fast. I've cleared channel five, so report as you go. Okay, get moving.'

Men hustled off with their guns and boots and bulky utility belts and holsters, dispersing in all directions like seekers in some schoolyard game. An incongruous ancient farm truck with a wooden plank-sided bed rattled up Ridge Road, heading for town, and was stopped at the barricade and turned back, the farmer removing his hat and holding it out the open driver-side door like a flag of surrender, peering up the hill that blocked the view of Wayne's house and over at the dead bear.

Whenever an animal was glimpsed atop the rise, the sheriff fired his gun into the air to startle it back from the doom of the fence line. In the thirty minutes before J.T. arrived, six animals—another wolf, a brown bear, a male and two female lions and a smallish tiger who may have been Zoya—were sighted and repelled.

Then J.T. tore up and leaped out of his truck and Will decided to disobey orders and leave the car.

The smell of smoke hung in the air, and J.T. was anguished and arguing with the sheriff, gazing in despair at the bodies in their stilled still-magnificence.

'Wayne is going to . . . oh Christ. This is terrible . . . this is terrible,' J.T. was saying, and he pinched between his eyes as if to catch the forced-back tears in the cup of his big palm. 'That's Lola,' he said with a crack in his voice, looking at the lioness that lay outside the fence.

'How do you know?' asked the sheriff.

'I *know*! I've known these animals for years. Most of them from babies . . . *Oh my god* . . . you didn't have to shoot her!'

'Do you reckon you could make an inventory of every animal owned by Mr Gage?' the sheriff asked.

'Sir,' said J.T., and his voice was pleading, 'these are *tame* animals. They're not dangerous. The bear, I get. But the lions, most of them I could just leash them and walk them back to their enclosures.'

'Mr Nash,' said the sheriff, 'within a five-mile radius of here, there's a high school, there's a sports field, a gas station and a family restaurant. I understand you're upset, but I need to protect the community as my first duty.'

J.T. looked down and nodded, a small nod for such a big man.

Soon J.T. and Will were writing out a list of all the animals, J.T. saying names as he unbent and touched each finger of his left hand and then balled his fist again, walking through each cage in his disbelieving mind and seeing each distinct beloved face. Steve stood beside them with his rifle keeping guard, though J.T. had let out a punch of laughter at the idea that he needed protection from these creatures, his friends. Will held a clipboard and wrote down the names and the species as J.T. recited them, and there was something reverent in the act, a bearing of witness. Fifteen tigers. Eighteen lions (two dead). Two brown bears and one grizzly bear (dead). Three wolves (one dead). One panther. Two leopards. Not counting the babies and the monkeys and the horses, that made thirty-eight animals potentially on the loose.

There had been no gunshot since J.T. arrived, but when a raven flew down and lit upon the bear's corpse, Steve pulled his pistol from his belt and fired it into the sky, and the bird wheeled away cawing.

Will and J.T. flinched, and J.T. shook his head. 'Seriously,' he said. 'Just waving your arms works fine.'

Steve replaced his gun and fixed his eyes on the hill, and Will saw that he had been trying to show respect for the corpse and had been hurt by J.T.'s response.

Thirty-eight animals.

The number was reported to the sheriff and his unruly eyebrows hoisted themselves towards his white-haired skull.

J.T. was insistent that he be allowed onto the property to try to cage as many creatures as he could and to try to locate Wayne.

'There's no way Wayne did this,' he said. 'Someone's come onto the property. Probably saw Will leave in the van and thought no one was home. It'll be one of those radicals, for sure. We've dealt with them before. One guy tried to let a tiger out and got himself mauled. People could be hurt up there. Wayne could be hurt, if he tried to stop them. I mean, I don't know why else he's disappeared like this.'

The sheriff agreed to let Steve drive the two of them up to the house again to search for Wayne, but they were not to try to capture or even approach the animals. And so Will climbed again into the too-clean scent of the patrol car's dark interior.

The spaces between the buckeyes that formed a thick border down the western edge of the property were beginning to fill with shadow and to merge with the trunks and fall-darkened leaves. The flats around the dam were still bare of animals but they saw many more than on their last mission, lions skulking and milling by the last row of cages, and a tiger sitting up on the old boat trailer above the spears of tall feathery grasses, as if advertising some safari adventure park. There was another tiger by the towel-hung clothesline, and two male lions prowling at the side of the house. From more than one direction they heard the still-disquieting sound of roaring.

'It's feeding time,' said J.T. 'They're hungry. Kind of good in terms of catching them, but it also makes them more risky to handle.'

They pulled up before the house and Steve leaned again on the horn in a long blast that scared off the lions and sent dusk-nesting birds rising into the lucent grey sky. Without warning, J.T. got out of the car.

'Hey!' Steve shouted.

As J.T. reached the door, one of the big male lions came back around the side towards him and Steve swore and pulled out his pistol, but J.T. was patting the thick-fringed massive head and then he gave the hip-high beast a gentle shove and it padded off. Steve swore again and holstered his gun, but he pulled his rifle from the dash and held it before him as he exited the car like someone stepping with an umbrella into rain.

He and Will walked with brisk caution to the front porch and Steve knocked with heavy futile authority on the open door through which J.T. had already vanished.

Will was afraid as he stepped into the familiar cool and monkey-smelling dusk of the tiled hallway. Not of Wayne, but in case there were other people in the house.

He could hear sounds from the living room and he moved inside with Steve too close at heel, his radio clicking and crackling. He saw J.T. standing by the TV, and at the same time he saw a low scuffling movement on the other side of the lounge suite and he could not help it, he sucked in with a loud breath of fright.

Steve held up his gun like a member of a TV SWAT team.

And then in a growling tumble the two tiger cubs rolled into view by the glass doors.

Steve raised his gun but Will leaped forward out of some fierce unknown instinct.

'Don't shoot! It's the babies.'

Steve let his gun hang down and stepped further into the room. J.T. and Will walked over to the cubs and bent and ruffled them as they tussled on, oblivious. From their cage, the monkeys screeched, startled by the presence of a stranger, and Steve jumped visibly at the sound.

'What the fuck *is* this place?' he said, his fear transmuted into embarrassment and then quickly into anger. 'It fucking stinks in here!'

Through the radio came the voice of the sheriff. 'Come in, LeRoy. What's your status? Have you located Mr Gage?'

At the sound, the monkeys launched into a full-bodied chorus, and Steve had to step out of the room to speak.

As Will and J.T. crouched with the cubs they saw a tiger—a huge Siberian male—pass close across the patio and head up the hill towards the horse paddock.

'What the hell is happening?' said J.T. in disbelief.

Steve returned and gestured for them to follow him and the three men went deeper into the house. There were rooms that Will had never entered here, and most were crammed full and alarming in their irrefutable evidence of disorder hidden only just out of sight. One room was crowded with perhaps seven or eight Harley-Davidson motorcycles, their tyre tracks visible in the peach shag pile carpet, and the peach chenille bedspread was stacked high with leather jackets whose protective muscled arms lay strewn about like some tentacled creature from the depths of sea or mind. It was cold in these rooms and in many the light bulbs had been unaccountably removed, leaving only bare plastic sockets like faucets through which might seep at any moment some noxious gas, and Steve had to light their way with his big black torch. In every room they called out to Wayne and were answered by silence.

Then, in what must be Wayne's room, they found the baby monkey in her box. Will picked her up and cradled her, and J.T. stroked her head with one finger.

'He's not here. Let's go,' said Steve. 'Put the monkey back.'

'She needs to be fed,' said Will.

'It'll have to wait.'

Will lifted the tiny monkey back into her crate. At least she had water. 'Hang on, can I at least leave her with some fruit?'

'For fuck's sake,' said Steve. 'Okay, be quick.'

Will ran to the kitchen and got a banana and ran back. He peeled it and placed it beside the cowering baby monkey. She was too little to be eating fruit yet, but it would have to do. Through sheer curtains that looked out on the near edge of the horse paddock, he could see two male lions—perhaps the ones that had been outside the house earlier—and two tigers.

Steve spoke into his radio, reporting their lack of success.

'Roger. Head back down then,' came the reply.

'Look at them—they're confused,' said J.T., pointing out the window. 'They're waiting for someone to come and feed them. If you'd just let me try to get them back in their cages . . .'

'Sorry, no,' said Steve. 'I need to take you back down. We have to avoid any chance of anyone getting hurt or, God forbid, killed.'

'But they *know* me. *Please.*'

'I'm sorry. It's out of the question.' Steve turned and walked off down the hallway. The monkeys were still shrieking when they shut the front door.

The light had changed even in the brief interval of their search and the sky was now a sickly hue, as if a fluorescent yellow bulb was shining through grey gauze. A thunderhead was launching like a zeppelin by slow degrees above the house.

'Storm's coming,' said Steve. 'Maybe even hail. Take a look at that sky.'

Just then they heard the sound of a wolf howl from some hidden place among the ominous scrap woods and wrecked cars of this junk kingdom, and Will felt a jag of deep dread that seemed to start in his teeth, as if he had bitten down on foil.

It was as the baby cop was backing the car towards the western side of the house that J.T. called out. He had been peering out the back windscreen, his body taking up most of the seat.

'Stop!' he shouted. 'I think that's Wayne!'

'Where?' said Steve.

'Over there. Down the slope. He's on the ground. He must be hurt.'

'Okay, stay in the car.' He swerved back around so they were pointing down the hill where J.T. had indicated.

The body was some way off down the slope, past Will's trailer and lying with its legs angled towards the dam. There was no doubt that it was Wayne. Beside him stood Snow, the white Siberian tiger. As they watched, Snow bent his huge thick-striped pale head and with the curved ivory hasps of his teeth he dragged Wayne by the thigh further down the slope.

'Snow,' said J.T. 'He must be trying to help him. Wayne's hurt.'

As Snow pulled Wayne across the grass, his torso rolled towards them and it was as if he had turned his head to look at his friends watching from the car. But where his face had been was now revealed a mash of red and bloody wound that swung in a gazeless arc across their excoriated field of vision and then turned towards the fading mirror of the dam.

There was a silence in the car that pooled and dropped, and like the shards of spilled water it would never be repaired.

Will heard with the part of him still present the click of four locks and he watched from some pinpoint distance the raging of J.T. against the door. As the car slunk away the cop said, 'He's gone, bud. There's nothing you can do for him. I'm sorry.'

J.T.'s forehead was pressed against the rear of the passenger seat and his wet snuffling inhalations were all that could be heard inside the car. As they reached the road, the young cop mustered his limited natural authority towards the back seat and said he needed to know before he let him out that J.T. would not do anything stupid like try to go back onto the property, and J.T. lifted his face and Will watched a thin cord of clear mucus stretch and land in a silvery line down the back of the dark upholstery. J.T. snorted up tears and gave a beaten nod and they were allowed to exit the vehicle.

J.T. walked to his own car and he slumped down against its side and leaned his head into the shelter of his bent knees and Will heard him retch and vomit onto the grass.

It was as though the dusk was bringing with it into the air some mist-borne drug of hazy stultification and, as in a long-forgotten childhood fever dream, Will felt his feet grow heavy and enormous, and he heard at the remove of translation Steve say to the sheriff something that made no sense: that there had been a gun by Wayne's body and his guess was that the cause of death would turn out to be a self-inflicted gunshot wound to the head and the damage done by the tiger had been post-mortem.

A gun? Had there been a gun? The sheriff spoke into his radio and said that the property was now a crime scene and he called for detectives and a paramedic team to be dispatched at once.

Wayne was gone? As if through the thickness of sleep the thought reached Will: was this Wayne's plan? But it couldn't be. He would never do that to his children. Will heard again Wayne's words to him: *I'm desperate here. Who's going to take care of them if you leave?* He shook his head and looked around. The road was clotted with vehicles and men moved about in all directions with serious faces and an energy of suppressed excitement. Two cops were strapping on bulky vests over their uniforms and Will's numb gaze drifted among the gathering of busy humans and cars and the stiffening bodies of shot animals in the dip of the road between the low hills that seemed at once too close, as though shielding him from the clear knowledge of what was happening here like a mother bending in to cover the eyes of a child.

Now a massive black Chevy Silverado pulled up in a showy spray of gravel and out of it climbed a man who would have played the role of warrior at any moment in history at which he manifested upon this poor and ravaged earth. He wore a thick armoured vest like the others over a blue hoodie and suspended from a kind of harness around his neck and chest was an industrial and enormous black rifle and another, some kind of terrifying machine gun, was strapped to his back. He had a sharp keen dog-like face and a thick neck the width of his close-cropped head that gave him a snubbed maggot-like appearance, the pale seamless digit of head-neck poking up from the bulky dark equipment of his uniform and video-game excess artillery. His name, called out around him, was Brock, and Will looked on him as the bannerman of advance into some new and deeper circle of hell, and in this assessment he was correct.

—

The sheriff began to marshal up the men who were stepping about in a restlessness of poured-out ready and now-cooling adrenaline. Will watched and glowered and tried to ascertain what plan of action was being launched like missile fire into this tiny kingdom. The three heavy-armed men lined up for orders and they named the weapons carried between them: M4 assault rifle; MP5 submachine gun; Glock 22; M&P15 assault rifle; Glock 17; AX308; Glock 22.

'You will be alone on the property,' said the sheriff. 'You have approximately fifty minutes of light. Your orders are to shoot every animal you see. There are three teams patrolling the perimeter, so do not fire into the woods or directly towards the fence line. Drive the animals out into the open first. Once the area is secured, we'll send the paramedics in. We will reconvene here at the control centre at nightfall. Is that clear?'

The three men, arrayed in their modern garb of ageless violence against the animal or subaltern other, climbed onto the dropped-down gate and into the tray of the tank-sized Silverado, and another man got into the driver's seat, and they checked their weaponry and nodded and the maggot thumped thrice the roof of the cab with a massive flat palm and they took off over the grate and out of sight.

Shoot every animal.

Will sat down beside J.T. where he was slumped over his own vomit. Already came in terrible quick succession the sound of gunshots.

'They're killing them,' said Will, and was surprised to hear his voice regressed to adolescence. 'What can we do?'

J.T. shook his unlifted head and would not speak.

Will leaned against the cold metal of J.T.'s truck and pressed the heels of his hands into his eyes. All was a-churn within him. And yet he knew that his guilt and stunned spectatorial pain were nothing to J.T.'s agony. The sound of shooting was constant and it moved about like a storm cloud, now so loud that Will was forced to cover his ears, and even the sheriff shook his white head; now further off, though still deafening enough, and gun smoke rose up from above the first hill and hung there in the cool gloaming. Between rounds Will heard the calls of the men in the truck as they tracked and tore after another of the terrified animals.

J.T. was straight out weeping now, pounding a fist into his big thigh and holding the other up to his mouth as if about to call out some loud demand, and Will felt the drops slip out warm from his own eyes, imagining the hazing out of hiding and the terrible chasing down of each crouched-running beast, each singular and stunning life no more, each petted bottle-fed and trusting creature killed in its mute and mad-dash fear within the bounds of its no-more home, and he felt in his constricted core that in this travesty he was implicated to an inextricable depth.

A man approached. It was Doc Hazel, the vet who had treated the animals for many years. He was pale and palpitant and he made clenching movements with his hands as he looked around at the cars and flashing lights and the black-clad sheriff and the passive downward-looking men with their ambiguous expressions that could be shame or thrill or the mere struggle to keep their features impassive in the face of such stark and sudden-met circumstances. Doc Hazel asked J.T. whether anyone had contacted Valerie. At the sound of her name, Will believed that he felt his stomach literally sink, and he was seized by a fast and thankfully brief pressing need to shit, and he contracted his whole body and his mind, too, so as to squeeze enclosed within the bowels of his brain any image of Valerie's face.

J.T. looked up and shook his swollen-featured head and said, so quiet that the vet had to ask him to repeat it, 'I can't,' and the kind old vet nodded and stepped away. Will saw him stoop towards the darkening fields, away from the cars and men and the bodies of the lions and bear, and he watched him pause a moment in which he seemed to meditate on his in-and-outward breath, and then pull out his phone and turn full away so that Will could only see his set shoulders and his long brown coat pacing the ditch line as he offered up the ruin of one woman's world.

Just before seven o'clock the truck returned down the driveway and pulled up only feet from where they sat, and as it slowed Will heard the myriad-clinking wave sound of the bullet shells rolling across the metal floor. The shooters let down the tray and began kicking out the shells: hundreds of them tumbling out, shining like currency.

'Out of ammo,' said one of the men. 'Man, we fired so many rounds we could barely stand up. It was like trying to balance on ball bearings.'

'I swear I've fired more rounds in the past forty-five minutes than in the rest of my life put together,' said another one.

The sheriff chopped his head towards Will and J.T. and the men dropped into chastened silence.

'Do you have a count?' the sheriff asked with a stern dispassionate voice.

'Yes, sir,' said Brock. 'Twenty-six so far.'

'Twenty-six. With the bear and the lions here and the wolf, that makes it thirty. Still another twelve out there.'

'I reckon we've got a quarter-hour more before we lose visibility,' said Brock. 'Then we could move to thermal.'

'Okay. Get back in there then,' said the sheriff.

Two of the men jumped down and each went to his own car to get more ammunition while Brock reloaded from a locked compartment in the rear of the truck and then with little fuss they took off again into the zone of massacre. Soon the shooting began again and soon, too, the dark fell in earnest.

J.T. got up and stood swaying. Like Will, he was wearing just a thin checked shirt and jeans, and he rubbed his arms and shivered. His face was a mess: blotchy white and red, his eyes puffed up, the irises dark and small and blank.

'I'm gonna sit in the car and call Tamsyn,' he said.

Will nodded. He raised himself and stretched his stiff legs, moving a few steps away to give J.T. his privacy. He heard on the radio that two more animals had been shot on the neighbour's property by the patrol sent down there.

Close to 7.30 pm three fire trucks arrived. The sheriff briefed the firemen and then two of the trucks drove off again to illuminate the southern and eastern perimeters, and the remaining truck reversed across the road and shone its lights up the fence line where the land was wooded and already thick with night.

Will thought in listless reflex brain-spark observation that the lit-up woods looked beautiful, would make a great photograph, the kind that might appear in an expensive square-format art magazine. The wind had risen into full tide and was thrashing the trees as if to strip them of their loose-held foliage, and leaves of orange and crimson and dark blood were swirling within the deep cones of light as though the earth was trying to remind them of the deathless undefeat and eternal persistence of beauty. Will let his gaze go slack and saw the leaves and the air through which they moved as one, and he felt some part of himself go out to be taken up and carried in that wild right system with no volition to retrieve himself, and it took a door slamming close by to make him reel his weightless soul back in on its gauzy frail umbilicus.

The detectives had arrived: strange costumed figures with their hooded white crime-scene suits whipping in the wind. They were driven onto the property by an armed escort to gather samples from Wayne's body before the paramedics were allowed to bag and carry him away.

Will watched them disappear over the hill, the ambulance following behind. It was very cold now, the wind coming in rough thumps of sympathy or threat, and the air wafted alternately the smells of rain and cordite.

Will approached J.T.'s truck and peered into the dark cab, but there was no one inside, so he paced the verge until at last the ambulance returned, bearing inside it Wayne's part-eaten corpse encased in its black and zippered coffin, and the sheriff gave the order to clear the way and the ambulance passed through the gate as the cars pulled off the road in chorus line formation to let the flashing hearse drive on.

Among the gathered men there was no uttered sound and all were united in their deep-sprung wish to put down bravery and plunge oblivious into the arms of wife or mother, to be enclosed in some indiscriminate female sphere of comfort.

Goodbye, Wayne, Will said silent into the night. *I'm sorry.*

*

The sky had been holding back its flood and hastening on the men with fulgurous flashes and loud threat and, now the task was done, the emissary intermittent heavy drops massed to torrent and the storm broke like a child giving way to held-in tears. All were drenched in seconds, and it was a cold and gusty downpour that seemed a pronouncement severe and opprobrious.

Will dashed towards the van, but as he neared it he saw J.T. running out of the field that faced Wayne's gate, and he turned back and ran with plashing footsteps to J.T.'s truck, and as J.T. wrenched open the driver's door Will likewise drew on the handle of the passenger side and the two men ducked in and the sound of water muted and changed tone, deepened now and hollowed by the metal roof, and both slammed their doors and bent inevitably to the task of wiping the rain from their eyes and hair and foreheads before they faced each other. They sat unspeaking, communicating nonetheless a mute kindred complex of pain and helpless forgiveness of whatever weight of implication they may singly or together hold. Through the rain-freaked and rivuleted windscreen they watched the fray of men continue all around them and they sat that way for more than an hour as the bowed figures moved among the headlights and the brief but brighter sky-thrown flashes, as the snipers in their truck made another incursion into the kingdom and were repulsed it seemed by the weather and then commandeered from somewhere two quad bikes and mounted up in pairs, revving off once more through the falling water in a convoy that looked no more official than a party of roo shooters come upon in the lawless outback of Australia.

'Where's Valerie?' Will asked at some juncture in their clamorous unspeaking.

'Doc said she's coming back from somewhere and it'll take her a while to get here.'

Will shook his head and looked down again. 'Did you talk to Tamsyn?'

'Yeah,' was all J.T. replied.

Will could hear J.T.'s teeth chattering over the sound of the rain, and J.T. just sat there staring straight ahead and let them clatter in his jaw.

Despite the adrenaline thump and thump of his veins, Will passed into a ghastly half-sleep. He woke when his head jerked up autonomous, and with a feeling of pure dread of the kind that had existed for him previously only following a nightmare. Apart from that, all was as it had been before he slept: the rain continued to sluice and runnel the windscreen and to thrum the metal roof and now and then there was the sound of a gunshot, a noise that had been invested in an interval of hours with a familiarity that would perhaps never leave him. J.T. snuffled and from time to time drew a sharp aspiration of two or three short gasps as though he had forgotten to breathe. The cab of the truck was freezing, but smelled rankly of the sweat of fear and stalled flight.

Will passed his hand across the windscreen and left a four-tined track on the fogged glass, as J.T. began to whimper again and then to sob. He hit his head twice against the side window and then he raised his hands to his face and through this screen he poured forth a series of heart-rent and rhetorical questions directed at his dead friend: why and what was he thinking and how could he do this to his animals, didn't he know this would happen to them, was he that dumb, or was this what he wanted and how could that be, had he lost it, and why did he not ask his friends for help?

Will watched him as he rode up and over this cold single crest of a grieving that was ocean-vast and in which such crests lay banked and dark and heaving as far as the horizon.

Eventually, he rocked in a necessary trough and revealed his mushy face. 'What are we doing here?' he said to Will. 'I thought we could save some of them but there's no way. I just want to go home now.'

Will nodded. 'You should go,' he said. 'I guess I'll try and get a bit of sleep in the van.'

'Shit, I'm not thinking. You come with me, of course. There's no way I'm gonna be able to sleep, but I can't stay here, I just can't.' As he spoke, J.T. tugged on the sleeves of his shirt, bunching and sealing his hands inside the damp fabric tubes in a boyish gesture of searching for comfort.

'Do you think we can just leave?'

'I'll go and talk to Sheriff Peck.' J.T. wiped his face decent with the shirt-stumps and then released his hands and opened the door. At once an insult of cold and rain flung in and Will had a minor flash of pity for the killers at their work under the pelting starless sky and then a sharper and enduring state of satisfied malice leaped up to replace it.

He mimicked J.T. in bunching his own hand into the sleeve of his shirt and with the knuckled cloth he cleared a porthole in the windscreen and watched J.T. go with swaying mud-sunk steps towards the region where a small open-sided tent had been set up, under which men stood hunched with dark and urgent purpose around a steaming tripod lantern. He had to clear the patch three more times and observed only the inarticulate movement of many heavy sets of shoulders before J.T. returned, re-drenched and shivering. His face in the overhead light was a terrible thing: blotched and boiled-looking, the eyes like burnt raisins in their sockets of wet dough.

'He says we can leave but we have to be back at five am.'

Will looked at his watch. It was 1 am. 'Why?'

'He wants us to help count the bodies.'

SLEEP WAS A BRIEF CLUBBED oblivion, suspended somewhere in a gel flecked through with the electric sparking of stressed nerves and spinning stars like those that circle a cartoon man knocked unconscious. Will woke in an almost-darkness that smelled of coffee and he could see a halogen glow in the doorway and hear the whispered voices of Tamsyn and J.T. in the kitchen. There was something in it that reminded him of childhood: his parents rising before dawn and filling the thermos and making banana sandwiches before a long car trip; lying in the dim warmth and listening to the hushed competent preparations until he was fetched and gathered up and carried to the car still wrapped in his quilt and squashed beside Tom in the packed-high back seat, the space smelling of closed bedrooms and mouth breathing.

The orange door was eclipsed now by a dark body and J.T. whispered that it was time to wake up. He flicked the light on and the room lit up a terrible grey, the gloss enamel walls and the cheap ceramic coffee cup that J.T. held out the colour of a dying tooth.

J.T. had changed and was rugged up in a Carhartt jacket and a blue beanie, but his face was the same yeasty pale and abraded pink, the membranes of his nose and eyes raw almost to bloody.

Will had slept in borrowed clothes after a hot shower that brought him stinging back to warmth at 2 am, just two hours before. His own clothes were draped over a chipped clotheshorse in front of the gas heater and he took them to the bathroom and put them back on, the dried-stiff jeans and the stinking shirt, and then in the nausea of sleeplessness and grief the two men embraced the weeping Tamsyn, who clutched her baby tightly to her breast, and like escapees recaptured, sunk low in impotent mutiny, they returned to the site of ruin that had once been Wayne's Wild Kingdom.

The roadblock at the exit off the I-70 was gone, but there were two sheriff's cruisers stationed either side of the pike. Something was going on: there was a black pickup truck parked off the road and three young guys huddled beside it in the glare of headlights while a cop stood with his radio upheld. In the back of the truck was the body of a lioness, her head lying open-mouthed and pitiful on the metal tray gate.

J.T. slowed and made a circular movement with his hand, and Will wound down the window.

'What's going on?' J.T. called out.

'Where you headed, sir?' asked the officer.

'Up to Wayne's. I work there. Sheriff Peck asked us to come back at five.'

'Okay, hold on.' The cop turned away and spoke into his radio and then nodded back at them.

'Excuse me,' said J.T. 'What's going on over there? With the lioness?'

'Dumb kids. They claim they found it on the side of the road. Up by Deever's driveway, I believe. Reckoned they were gonna make a rug out of it.' He shook his head in exaggerated disapproval, though he was barely older than the three cowed youths across the road. 'If we hadn't caught them, we would've been searching for that missing lion bitch until kingdom come.'

As they drove down Ridge Road and into the dip, they met a bank of fog and they entered it and were consumed. The fire trucks were gone and the road in their headlights and the verge on either side was a gouged-up field of mud with thin lines of torn grass between tyre tracks.

J.T. pulled up off the road and Will felt the wheels sink and hoped they wouldn't bog. The two of them got out and walked through the mist and mud like men approaching the gallows.

At the control centre there had been a changing of the guard. The sheriff was still there, but Will didn't recognise any of the other men. There was a group of about ten still gathered under the white crime-scene marquee, the roof of which was bowed and sagged with rainwater. The lamp shone eerie in the foggy air. Two cops who had evidently arrived just before them were handing out takeaway coffees from cardboard trays. The sheriff saw them and he held out an arm as if to hug J.T. and then dropped it again.

'J.T., Will,' he said. 'Thank you for coming back. I appreciate it.' His manner had changed; it was as if he was being recorded or speaking in front of the media. He turned to the tent. 'These boys work on the property. They're here to do an inventory so we can check if there are any animals unaccounted for. Boys, this is Dr Susan Hillier and Dr Murray Smith from over at the Range animal sanctuary, and this is Peter Morton from Columbus Zoo. They're here to lend a hand. We've made the decision that once it's light again, if there are still any animals on the property, we'll do our best to try and tranquillise them instead of euthanising them. Transport them back to the zoo if we can get permission from Mrs Gage, who's on her way here now. Same with the remaining animals inside the house.'

'Okay,' said J.T. 'That's good. There's no way Valerie'll surrender any of them that *are* still alive, though.'

'Well, we'll see,' said the sheriff.

The people from the sanctuary were subdued in their greeting, like funeral directors meeting the bereaved. The man from the zoo was a big outdoorsy-looking guy wearing matching khaki shirt and trousers. He looked like someone who might star in a reality television show in which he had to navigate a variety of treacherous wild terrains.

The sheriff began to lay out the plan. He was holding an enormous cup of coffee, the size of a child's bucket, and Will watched as he gestured about with it and a bubble of brown froth bloomed from the sip hole in the lid. The woman from the animal sanctuary removed the lid from her coffee as the sheriff spoke and licked the chocolatey suds from inside.

Will was shivering again already, standing in the square of steaming orange light, an island of careful human order and tactical logic in the surrounding dim and fog and mud in which the bodies of dead animals lay everywhere, invisible and cold, their striped or tawny hides slick and matt with the cleansing or condemnation of rain.

'We've had men on the perimeters all night and we're as certain as we can be that no animals have escaped from the property,' the sheriff was saying. 'Our guys have gathered up all of the animals that have unfortunately had to be euthanised. They've got most of them in one spot up on the hill there. So what we're gonna do is we'll get you two'—here he brought his outstretched arm with its coffee cup around towards Will and J.T.—'to go up there . . . escorted by our guys. You'll be perfectly safe. We think we've got them all anyways, but they'll . . . you know, just in case . . . and then we'll check off the animals against the list we made last night. Make sure you didn't miss any of them. Because I know it was'—he paused, checking his tone and coming up apparently short—'well, it was a difficult night for everybody.'

'A *difficult night*?' J.T. muttered beside Will.

'These folks'—he nodded at the other three, who nodded in return—'will be on standby down here, and if it turns out we've still got any animals at large, then we'll do a line search and if it's at all possible we'll try to tranquillise them so we can save a couple at least. After that we can move on to the animals in the house. I believe there are two tiger cubs and a couple of monkeys.'

Will thought of the baby monkey in her crate in the dark unheated house.

'What about the other cubs?' said J.T., and now Will thought of Nala, his little sweetheart. Oh, cruel fate, what portion of this vast estate of guilt was his own allotted part? He saw within his scarred imagining the frown-darkened face of Wayne in its desperation of ruined fellow feeling and belief in his agency over destiny.

'What other cubs?' said the sheriff. 'Were they in the house?'

'No. In an enclosure up behind it. Just a pen. They're still little.'

'Not sure about that.'

'We'll do our absolute best,' said the man from the zoo. He stood there in his cargo pants, his thick thighs spread wide, his arms crossed.

The sheriff gave an awkward cough and continued his briefing, explaining that they would wait here until first light and then embark upon their mission.

'Why did we have to get here so fricking early then?' J.T. mumbled.

The three vets or animal experts, whatever they were, clumped by one pole of the tent and spoke quietly and drank their coffees, and the rest of the group disbanded, leaving Will and J.T. standing in the centre with the clipboard inventory they had made last night in that brief deluded blink of waning hope.

The sky did not grow light so much as it intensified from black into a menace of purple, and then paled to the same contagious yellow-grey it had been twelve hours before. As they passed with their armed escort across the grille and broached the first hill it was clear that today would not be a better day than yesterday. What had been a scrappy realm of mown grass and weed-sunk vehicles, cut through by the gravel driveway and badged by the small dam, was now a torn-up field of mud, gouged and scored with deep rain-filled wheel tracks as if a giant had stirred about in it with a huge pronged instrument with no intention save sheer delight in destruction, and it was altered to the edge of recognition.

In the bowl of land above the dam lay a splayed mound of the chain-dragged and desecrate slain. The bodies of the furred and still beautiful once-menagerie had been arrayed in their species and laid out with their heads all visible but their hinds piled and tangled, and it was all Will could do to look.

The air was strangled with the smell of death and with the unburied stink of turned mud, and after mere steps their shoes were clodded huge and heavy with clay, and they stepped horse-kneed and clownish with a terrible comedy.

Will felt condemned, arrested, within their escort of lawmen: a captain or lieutenant beside them, carrying the clipboard, and two new shooters fore and aft the little group, their gun-raised swivelling adding to the bleak farce of their mud-slow ascent.

It was very still and a fine cold rain seemed to hang rather than fall about them, leaving on the dark wool uniforms a thin glint of silver like the glimmer-leavings of a snail. In the far woods the birds were calling as if it were just another day, newborn, amnesiac and ruthless-full of promise.

J.T. walked beside Will with his head bowed. He would not look ahead, but as they passed the row of cages he had built and tended with his own free-given labour he turned and saw as Will did the animals that had remained within their open prisons and been shot there regardless. It was mainly the older ones, those long-tamed and accustomed to their bars. There were three such bodies visible in the foremost row of cages: Lambert, the old lion whose hips were as bad as Simba's and who, like him, was often let out to roam the property and sometimes rode in the passenger seat of the van with Wayne as he carted hay for the horses or carried out some other task about the place; Elsa, the oldest of the lionesses; and in the cage beside her, Sabrina, the pregnant Siberian tiger. At the sight of these, J.T. crumpled and the party halted in shamed or embarrassed respect. Will stood and burned in his weighted boots until the superior officer caught his eye and coughed and Will walked heavily over to J.T. and put his hand upon his back and spoke gently to him, and they rejoined the party.

There was no way to set about the task but stone-wise and comatose and dead to themselves in some deep and perhaps abiding way, and they set about it thus, lifting with their living hands the weighty cold and ground-damp heads of each poor lion and lioness, tiger and tigress, wolf and bear and leopard and the single panther whose mythic power had elicited such reverence in Will and whose face was now a wreck of mud and prophesied, Will thought, with a fatalism that did Wayne proud, the sure and terrible ruin of all things at the hands of man. They gazed in numb clay witness at each stilled face, at the silt that caked unblinking eyeballs and at the pink hard tongues protruding from once-fearsome mouths, and they saw the places where the rich fur had been shot away, revealing bone or red muscle or purple viscera, and the marks of chains where the heavy bodies had been dragged through the mire and now lay at unseemly angles like so many broken terracotta creatures, and they said aloud each sweet and corny name—*Winnie* and *Pooh Bear* and *Bongo* and *Simba*—and the captain stood by and checked them off: that long and permanent list of the dead.

And then among the mud-sunk bodies of the lions Will saw her by her size, his Nala: soft-suckled darling of the milky breath; biscuit-eared nuzzler and velvet tumbler; big-pawed loving pouncer and sweet-tempered little animal sister who had clumsed and nestled and play-growled her soft way into his heart. And from this, in cowardice, we turn away.

—

The people from the sanctuary stared at them in apparent dread as they returned, wet and filthy and damaged, too, in other ways that were beyond the help of warmth and shelter. The maggot had returned with his slung machine gun and his rifle. His eyes were ringed purple with tiredness, but his uniform was fresh. There remained, besides the tiger cubs and monkeys in the house, and the bear and lioness who lay where they had fallen by the roadside, one lioness and one tiger apparently still at large, and the list of the dead numbered forty-three.

Will went over to the woman from the sanctuary and told her that there was a baby monkey up at the house that needed feeding, and she thanked him and went to speak to the sheriff, but he would not let her go yet, and he set about readying the men to carry out the line search of the property. He excused Will and J.T., but with grit and zombie newfound strength J.T. asserted that he would not stay behind and let another animal be shot, and Will could not stay back alone, and so they joined the milling still-armed group as they waited for the woman from the sanctuary to prepare the tranquilliser gun and then, like a party searching unaccountably for a body, when corpses lay before them in impossible number, they entered again the once-wild kingdom. They formed a human chain and began to trudge the wooded regions down the fence lines, the only remaining places where a terrified animal might have escaped the slaughter of the previous night.

In every quadrant of the land they tramped were littered the bright casings of bullets and they glinted in the mud like lost precious objects and Will could not believe how many there were. He lagged a step behind and bent and picked one up, slipping it into his pocket, for what reason he could not guess, and then he wiped the guilty mud from his hand and walked on. His mind was like a thing stunned by electric shock: it sat twitching but to no effect. It seemed to him that the haze that lingered from the lifted fog was perhaps some issue of his eyes or brain and he blinked incessantly in the cold damp air that stung like wood smoke.

The group went on unspeaking, alert for any sound, and at length they approached a deep thicket of trees and thorn bush, an outcropping of the deeper woods that continued down the fence line all the way to the road, and they heard from within a crackle and a rasped repeated sound, half growl, half cry. Will had not heard the sound before and did not know from which animal it issued. It was a haunting, hackle-raising noise and the men in their fallen-back positions looked from each to the other and shivered.

'That's a tiger,' said J.T. softly. 'It must be Kahn. He's calling out for his own.'

'That's a wicked sound,' said the deputy who stood by Will. 'My blood is running cold right now.'

The sheriff whispered for the group to fall back ten paces and he turned to confer with the people from the sanctuary while the officers trained their guns on the patch of brush. The tops of the saplings some ten metres within the thicket were moving, shaking their yellow leaves with a festive sound. To their left, Will could see the perimeter fence of the property, and beyond that there was a distant glimpse of the highway. The sheriff called out to the maggot and he came at a quick crouch towards the ones who would decide, both hands wrapped around his gun. Will watched as he nodded at some unheard command and then began his hunched return towards the trees. He stopped at the edge of the vegetation and raised his rifle and Will thought he was going to shoot, but he was only looking through the scope and he dropped the weapon again and came back. The woman from the sanctuary readied the tranquilliser gun while around her armed men rotated with their feet planted like heliotropic flowers.

J.T. walked over and spoke to the sheriff. When he came back he whispered to Will that it was indeed Kahn, and that the lady from the sanctuary was going to tranquillise him.

'It takes ten minutes to kick in, though, so it's risky. And there's still Kimbra they're worried about, too—although she'll stay hidden for sure. They think Kahn might be injured—the Narco guy says he remembers shooting something in those trees last night.'

It began to rain again. Will was shivering hard in his shirt and t-shirt and his feet were wet and cold inside his boots. He watched as the vet crept towards the bushes, Brock and another man covering her. Brock halted at the edge of the undergrowth and she entered the trees on her own, slow between the thorny branches. Everyone watched in utter stillness and silence. She was a small woman, dressed in the sand-coloured uniform of the sanctuary, her hair pulled back in a ponytail. She turned and nodded and then kept going deeper into the brush. When she was some way in, Brock also began to make his way among the trees, with more evident difficulty because of his bulk and raised gun. The other officer circled around towards the fence line, peering in to where the tiger was presumed to lie in hurt or frightened hiding.

Will found himself incanting a kind of inner prayer, such as he had long ago abandoned, that the tiger—just this one last tiger—would be saved. He could still see the woman where she stopped and crouched and raised the tranquilliser gun, and he heard the pop when it released, so much more benign than the dread endless sounds of bullet fire that would echo in his mind for who knew yet how long. The woman remained squat and still, her eye to the scope, and some ten seconds passed.

'She got him,' Brock called back to the sheriff. 'I saw him flinch.'

At the sound of the man's voice, the tiger stood into visibility within the trees and then it leaped, displaying one desperate final time and for its very life all the mighty strength and glorious power of its being, its front paws extended as if for flight and the huge chest spread and pale and magnificent, and as the woman fell back contorted in a twist of panic the arc of the tiger's leap seemed magically extended and it rose higher still within the air and Will did not hear the shots and saw only that his prayer had been answered, that the tiger was rising up by some miracle of rectitude and fate, and he saw it rocket up into the sky and its wild soul fly to freedom, and it was gone.

—

Back at the road, a fresh body lay by the tent—Kimbra the lioness, whose corpse had been taken by the young thieves in their truck—and the sheriff declared that each last animal was accounted for.

Something made Will turn and he looked across the road and saw her: Valerie. She was clasped in the arms of Doc Hazel, and when J.T. ran to her she passed into his broader arms and the two of them stood thus clenched together and Will went alone to the tent, where he took a donut from a box and sat down on a folded blue tarpaulin, while all about him men pretended deafness to her loud and abject loss. The difference between this woman and the Valerie with whom he had spent three nights and days so short a time ago filled Will with a new and awed respect for the changes that calamity may wreak so swift and ambush upon a person.

Now the sheriff drew near to where J.T. and Valerie stood in bereft small comfort, and the big outdoorsy man from Columbus Zoo followed, and Valerie emerged from the arms of the boy she had mothered lightly these years and who now mothered her in her need, and she gulped herself silent and wiped her eyes. The sheriff and the zoo man stood in lame poses of deference, their hands identically clasped at the level of their groins as if the custom before a widow was to cover any reminder of their husbandly parts.

From where he sat, Will could not hear the conversation, but he sensed that it was portentous. He studied the faces that he could see: Valerie's as pale and swollen as J.T.'s had been last night; the zoo man's full of unconvincing humility; J.T.'s showing first its native submission and then a fierce rage induced by whatever the zoo man was saying.

The zoo man put a hand on Valerie's shoulder and he looked into her face and then took the same hand and laid it on his heart.

J.T. turned and put his own hand onto Valerie's shoulder and he bent his big kind head and spoke with obvious urgency and she, poor focus of this vexed attention of crowding men, nodded and shook and looked around with dazed and seeming blind expression and there was more remonstration and mute words from both J.T. and the zoo man, and then from the sheriff too. Finally Will saw Valerie concede in an attitude of utter hopelessness to the zoo man, turning up her face towards him and nodding a small assent as if to death itself, and he reached out again in his grief-entitled laying on of hands.

Will saw J.T. convulse with emotion and stride towards him.

'She's agreed to let the zoo take the animals that are in the house. The tiger cubs and the monkeys.'

'Even the monkeys? But they're her babies.'

'I know,' said J.T., holding out his palms as if beseeching Valerie still.

'What about the little one? Do you think she's okay? She's been up there all night without being fed.'

J.T. only shrugged. 'I said I'd look after them here until she decides what to do, but she said she doesn't ever want to come back here again.'

Already now they saw her, head down, a hand clamped over her mouth, make a run towards her car. She got in and slammed the door, and with a spinning of mud-lodged tyres she drove away.

After she left, the transport vans arrived from Columbus Zoo, bedecked in their cheery animal decals, and some planks were dragged by mule and laid down on the driveway so that they could reach the house to tranquillise and transfer the monkeys and the tiger cubs into the cages that would take them to their unfamiliar frightening new home.

The men were leaving gradually, and as the day drizzled on the news crews began to arrive, and dark birds circled in their carrion vortices around some unseen pole where perhaps the moon lay hidden by the grey scrim of cloud. The sun was but a paler patch above the hills, a section of the sky's upholstery worn out by repeated circular rubbing.

Will watched from the tent as the sheriff and the zoo man gave interviews to the clutch of cameras, and when the sheriff walked back to the tent he asked if they could leave, or at least go somewhere away from the reporters, some of whom were local and knew J.T. and had sent him into hiding in his truck and even tried in vain to knock on the windows and locked doors to ask for comment.

'We can drive back up to the house when the animal transports are gone,' Will told J.T. 'But we can't leave yet.'

'The fuck?! Why not? It's all over, isn't it?'

'Sheriff said he wants to come up and talk to us before we go. About the bodies and the property or something.'

'What are they going to do with them?' J.T. asked.

'There's a ton of chicken guts sitting in the van right there, too,' Will replied in dumb practical non sequitur.

The zoo transports left in funereal procession, and J.T. started the truck and they pulled once more across the rattle of the grille and in the clarifying light of slow-dissolving clouds drove up and over the first hill and through the ruined land: past the open mausoleum cages and the dam where no duck rested on the wind-frosted water; past the welter of named and catalogued corpses, and the place where Wayne had lain and where now a staked square of crime-scene tape flapped with a rapid audible beat in the new-day breeze.

The house was dim and desolate and cold. J.T. went about switching on the lights and Will put on a pot of coffee, feeling a sense of trespass in this dead man's home where he had lived the past four weeks. J.T. put on 'The House of the Rising Sun' for Wayne, and they stood in their socks and toasted him with mugs of coffee and then, because that did not feel right, with Jack Daniel's.

'Goodbye, old friend,' said J.T.

They kept at the whiskey and when the sheriff arrived Will felt so multiply numb that he could barely focus on the man's face; his vision seemed to track and pile upon itself like the terminus of an escalator where the grey lines flatten and follow one another unceasingly into the void.

Sheriff Peck had two things on his mind. One was what to do with the bodies and the other was to stop J.T. and Will from giving an unfavourable account of events and the role of local law enforcement to the media.

'I'm not fucking talking to the media, okay?' said J.T. 'And that's not because I care about protecting your reputation; there's just no way I'm talking to those vultures, so you can quit worrying about it.'

The sheriff shifted his muddy boots. His hands were awkward at his belt loops and he looked at Will, who held up his hands and said, 'No way! Me neither.' The sheriff cleared his throat and nodded his white moustache towards them and then moved on to less undignified subjects: the forty-two corpses of exotic animals laid out at this moment in the mud some twenty metres from where they sat.

'Mrs Gage left before I had a chance to ascertain her wishes on the matter, and I'm reluctant to trouble her again, so . . . I'm asking your advice regarding what you think she would want. We could either cart them away for . . . disposal. Or we could bury them here on the property.'

'Bury them here,' said J.T.

And so the bodies were buried. From somewhere—perhaps the scrap metal yard—arrived an enormous yellow excavator with a digging arm on one end and a clawed bucket on the other, and it appeared to the two young men, watching sickened and compelled, to be the natural issue of such industrial end-days cataclysm in the age of iron. Through that strewn waste it lumbered, churning up still further whatever ground it passed over with its awesome wheels that seemed, too, excessive dark symbols of the futile zenith of human invention and ascendency.

Where J.T. had directed, in the swale below Will's RV bedroom and close to the taped-off square where Wayne's dishonourable corpse had lain, the excavator dug a pit some thirty feet deep into the seeping mud, and then it scooped and gathered up the once-majestic striped and maned and tailed poor bodies with the help of the remaining men, who lugged and hefted the corpses like sacks into the hungry metal mouth of the tractor, and it raised and tilted its tray above the hole and the bodies slid and tumbled to the pit, their mythic size reduced to nothing in the maw of the mechanical beast. They were buried by the bucketload and the earth backhoed over them, and it was done.

'I'd like to go and get Tamsyn and Kaylee,' said J.T. as they stood at the window, the cold still empty house behind them, Wayne's guitar lying across a leather sofa and the door of the monkey cage wide open. 'I'd like to say some words over the grave. Something.'

Will nodded, though he dreaded the very thought of this ceremonial grieving and wanted just to sleep or drink or get so high that he forgot every single thing about himself.

'Also, we have to feed the horses,' said J.T.

'Shit. Where are they?'

'They'll be in the barn. But they've missed two feeds. Do you want to come with me, and then we can feed them together? Or if you're happy to stay you could maybe feed them while I'm gone.'

'Okay,' said Will, sensing that this was J.T.'s preference. 'I'll feed them. You go get Tamsyn. You're coming straight back, though, yeah?'

'I'll come straight back,' said J.T.

*

Will stayed in place as J.T. drove to where the sheriff stood talking to the men. There was some exchange of words and a display of earnest gestures on the part of the sheriff, and then J.T. walked back to his truck and drove away.

Shortly after, the excavator departed too, and then the men in their cars lined up by the cages, but the sheriff's car turned towards the house. When it had made the round of the driveway and stopped outside, Will walked to the front door and opened it, watching the tired man as he approached with his hat in his hand, as if to deliver some inconceivably worse tidings.

'J.T. told me he'll be coming back shortly,' he said. 'Is there anything else I can do? We're about finished here, and it's been a long night for the men, but if we can help with anything more . . .'

Will shook his head.

'I've stationed a patrol at the gate,' said the sheriff. 'To stop anyone . . . the media or whoever . . . from coming onto the property. I'll keep that in place as long as necessary. So if you need anything, my men will be just down the hill.'

Will nodded.

'Alright then,' said the sheriff. 'Obviously this property still belongs to Mrs Gage . . .'

'Of course!' said Will, flushing with quick rage.

The sheriff lifted each of his soiled feet in turn and placed them a few inches from where they'd been, and then he smoothed a hand across his scalp and put his hat back on, a gesture that evoked Wayne in a scalding flash.

'Alright then,' he said again. 'I'll take my leave.'

Will stayed where he was as the sheriff slammed his door and started the engine. He glanced at his watch. It was close to 1 pm and the sky was still grey and wholly clouded and the air was humid and thick with the smell of dug mud.

He let his eyes travel left to right across the near-unrecognisable landscape, from the undamaged woods at the western border into the void of clay where the only green remaining was the reeds around the little dam, the unmarked surface of which was the single point of soothing for his gaze, and it was all just so much waste. He followed with his welling eyes the black car as it too vanished over the limp horizon.

And then at once he was alone, in the wreck of an extravagant and hopeful ruined dream, standing in the doorway of a dead man's house, somewhere in America.

WILL WOKE TO A TOUCH on his shoulder like a bright sharp hook hauling him too fast from the dream deeps back again into the new old world.

'Sir, we're serving breakfast,' came the voice.

He shrugged off the thin blanket tucked bib-like around his throat and removed the flimsy eye mask. They'd turned up the lights. He wiped his mouth and felt the crust flake off against his knuckle.

'We have a seasonal fruit platter or gourmet chicken sausages with scrambled eggs and wilted spinach,' said the hostess.

'Umm . . . the sausages, please,' he said, knowing it was a bad decision.

The tray came at him with its jigsaw of square plastic dishes crowded around the central foil-capped rectangle.

'Is there coffee?'

'Tea and coffee will be coming through shortly, sir.'

He nodded and the cart moved on to the next row, where

the hostess was obliged to wake some other poor fool and offer him a sausage.

So goes the world. No respect or halt for pain, just the onward-rushing cruel or darkly comic or plain oblivious random in which we cannot help but search for pattern, for as Will pulled back the foil and saw the pale and stubby pair of jellybean-shaped sausages in repose beside the colourless eggs, his mind went straight there—to minced chickens; to chicken nuggets; to Wayne—and his head reared back in refusal against the seat.

His feelings were a Ferris wheel inside him, each swaying car of grief or anger or despair rising to replace for a brief ascendency its forebear and then lurching down and followed in its turn by some fresh obliterating emotion.

He closed his eyes until the pitching ceased, and then he pressed the foil back over his meal. He peeled open the little fingerbowl of water and drank it. It tasted strongly of plastic and he imagined the microparticles accruing like debt in the soft membranes of his body, the slow death from cancer that his entire generation most likely had to look forward to.

You were probably smart to get out early, he thought to Wayne, as he had found himself doing with increasing frequency and slight concern this past unprecedent of days.

He had been so stupefied with sleeplessness and grief and unbelieving that when his phone woke him on the morning after, he had registered the name only as the cool screen touched his bed-warm face and it was too late.

'Hello,' he said, his voice betraying the word as his first of the day.

'Will. It's Paul. Sorry, did I wake you?'

'No. Well, yes. What time is it? Fuck, it's almost midday.'

He sat up, feeling once again the hard wooden floor of Kaylee's room against his hip where the sofa cushions had slipped apart in the night, and waited for the blast of abuse.

'I just saw you on the news,' Paul said. 'What the fuck happened? My god! Are you okay?'

'The news?'

'You're all over the TV.'

'Me?'

'Well, you're in the background, but I saw you straight away. Are you still there? In wherever-it-is? Ohio?'

'Yeah, I'm still here.'

'Look, do you need me to come and get you? I can leave right now and drive out there and pick you up.'

Will felt his throat thicken with inarticulate emotion at this kindness, as shocking unexpected as if Wayne himself had woken him on the phone.

'Paul . . .' It was all that he could say, and it came out phlegmy and obviously near tears.

'Hey, it's okay,' said Paul.

'Don't you hate me?'

'Oh, look . . . we don't need to go there right now . . . You're still family.'

At that, the sobs came, breathy and humiliating, and they would not be held down. 'I'm sorry,' he gulped.

'Hey, it's okay,' said Paul again. 'Like I said, let's not go there.'

Will had meant for crying like a baby, but Paul continued.

'It's all over with Justine, and I'm actually feeling okay about that, so . . .'

'Really?'

'Yeah. I am. Anyway, enough. I'm calling to see if you're okay, and you're clearly not, so should I come get you?'

Will thought for a moment, and he felt within him the kind of gut-lodged certainty that he had rarely known before. 'Thank you,' he said, 'but I think I need to go home.'

The events of Tuesday—the suicide of the gun-toting Midwest veteran Kubla Khan and the massacre of his inconceivably legal menagerie—had been on the news all over the world, and there in the background was Will, hunched and muddy on the folded blue tarpaulin while in the foreground the man from the Columbus Zoo, the Bear Grylls or American Steve Irwin figure, who Will learned *had* in fact had his own wildlife television show, repeated again and again his perfect soundbite couplet:

'It's like Noah's Ark wrecking, right here in Littleproud.'

In the numb following days Will had been deluged with messages on Facebook and via SMS from those who had his American number and he knew there would be more waiting when he put his Aussie SIM back in, that he would be returning home a minor celebrity of human-interest trauma, and he was wrestling in a moral trial of the soul to determine how he felt about that.

In such a brief annihilation of hours, his relation to his former life had shifted. A shamed miracle consequence was that he could now think of seeing Laura again as other than catastrophe, and in this his journey had served its base intended purpose. He wanted to believe that it was because the affliction of experience had humbled him out of his microcosm self-involvement, that he had a new measure of catastrophe that put his little heartbreak into its right perspective. But it was not that. He knew that his involvement in this world-news tragedy had drawn around him a charm of protection, that he would no longer have to suffer her coldness and distance. She would ask—everyone would ask—about what he had been through, and he would respond with quiet stoicism, downplaying the significance of the horror and its impact on him, but she would see it.

Oh god, what kind of monster was he?!

It was as if Wayne had given him a terrible gift: an undeserved free pass from the reckonings he should have faced, for there would be no need now to revisit that phone call, to hear that glass-hard tone of self-protection in her voice, nor to face head-on, as Valerie had urged him to, the lessons of her words or the truth of his pathetic self-delusion. He understood that he had shirked too easily the more quotidian trials that had been laid out for him, and knew with relief and enormous shame that now he would not turn back and look.

'Why not go home a hero?' he heard Wayne say to him, in that pushy optimistic episode of wisdom-giving. Well, he would not go home a hero, but instead the vulgar cheap equivalent that must serve for his own soft non-combat generation.

Oh, Wayne! Oh, dude, what were you thinking? You who hadn't hurt a living thing since the war. Did you think you were giving them freedom? Were you that stupid; that crazed with sadness? Did the prospect of your own soon-caged new life change your mind about your poor caged children? The answer, of course, was right there; it had been there from the start. The war. It was as banal and profound as that.

The war: that was as far as our young protagonist's understanding would reach in the aftermath moment, and it would not be until years later, when he heard on the news about the Australian man who shot and killed his own teenage children after their mother left him, that he began to comprehend that some men kill their own young with the very aim to inflict precise and maximum pain on the mother of those young, and that in this we are surely worse than all the other creatures of the earth over whom we claim ourselves supreme.

For now, he chiefly felt an overwhelming sense of all that he had failed to learn and do on this short aborted quest. At helping Wayne, he had failed. At staying ninety days, he had failed. At forgetting Laura, failed. At the gaining of self-knowledge of the kind to make a man of him, he had miserably failed.

Will looked at his phone, at the image he had set there on the screen: a beaming Wayne with Charlie the lion cub, taken on that innocent early night that seemed so long ago. His heart ached, literally—he didn't know it could do that—when he thought of Wayne: his wide hunched shoulders and his thinning hair and turned-down mouth that tipped seesaw into such child-open gladness at the sight of one of his animals or in conversation with his friend J.T. His skinny ankles and his chicken nuggets and his rare and wondrous headlong-dashing energy for life and his strange cosmology of conspiracy and fate in which Will seemed to occupy some significance for the poor doomed man. What role *had* he played in the life of this man, whom he had so lightly cast as a minor actor in his own drama, an anecdote to ease the angst of his return? Oh god, if only he had tried to help. If only he had been a better human.

On the screen in front of him, the plane inched forward in halting stop-motion over the empty blue space of the Pacific Ocean. He was literally *nowhere* right now, and he realised with no real surprise that he wanted more than anything to stay here, to remain in this cramped non-place with these incurious strangers for a while—maybe a month—before the plane landed and he walked back into his old life, a prospect more terrifying than the utter void that was the alternative. He wished he could have returned home by some slow, freight-carrying boat. He wasn't ready.

The question of what to do with his experience hung over him like a cloud containing all of weather's stored ambivalent potential for lifegiving or destruction. Would he close now against the world that had shown itself so cruel oblivious to his sweet naive and open *Yes*? Would he ever know again that awed and overawed receptiveness to surrender? Would he gain at least the chastening of knowledge, with its concomitant humility? Or would he brandish this story of his cut-short trip like his father before him, for all the days of his life? Perhaps he too would stoop to that; what else had he? All this coexisted within him, and time alone could tell the outcome, for there were many things he kept from himself, and he cherished still the myth of the young man's journey and its invariable success, the relinquishment of which is more difficult by far than religion or father worship.

In the too-short limbo present, he simply tried to make of his mind a tribute. To think with clear-eyed bravery and undiminished sadness of Wayne, exuberant and stubborn and fully himself. To think of Nala, his sweet dead darling. Of Valerie. Of Bubbles and Bam-Bam at the zoo. Of the baby monkey whose fate he had not learned. Of Cissy and Tootsie in who knew what harsh enclosure without the comfort of their mother's arms. Of J.T. and Tamsyn and Kaylee, as they had stood at the grave of Wayne's Wild Kingdom, while J.T. intoned his good and earnest prayer for his friend and his lost beast family. Will steadied his mind and guided it towards them, but it would not go. It lurched forward and then bounced back as if from a padded door.

There was a soft ding from the intercom and an announcement that the captain had turned on the fasten seatbelt signs, and the plane gave an immediate buffet, as if passing a semitrailer on a windy highway, to demonstrate the necessity of this directive. The flight attendants paused in their clearing of breakfast, and Will turned in haste to his uneaten food. He wondered what time it was at home, and if he really should be eating now, and if his guts would be as messed up when he landed as they had been when he first arrived in New York.

And so, despite himself, his thoughts moved inexorably homewards and he moved, like all living things, inexorably on. He would at last stop thinking of Wayne, and of Laura, too; stop writing to J.T., who would send him one last email to tell him that Bubbles had died in the Columbus Zoo, trapped in a faulty sliding cage door; and yet another year would step up to take the place of its predecessor, and the poor earth turn again like a time bomb counting down; a new apartment block would spring up across the street and the tents in Zuccotti Park would be packed away, and a new president replace the old; and the monkeys, Tootsie and Cissy and the unnamed baby, would be sold and sent across the world to a zoo in Dubbo, Australia, where one day Will would see them with his wife and children and would never guess that they were the same creatures with whom he had shared a brief and loving home. And only the dead would not continue to move heartless and inexorable onwards, for the place to which all moved was the very place at which they had already, and at last, arrived.

Coda

WAYNE HAD TO ADMIT THE sunsets here were incredible; by far the most spectacular he'd ever seen. They had spent the past week—Wayne's first in Vietnam—making flight after flight into the A Sâu Valley, dropping off five battalions at landing zones in the valley floor and taking in engineers and supplies through a hole in dense three-canopy jungle to make another landing zone, or LZ as he'd learned to call it, on higher ground, where the VC were dug in and invisible and where they would have to pick up the wounded and do supply dumps once the assaults started tomorrow.

Wayne thought they were going to crash when they'd first gone in to what would be the new LZ. They had four gunships defending them, but the spot was nothing more than a hole in the jungle. As they'd approached, Jay, the best pilot in the company, had turned the Huey on its side, almost one hundred and twenty degrees, and he spiralled it down towards the branches, which rushed up at Wayne like some kind of tree-dwelling former life flashing before his eyes. Suddenly the whole chopper shook and there was a sound like tearing metal.

Wayne had yelled out, slammed back in his seat and sure he was about to die. But it turned out that Jay was using the main rotor as a saw to cut away the canopy and widen the LZ. Holt and Milch had laughed at him, of course, but Milch also admitted he'd been shit-scared when he'd first seen it done.

Wayne lit a cigarette—he'd already gone from one to two packs a day since he started basic training. They were flying back to base with an empty ship, having done their last supply drop for the day at the lower LZ. They'd been flying ten- or twelve-hour days all week, and from tomorrow it was about to ramp up even more.

There were thunderstorms pretty much every afternoon here, and today had been no exception, and now Wayne sat behind his M60 and smoked and stared out at the post-storm sunset, looking for shapes in the banked-up enormous cloud formations, silhouetted at their rippled edges and glowing that lustrous creamy colour inside like the thick petals of magnolias in his mother's garden. Behind those grand and constant-shifting clouds—like explosions in extreme slow motion—the sky was the crazy colour of canned peaches, and the sun's still-visible segment was a red so hot it branded his blink-vision for a full half-minute wherever his gaze travelled.

Wayne had existed in a kind of blurry dissociated and unreal haze since he'd got here, as if a shroud hung between himself and this place that he'd been imagining for months and now felt he wasn't really *in*. He couldn't seem to shake himself out of it.

Back at the base, he stood around smoking while Jay and Holt tied down the main rotor blades and then they all hustled to the mess tent. They'd been at the rear of the formation, in the last company back, and when they'd eventually found a free landing spot it was a half-mile hike from the tents through full puddles.

He wondered if he'd missed a visit from his little buddy that evening, the young monkey that had started coming almost daily for the bread rolls he smuggled back in his pockets to feed it. It was a macaque, and must have lost its family, because it was always alone, and seemed to live in the trees at the back of his tent. At first he'd torn off bits of bread and thrown them, and the monkey had waited until he was well back to scamper down and snatch them and then dash off and crouch on a branch to eat, with its clear and canny eyes trained always his way. Now, though, it came right up to the tent and sat and ate the bread on the ground where he tossed it, then chittered at him for more. He was hoping he'd be here long enough to tame it; have it sit on his shoulder and eat from his hand. That would be something. He brought a bread roll back with him from dinner, but it was dark already and he knew the little monkey wouldn't show up now.

During dinner, the booming sound of heavy artillery had broken out from the valley, and the men hushed and exchanged glances. Some had even cheered. The artillery would continue through the night, followed by air strikes at dawn, and then the infantry would move.

The helicopter crews would wait until they got the call to fly, and then go in to extract wounded troops. The LZs would probably be hot, and it would be the first time Wayne would see real action. By rights, he should be shitting himself, but he couldn't get his head around it, and felt only the same buzzing jaw-clenched flatline. He was worried that he wouldn't be able to react quick enough, or at all, when the time came, and he lay awake for what felt like hours trying to bring himself back into the sensory world, concentrating on the sound of the artillery and then on the rain on the tent, and then just even on feeling the presence of his own hands and feet against the blanket.

They were woken at dawn but then nothing happened and they hung around listening to the air strikes and waiting for the call. They watched the massive plumes of black napalm smoke boiling up out of the valley. After that, there was an interminable lull while the infantry moved in.

And then, with so much warning and somehow none at all, it was on. He was flying with Jay and Holt again, but with Jackson as co-pilot. They flew north at three thousand feet, parallel to the river that ran blinking along the valley floor, flying in formation with fifteen other ships, with Brad Rose, or Rosie, in Alpha One position because he was a crazy motherfucker and had switched with Kinsey, who'd drawn the short straw. Their first flight in was just to the lower LZ, picking up grunts who were injured but fine to walk back down the hill.

Wayne felt sorry for these grunts: it had all happened so fast, and now it was over, for the moment at least, and they were headed back to base to get patched up. Wayne and the crew were all eager to know what it was like on the ground, and hassled the grunts for details. It was bad news. It looked like there might be a crap-load more VC on the hill than they'd thought.

The napalm and delayed-action explosives had exposed spider holes, bunkers and tunnels dug right through the jungle. They'd seized tons of ammunition already, and documents found on a dead VC had revealed there might be as many as two thousand of them in the valley, coming in and out through Laos.

The first few flights went fine, and Wayne started to relax a bit. Because of the temperature and humidity, they could only carry eight troopers at a time, and it was going to be a long day. Then they got an urgent call to do a single-ship landing at the hot upper LZ. A medevac chopper had been hit with an RPG while hoisting in a wounded trooper, and it had crashed, killing the grunt as well as the medic on board. The rotor blades had decapitated another guy on the ground. The crew chief, pilot and co-pilot were able to escape, but both pilot and co-pilot had sustained burns when the chopper caught fire.

Jay looked back at Wayne and Holt and said over the intercom, 'This is the one.'

They flew back north along the same route. The river was a dull iron-grey now, lying unmoving along the valley floor, and there were thunderclouds over the far range. The jungle was dark green in the cloud-shadow, no longer the myriad random-patterned pale and deepest green and every conceivable intervening shade revealed in sunlight.

Two gunships were ready to accompany them to soften up the LZ, but it was too tight with the crashed medevac chopper for more than one ship to land at a time. As they approached the hole in the canopy, the gunships started raking the jungle and Wayne saw muzzle flashes from below. Jay said over the radio that they were receiving fire, and then one of the gunships reported that it was taking hits, and then the other.

This is the one; this is the one; this is the one, Wayne was saying over and over in his head, and he realised he'd been repeating it ever since Jay had said the words back at the base.

'Going in,' said Jay over the radio. He brought the Huey over the LZ, staying at about two thousand feet, and then pulled the nose up and banked steeply and very fast. The trees rushed up at Wayne and revealed all their impossible detail of bark and twig and billion-brothered leaf, as the ship did a full revolution and then righted.

As soon as they levelled out he started firing rounds, his hands jarring into instant numbness. He could see the grunts all around the LZ and the burnt-out medevac chopper in the trees to the left, but as they got closer he couldn't see the jungle anymore, just the flashing gunfire and smoke and the tearing obliteration of what used to be trees at the edges of the LZ.

They made it in without taking a hit, and as soon as they were six feet off the ground the wounded men began to rush the ship. Two guys were carrying another on a litter who was bandaged around the abdomen and covered in blood; Jay brought the ship down and they lifted him in, and what Wayne saw in the eyes of the three men was some germ of airborne fear, and it leaped the gap between them and Wayne felt it writhe down into him and kick his body into a new mode of adrenaline arousal that he'd never experienced before. It was like he'd had earplugs in, attached to strings, and someone had jerked them out and now the sound gushed in and threatened to deafen him.

He fired over the heads of the two men as they scrambled in and pulled the litter away from the doors, and behind them were two more carrying another whose legs were badly burned. Wayne recognised the two men carrying the burned guy—they were the pilot and crew chief of the medevac chopper. Where the pilot's hair had been on the left side of his head was now a charred red mess and his left hand and arm were bandaged and it looked like he couldn't use them.

'We can only take eight,' Jay shouted over the intercom. 'There'll be more ships coming after us. We need to take the worst ones.'

Behind the guys in the doorway Wayne could see three men on the ground at the edge of the LZ who looked badly hurt.

'The load is eight,' he shouted, and the pilot and crew chief nodded as they lifted in the burned guy.

Everywhere around them was a cataclysm of noise that widened in concentric rings like a hurricane: the chopper blades in their never-ending ear-buffet monotony; his own gunfire and the firestorm going on around the LZ on every side; and further out the featureless commotion of battle from no one quadrant.

'Bring those guys first,' Wayne shouted, pointing at the three prone figures, one of whom had begun to drag himself through the mud towards the chopper. The medevac pilot and crew chief nodded again and crouched and hurried back under the rotor wash over the wild-rippling puddles. Wayne saw one of the grunts defending the LZ get hit and go down, and then suddenly there was another guy who'd come from behind them, crouched in the mud and waiting to climb on. He had been shot in the face and his whole mouth and jaw were bandaged over and the bandage was soaked in blood

'We need to get out of here,' Jay yelled over the intercom. The pilot and crew chief reached the two men lying on the ground as the third was still dragging himself through the mud to the chopper.

Wayne stopped firing and turned to the two grunts who'd lifted the bleeding guy in. 'Go grab him,' he shouted, pointing, but one of them had his hands over the bleeding guy's stomach and the other one was sitting on the deck as if he couldn't hear or see.

'Hey!' Wayne screamed, but the guy just huddled there, ignoring him or in shock.

The pilot and crew chief returned, hauling a grunt who seemed to be unconscious.

'Is he alive?' Wayne shouted, and the pilot nodded. He was big and they couldn't lift him in, and Wayne had to jump down into the mud and together they rolled him up onto the deck, revealing a mess of dirt and blood on his back. Wayne felt as if he was floating above the ground; he couldn't feel his legs where they held him in the churned-up mud of the LZ.

The trooper who'd just gone down was being attended to by the guy beside him, who had his mouth open in an inaudible shout, and Wayne waved at him and he dragged the shot man up and another ran over to help bring him to the chopper. The pilot and crew chief crouched and ran back again, heads tucked low, towards the guy still lying at the edge of the LZ.

'We've got seven,' came Holt's voice over the radio, and he turned and saw that another badly injured grunt was being lifted in through the left-side door.

Wayne jumped back onto the deck and grabbed the shell-shocked grunt by the shoulder. 'Hey, you gotta get out, man, there's worse-hit guys we've gotta get back.'

But the grunt looked at Wayne with that doomed stare and shook his head.

Wayne was about to slap him when the burned man shouted to Wayne, 'Hey, help him,' and Wayne looked down and saw that the guy dragging himself across the mud had reached the chopper and was trying to haul himself in. He didn't seem able to use his legs, and Wayne reached down and grasped the guy's hands and pulled him onto the deck.

'That's eight,' Holt yelled. 'We can't take nine. We won't make it over the trees.'

'I know,' Wayne yelled back. 'But this guy's not coming.' He jerked his head at the mute.

'Hurry the fuck up!' Jay shouted over the intercom.

The two guys with the shot trooper were close, and right behind them the pilot and crew chief were hobbling back with the final guy from the edge of the LZ.

Wayne waved them all to go back. 'We're full,' he screamed. 'You'll have to wait for the next one.'

But they couldn't hear him and kept coming.

'Are we good to go?' Jay yelled.

'Hey,' said the guy who was holding his hand over the bleeding grunt's stomach. 'Take over here. I'll get out.' He jumped down and ducked out under the blades of the chopper and helped lift in the shot trooper.

'That's eight!' Holt shouted. 'Go! Go!'

Jay began to lift the chopper off the ground, just as the other three men reached them, the burned pilot and the crew chief and the grunt they'd been carrying, who was missing a leg below the knee. All three of them grabbed onto the chopper as it rose, utter unholy panic and scalding desperation in their eyes.

'Wait,' Wayne shouted. 'That guy's bad. We need to take him.'

'We can't,' Holt screamed back. 'We're full!'

Wayne turned around once more to the crouching shell-shocked grunt.

'Get the fuck off!' he shouted above the rising sound of the rotor.

But Jay was lifting off, with the three guys still holding on. The pilot, who could only use one arm, dropped off as soon as his feet left the mud, but the other two clung on. Jay was hovering ten feet above the ground and shouting at Wayne to get them off and Holt was shooting into the trees on their left side and Wayne knew he had to get back on his gun because right now was when they were most at risk, and if they went down they were all fucked, and right on cue he saw muzzle flashes coming from the trees.

'Fuck!' he shouted, looking back at the weak grunt still cowering there like he couldn't see a foot in front of him.

'Get them the fuck off!' Jay shouted over the intercom.

'Come on, man,' yelled Jackson. 'Or we're all gonna get it.'

It was the first thing Jackson had said since they'd landed, and Wayne knew he was right, and so he hunched back as best he could to avoid the eyes of the two men hanging there, and he prised the two sets of white-gripped fingers from the edge of the deck. He felt the pressed-hard softness of the pads of their fingers, and the edge of one of the nails as he pulled the finger up, and he felt the resistance give way quicker than he had expected.

The chopper lifted with the extra weight gone, and he yelled out, 'Go!' and Jay took them up fast as Wayne jumped behind his gun and began firing into the trees. He couldn't see the men below them until they had cleared the canopy and he glimpsed them for just a second, the two able men dragging the legless third back to wait for the next ship. Jay was already radioing for another slick to come in and pick them up.

Wayne stopped firing as they reached height and he crouched down at the end of his harness and applied pressure to the bandage around the bleeding grunt's abdomen.

As they neared base the rain started and there was lightning and thunder close by, and by the time they landed and got the WIAs loaded out and on the way to the hospital tent, they were in the middle of the biggest thunderstorm they'd seen here yet, and they were told to stay grounded, and soon the assault had to be called off because there was zero visibility.

Wayne was still full of rage—he was shaking with it—and he went back to his tent and stood in the doorway and smoked cigarette after cigarette and tried to calm down. For a second there, he knew he had hoped the coward grunt would die, and he tried hard now to take it back. *I take it back*, *I take it back*, *I take it back*, he repeated in mute compulsive penance. He couldn't stop thinking about the legless guy and the crew of the medevac chopper, maybe still stuck out there in the storm.

*

The rain kept up pretty much all night, and again Wayne lay awake on his cot for a long time. At some point, he realised that he was still saying over and over in his head, *I take it back*, *I take it back*, *I take it back*, and he wondered if he had just started doing this strange repeating thing over here, or whether he'd always done it and just never noticed before, and he wondered if he would ever be able to sleep again.

He thought about what he'd had to do today, and he thought about the guys out there in the mud, and he thought about the fucked-up coward grunt, who he may or may not have laid a curse on. It was dumb, he knew, as well as destructive to think that way, but he'd always known there was something about him that was different from other people, that his life was governed by forces of luck and fate more than theirs, and that he was somehow held within the sights of the universe and, if he truly wished for the death of the grunt, the guy would probably die. He remembered the time he'd made a deal that, if he did something good every day for the next week, Lori would start liking him, and he had, and it had happened, like magic; she had never even noticed him before then.

In the humid dawn, Wayne sat on his cot by the open back of the tent, where the water was dripping in quick glinting sporadic bursts of droplets that leaped the edge in weighted synchrony, and he willed the monkey to come, and after a while it appeared, all slicked-down tiny like a wet cat. He could see the pink skin beneath its pale drenched hair.

Wayne got up slow and fetched the roll from where he'd stashed it yesterday—was that only yesterday? It felt so long ago—and he sat back down and tore off a chunk of the hardened bread and tossed it over.

The monkey looked across to where the bread had fallen and then back up, bird-quick and vigilant in the movements of its eyes. It scuttled forward and snatched up the bread and its eyes flicked straight back to where Wayne sat unmoving and silent-praying for it to stay. And it did stay, eating piece after piece of the unwholesome bread, which it held in its tiny perfect little hands, until there was no more to throw, and it studied Wayne from out of its serious small pink face, so old and so young at once, and for those minutes Wayne felt something close to calm.

Acknowledgements

Although *Wild Abandon* is a work of fiction, and none of the characters are based on actual people, the second part of the novel was initially inspired by real-life events that occurred in Zanesville, Ohio, in 2011. I would like to particularly acknowledge the following sources, on which I drew in the process of researching these events and creating my own story:

Teresa Headley and John Moore. *Eighteen Days to the Massacre: An Exotic Caregiver's Perspective.* 2013.

Chris Heath. '18 Tigers, 17 Lions, 8 Bears, 3 Cougars, 2 Wolves, 1 Baboon, 1 Macaque, and 1 Man Dead in Ohio.' *GQ* magazine, 2012.

Chris Jones. 'Animals: The Horrific True Story of the Zanesville Zoo Massacre.' *Esquire* magazine, 2012.

Enormous thanks to my agent, Clare Forster of Curtis Brown, who was endlessly patient and encouraging while I worked on this novel, and who understood, from the first reading, exactly what I was trying to do with it. Thank you for your unwavering support, Clare!

I'm so thrilled that Jane Palfreyman at Allen & Unwin loved this novel, wanted to publish it, worked so closely on it at every stage, and let me keep (almost) all of my baroque sentences intact. It has been such a pleasure to work with you, Jane, and with the superb team at Allen & Unwin. Thank you to Christa Munns and Ali Lavau for your work on the copyedit and proofs, and to Sandy Cull for the cover design.

This novel was a long time in the making, and I am deeply grateful for having received such generous support from so many individuals and organisations along the way.

Thank you to the University of Melbourne for a Felix Meyer scholarship, which enabled me to travel to the US in 2016 to conduct research for the novel, without which the project would not have been possible.

Heartfelt thanks to the Australia Council for the Arts for an Arts Project Grant in 2016, and for awarding me the BR Whiting Studio residency in Rome in 2018, which was truly life changing. Thank you to the extraordinary Lorri Whiting, who created the residency.

To Creative Victoria for a VicArts grant in 2019, which gave me time to edit the manuscript.

I was also fortunate enough to be awarded a number of writing residencies while working on this novel: a Grasstrees residency, provided by the Stella Prize with the generous support of the Trawalla Foundation; a Fellowship Residency at Varuna, The National Writers' House; and a residency in the Leighton Artist Studios at the Banff Centre in Canada. These residencies gave me the precious gift of unadulterated writing time, and in such stunning locations!

Thank you to the brilliant Michelle De Kretser, who read an early draft and provided encouragement, friendship and sage advice. I'm eternally grateful!

To Sophie Cunningham, Antoni Jach, Nam Le and Emma Schwartz, Lucy Treloar, Omar Musa, Claire Thomas, Tony Birch, Kevin Brophy, Amanda Johnson, Bonny Cassidy, and the Masterclass gang, for friendship, writerly support, publishing industry know-how and great conversation. And to my reading group, for being inspiring and wonderful.

To Nate and Matt, for letting me stop working shifts at the bar so that I could get back to writing, and for your friendship and support—thank you, thank you!

To Ali, Joh and Jase, Sarah, Jackie, Chris, Sam, Lucy, Anthony and Juliette, Jerome and Steph, Jon and Jigna for being such great friends, for giving me so much love and putting up with my flakiness while working on the book.

To my family—especially Mum and Dad, who both read early drafts and were surprisingly enthusiastic, despite the 'adult themes'—and to Alan, Sandra, my dearest ant Annie, Elwyn, Andrew and Cath, Nattie and Josh, my adorable nephews Noah and Zeke, and Nooshin and Sepand.

Last and most: Hootan, my love and best mate. I will never be able to thank you enough, for believing in me, for being my absolute rock, for making me laugh, for taking on the terrible job of first reader, and for so, so much more. This is for you, and for Wilma and Ellie, our own little 'exotics'.